LADY OF THE DROWNED EMPIRE

FRANKIE DIANE MALLIS

SEVEN QUEENS PRESS

CONTENTS

For anyone who ever believed they were unworthy, or undeserving of love. You are so worthy of love.

And for Asha and Marcella. I might not have finished without the both of you.

In memory of Frank: Grandfather, Namesake, and Published Author.

And to Michael, thanks for sharing your birthday with the release. Also, happy birthday!

GUARDIAN OF THE DROWNED EMPIRE

PREVIOUSLY

HAVING SURVIVED THE IMPERATOR'S cruel test and lashing, Lyr is more determined than ever to train as a soturion, and prove she deserves to stay in Bamaria. She now only has three months to prepare for the Emperor's test in winter, and has agreed to additional secret trainings with her bodyguard and apprentice Still haunted, by her last interaction with the immortal Afeya, Mercurial, Lyr debates telling Rhyan his cryptic words to her, "You're the fire." But before she can, she is summoned by Arkturion Aemon for a trial.

Tani has been accused of being a member of the Emartis, the terrorist organization determined to replace Lyr's father as arkasva with her Aunt Arianna. Many believe Arianna to be the rightful ruler, and identify themselves with black seraphim feathers—a symbol Tani recently had on her when she engaged Lyr in a fight. Lyr has been called as a witness, and believes Tani will be found guilty, but when the Imperator appears, Lyr is suddenly the one being questioned until she's once more publicly humiliated and tortured. Fearing that Tani will tell the Imperator and Aemon her suspicions of Rhyan and Lyr's affair, and illegal use of kashonim, Lyr defends Tani despite the damning evidence, and they are all dismissed.

Rhyan is furious he was forced to watch helplessly as Lyr was injured again and blames himself for what happened. Tristan arrives to see Lyr but finds an angry Rhyan who accuses him of physical abuse. Knowing the subject must be dropped before Tristan grows suspicious of her cuts and bruises— a result of Lyr hiding Meera's vorakh, Lyr ends the fight by lying to both Tristan and Rhyan—it's the only way to uphold her blood oath and keep Meera and Morgana's forbidden magic secret—exposing the secret would mean death.

Rhyan tries once more to understand where her wounds have come from, and when Lyr won't answer, he pulls away. Lyr later invites Tristan to be intimate in her apartment. But Tristan is also pulling away, sensing Lyr is keeping secrets. Knowing she can't count on Tristan's Ka to protect her, and feeling uncertain of her standing with Rhyan, Lyr looks deeper into the mystery of her missing power. The scrolls she believes hold the key have been returned to the Great Library by Mercurial. But Ramia, the half-Afeyan who gifted Lyr an ancient necklace, shows her the scrolls have been made unreadable and her research is cut short.

Rhyan mysteriously misses their first day of secret training but reveals he was summoned to the border to hunt akadim. The undead beasts have been growing in number, moving farther south, and for the first time in history, have been organizing. Rhyan and Lyr train, and the tension is smoothed between them. But they aren't the only apprentice and novice spending additional time together as Lyr finds Tristan's cousin, her friend Haleika, with her own off-limits apprentice, Leander. Haleika blackmails Lyr to keep her affair secret, or she'll expose Lyr and Rhyan to Tristan.

Months pass and Valyati, the winter solstice, and the Emperor's final test are quickly approaching as Lyr's strength increases. But so is her growing attraction to Rhyan the more they work together. When an Emartis attack forces Lyr to stay at Rhyan's apartment for the night, the boundaries they'd so carefully constructed fall apart. Rhyan's intense nightmares force Lyr to intervene and wake him. She asks Rhyan to come to bed with her, just as friends, so they can both rest. Still emotionally raw from his nightmares, and a brutal night of fighting, Rhyan admits he can't. He presses her against the wall, admitting he doesn't trust himself, and almost kisses her.

But Lyr tells Rhyan how deeply she trusts him and finally he calms and they go to sleep. In the morning, Rhyan apologizes for his behavior, then suddenly, they're kissing until Aemon arrives to check in. She tries to forget the kiss happened as she attends the Days of Shadows celebration with her sisters and Tristan. But Lyr's worst fear comes to light as Meera begins having a vision. Barely making an excuse to leave Tristan, Lyr runs to Meera and pulls her from the party. Just before they can escape to safety, their escorts catch up to them along with Rhyan. To save Meera, Lyr finally breaks her oath, and tells Rhyan about the vorakh as they take off in a seraphim carriage.

Landing on Gryphon Island, Meera has recovered and takes off to calm down, while Lyr panics over breaking her oath. But Rhyan comforts her, and swears to keep her secrets. They walk the beach to find Meera, and run into Mercurial. Lyr's blood oath begins to burn, the magic punishing her for breaking the blood oath. Mercurial admits nothing can save her from the debt's final punishment unless the oath is changed. He also reminds her she should be wearing the necklace she received from Ramia. As he leaves, a storm hits the island. Rhyan and Lyr find Meera and run to their seraphim. As they fly home, the Emartis attack, upsetting the seraphim and Lyr is flung from the carriage, but saved by Rhyan. Until the blood debt is changed, her life will remain in constant danger, and her body in pain.

They arrive at Cresthaven along with all Bamarian nobility—there for security purposes during the terrorist attack. Lyr tries to conceal her pain and fear from Tristan, as they are briefed on the attack. Once dismissed, Rhyan alerts Lyr's father as to what happened. To save Lyr, her father makes his own deal with Mercurial, and the blood oaths vanish. Rhyan and Lyr agree to ignore their kiss, and focus on training for one more month. He also swears to keep the vorakh secret, and offers Lyr and Meera two illegal vadati stones from his mother, as tokens of his oath.

Lyr attends the Valyati ball, where the Imperator hints that Lyr's cousin, Jules, suffered mistreatment with him before her execution, sending Lyr into a panic attack. She must be carried from the party to be calmed down by Rhyan. But after, Lyr can no longer resist Rhyan, nor can he resist her. They begin removing each other's clothing until Mercurial interrupts, finally forcing Lyr to make a deal in exchange for his silence. But before she can finalize the contract, akadim attack. Rhyan manages to kill one, but before he can get Lyr to safety another appears, and Rhyan has no choice. To save Lyr's life, he reveals he's vorakh and travels Lyr to safety in a cave. They confess their love for each other before returning to Cresthaven. There they discover not everyone survived. Leander was killed by the akadim. The one Rhyan let live to save Lyr's life. Haleika's soul was eaten by the beast, leaving her in the process of transforming into an akadim herself.

Heartbroken and full of guilt, Lyr is taken to the arena for the Emperor's test. To prevent her from using kashonim, Rhyan is bound by rope, unable to access his magic. Haleika is brought onto the field, just as she turns into a full akadim, revealing she is the test. Though horrified she must fight her friend, Lyr is determined to survive and protect Rhyan. But Haleika is too strong. She punctures Lyr's necklace, breaking three of the red diamond centers as Lyr bleeds. To Lyr's surprise, she feels strength and power rush through her, and defeats Haleika. But before she can receive the Emperor's pardon, the Emartis attack. Lyr's father is assassinated. Weak and in shock, Lyr faints.

She wakes the next day at Cresthaven. Though Meera is Heir Apparent, she has decided to abdicate rule to Arianna—knowing her vorakh will prevent her from being arkasva. Lyr attends the announcement, still grieving her father and friends. Tristan's grandmother pulls her aside, and tells her their engagement is off now that Lyr's lost her status. Rhyan escorts Lyr outside to get some air and admits he needs some time alone. He feels he betrayed his oath as a soturion by saving Lyr, instead of killing the akadim. He feels responsible for Haleika and Leander's deaths, but he has no regrets. He still loves Lyr more than anything. Mercurial arrives to finalize the contract just as Rhyan heads to the fortress walls for duty.

Mercurial demands Lyr find her magic power, and complete a favor for him. She agrees, and then Mercurial finally explains what saved her in the arena. Ramia didn't give her a necklace, but an ancient piece of armor, one that belonged to, and contained the blood of the goddess Asherah. Lyr accidentally formed a kashonim with the goddess, when their blood mixed together. Not believing this is possible, Mercurial reveals it is because Lyr is the reincarnation of Asherah.

He puts the Valalumir star—part of the original light mixed with part of his soul into Lyr's heart, a process so painful she faints. When she wakes, she stumbles upon Arianna preparing for the announcement that she will rule Bamaria. Arianna covers up a tattoo of black seraphim wings. And Lyr finally knows that her aunt was the leader of the Emartis all along, and her aunt was the one who murdered her father.

DROWNED EMPIRE SERIES READING ORDER

Dear Reader, please be advised of the following topics before you begin reading:
Grief
Misogyny
Violence
Sexual assault
References to off-page rape
Recounting childhood grooming/attempted assault (this comes toward the end of Chapter Thirty-One if you need to skip or skim)

THE LUMERIAN EMPIRE
LUMERIA NUTAVIA

THE FIRST SCROLL:

SEKHIUM

CHAPTER ONE

MORGANA

(ONE YEAR EARLIER: THE night of my Revelation Ceremony)
I thought I'd known pain before. I was wrong.

My knuckles matched the white of the marble banister beneath them. I stood at the edge of my balcony outside my bedroom. My shoulders were tense and my gaze unfocused on the crashing waves of the Lumerian Ocean. A full moon cast light on the fortress of Cresthaven, but the headache pounding through my skull blurred my vision, making the familiar towers appear foreign.

In the distance, a seraphim squawked, and the rolling sounds of waves rushed forward over the sand. I swayed, dizzy from the pain. Still, I gripped the banister. Harder. Harder.

The clocktower began screaming the new hour. Ashvan fled to the sky, riders on the backs of the jewel-toned horses scouting over Bamaria.

It's late. So fucking late.

When I'm done here, shit's going down!

Buy more rice tomorrow.

I slammed my hands on the railing. The Godsdamned voices. I couldn't escape. I'd been hearing them for hours now, ever since Arkmage Kolaya had removed my Birth Bind. The blinding torment of the incessant thoughts had begun on the dais in the temple, and it was unrelenting. Nothing seemed to relieve the pain; nothing stopped the noise. I couldn't hide, couldn't find a moment of fucking silence. My own mind was no longer safe.

The backs of my eyes burned. Shit. Shit. The voices were coming faster now. Louder. Interrupting my own thoughts. The ashvan riders in the sky were too close for me to ignore.

Fucking Ka Batavia, stupid blue palace.

If I ever get to Lady Morgana...skirts going up....

I released the banister, pressing the heels of my palms into my eyes. I would not cry. I would not cry. Between my two sisters, enough tears had been shed tonight, enough tears for an Afeya's lifetime. I wouldn't add one single tear more. Tears didn't change shit. Tears didn't get you what you wanted. They made you weak. They forced you into a ball on your bed with your fingers digging into your belly as you sobbed in agony, crying like a child, waiting and waiting while no one came to help.

I've kept the secret this long....

The voices pounded through my thoughts.

They don't know she's a traitor. Soon they will.

Fly faster, you Moriel-horse. Fucking tired....

I covered my ears. It didn't help.

Shekar arkasva!

I pressed harder into my temples, pushing back the tears. I could see my father's dagger in my mind's eye, covered in my blood, in his blood, in the blood of my sisters.

Picking up the dagger and sliding the blade down the skin of my wrist—slicing off the scars of my second blood oath—had been on my mind all night. The thought overwhelmed me, its grip like a vice on my soul.

I hadn't done it. I wasn't stupid. The act would be nothing more than useless violence with no result. The magic my father had invoked ran far deeper. I could cut off my arm, and I'd still be bound for life.

Even without the oath in place, I would remain vorakh. I was doomed to this pain.

I shut my eyes, leaning forward against the cool stone of the banister, listening to the waves crash in the night.

Need a Godsdamned drink.

Final shift tonight. Thank fuck.

So many thoughts. All in my head. All at once.

Gods, I want....

Fucking gryphon-shit....

Emartis....

Releasing my grip, I stumbled backward. My back slammed into the wall, and I slid down to the ground, to my knees, with my head in my hands. A hammer pounding in my mind.

Why was it all so loud? Shut up! Shut up! Shut the fuck up!

The blue lights faded. The patrol was over. But the thoughts of the riders and every other person awake within the walls of the fortress continued.

One red, one blue....

Need to piss!

Hurts, doesn't it?

My fingers tangled in my hair as the new thought entered my mind. The voice was smoother and louder, standing out for just a moment before mixing and joining the thousands of others.

I groaned, wanting to slide a blade into the heart of whoever had thought that. Whatever they thought was hurting them, they had no idea. They didn't know pain.

You're wrong, said the voice again. *I know pain. I know it well.*

The thought rang so clearly in my mind, sweat beaded at my forehead, dampening the thick hair at the nape of my neck. An ashvan rider? A sentry on duty below? It sounded like they were responding to me. To my thoughts. But that...that wasn't possible.

Isn't it, though? Possible? Because here I am. Responding.

His voice felt like a shadowy fog, deep and smoky.

I stood up and rushed forward, searching beyond the balcony and fortress walls for him. But the grounds were empty, the neighboring balconies abandoned at this hour. I raced back inside where the torches were lit, fires crackling and spitting and dousing the room in a golden fiery glow. Not one soul was in sight. No escorts or sentries were allowed up here.

Don't try to look for me. You won't see my face. Not until I want you to.

I clutched my head. Was I farther than Lethea? Was this actually happening? Had the pain twisted and ruined my mind to play tricks on me?

How many times have you heard of Lumerians being arrested and taken away for vorakh? Taken to Lethea? Stripped? Or worse? You don't think it's possible that this is happening? Did you think that you were that special? That you were the only one? Your sister and cousin were cursed with the same affliction.

I shook my head. *No...no.* This wasn't real.

I assure you, this is very real, unfortunately for me and for you. I hear you quite clearly, just as I know you hear me. You're not the only mind reader in Bamaria. You're not the only one in the Empire. Not by a long shot.

I searched the shore for movement, for signs of life. But there was nothing more than a seraphim resting on her belly, her wings, bronzed beneath the moonlight, rustling against the sand and the water rushing back and forth across the shoreline. Not even a set of footsteps marred the beach.

How many are there? I asked.

Too many. Too many who found far worse fates than the pounding in your delicate noble skull.

I sucked in a breath, my chest rising and falling. *How are you doing this?*

How can I hear you? came the response. *Stupid question. We can both hear. Doesn't take much to focus. The same way you have a conversation in a crowded room and still hear the person you're speaking to.*

I could feel their vitriol and lack of patience in my mind.

So you really are like me? The moment I had the thought, I checked my wrist, expecting the scars of my blood oath to redden, to burn me.

You haven't broken your oath. And before you ask, I already knew. Knew the moment it happened. I knew about Meera. There was a long beat, and a shadow swept through my mind. *I know about Jules.*

My heart pounded, sweat dripping from my neck to my collarbone.

Who are you? I asked.

If I won't let you see me until I want you to, you won't know my name either. Until I want you to.

What will make you want to?

He was quiet as my mind raced.

How do you do that? I asked desperately. *Go silent. Stop thinking. Tell me.*

That wasn't what I came to teach you tonight. Nor was it my intention to see you. Or to tell you my name. You must learn patience first. For some time now I've been watching you, listening, and I know you have none, Morgana.

I shook my head. He'd been spying on me. How long? How many thoughts had he stolen from me? My family?

You go too far when you speak my name informally, I thought.

I didn't speak. And all things considered, I think we're far past formalities. Don't you?

What do you want? I asked.

He was silent again. I couldn't tell if he'd decided to end our conversation or was refusing to answer.

I bit my lip, fighting back the anger inside me. *I don't want to play games. Speak, or end this now. I see no point in you revealing this much of yourself if you don't intend to help me.*

You dismiss games too easily. Games can be fun. This is all so you know you're not alone.

Gryphon-shit! I stared again at the empty shore, the abandoned balconies. *I'm still alone!*

If a thought could translate into a shrug, he'd done just that. *You're powerful,* he thought. *Perhaps more so than any other vorakh I've met.*

I sneered. *I wouldn't exactly call this a meeting. And I've been vorakh mere hours. How could you know anything of how powerful I am?*

Because of who you are.

Ka Batavia? So?

Your power comes from something far deeper than your bloodline and name.

I returned to the edge of my balcony, staring at the waterway beneath. A smooth sheet of glass covered the running water that fed magic from the Lumerian Ocean throughout Bamaria. I wasn't too high up. If I drank myself into unconsciousness, that would solve tonight. But tomorrow, I'd still be here. And hungover. I eyed the glass, calculating the distance below, my leg already lifting to straddle the ledge. Maybe it was far enough. I eyed my tower. Maybe I could climb until I inevitably slipped—

Stop! the voice shouted. *Put your Godsdamned foot back on the ground.*

Why? I shifted my weight back until both feet touched the floor. *I don't want this—this life, this pain, this whole conversation with you.*

You'd rather break all your bones? That's all that will happen if you jump. You won't die. I'm sure of it. If you think you're in pain now, just wait until you're healing every single broken bone in your body, feeling them mend and reshape, all while listening to the endlessly inane thoughts of the healers caring for you day and night.

Go away, I sniffled. It was too much. It was all too much.

I can take your pain away.

I froze.

But only briefly, he thought. *There are ways to manage vorakh. They don't want you to know, they don't want you to hide from them, to learn their secrets. I can help you. I don't mind, especially for someone with your...qualities.*

There was a seductive edge to his words.

Are you going to bring me a glass of wine to numb my pain?

You can drink yourself to oblivion if you want. Smoke moon-leaves until you're higher than a seraphim. I have another method to ease your suffering. His words were like a caress in my mind.

What method? I asked, my throat dry.

Let me come to you. Let me show you.

You said you wouldn't show yourself to me.

There was a smile in his words as he thought, *I won't. It's dark.*

How do I know you won't hurt me? I crossed my arms over my chest, a chill spreading across my body. The hairs on my arms stood on end.

If I wished you harm, I'd have let you be. Watched you climb to the top of your little tower and fall. You're the only one trying to hurt yourself tonight, acting out, imagining blades on your skin, falling, hiding from your fate. You're acting as scared as a helpless kitten.

I squeezed my eyes shut. I couldn't let him come to me alone, but what other option did I have? I couldn't explain this to an escort. Certainly not to Meera, definitely not Lyr. Not without them becoming suspicious and scared and hurting my head with their thoughts more than they already had.

This was a bad idea. Too dangerous. Too unknown.

And yet, as much as I was afraid, something inside me wanted to say yes.

If this was a trap, if he were to hurt me, to kill me.... I squeezed my hands into fists, my nails cutting into my palms. Lyr had things under control. She'd care for Meera—far better than I would. I wasn't necessary. I wasn't needed. And I couldn't take much more of this pain.

How will you get into the fortress? I asked. *We're surrounded by walls, guards. Only one entrance will open. The rest are warded and have been impenetrable for a thousand years.*

I'm aware of Cresthaven's protections.

Are you Ka Batavia? I asked.

I am beyond the Kavim.

Lumerian? I asked.

I consider myself beyond that as well.

I frowned. *Afeya?*

Don't insult me.

Then don't come.

I'm afraid it's far too late for that.

There was a knock on my door, the thud loud enough to steal my breath. I stepped back as wind gushed through the doors of my balcony, swirling my black gown against my bare feet.

"Lyr?" I called, my voice shaking. "Meera?"

You're vorakh. You'd have heard your sisters approach. You know Godsdamned well it's me.

I stepped back, shocked he was inside the fortress, shocked he'd gotten so close so quickly. *There are guards downstairs.*

A fine threat indeed. I walked right past them as I came inside your little fortress. I'll walk past them again when I leave.

The backs of my legs hit the bed. I stared down at my discarded diadem at the edge of the covers. Nothing else was in sight to use to fight—

I told you I wouldn't hurt you. But you're well on your way to doing that on your own.

I don't trust you, I thought, fear overriding my desperation.

That's good, came his response. *You shouldn't trust anyone. Men lie. Most often to themselves. Thoughts aren't truths. Just thoughts.*

I squeezed my eyes shut, grabbing the folds of my gown. I didn't know what to do, only that I'd been in pain for hours, and my future held more of it.

It's your choice, he thought. *Say yes, and I enter. Say no, I leave you to your suffering. But you will succumb to me sooner or later. One day, the pain will be too much. Too hard. Too blinding. You won't be able to take anymore. And on that day, you'll take things into your own hands. Or someone else will. Someone will notice. Vorakh hunters stalk your fortress; one is already too close. You know of whom I speak: the young Lord*

Grey. If you do not gain control, the secret will cease, and your greatest fear will come to pass—your sisters will be exposed.

I stared at the door, the only thing separating him from me. It was unlocked. If he'd wanted to enter, he would have by now—with or without my permission.

Exactly, he confirmed. *You're showing a real talent for reading and discerning thoughts.*

Men lie, I thought.

They do. Now make your choice.

I squeezed my eyes shut, my chest heaving. *You can really help me?*

I don't allow other vorakh to suffer.

I could feel the truth resonating in his words, the thought carrying far more conviction than anything else he'd communicated. I nodded. *Come in.*

Turn off the lights. Use your stave, the one you left on your nightstand. Every single light. Don't just extinguish them, make it black. Call the darkness to you. You know the spell.

He not only knew my thoughts, but he could see through my eyes. He knew my name, my secrets, my fears....

And I knew nothing of him. Why couldn't I see through his eyes?

There was no answer from him. I was sure he'd heard me and was choosing not to reply, going silent like he had before, keeping me locked out of his mind.

My head was screaming, my heart hammering. But nothing could be worse than this. This pain, this agony.

My hands shaking, I walked alongside the bed and retrieved my stave, the twisting of moon and sun tree branches cool and smooth against my palm.

This was to be my first true show of magic. My first spell, my first act as a mage. Perhaps my last.

I lifted the stave and winced. Every movement worsened the pain in my head. I pointed at the first torch, the stave warming to my touch, the tip glowing with blue light.

"Ani petrova lyla." A spark shot forth, smothering the flames. A hiss of smoke on a charred stick was all that remained. I turned, directing the stave's light to the next torch and the next, repeating the spell until I saw nothing but black and heard nothing but the sound of my heavy breaths against the whisper

of extinguished flames and the wind hissing across the waves of the ocean.

Good, he thought. *Now I ask one last time. Are you sure?*
Yes.
Will you let me into your room, Morgana?
Yes.

The door creaked open, filling with his dark shadow.

My heart hammered even louder, as he stepped inside with another caress of his thoughts against my mind.

Hello, kitten.

CHAPTER TWO

LYRIANA

(PRESENT DAY)

Control what they see.

A black seraphim tattoo hidden beneath the cuff on her arm.

Control what they think.

Leader of the Emartis. Traitor. Our new Arkasva. Bamaria's High Lady.

My aunt Arianna.

I must control what she sees.

I tried to catch my breath. The golden doors of Cresthaven's Seating Room loomed over me. This was the room where my mother had held court until the day she died. The room where my father had once ruled our Ka and country.

I'd survived the Emperor's test and been granted clemency to continue training as a soturion to avoid exile. But the price had been Haleika. The price had been my friend—her life, her memory, her soul.

The price had been the life of my father, my High Lord and Arkasva.

He was dead. Murdered. Assassinated by terrorists, traitors, followers of the black seraphim—my aunt Arianna. Our new High Lady.

I clenched my fists at my sides, willing myself to remain calm, to breathe.

I wasn't supposed to know Arianna was a traitor. I couldn't let that knowledge slip. I may have survived the Emperor and the Imperator, even survived making a deal with the immortal Afeya, Mercurial, but Aunt Arianna held my life in her hands now. Aunt Arianna had to believe I had no idea that she was a traitor—a murderer. She had to believe with her whole heart that I still loved and adored and trusted her.

I had to control what she saw.

I rolled my shoulders back, held my chin up high, and centered the golden diadem across my forehead. The diadem, an emblem of my power and status as an Heir to the Arkasva, third in line to the Seat of Power, had been such a constant companion and accessory that I could adjust the piece with my eyes closed. I knew exactly how to pin it, had grooves in my scalp from years of wearing it in the same position.

But in that moment, the golden circle felt unnaturally cold against my skin, unlike the necklace—no, the armor, Asherah's armor—I wore. The gold of the chest plate had warmed to my collarbone and shoulders. I'd acquired it from Ramia on my birthday at the end of summer, had owned it for months believing it to be an ancient piece of jewelry until tonight, when Mercurial had told me the truth.

You are not human. You are no one's daughter. No one's sister. No one's friend. No one's lover. No one's slave. You are a goddess, made of the very essence of life itself. You are the sun, you are the moon, you are the stars. You are the water of the ocean, the dust of the Earth, the very air you breathe. And you...you are the fire.

I stumbled forward, my hands hitting the wall for balance as Mercurial's words pounded in my head. He'd revealed a secret I'd never known or dared to suspect. He'd unlocked a memory I could barely grasp.

I was Asherah reborn, a goddess in mortal flesh.

The armor across my chest, the armor which had belonged to the Goddess Asherah—to me, a thousand years ago in my past life—shined beneath the torchlight above my head. Inside the seven-pointed Valalumir stars were red diamonds that held Asherah's blood—my blood. Our blood.

The chest plate seemed to pulse against my body. My heartbeat vibrated with the light of Mercurial's Valalumir—with a piece of the Afeya's soul inside of me. A golden star branded on my chest completed the bargain.

Though I'd revealed nothing at my Revelation Ceremony, though the nahashim sent to test me had found no evidence of power, Mercurial had said I had magic and that there was a way for me to get it, to claim it, to make it mine.

I was going to need it in order to stand any chance at exposing Arianna, defeating her, and taking back the Seat of Power for my Ka, my family. It was the only way I'd have justice for my father, reclaim the Seat, and right the lines of Bamaria's succession.

But I needed more answers, more guidance. And I needed allies. I didn't know what to do or where to begin. I just knew I needed to survive this announcement and keep pretending I was ignorant of the truth long enough for Arianna to look the other way while I gathered my strength and formed a plan.

The front doors of Cresthaven opened at the end of the hall. The echoing sound was distant but clear.

My enemy approached.

Footsteps echoed, signaling the marching of the soturi, Aunt Arianna's own personal sentries, who surrounded and guarded her. The clack of her shoes against the marble floor—the familiar, specific rhythm of her gait—grew louder. She was close.

I pushed open the door before me. The entire room silenced at once. Nobles of my father's court crowded around the golden Seat of Power in black gowns and tunics, leathered boots shined to perfection for winter. They were all holding glasses of wine and staring at me with intrigue and concern.

At the opposite end of the room, standing away from the sea of prying nobles, were Morgana and Meera, both looking stoic and weak. My sisters, though they appeared to be ignored by the crowd, were being considered in sidelong, covert glances. No one ignored those wearing diadems, as no one could ignore those in line to the Seat.

I held up my chin and walked forward, the sensation of the eyes following me crawling up my spine. My skin tingled from the power of the auras swirling and rising with interest; the dark sadness from Tristan, the anger from Ka Grey, and the predatory surge of power from the Imperator all seemed to hit me at once.

I wouldn't falter.

My back straight, I nodded once toward our acting arkasva, Eathan, my father's Second, as I passed him. Shoulders tensing, I took my place beside my sisters, schooling my expression to appear noble, neutral.

"Lyr?" Morgana asked, pulling me closer. Her fingernails pierced my arm. "What's wrong with you?"

My nostrils flared as I snatched my arm back. I couldn't tell her, couldn't think it. She couldn't know. I couldn't predict how she'd react or if she'd accidentally give us away.

Do you really need to ask? I thought.

"Yes," she hissed, her dark aura flickering behind her. "There's something new. It wasn't there the last time I saw you."

I rubbed my arm, stepping back in case she tried to grab me again. *You're so dramatic. You saw me ten minutes ago.*

Her dark eyebrows formed a V. "You've been gone twenty." She stepped toward me, recapturing the space between us. Cornering me, her eyes darted to my chest, to my heart, to the place where Mercurial's Valalumir had entered, sealing my fate with his. She couldn't see the mark, the star, only the armor I wore. I had not been wearing the armor of Asherah—broken in my fight with Haleika—when I'd left this room, but now it was around my neck and shoulders, intact once again.

"Something changed. Something happened out there," she said.

A lot of things happened tonight.

Meera was leaning in now, her hazel eyes filled with a mix of grief and concern.

I stared forward, refusing to acknowledge her, not wanting to bring her any additional worry.

I'd tell my sisters as soon as this circus was over. They needed to know to truth—we had to prepare, to plan. To get our revenge. To fight.

But not yet.

I looked across the Seating Room to Tristan and his grandparents on either side of him. Lord Trajan sipped a glass of water. Lady Romula, Master of Finance on my father's council, clutched a glass of wine in a hand dripping with silver rings and bracelets.

Tristan's grandmother was one of the most prominent leaders on the Bamarian Council, the Council Arianna would soon head.

I could only focus on the soft brown eyes that made my heart ache all over again. Tristan. Loving and losing a cousin sentenced to death by the Emperor because of magic outside their control—magic society deemed evil—wasn't something anyone should endure. Not being allowed to grieve or mourn, being forbidden from honoring the dead because by Lumerian decree, they were monsters—that had been my fate for two years with Jules.

Now, Tristan faced the same pain at the loss of his cousin Haleika. And on top of his grief, on top of mine, we were being torn apart.

Lady Romula had already ended our engagement earlier tonight—or, at least, she'd ended the possibility of our engagement. Tristan had never actually given me a ring even after two years. And from the look on her face—cracked lips pressed into a smirk, eyes narrowed in disgust toward me—I knew she'd already spoken to Tristan. Despite the hurt and pain she'd caused him and me, she looked rather pleased with her plan.

I needed to talk to him, to make sure he was all right, to find some closure for what we'd been and what we'd tried to be. I needed to be there for him—especially because Haleika's death, in so many ways, was my fault.

I wasn't sure I'd ever fully forgive myself for the role I'd played in it. When I closed my eyes, I saw her lying dead, her body broken by the akadim that had killed her—that had eaten her soul. I could see her lover, Leander, dying while trying to save her. I was haunted by the vision of her transformation in the arena and could so clearly see her becoming a monster. I could see myself driving a burning stake through her heart. And I could hear the agonizing screams she'd made, screams that had stopped when Rhyan—my apprentice, my guard, my friend, my love—had ended her pain by cutting off her head.

I clutched at my heart, my breath coming short as the whole scene played before my eyes. The fear and adrenaline I'd felt in the arena still pumped through my veins.

I'd done what I'd had to do to survive and protect Rhyan's life. But I didn't know how I was going to live with it—the knowledge of the lengths I was willing to go to in order to protect those I loved.

Or the knowledge of what I'd done to Tristan, the boy I'd known my whole life, the boy I still loved so deeply...just not the way I was supposed to. Only one person had ever owned my heart like that.

A dark shadow pierced through me, pulling my attention away. It was the shadow that had haunted my nightmares since I'd last seen Jules. The dark swirl of energy emanated from the powerful aura of the Imperator.

His dark eyes met mine, as his fingers flexed at his side, dancing over the hilt of his sword. A small grin played on his lips. He sent out a sensation of victory—he'd wanted my attention, and he'd gotten it. A shudder ran through me.

Phantom fingers pressed into my back, into the open wounds he'd ordered and reopened when he'd tortured me months earlier. My hands automatically squeezed into fists, and I had to fight to uncurl them, to not reveal the effect he had on me. He wasn't touching me now. He wasn't close enough to touch me. But I wasn't safe from him. Nor was I safe from his warlord, the Bastardmaker, or the Imperator's horrible son and heir, Viktor.

Being removed from the line of succession and losing my status and station as heir meant I was more vulnerable than ever.

I pulled my gaze away and automatically searched the room for the one set of eyes I knew would bring me comfort, would make me feel safe. Emerald green eyes.

But Rhyan wasn't here. He'd been called away in the last hour, sent to guard the outer walls of the fortress.

There was so much happening in Cresthaven that I hadn't considered how odd it was for there to be such a last-minute change in guard. Or how strange it was for Rhyan to be ordered away from my side. Since he'd been placed on my security team as one of my personal bodyguards and escorts, he had rarely been called away from me—unless he was needed to hunt akadim.

Over a dozen soldiers stood guard before me now. Not one wore the gold of Ka Batavia; not one served Bamaria or was loyal to my family and country. My father had been publicly murdered, my sisters openly attacked, and instead of increasing my protection detail, I'd been left more open and exposed than ever. Where was Aemon, the Ready? Or our soturi, our army?

I was surrounded by the foreign Soturi of Ka Kormac, men loyal to the Imperator—my enemy. Every soturion before me was male and wore silver armor styled like the pelt of a wolf. About half had the black beady eyes of the Bastardmaker, the disgusting excuse for a man who'd carried Jules away on the Imperator's orders. He was the monster who led Kormac's soturi.

The foreign army of Ka Kormac had been occupying our country for as long as I could remember, their numbers growing each year. But they'd never been armed within Cresthaven. Never before had we been so outnumbered.

Even Arianna had been surrounded by the soldiers of Ka Kormac.

Something was wrong. Something was so very wrong.

I turned back to Morgana, who'd reached forward to squeeze my hand. One squeeze—hard, painful—then she released me, resuming her posture.

Eathan adjusted his position on the golden Seat of Power, his gray robes a near perfect match for his hair. He'd become the acting Arkasva last night—placed on the Seat the moment my father had taken his last breath. A silver laurel sat atop his head. On a small table beside him, nestled over a golden plate of red rose petals, was the golden Laurel of the Arkasva. It had been the laurel of my father, the rightful ruler of Bamaria, and was about to be claimed by Arianna.

The doors to the Seating Room opened, and the dozen soturi guarding Arianna marched through the entrance, their hateful presence filling the room.

Naria entered next with the usual scowl on her face but also a darkness in her eyes I hadn't seen before.

I straightened. My mouth was tight, my heart pounding. I couldn't do this. I didn't want to do this. I didn't want to see my aunt. I couldn't stand to look at her, not when I knew the monster within. I wanted to run and hide. I wanted Rhyan to come and take me away. But he wasn't here. And I couldn't call him without risking another secret—the illegal vadati he'd given me, an heirloom of Lumeria Matavia his mother had kept until she'd died.

I clutched at the stone incased in a golden charm around my neck, concealed behind Asherah's armor.

Inhale...exhale...inhale.... His voice was clear in my mind, commanding me, calming me.

The door filled with Aunt Arianna's aura. Her red hair was styled into a crown with little golden beads, ready to accept the Laurel of the Arkasva. Her golden seraphim arm cuff was back in place, shining on her arm against her glittering black dress.

The eyes of the black seraphim met mine.

CHAPTER THREE

ARIANNA'S BLUE EYES WERE piercingly intelligent and observant, looking me up and down in that assessing way she had. I froze with fear, my entire body locking. She swept her gaze to Morgana and Meera. My throat went dry as I prayed they didn't reveal anything, that I'd kept my mind blank enough for Morgana not to know what I did.

Then Arianna's eyes softened, her expression filling with sorrow and motherly concern.

She didn't know. I exhaled. She didn't know I knew.

Her mouth lifted into the soft, sympathetic smile she'd given me hundreds of times before. The smile that had once comforted me, that I'd longed for when I'd been locked up in the Shadow Stronghold. Now, my stomach twisted as I watched her. She was my blood, her face one I knew better than my own—one that had been identical to mine when I was younger. We had looked so alike at my age that when Meera first had the vision of Arianna's treachery, we'd all believed the girl in her vision to be me.

But I no longer saw the resemblance. I no longer saw my aunt. Only a snake. A viper.

A black seraphim.

My sisters and I moved forward as one, standing beside the Seat of Power in a neat and tidy row. Meera, Heir Apparent, was next in line to the Seat, then Morgana, second in line, then me, third. Three perfect ladies, three sets of diadems.

On the other side of Eathan were the Imperator and the Bastardmaker. The Imperator's son and heir, Viktor, finished the lineup, his black eyes slitted as he sneered.

Eathan stood, glancing uneasily around the room as we all bowed. He'd always had a quiet strength to him, a commanding presence. But he was not made to be Arkasva, and it was clear he had never expected to be in this position.

"Tonight," he said, his voice deep, "we must pause our mourning of Arkasva Harren Batavia, High Lord of Bamaria, Bar Ka Mokan."

"His soul freed," came the response.

Eathan cleared his throat, his eyes reddening. "I will not name our High Lord's murderers." He spoke quietly, like he was barely able to control his emotions. "These criminals, these killers, tried to remove him from power eighteen years ago." He swallowed, and when he spoke again, it was in a near shout. "They failed. Ka Batavia was stronger. And Ka Batavia remains strong. No matter the crimes they committed last night, they will not win. Not while I draw breath."

I pressed my hands against my hips, using every ounce of willpower I had to keep from sobbing and screaming out that they already had won, that we needed to fight back, to do something.

We couldn't do anything, not while openly surrounded by armed enemies. Not when I wasn't sure who my true allies were and who was a disguised foe.

"Before I may fulfill my duty to Bamaria," Eathan continued, "I offer my sympathy to my dearest cousins, Lady Meera Batavia, Heir Apparent, and Lady Morgana Batavia and Lady Lyriana Batavia, Heirs to the Arkasva." Eathan paused, turning toward us, bowing his chin in reverence.

Meera stiffened, and Eathan's eyes met mine. A wave of sorrow flashed. His aura was always quiet and calm, a steady, reassuring contrast to the intricacies and overwhelming shows of power by others in Court. But now, his aura was full of grief and sadness.

"For eighteen years," he continued, "I've been his Second. I proudly stood everywhere he was not. I take no pleasure in holding the Seat of Power. He should be here tonight. He should be wearing his laurel." Eathan's voice shook as he gestured to the golden leaves on the table beside him. "But it is my sacred duty to wear the silver, to rule in his stead for one month. And when our next High Lady takes her Seat, we will mourn him and grieve in the manner befitting our High Lord."

I closed my eyes, knowing what came next: the announcement. Once spoken, this could not be undone.

Not until I claimed my magic.

"Lady Meera Batavia, Heir Apparent to the Arkasva, High Lord of Bamaria," Eathan said. "Please join me at the Seat."

Meera stepped forward as Arkmage Kolaya emerged from the crowd. Her thick white braids fell down her back, and her white robes trailed on the floor behind her. The scent of incense clung to her as she came forward and steadied her stave of twisted moon and sun tree branches on the ground, the crystal on its top alight with color.

"Lady Meera Batavia," she said, her voice deep and ancient. She tapped her stave against the floor, the sound echoing through the silent room. Her stave's crystal glowed, flashing red, orange, yellow, and every other color of the rainbow until it settled at last on Batavia red. The light blinked out and then shined Batavia red again and again.

It felt like a warning.

There was a final flash, and the light dimmed to black, glowing bright as obsidian. It seemed to cast a black shadow across the room.

Arkmage Kolaya's eyes focused on Meera. She leaned forward as she asked, "Are you prepared to wear the Laurel of the Arkasva and fulfill your sacred duty?"

Meera wrung her hands together then rolled her shoulders back. Her chin lifted high as the trembling of her lips stilled. "No."

Though I knew that nearly everyone in the room was aware of what her answer would be after the earlier Council meeting, the reality of her words still seemed to come as a shock, and a stilled hush fell over the room as it became even quieter.

The succession everyone had planned for and believed to be coming for the past twenty-one years was finally coming to its end.

A small smile played on Arianna's face, anticipation brimming against the power of her aura. It was subtle and tempered with feelings of weighted sadness, but I felt it, and it only confirmed what I knew.

The blade of my dagger felt heavy against the leather holster strapped to my thigh. My hand itched to push aside my dress, slide around the hilt, grab it, and slice it through Arianna's heart.

I seethed, trying to stay focused, to remain calm. But my heart was pounding with the knowledge that my father's murderer stood merely an arm's reach away. After months of training with Rhyan, I knew exactly where to stab her, what amount of pressure to use. In less than a minute, I could bring my father justice.

But to what end? A dozen soturi stood between me and my escape. I'd be caught before she closed her eyes.

I took a deep breath, wringing my hands in front of me. It took all my willpower to still myself. To remember I couldn't act without a plan.

Without my magic.

Meera coughed, clearing her throat—she looked too frail to go on, too upset to make the speech she'd prepared. But as Heir Apparent, she had to announce her replacement.

"I've spent my life preparing to be your High Lady." Meera's delicate voice shook; she was barely holding back her emotions. "But in these times of troubles and political...political...." A tear rolled down her cheek. "In these times—" Her voice caught, and then the tears were falling without abandon. Her hand, holding the small scroll with her carefully prepared speech, fell to her side.

I started forward, ready to grab Meera, pull her back from the crowd, and hide her from the disapproving, judgmental eyes of the Bamarian nobility. But Morgana beat me to it. There was a furious determination in her eyes as she grabbed Meera's speech from her.

A dark shadow cast itself over the Seating Room as Morgana turned to face our audience, her eyes daring anyone to challenge her for stepping forward. "I'll speak."

Meera's face reddened with anger. The moment she'd told us she'd abdicated, Morgana had screamed at her—denouncing her decision even though we'd all known none of us were capable of becoming arkasva, not yet, at least. Morgana and Meera's relationship still felt strained, but Meera gave a small nod and took a step back.

I held my breath, my skin crawling with fear. Morgana never made public speeches—not since her vorakh. She was easily distracted in large groups, sometimes too loud, sometimes saying the wrong thing because of what she'd heard. One misstep, and Morgana could give us all away.

She unrolled Meera's parchment and began to read. "In these times of troubles and political unrest, of domestic terrorists rising in our country and attacking our leaders, and of akadim breeching our borders," Morgana paused, swaying on the spot.

I fisted the folds of my gown. Come on, Morgs.

Morgana coughed, clearing her throat, her back straightening as her eyes ran across the parchment. She rerolled it and stared out at the Council. "Lady Meera must do what is best for our people. She's putting Bamaria before her own ego and desires. Though she sacrificed and prepared her entire life to become your High Lady, she doesn't believe she's what you need now."

Meera leaned toward me, her shoulders shaking with silenced sobs as she tried to remain composed. I placed a steadying hand on her back. She had no idea she'd handed our country over to Father's murderer and given Bamaria to our traitors in a giant bow. It was probably better this way, that she didn't know yet. I'd tell her after, and we'd plan.

"Bamaria needs strong leadership, someone who can tackle these crises head on, someone who already has years of experience." Morgana paused, and a wave of silence swept across the room. "Lady Meera Batavia, Heir Apparent to the Arkasva, officially abdicates to our aunt, Lady Arianna Batavia."

My mind flashed again to what I'd seen outside: Aunt Arianna's bared arm. Her black seraphim tattoo. The traitorous soldiers protecting her.

A few nobles gasped in feigned surprise while others shouted cheers of support. A round of applause drowned out Morgana's sudden cry as she stumbled back to my side. Her dark eyes widened, staring into mine. The color drained from her cheeks as she blinked rapidly, her bottom lip quivering, pure horror spreading across her face.

You know? I thought.

Her chest rose and fell in rapid breaths, her nostrils flaring.

Why didn't you tell me? she mouthed.

Be still, Morgs, I ordered. *Control what they see.*

Morgana closed her mouth, her bottom lip still quivering, her eyes searching the room with a kind of focus she only had when she was actively listening—reading minds, trying to learn more.

Arianna smiled widely and stepped forward, her arm extending out to beckon Meera to join her. Stumbling, Meera did, her body stilling as she endured Arianna's tight embrace. The golden cuff on Arianna's arm dug into Meera's skin before Arianna leaned back just enough to press a kiss each to Meera's cheeks. Her hand tightened around Meera's, holding it like she was a prisoner. Bile rose in my throat.

"Do you accept this honor, Lady Arianna?" Eathan asked.

Arianna bowed her chin. "Lord Eathan." She turned and curtseyed. "Lady Meera." Rising, she adjusted her dress, her hands before her in supplication. "I always believed in my sister Lady Marianna's knowledge, believed in her choice for successor. But I, too, am bound by Ka Batavia to protect Bamaria. I will hold it my sacred duty to take on the role of Arkasva and High Lady as my many ancestors did before me."

"We honor you, Lady Arianna," said Arkmage Kolaya. "As custom, a month will pass to allow for the smooth transition of power. Lord Eathan, Bamaria's acting arkasva, will rule in the interim, making decisions he believes would have been made by our late High Lord. During that time, Lady Arianna will be preparing and making her arrangements and finding her own successor to be the Master of Education on the Council of Bamaria."

Kolaya tapped her stave on the ground. The crystal atop flashed with light as Eathan stepped forward, his arms wide. Meera stood to one side as Arianna walked to the other.

"Lady Meera," Kolaya said, her voice commanding and echoing through the room, "you shall still carry the title of Heir Apparent until the anointment of Lady Arianna, at which time you will step down as heir, and the line of succession will be redrawn."

I swayed, feeling Morgana's hand on the small of my back.

Meera wasn't the only one losing her title as heir. Morgana and I were, too.

Eathan took Arianna's hand and then Meera's, holding them together before him so their wrists touched. Kolaya produced her blade and slid it quickly underneath their joined wrists. She held a small silver bowl beneath to catch the blood. The cut made, she waved her stave, and instantly, the two wounds were healed, leaving small red scars in their wake. With another wave of her stave, Kolaya floated the bowl in midair, guiding it above

Arianna and Meera's heads. Two droplets fell upon each of their heads.

As Kolaya stepped back, Eathan picked up my father's laurel and held it over Meera's head, where it was supposed to be, then moved it ceremoniously over Arianna's.

I had one month until the laurel rested permanently on her head.

"I present your next Arkasva Batavia, High Lady of Bamaria."

I squeezed my eyes shut and held my breath as I sank into a curtsey.

"It is done," Eathan said. "I humbly wear the silver laurel, the color of the moon to show the cycle of my own reign. In one month, I shall pass the golden Laurel of the Arkasva, of the constant sun, onto Lady Arianna. May you rule for the rest of your days."

"Thank you, Lord Eathan." She retreated, neck craning as she observed her subjects.

Eathan's expression hardened, as he once again took his seat, leaning back against the golden chair. He looked bone-weary and exhausted, but there was determination in his eyes. "I plan to use my time on the Seat to bring the Emartis to justice. The Shadow Stronghold has already been filled with these villains. But we know more of them are out there now. Each one must be found and brought to justice."

The Imperator stalked forward. A small sneer crept across his lips, as he turned toward me. His eyes dipped down the length of my dress then rose back up, tracing my every curve.

He smoothed his cloak, black with a golden border. The markings gave him power and jurisdiction outside his country, and being nephew to the Emperor allowed him to abuse that power. "Lord Eathan, before you use the command afforded you by the silver laurel of a temporary arkasva," he adjusted his own golden laurel, "I must address the Council." Eyeing every noble in the room, his aura flared with predatory shadows. "I am happy to see our traditions honored and the will of Emperor Theotis obeyed. But, as Lady Meera said, this country faces crisis after crisis.

"We will maintain the formalities and rituals. But with so many threats against your country, I see no reason for Lady Arianna to delay taking her Seat."

I stiffened. My understanding of why Aemon was missing, why the only soturi in here were loyal to the Imperator, came like a strike of lightning.

He was going to break protocol. He was going to use Arianna and claim even more power for himself tonight.

"Bamaria faces threats on their border from akadim, akadim who not only breeched your walls, but maimed, killed, and turned innocent citizens of Bamaria forsaken. No one is safe from their threat—not even the noble members of the Bamarian Council."

I caught Tristan's eye, a tear escaping. He turned away. Lady Romula's hands shook with fury. It was a low blow—using their pain for his political machinations.

The Imperator's feral eyes rested on this display of grief. He knew exactly what he'd just done. "The Emperor has ordered me to face this task head on, and I am more than ready," he drawled. A few of the soturi in the room snickered at his play on words, which hinted he was a stronger warrior than Aemon, the Ready. I eyed the room again. Where was he? Why wasn't he present for these proceedings?

Several of the nobles before us seemed to be thinking this as well, their own eyes wandering, their weight switching uneasily from foot to foot as whispers began to fly back and forth.

I hadn't seen an order be visibly given, but the Imperator's wolves all began to shift, taking slow, measured steps through the room, adjusting their gazes and their stances and embedding themselves more fully into the Court.

"It is of the utmost importance that we take a delicate approach to the issue of the Emartis. With such division in your country and threats from outside, we must avoid dissolving into chaos, into civil war. Arresting anyone who disagreed with the Ka's rule is not the answer. Further dividing the country will not lead to peace. We must all come together. Ka Batavia and the Council of Bamaria must unite behind Lady Arianna and honor the alliance created with Ka Kormac in order to protect your people. A month is too long for the crisis you face." He stepped before Eathan and snatched the silver laurel from his head.

Eathan's hands rose up as if to take it back before he forced them down to the golden armrests, his fingers tensed.

"Lord Eathan," the Imperator's voice shouted across the Seating Room, "in the name of the Senate and Emperor Theotis,

High Lord of Lumeria Nutavia, I declare your services to Bamaria complete. I place the silver laurel of the acting Arkasva on Lady Arianna's head until we may replace it with the gold. Lady Arianna shall begin her rule of Bamaria tonight."

My throat went dry. The Imperator's soturi were still moving about, beginning to surround the entire Council. Two of his wolves were approaching my sisters and me.

I schooled my expression as my heart pounded through my chest.

The doors to the Seating room exploded open, slamming into the walls with a bang. A dark shadowy presence gusted through the air—an aura of power, death, and readiness. Golden armor and a red arkturion cloak glowed behind the shadows spilling forth.

Morgana gasped, as a small cry of relief escaped my lips.

Finally, Aemon was here—and he had an army of Ka Batavia soturi behind him.

CHAPTER FOUR

"Apologies for the interruption, my lord." Aemon strode forward, bowing before Eathan. "Or is it your grace now? For one month, yes?"

The room stilled, and my heart lightened at Aemon's presence. The Ready had squashed the rebellion last time. He had single-handedly stopped the Emartis, saved my father from the mob, and defeated Arianna's husband, my uncle Tarek. Because of Aemon's quick acting, Arianna had first been arrested. The event had earned him his nickname and his reputation as a God of Death.

From the presiding silence of every nobleman and woman before me, the Imperator himself, and the Bastardmaker, I knew that this fact had not been forgotten. If anything, Aemon's presence tonight seemed to remind everyone of what exactly had happened eighteen years earlier. The parallels could not be ignored, especially when Turion Dairen, Aemon's cousin and Second, appeared at his side, his eyes blazing with fury. Dairen had taken my father's killing blow during the rebellion—he was the reason my father had survived with only a limp.

"Arkturion Aemon," drawled the Imperator. "Welcome to the proceedings."

The Ready bowed once more, the movement deep enough to avoid censure but brief enough to assure insult. His eyes darkened as he assessed the scene before him: Eathan, laurel-less, sitting in the Seat of Power, and Arianna, standing beside him, adorned with the silver laurel of the arkasva.

"The hour is later than I anticipated," Aemon said. "I apologize for my tardiness. I should have liked to witness these proceedings from the start. Unfortunately, we had something of a commotion outside, your highness. Hundreds of Lumerians gathered beyond the fortress wall under the impression they were to receive a special announcement." His fingers danced along the hilt of his sword, his aura pulsing.

The Imperator glared, and at once I knew he'd been behind it.

Aemon shrugged. "However, I was not informed of any such special announcement, particularly since the city had been ordered into lockdown and every last Lumerian has been sent home. Or they've been sent to the Shadow Stronghold after some," he coughed, "debate. I commend the soturi standing behind me. Thanks to their efforts, we all came to an agreement." The silver starfire blade in his hand reflected the flames of the torches in each corner of the room. Aemon turn the hilt in his hand, the steel shining before he slid the weapon back through his scabbard.

"Agreement?" The Imperator leaned back on his heels, both hands sliding across his leather belt.

Aemon nodded. "Lumerians who'd approached the wall could choose their bed for the evening—their own or the prison beds. Lady Sila, you must forgive me if you find your quarters overburdened tonight. I know the Stronghold was already full. However, Emartis were not given the choice. We do have some soturi of Ka Kormac that appear to be without assignment. Perhaps they may take the additionally needed posts we need covered." Aemon's eyes settled on the Imperator, the challenge clear. "I, of course, defer to your judgement, your highness."

Every soturion in the room wearing silver armor of Ka Kormac took a fighting stance, their legs widening, their hands on their sword hilts and daggers, their shoulders tensed. They were slowly extricating themselves from the crowd, stalking forward and center, coming into formation.

The Imperator's lips quirked, giving me a sinking feeling in my gut. The Imperator looked...happy. As if he'd expected no less—as if this were a trap he'd set for the Ready.

The small army that stood behind Aemon at last filed into the room. They all wore the golden armor of Ka Batavia with their shoulders covered in sharpened seraphim-feather-shaped metal. The sigil of Ka Batavia—the proper sigil, a silver moon above golden seraphim wings—was emblazoned across their chests.

Nothing was right. Nothing was going according to plan. I should have been in my apartment with Rhyan celebrating my victory over the Emperor's test. Not grieving Haleika, Leander, and my father. Not watching the Imperator usurp power with Arianna.

But at least our soturi still stood strong. At least they were here now, armed and more than capable of fighting the soturi loyal to the Imperator.

I held my breath until the last soturion made his way into the room, and my heart stopped as he did. This soldier stood tall, his presence commanding, the muscles of his arms clearly displayed beneath his green cloak and armor, but he did not wear gold like the others. Black leather covered his chest and abdomen. It was singularly unique armor that only he wore, armor that had originated in the north with an original sigil design that bound him to me.

His sigil showed a seraphim's profile facing a gryphon. A sun and a moon had been filled in with blood—the blood of a kashonim. My blood. And his.

Rhyan's green eyes found mine across the room at once, and for a second, time stopped. The scar running through his left eye was more pronounced than usual, his skin pale. His deep brown curls stuck to his head with a mix of sweat and snow. He'd been fighting hard out there, defending our fortress.

Defending me.

I tried to scan him for any sign of injury, but from where I stood, he only seemed to be sustaining the few he'd received the previous night. His boots were muddied, but his soturion cloak was perfectly wrapped around his waist and shoulders, held in place by his black leather belt. Seven straps hung past his thighs, each one with a shining and sharpened Valalumir star at the end.

There was a white bandage on his neck—an injury he'd gotten after taking me home last night. I'd been unconscious after defeating Haleika and watching my father die.

Beneath the cuffs on his wrists was another set of bandages helping to heal burn marks from the bindings he'd been tied up in while I'd fought in the arena.

It took all I had not to go running into his arms to throw my arms around his waist, feel his solid sturdiness, breathe in his pine and musk scent. I remained in place, held by his gaze and warmed by the reassurance of his presence.

"I commend all of you for your efforts," the Imperator said. "It is more important now than ever to keep Bamaria safe, to defend Ka Batavia and show a united front. And this is why we have all decided to forgo the month's long wait for Lady Arianna to take her Seat as Arkasva."

Rhyan stiffened from across the room, the look on his face indicating he immediately understood the situation.

Only he didn't—not fully. He didn't know that Arianna was a traitor. But he understood the terror and overreach of Imperators better than most Lumerians ever could. Even without knowing Arianna's role in leading us here, I could see in Rhyan's face his awareness that if Imperator Kormac wanted her to rule tonight, it was for his benefit—no good could come of it.

And while Aemon's presence in the Seating Room seemed to have placed the Soturi of Ka Kormac at a standstill, it was not enough to stop the proceedings.

Eathan was still being stripped of his duties as acting arkasva. A weight settled on my heart as he stood from the Seat, something final in the slope of his shoulders.

It was like seeing my father die all over again.

Eathan lowered his head, his expression grave. He looked so bare without the laurel even though he'd only had minutes to wear it. He walked past us, his aura heavy.

I'm sorry, he mouthed.

"Lady Arianna Batavia," said the Imperator, "please take your Seat."

Every Ka Kormac soturion in the room tensed. Their feet separated into fighting stances, their arms strained, their hands reached for their blades, and their eyes shifted between the members of the Bamarian Council, me and my sisters, Aemon, Rhyan, and the soturi who remained loyal to us.

I sucked in a breath, my hand sliding down my leg as I found Rhyan's gaze. His jaw was tensed, his fingers wrapped around the hilt of his sword, his arm flexed. One word from the Imperator or Aemon, and war would break out in the room.

The Imperator's aura swept out. I felt his predatory energy poking and prodding, looking for an objection—a reason to call his men to action.

Everyone remained still, silent, watching as Arianna swept her gown out from beneath her. The skirt fell in delicate folds as she sat, elegant and regal, on the Seat of Power.

Aemon's posture remained stiff, but his hand fell from his sword to his side. Rhyan pursed his lips in response, watching the movement. Many of the soturi wearing gold seemed to take this as a signal to relax and released their grips on their sword hilts, but Rhyan remained tensed—his fingers locked into place, his eyes sweeping the room. I watched his gaze land on Arianna, and I followed suit, saw her carefully eyeing the golden Laurel of the Arkasva, embedded in its roses, a hint of longing in her expression. She lifted her piercing blue gaze back to the Imperator, who was approaching with the silver laurel.

"Lady Arianna," he said, "this act restores order to Bamaria and, at last, returns your country to its traditions of female arkasvim in power."

The Bastardmaker smirked. Several of the nobles, either clueless to what was truly happening or secretly having support- ed Arianna all along, grinned widely and clapped quietly. The Godsdamned Moriel traitors. The snakes.

"I place the silver laurel on your head. And I trust you will know the right choices to make over the next month before we can replace your laurel with gold." The silver leaves nestled over her crown of braids, a stark contrast to the golden beads she'd threaded through them.

Arianna smiled solemnly. "I will make Bamaria proud and secure our borders. I promise to calm the tension within."

There was another round of applause. I tried to clap to keep Arianna from harboring any suspicions, keep the soturi in the room from turning against me, and Rhyan from alerting to my unease. But my hands were glued to my side. Morgana wore a horrified expression, her face paler than usual. Only Meera was capable of playing her role correctly.

Only Meera didn't know.

"Your grace," drawled the Imperator, his voice mocking, "to- gether we shall expose the negligence of the Soturi of Ka Batavia. Whoever allowed the beastly akadim in, blood is on their hands."

Haleika's blood is on your hands. And Leander's! Ka Kormac let them in, not Ka Batavia! My teeth grinded.

Morgana pinched my hip.

I sucked in a breath, straightened my back, and forced my mouth into a small smile.

Control what they see. Gods. I wasn't going to last much longer. I was too angry, too emotional, too hungry for vengeance. I wasn't the girl I'd been the past two years, able to smile prettily no matter what. Sit still, follow orders, maintain our reputation at all costs. I needed this to end. I needed to get away, to be alone.

Arianna nodded. "Your highness," she said sweetly, "I spare no soturion to this cause of keeping the demons out, ensuring we never let such a tragedy as the one borne now by Ka Grey befall us again. You have Bamaria's resources and our soturi at your disposal, including Arkturion Aemon's legions."

Aemon's eyes narrowed, his aura pulsing with darkness.

Morgana shook her head, watching him carefully before she turned back to Arianna. "Shit," she muttered.

"Turion Brenna," Arianna said. "Please step forward."

Brenna approached the Seat, bowing before Arianna. "Your grace." She rose. "What do you command?"

"I know your passion for bringing the Emartis to justice is strong, and I trust your ability to do so. Our prisons are already overrun with those suspected of being members. Naming the Emartis terrorists by the Council was also an important step in national security. But I do not believe them a present threat. Though I never sought out the Seat of Power, they wished me to have it. And right now, to avoid chaos, we need Bamaria to rally together, to support me. Will we now punish those Bamarians who desired to see me in the Seat?"

My heart pounded. She was practically admitting she supported the Emartis. By the Gods. How secure was she to be so bold now?

"Your grace," Brenna said, "none of us would think to punish those happy to see you as Arkasva Batavia. I include myself as one. But the Emartis murdered our High Lord, have committed multiple acts of terrorism, and have on more than one occasion threatened the lives of the heirs. They must be brought to justice. Otherwise, we allow them to set a dangerous precedent."

Arianna leaned forward, her black dress glittering, her hands gripping the golden armrests on either side of her. "We will find those guilty, I swear it. And when we do, Gods have mercy on them. But I do believe many of the Emartis to be innocent, uneducated Bamarians who were merely swayed by public opinion. No ruler is perfect. Harren had his faults. Our people were not always happy and fell prey to negative stories of his rule, easily enticed to support another—to support me. We cannot punish our people for such things. I cannot have that be my first act—to forsake those who show me allegiance."

She'd publicly referred to my father with no title attached, no address. Morgana's aura flared, and I dared look ahead, meeting Tristan's eye across the room. His head was cocked to the side, and there was a frown across his face as he played with the silver sigil ring on his finger. Beside him, Lady Romula was looking up with the tiniest smile on her dry, cracked lips, her hands pressed together before her gown, her glass of wine long finished and discarded.

"We must remember," Arianna continued, her long fingers wrapped around the golden chair beneath her, "there are good and bad people on both sides. I will not categorize those who celebrate my ascension tonight with those who sought the means to make it happen." She sat back, resting her chin in her hand. "Arkturion Aemon, I know you led our soturi bravely tonight, but I cannot thank you enough for allowing those who clearly only offered support to me with no ill will toward Ka Batavia to remain untouched."

Aemon bowed. "Of course, Lady Arianna. I certainly have no wish to conflate the two." His hands remained flexed at his side. He was playing his own role tonight. I understood—even if I wanted him to cut through our enemies right here and now, we had to be patient, to gather our forces and when we were ready, then we would take back what was ours.

And when the time is right, you will strike and have your revenge. And then you will retake the throne of Bamaria.

Mercurial's words ran through my mind. They were becoming clearer and clearer. I had to claim my magic. When we removed Arianna from the Seat, we'd need an alternative to rule in her stead.

Not Meera. Not Morgana. Me.

And how somehow, I knew that it was going to come to this. The deep dark parts of me that wanted to rule, that studied for this without any reason to suspect I might ascend. I'd been preparing my entire life to step into my power. But my magic—that was step one.

"Right now, our priority is the border," Arianna said. "Valyati made that clear. Turion Brenna, you wish to serve me?"

Brenna bowed. "Yes, your grace. More than anything."

Flames crackled from the torches behind Arianna until there was a small pop that made me jump.

"Turion Brenna, we will require all of your resources as Master of Peace to protect Bamaria against akadim. After our borders are safe, we'll find the villains."

"Yes, your grace," Brenna said stiffly.

Arianna waved. "Let it be so." She turned to Lady Sila. "You'll watch the Emartis. Keep an eye on them and report to me."

"Exactly as you wish." The spy master stepped back, her shimmering cloak of invisibility causing her to vanish into the crowd.

"Good," the Imperator drawled, clapping slowly. "We now have our ruler in place. We have a plan to secure the borders and an effective way to approach the Emartis." He grinned at Aemon.

"All is well," Aemon said carefully. There was something dangerous in his aura and expression, like a dark shadow had fallen over him. "I understand we are doing things by the book to ensure a smooth transfer of power. However, given the contention between those who support the Emartis and those who don't, I believe it is in the best interest of the former Heirs to the Arkasva to have additional protections in place. Particularly since the attack did not simply stop with Arkasva Batavia's fall."

I shuddered. I'd been unconscious for that. I still wasn't sure what had happened to Morgana and Meera on their way back to Cresthaven—each with ten escorts protecting them. Or what Rhyan had gone through to get me home. I only knew he was sporting a large bandage on his neck as a result.

"I'd like to take charge of the heirs' protection if it pleases your grace." Aemon nodded toward Arianna.

She turned toward us, her eyebrows lifted in question. "Do you wish Arkturion Aemon to do this for you? I am more than happy to assign a team of escorts on your behalf."

My eyes caught Morgana's, and she offered the slightest nod of confirmation before her dark eyes flicked to Meera. There were unspoken words between them before Meera nodded. Stepping forward, Meera publicly accepted Aemon's offer of protection.

Warmth rising up my body let me know Rhyan's gaze was on me. One eyebrow was furrowed in concentration. He was my bodyguard, along with a team of soturi and escorts who'd trailed me my entire life. I already knew he was going to want some say in my protection moving forward.

"Before I leave for the capitol," announced the Imperator, "I'd like to know matters here are settled. To avoid any further dispute, false claims, or rising rebellions, Lady Meera must publicly proclaim Lady Arianna as Arkasva and High Lady of Bamaria tomorrow."

Publicly. So no other claims would be considered legitimate. So there'd be no going back, no changing our minds, no bringing forth evidence of her treachery.

Meera nodded and curtseyed to the Imperator in response. "Your highness."

"Thank you all," Arianna said, "for welcoming me, for your support. We've done enough for tonight. I believe Bamaria to be on the mend.We shall convene in the morning and begin to make further arrangements. Now I shall retire to the Arkasva's rooms."

My stomach turned. Arianna was going to sleep in my father's bed. She was going to stay in Cresthaven. She'd have access to every floor, every hall, every room—including ours.

Including Meera's, with her paintings. The proof of her vorakh.

Meera's vision of Arianna as the black seraphim was painted from floor to ceiling in full color in her room. I had no doubt in my mind that if Arianna saw it, she would not make the same mistakes we had—she'd know exactly who was in the painting. She would recognize herself, her treachery.

Morgana stiffened, her eyes following some soturion I wasn't familiar with, before she whipped her head back at me, her dark eyebrows furrowed into a V and her mouth tight.

Arianna was surrounded by a host of sentries and escorted outside, as the Seating Room was slowly beginning to empty. Tristan looked up at me, his eyes red, his bottom lip quivering. He was duty bound to follow his Ka from the room; most likely he'd go home to the Grey Villa, where they'd mourn Haleika in secret. At least, I hoped they would. Someone had to mourn her. Someone had to remember who she was—who she'd been before her soul had been stolen. If Tristan didn't grieve, he'd shut down even more than he already had, turn into an empty mask like I'd been after Jules—until Rhyan had pulled me back to myself.

Tristan offered a sad smile and left the room, his feet heavy on the ground.

I turned back to Morgana. We had so much to discuss, but first, we had to protect our own secrets.

We need to remove all of Meera's paintings.

Morgana nodded and pulled Meera toward her. She took Meera's hand in hers, and then she took mine.

Across the room, Rhyan stood guard. His eyes moved slowly down my body, lingering on my chest, on the armor I hadn't been wearing when he had left me outside—on the armor concealing the mark Mercurial had branded onto me. Rhyan frowned and bit his lip, his good eyebrow furrowed with concern.

I could still feel his touch from just an hour ago, his fingers brushing against the sensitive skin over my heart, over the place where an akadim had tried to suck out my soul. It was the same place where Mercurial's bargain had entered me—and now trapped me.

Even at this distance, I could see the anguish in his expression. I could sense the worry he felt over what exactly had occurred in my meeting with Mercurial after he'd left.

For a second, I wasn't sure if it was my heart or the piece of the Afeya's soul that was beating so profusely against my ribcage. I didn't want Rhyan to see what had been done to me. I didn't want it to hurt him. I didn't want it to be real.

Aemon called out to Rhyan, ordering him to more guard duty outside in case any Lumerians were still riled up by the Imperator and decided to return.

The longing expression in Rhyan's eyes made me ache for him, and it took all I had not to break free of Morgana's grasp and run to his side. But we still had roles to play, duties to perform.

He lowered his chin, his eyes blazing, before he turned on his heels and headed through the door, his hand already reaching for the hilt of his sword.

I stared after him, watching his body vanish beyond the threshold, wanting to call him back.

"Lyr," Morgana hissed. "Not now." She turned her head toward Meera.

I nodded.

"Lady Lyriana, Lady Morgana, Lady Meera," Aemon said, turning toward us. He reached for his belt, as he frowned. His aura darkened, and I could feel the guilt coming from him for having failed his arkasva, for having failed in his duty as the Ready.

Morgana's eyes narrowed in annoyance, as she released our hands, her arms folded across her chest. She despised these types of gestures, the formality and expectation of condolences.

"I am sorry for your loss, your graces," Aemon said, his words conveying all the heaviness I felt. "I am sorry I did not stop them this time. I will carry that knowledge my entire life. I lay my sword at your feet."

Meera sniffled again, but Morgana's impatience was growing. "Thank you, Arkturion," she said coldly.

"I'll be in touch. We should discuss your security details as soon as possible. Know that the fortress is well protected tonight." He nodded once at us, throat bobbing, and turned.

We were protected from the outside perhaps, but not from our enemies within.

"Gods. We need to get upstairs," Morgana said urgently, groaning as she spoke.

I turned toward her, my heart stopping. A sudden sensation of freezing rain poured down on me.

Meera's aura.

By the Gods.... We were surrounded by so many people, so many enemies.

Meera paled, her eyes rolling back.

Fuck.

Morgana and I switched positions, putting Meera between us, both taking one of her arms. Her head rolled back, and Morgana winced, gasping in pain. Fuck. Fuck.

I switched my hold on Meera, grabbing her with my other arm, using my hand to prop up her head, my grip tightening in her hair.

"Run," I said to Morgana. "Now!"

CHAPTER FIVE

MORGANA

GODS. MY HEAD FELT like it had been split in two. Since last night, since Father died, my vorakh had felt more sensitive. Harder to shut off, to ignore. We'd just barely made it up the stairs to Meera's room without notice and before her strength had become too much for me to handle. By the grace of the Gods, we were in her room before all the nosy ass-kissing nobles crawling the fortress for my father's scraps could hear. But just barely. My legs gave out the moment Lyr closed the door behind us. Meera's vision was already too loud, too intense, too much. My back bowed in pain as my ass hit the ground, my head slamming into the doorframe.

Fuck.

I tried to open my eyes, to crawl to Lyr, to help her. She'd hauled Meera onto her bed and was pinning her down, her arms straining.

Meera's mouth was open, and she was screaming. Too loudly.

Lyr tried to cover Meera's mouth then grabbed a pillow to muffle her cries before anyone could hear.

I tried again to help my sisters, but I couldn't move. All I could do was try and take my stave from my belt to cast a spell on the room that would silence our voices. But white flashed across my vision, and I was gone. No longer myself.

Akadim. Bright red eyes, sharp, long teeth, clawed hands...the beasts towered over me...over Meera. In the distance, I could hear her scream, feel her fear and terror. A claw slashed across my face, and fire erupted beneath my skin. I was burning and bleeding, the blood dripping down my body hot as flames.

I scrambled back. Or, Meera did...I was still her. I saw what she did, trapped in her vision. Trapped in a way I never had been before. Meera hit a stone, and I felt the sensation of it slamming into my spine. I also felt the Godsdamned door again. I felt everything at once—my vorakh, her vorakh. It was too much. Too painful. Too terrifying.

I tried again to grab my stave, but my hands weren't working. I was Meera. And I was hearing Meera. And I was Lyr. All at once.

No! Please. Lyr was crying, losing the battle to keep Meera silent, losing the battle to keep her from pain, to do what she had to to stop the vision. To pull our sister back to us.

My mouth opened, but no sound came out.

The akadim in my mind struck again, a blow to my jaw that left me seeing stars. Meera was lying unconscious, the front of her body on fire, the back freezing as she—I—sank into a bed of snow.

We were surrounded by roughened, craggy, snow-capped mountains, nestled in a valley.

My eyes closed, the vision going dark. My veins burned. Something was inside me, changing me, killing me.

When I opened my eyes again, I was still trapped in Meera's vision. The snow was melting, the mountains bare, the cliffs reddened by flames burning in the distance.

I stared down at my hands—at Meera's hands. Her nails had elongated into claws. I screamed, recognizing them as the same claws I had seen last night on Haleika Grey. I was an akadim.

Meera turned, frantic, screeching with terror at her transformation, still in pain. I turned with her. I still was her. A goddess lay on the mountaintop. Fires burned everywhere, but she remained untouched, unburned. Snow fell in a protective circle around her body.

The goddess opened her eyes, yawning as if she'd slept a long time, as if she'd been asleep since the birth of the universe. Meera's heart was beating too quickly. Each thud against her chest was like a punch to the gut. I cried out, hearing my actual voice rise against the noise inside Meera's head.

I pulled myself from the vision by sheer will and forced an eye open, using all I had to tear myself away from Meera's mind. I was out just long enough to see her lunge for Lyr and get her hands around Lyr's neck. They struggled until both of my sisters were flying off the bed.

Lyr cried out as her back hit the ground. Meera landed on top her, fingers squeezing her neck, prying off the necklace Lyr had put back on tonight.

Then I was torn away from the world, thrown back into Meera's mind.

"Asherah," I said, Meera said, the akadim we were trapped in said.

The goddess stood, her hair fiery red, her eyes hazel and clever, her—

That wasn't Asherah. That was Lyr.

We lunged for her, clawed hands slicing through the necklace across her chest—no, no, it was armor.

No! Someone was crying. Me? Lyr? Both of us?

Lyr screamed in pain. *It's burning! I'm on fire.*

We had to stop. We were hurting her. Me and Meera as this monster were hurting Lyr inside the vision. And Meera, possessed by her vorakh, was hurting her in real life.

"You remember who you are now," we hissed, our voice gravelly, inhuman, male and female. Ancient. Powerful. Terrifying. A combination of too many voices at once—voices that should never have been mixed. Lyr's eyes widened, true fear behind them. "But we've always known. We have tracked you for centuries, Goddess. And we've always been ready for your return. Our army is ready. And this time, you will fail."

Both Lyrs cried out—the Lyr in the vision and the real Lyr here in Meera's bedroom.

Lyr yelled out again. The Lyr in the room. She called out a name I couldn't decipher. She was crying, pleading. Begging him to come. And, suddenly, there was another voice here with us, a male speaking low and urgently with a northern lilt....

I knew who it was. I'd heard his voice before. But I couldn't recall his name or his face while trapped in the vision.

"Auriel won't save you this time, Asherah," we spat.

Our akadim hands ripped the armor from Lyr's neck. She wore it inside the vision, too, along with a floor-length white dress, a low V cut down the center—her dress from Valyati.

The skin between her breasts burst into flames, and she screamed, stumbling back. We chased her forward, and the fire cleared, revealing a seven-pointed star on her skin. The Valalumir.

The Lyr in Meera's vision looked down. There were two versions of her body now. One was standing and one was asleep, curled up by her bare feet.

The one on the ground was clutching a crystal in her arms. It was red against the flames and glowing, too bright to look at directly. The light was unlike anything I'd ever seen. My akadim claws rushed up to my face to cover my eyes. It was too much. I didn't like it. The light hurt me.

I knew the crystal was a lost shard of the Valalumir.

The awake Lyr in the vision bent down to pick it up. I screamed. The crystal in her hand glowed brighter and brighter. Too much. Too much.

I tried to cover my eyes. Meera was screaming, the akadim we'd become was screaming. Pain seared through my head. My eyes were closed, and still I saw the light, still it set my eyes on fire.

I lost consciousness. I was no longer Meera. I was no longer Morgana. I was no longer....

Drool slid down my lips as I woke. My head was pounding and my arm and back sore as if I'd been hit. Lyr hovered over Meera's bed, her cheeks streaked with tears. Her dark hair, wild from being pulled, stuck up in odd places around her diadem. Her apprentice and bodyguard, Rhyan—*Rhyan*, right, why couldn't I remember his name before—was standing behind Lyr in his leather armor and green soturion cloak, his arms crossed over his chest. One eyebrow—the only eyebrow he seemed capable of moving—was narrowed. His aura was pulsing and seemed to wrap around Lyr from behind, like he was cloaking her in it. His gaze was full of such a heavy intensity and intimacy as he watched her, I wanted to look away, like I'd seen something private. More intimate even than when I read another's mind.

"Meera?" I croaked, my voice hoarse from screaming.

I crawled to my feet, stumbling to the bed, my legs giving way before I made it. I clutched at her blankets, knees still buckling as I hauled myself to her side.

Blood streaked her face. Her nose bled.

Morgana? she thought. She was terrified, her entire body shaking. *Did you see? Akadim?*

I clutched her chin, pulling her face toward mine, trying to reassure her. "I know. I was there. I saw," I breathed.

Her lips quivered, her gaze holding mine as more blood dripped, running over her pale pink lips. *It's never felt this intense before.*

"Morgana." Rhyan moved to my side of the bed. "Here, let me help you." He extended a hand for me to grip.

I waved him off. "I got it." I only wanted to get to my sister. To make sure she was all right. With a burst of energy, I pushed myself all the way onto the bed and crawled to lay beside her.

Meera's eyes were closed, but she was breathing. Lyr was wiping the fresh bout of blood from her face. Behind her, a pile of dirty clothes was topped with a bloodied towel. Lyr's arms were scratched up, and a trickle of blood ran down her elbow from the golden cuff she always wore. Within it was the log she kept of Meera's visions.

She protected that thing with her life, though I honestly didn't know what good keeping a record of every vision did aside from stress her out. Meera's vorakh would, at some point in time, drive her mad, break her mind. No amount of recording times and dates or brewing oils was going to stop that from happening. Lyr wanted to save her as much as I did, but she was so focused on putting a bandage on top of the wound. Bandages bled through unless the cuts were sealed, the poison extracted, the infected limbs removed.

But that was what I had been quietly working on.

Getting to the heart of what *they* knew was our only hope.

"Did anyone hear anything?" Lyr asked urgently. "Morgs?" *Were we too loud? Are we safe?*

I glared at Lyr before I closed my eyes, wincing and bracing my hands against the bed. I spent so much time trying to block out the voices, to silence the noise, I rarely opened myself up to hear them. Every time I openly listened, I nearly blacked out from pain and suffered a migraine for days. And since my vorakh felt extra sensitive, a part of me balked at the task.

But it had to be done. I imagined a black wall in my mind, onyx and thick, holding the sounds out, keeping the voices away. It never fully did. It only blurred the speech, softened the volume.

Only one thing in this world so far had brought me true silence. But I had to wait for that.

I imagined a crease in the wall of my mind, light shining through it as the onyx groaned and pulled apart. The light grew brighter, and immediately, the influx of thoughts attacked me.

About time we got new blood on the Seat.

That Batavia bitch looks too weak to hold a stave. The fuck was she going to rule?

One hour till he notices I've abandoned post.

I winced, gagging from the volume of the voices. Some were in the Great Hall, some downstairs, close to the Seating Room. My skull felt like it was splitting into two, but I kept pressing further.

Owes me a silver coin.

From this exact angle, he really does look like a dog....

Shekar arkasva!

"Morgana!" Lyr shouted. "Did anyone—?"

"Shut up," I seethed from gritted teeth. "I'm listening."

"Sorry," Lyr said, her voice shaking with hurt.

"Partner." Rhyan squeezed her shoulder. "Give her a second."

I glared at Rhyan. "No one asked you."

His jaw tensed, but he lowered his chin, bringing his gaze back to Lyr. He continued rubbing her shoulder until she leaned back against him.

I closed my eyes, tilting my head back on the bed pillows, my knuckles numb as I gripped the blanket, listening further, trying to pull out Arianna's voice or that of a soturion from Ka Kormac—those would be the most concerning if they'd heard anything amiss. Wind howled outside the fortress, and I retreated deeper into my mind, straining to listen for what I'd spent more than a year trying to shut out.

But I couldn't make out a single coherent thought that felt relevant.

Wonder if Arianna will remarry at last.

The Imperator's definitely fucking her.

Blue rhymes with shoe, and you, and two, and....

I winced at each new voice that came into my mind. All self-absorbed idiots—all Lumerians either thinking absolutely mindless, unimportant thoughts, or completely focused on how tonight's events benefitted them. Pulling myself back, I listened for any signs of anyone in our wing, anyone on the stairs, anyone close enough to be dangerous. But we were alone.

"We got lucky." I opened my eyes. "No one seems to have heard a thing—all wrapped up in their own gryphon-shit or too far away."

"By the Gods," Lyr groaned in relief. She sat on the edge of the bed and pushed back Meera's hair while pulling more blankets over her. "Do you want to talk about it?"

Meera only shivered in response. She went cold after visions. Goosebumps ran down my arms as well.

"No, she doesn't," I snapped.

Lyr's eyes were wide and full of hurt. But it was enough already. Meera was half-conscious. The last thing we needed her to do was talk about her latest terrifying vision and add any more Godsdamned paint to this room. In fact, if we didn't start removing every painting from her walls soon, we might as well hand ourselves over to Arianna now.

I stared at the paintings of her visions from the last two years, at the ridges of texture from layers upon layers of paint. Myself to Godsdamned Moriel.

I wanted wine. I wanted to smoke. I wanted to fuck. Anything but this. But Meera's vorakh would be exposed if we didn't remove the paint.

I stared at Meera's rendering of Aunt Arianna, her red hair, her clever eyes, her uncanny resemblance to Lyr before turning into a black seraphim. The truth had been in front of us this whole time, but we hadn't seen it. We hadn't known we were looking at Arianna.

But Meera's vision tonight? That had been crystal fucking clear.

Still, I wasn't going to be fooled a second time. I needed proof.

I leapt off the bed, lunging for Lyr's neck.

"Morgs!" she shouted in surprise just as Rhyan vanished and reappeared without warning behind me, breathing down my neck.

"Morgana," he warned. His aura pulsed with a level of anger and restraint I didn't think possible. He was tense, seconds from attacking me the moment he believed me a threat to Lyr.

I twisted my neck to look back at him, venom in my eyes. "I'm her sister, not an akadim. And you are in my fortress. In my sister's bedroom. Back off."

The muscles in his jaw worked, his strangely green eyes burning into me. I realized in that moment how relevant my words had been. In Meera's vision, Lyr had been there. And Meera, and me by proxy, had been an akadim. Had Rhyan sensed that?

No, he was just so in love with Lyr, so protective, his instincts got away from him. He saw a threat and moved to stop it.

Only I wasn't threat. I was exposing one.

Sorry, he thought. *Reflex. I know you'd never hurt her.*

My stomach twisted. I'd known the forsworn lord half of my life, but we'd only truly spoken a handful of times. We knew each other's deepest secrets, and we kept them. We were both vorakh. There was a kind of bond and understanding between us from that fact alone. But we weren't friends.

"No shit I wouldn't hurt her." I rolled my eyes at him and turned back to Lyr. "We saw you," I said. "You were in Meera's vision again. And this time, I'm sure it was you. Because you were wearing this," I said, pointing to the collar of Valalumir stars around her neck. I ran a finger over the gold stars, the red diamond centers. Three were now white—missing the red material inside. "Tell me the truth, Lyr. It's not a necklace, is it? It's armor."

Lyr gasped, her eyes widening. Her mind was forced blank, the kind of blankness she'd so desperately tried to achieve downstairs. That was all the confirmation I needed. I reached for the nape of her neck before she could react, my fingers finding the metallic clasp.

"Morgs! No," she protested.

Rhyan made a sound of protest, and tears sprang to Lyr's eyes as I bit my cheek.

But I already had the collar off. She was wearing a black mourning gown, a V cut down the center. Without her armor, her cleavage was on full display. When I'd last seen the skin of her chest bare like this, it had been smooth. Unmarked. The skin of a noblewoman.

But that was no longer the case.

Meera's visions had always been nonsensical, but now they were coming true. I didn't want to be right. But I needed to know what the hell this vision meant before the next tragedy struck.

My eyes fell on the golden seven-pointed star branded between her breasts, glowing with light. Just like she'd had in Meera's vision.

An Afeyan contract.

CHAPTER SIX

MORGANA

RHYAN PUSHED PAST ME, stopping in front of Lyr. One hand reached out before he slammed a fist at his side. His eyes were blazing with fury as he stared at the mark.

"That's where he...where...." His shoulders rose and fell with uneven breaths. The room grew colder. His hands reached for her again and again retracted. "Lyr, I'll kill him."

Lyr closed her eyes, her breathing labored as she placed her hand over the mark, trying to conceal it. Staring back up at Rhyan, she shook her head, grimacing in pain. "It's done. You can't change it. You...I...." She bit her lip. "Rhyan, please. It's done."

"Like hell it is! It should have been me. This was my fault. I should have stayed. I should have—"

"No," Lyr said, squeezing his arm. Her hand slid down to his, their fingers entwining. "It's not your fault. Don't blame yourself for this. I had my part." Her eyes watered. "There's nothing you could have done. He wanted me, you know that. He was only willing to treat with me."

I frowned at this. The Afeya—Mercurial—had something on Lyr and Rhyan, but he only wanted to make a deal with one of them? It made no sense.

"What the fuck?" I asked. "Why did you make a deal with him? You knew what he was, what he did to father."

"I know. I didn't want to, but...." Lyr's cheeks reddened, her eyes meeting Rhyan's then staring down in shame.

Lyr was emotional—her thoughts were all jumping forward, almost chaotically. But they were clear, and I could see. Within a minute, I began to piece her memories together, and from them what had happened, what had led to the bargain.

Mercurial had caught them together at the ball. I saw her lying underneath Rhyan, their bodies straining to be together, her attempting to tear off his clothes as he pulled the straps of her dress down, his mouth all over her, very clearly breaking their oath. And then Mercurial walked in, catching them. He'd blackmailed them into a deal.

"His silence for what price?" I asked.

Lyr looked from me to Rhyan and then Meera, her thoughts erratic, her desperation to hide them now almost blocking out every coherent idea in her mind. She was hiding the truth from Rhyan of just how badly the star had hurt her. When it had entered her body, it had done so with a burning hot pain that had numbed to a dull warmth. She was protecting this information, keeping it deep in the recesses of her mind, and yet, she was guarding even more tightly the secrets she'd learned from Mercurial. She'd been doing this earlier with her knowledge of Arianna—hiding from me that our aunt was the traitor, the murderer. She had been trying to protect me.

But she couldn't protect me from this—nor could she hold the secret in her mind much longer.

"Lyr, stop hiding your thoughts. We're all in this together. You need to come clean now. To all of us."

Lyr sobbed and nodded, her eyes closing, her mind reliving what had happened.

I winced as I saw the moment Mercurial had explained to her how she'd powered up in the arena, breaking the stars on her necklace. She thought of the moment she'd learned the diamonds weren't made of starfire but of blood—ancient, powerful blood. The blood of a warrior, of an arkturion. Of a goddess. I heard it then, the truth Mercurial had whispered to her, the way she'd appeared in Meera's vision.

You're the fire.

"Lyr," I said, my throat going dry. "You're...."

She shook her head. *I'm not ready. I...I don't know what it means yet or what to do with it. I'm scared of it. I can't...I can't....*

"Lyr," Rhyan crooned. "Come here. Come here to me." He wrapped his arms around her, rubbed her back. "Whatever his price, whatever he told you, we're going to figure this out. Together. I swear."

"And the price, Lyr?" I demanded. "The price for his silence? For telling you this?"

Rhyan glared at me, but I didn't care. We needed this out in the open. I had no patience for being soft or gentle. People were dead. Our father was dead from treating with this monster. And now Lyr had walked into the same Godsdamned trap even though she had known better. Even though I'd warned her.

She nodded, thinking the answer.

I narrowed my eyes. "The Afeyan messenger is forcing you to claim your magic?"

"What?" Rhyan stilled at this news, looking past Lyr to me, one eyebrow lifted in shock. He turned back to her, pulling her closer. "That's what he wants? Is that even possible?"

Lyr shrugged helplessly. "If you trust his word. I don't know. Remember when he'd said before I could be a powerful soturion? He said there was a way. That there was a...a map or something to get to it."

"Map?" Rhyan ran his fingers through his hair, his mind sorting through all he could remember about maps and the Afeya, but he drew a blank and tightened his hold on my sister as she leaned instinctively into him. The trust between them was so palpable, so strong, it was like a living, breathing entity outside of them.

For a second, my heart felt heavy. Jealous.

I pushed the thought down. Trust could be broken. I didn't need that gryphon-shit in my life. I needed something much simpler. I eyed Lyr carefully, still pulling out the pieces of her thoughts I could find and pairing them with what I knew, what I'd already heard.

"You were considering going to the Afeya after your Revelation Ceremony," I said, remembering the desperation she'd felt months earlier. I'd warned her not to go to them, not to put her faith in them. I didn't trust a single slippery word Mercurial had uttered to her.

Afeya, the immortal fuckers, were immune to my mind reading. For this, I would have wished to be around them all the time, save for my hatred of their games and lies. They couldn't be trusted and were always attempting to get something, bargaining to extract a price far too high for anyone to pay. Around them, my head would be clear, but I wouldn't last a day in their courts. And I wouldn't want to.

Lyr nodded, admitting how she'd considered making a deal to get her power so she might stay in Bamaria and protect me and Meera. Any Afeya she'd crossed paths with would have struck this deal with her in an instant. I would have bet there were Afeya stalking Bamaria, hoping for a run-in with her—a chance to extract a price. And the price...Gods knew what it could have been.

"This Afeya," I seethed, "is keeping both of your secrets, and in exchange, he's giving you exactly what you most desperately want? And he lets Rhyan off without having to do shit? Do you see how messed up this sounds? Afeya don't work this way. And I guarantee that Mercurial is not some exception to the rule. There's something in this for him. Something very valuable. I can't believe you were so stupid."

"What would you have done? You don't know what it's like. He's been stalking me for months—literally waiting to waltz in on me, to find me in any compromising position he could, all so he could use it against me. It was just a matter of time. And you were the one who told me he was here to begin with," she shouted.

"Yes, and I said stay the fuck away from him." I turned on Rhyan. "And you. You knew he was after her. But no, couldn't keep your hands to yourself."

"Morgs, stop!" Lyr yelled, standing protectively in front of him.

"He's not acting like an Afeya, but he is one. The only reason the Afeyan bastard wants you to have your magic is so he can use it for himself." I frowned. "But then this begs the question, why would an Afeya need the magic of a Lumerian?"

Rhyan drummed his fingers along Meera's dresser, one hand still on Lyr's back. "He wouldn't. Their power far exceeds our own. You're right. It doesn't make any sense."

"No," I said, watching Lyr, the turn of her cheek, the darkness of her hair in the moonlight a contrast to the way it shined as red as fire in the sun.

It was starting to come together. Meera's vision. The goddess. Calling her Asherah. The red shard glowing bright—bright enough to have been the Valalumir in its original form.

I turned to Meera. She'd been following along the whole time—too weak to speak but interjecting her thoughts to me. And in that moment, her thoughts were identical to mine.

My heart pounded as I turned back to Lyr. "You're her, aren't you? Reborn."

I felt dizzy and winded. If I was right, if Lyr was the reincarnation of Asherah—and was indebted to the Afeya with a bargain to find her magic power—the moment she was successful, we'd be handing him the most dangerous weapon of all time.

Tears streamed down Lyr's cheeks in confirmation. In a flash, her memories came to me, confirming everything. She'd seen herself in her mind. She'd had, not a vision, but a memory. She'd seen her past body, looked down at her hand—larger, darker. She'd felt herself on a golden beach. She'd felt the connection the first time she'd worn the armor.

Then I saw Ramia, half-Afeyan, giving Lyr the armor at no cost—on the orders of Mercurial, First Messenger of the Star Court.

"Fuck," I said.

"Out loud," Meera rasped. "What do you mean?"

In the same moment, Rhyan asked Lyr, "You're who reborn?" His eyes searched hers, but Lyr wasn't responding. She'd gone pale. Rhyan swallowed, one eyebrow furrowed in concern as he looked to me.

What's going on? he thought.

I ignored him, staring at my sister. If we were going to help her, we all needed to know what she knew. She could not hold this secret herself.

Lyr nodded slowly, looking like she was in disbelief. *Say it, Morgs. Tell them.*

"You're Asherah," I said. "You're the goddess reborn."

No! Rhyan nearly roared the thought, his heart heavy as a wave of dizziness washed over him. The thoughts in his mind, some moving too fast for me to hear, were all clicking together. His eyes widened in horror, and there was a flash in his mind of his father, of ropes tied around his hands, binding his body, and of Lyr leaning back against a tree.

Lyr nodded again. "I think I am."

"Gods," Meera gasped, struggling to sit up.

Rhyan shook his head. "Lyriana." His eyes searched hers, his mouth open as he ran his fingers through her hair, imagining the locks in the sun. Red. Batavia red. Red like Asherah. "Lyr, shit. Shit."

Rhyan pulled away from her, his hands fisted at his sides, his aura storming with such force, Meera's glass doors flew open. Snowflakes exploded into the room, leaving me shivering until I grabbed my stave.

"Lisgo deletim." The doors snapped shut. "Does anyone else know?"

"Besides Mercurial? No one outside this room, as far as I'm aware. But I don't know." She shrugged again.

"We need to keep it that way," Rhyan said fiercely. "Mercurial isn't the only one we need to worry about. This knowledge in the wrong person's hands, even just speculation of it...." His nostrils flared, the energy in his aura swirling with cold. I saw in his thoughts a vision of mountains, mountains that looked so similar to the ones I'd seen in Meera's vision. "Lyr, there's no way for you to be safe if this gets out. Not until you take control of it."

"She's less safe than you know," I spat. Our aunt had murdered our father, usurped the Seat of Power, and stolen Meera's inheritance and destiny from right under our noses.

Myself to Moriel.

I looked to the bed. Meera was starting to pass out, exhausted after such a violent vision.

In this room, only me and Lyr knew the truth of Arianna. But others had to know. There were traitors amongst us, allies to her cause, and most likely those who dealt in secrets, who took no single side and felt no allegiance, concerned only with being paid.

But who? That was the part I hadn't figured out. That was even more infuriating than being blindsided by Arianna's treachery. Who on the Council had worked with her? Who else had betrayed us and managed to keep their secrets safe even in their minds?

Even from me.

I stared down at my left wrist. The two scars that had been there for two years were gone now, thanks to that Afeyan bastard. And because Lyr had let Rhyan in on our secret.

I scratched at the skin, bare and pristine, with no sign of ever having been marred. I'd railed against the blood oath that had sworn me to secrecy for years, done all I could to find a way to undo it, but I had to admit—my instinct now was to keep this new secret only between me and Lyr. And Meera when she woke.

But I knew we needed to tell Rhyan, too.

Lyr was thinking the same thing.

He was too close, too protective. And he was a strong and powerful ally to have in our corner. And...Lyr wanted him to know.

But I'd already been present for enough revelations tonight. I had one more job to do for my family, and that was it. I couldn't do one more thing without my head exploding.

"Listen," I said, reaching for Lyr's arm. "Meera's asleep. She needs her rest. I'll fill her in on everything tomorrow morning. But right now, the most pressing emergency we have is getting all the paint off her walls."

"You're right," Lyr said, putting on a brave face though she also looked completely exhausted. Rhyan watched her carefully, preparing to step in and tackle the physical labor on her behalf.

I shook my head. "No, I'll do it." I brandished my stave. I barely had the energy, but I was the only one capable of doing this in the timeframe we needed. Relying on the soturi in the room to do manual labor wasn't going to cut it. "You go to your room. Fill him in." I glared at Rhyan, letting my own aura of shadows unleash itself on him.

He froze, palms up in surrender, though his face showed his annoyance. Rhyan absolutely hated being told what to do. He only seemed to tolerate it from Lyr.

"I don't need to threaten you with a blood oath, do I?" I pointed my stave toward his upturned wrists. "I hate them, but I'm also not above using them to protect my own."

His fingers curled into fists. "I gave my oath to protect Lyriana a long time ago. There's nothing in this world or the next that could make me break that. I keep her secrets, and in turn I keep yours. As I trust you with mine, Morgana. But you choose. You want me to submit to a blood oath? Ask."

"Go," I said, my stave warming in my hands, the incantation on the tip of my tongue.

Meera's door shut behind them, and I closed my eyes, allowing their voices to soften behind the expanse of hallway and Lyr's bedroom door.

I gripped my stave, my palm warm from its heat, the tip glowing with blue light as I uttered the incantation, pulling the paintings of Meera's visions apart, removing each layer of color until two years' worth of visions were gone. Afterward, Meera's walls were bare, as white as they'd been when Jules had walked these halls.

I sucked in a breath, sweating from exertion, my head pounding. I checked Meera one more time. Maybe she wasn't as expertly tucked in as she would have been with Lyr, but she was safe. She was in her bed and had enough blankets to keep her warm. She was breathing. It was good enough.

I'd felt the vision, too, but no one was tucking me into bed. And I'd been the one thrown into the ocean with far too many revelations tonight—from Arianna's truth to Lyr's ridiculous Afeyan deal to the knowledge of who she was—all while hearing every idiotic thought in the fortress on top of it. All while having the worst fucking headache I'd had since the night of my Revelation Ceremony.

I made one more sweep of Meera's room, making sure there was not one sign of treason, of vorakh, and then I left her to her dreams.

I lit the torches in my bedroom a minute later. I was too sober for this. Too Godsdamned alert.

Yes! Yes! Ugh. Some Korterian soldier had a girl against the wall beneath my room.

Gods, he could hurry it up. The bored thought was courtesy of the girl he was fucking.

I eyed my dresser. An empty decanter of wine sat atop it. Three empty bottles were beside it, the glasses reflecting the flames above them.

With a scream, I slammed my fist against them, pushing them away. The glass crashed and shattered against my floor.

Tonight had been too much. With the betrayal I felt from Arianna, I wanted to strangle someone. And yet...it was all my fault.

I should have known the betrayer was Arianna. I, of all people, had the means to discover the truth, to stop this from happening. And I'd failed. She'd never had a single thought to tip me off. Not even tonight. From the moment I'd known downstairs, I'd been listening, straining, and not for one second had Arianna's thoughts faltered. Or, if they had, there had been no way I could have heard them.

She had protection. I was sure of it now. She was one of them.

The only bright spot in a very bleak-as-shit night was the fact that Lyr hadn't questioned me. She hadn't asked me how I hadn't known Arianna was a traitor from the start, why I hadn't read Arianna's mind.

She should have asked me. The Lyr who wasn't grieving, who wasn't in shock over all she'd learned and experienced tonight, the Lyr who thought too much and was too smart for her own good—*she* would have questioned me at once. I could read minds. Why couldn't I read Arianna's?

I swallowed, moving across my room in search of wine. I undid the black belt at my waist, feeling my stomach expand as the belt fell to the floor. With a groan, I untied the strings behind my back. My dress fell open in the front, still covering my breasts but no longer holding them up. My diadem went next, tossed onto my dressing table.

Kitten? His voice was deep and shadowy but so clear and loud I knew he was close. Already past the sentries, already deep inside the fortress.

Now you come crawling to me? I thought. I'd needed him hours ago.

Don't be petulant, he chided. *It's been a busy night.*

My father was murdered!

Which is why I've been busy.

My face heated, anger coursing through me. *If you think I'm in any mood for your games—*

I wouldn't presume. There was a soft knock on my door before it creaked open.

I retreated to my bed, lying over the covers, fully aware half my breasts were exposed. I didn't look at him. I never did. Partly out of habit; our relationship had begun with my eyes closed. I'd begun to see him as two different beings. The one he presented in public, and the one he was with me.

You left out some important information, I thought, staring pointedly at the ceiling. *How could you leave me in the dark like that?*

Me and you have always been in the dark, existing in the shadows. He closed the door behind him, not gently, and I could feel his annoyance and irritation spiking through both his mind and aura.

As if he had any right to be annoyed.

I said no games. I grabbed at my shoulders, the tension in them paining me. *Did you know? Did you?*

Know Arianna was the traitor? he asked.

Answer the Godsdamned question.

He sighed audibly, irritably. *I suspected Arianna had the elixir, in the way all high-ranking nobles with secrets and access to wealth do.*

I'd thought you'd have more than just a suspicion. I closed my eyes.

I'd thought you would, too. The lock clicked into place. *You knew the elixir existed. You knew what it did. And you knew your aunt. She was noble, after all. Not one of them is without secrets, without some crime behind them. So ask yourself this—why didn't you know? Why did you allow yourself to be blinded?*

Arianna was the queen of controlling what people saw. She was always thinking the right thoughts. She'd think in anger at how her husband was a traitor. Or she'd worry for Naria. She'd think of how much she loved me and Meera and Lyr. Sometimes she even missed Jules. She thought about paperwork, meetings, the Council...everything but her plans for assassination, usurping the Seat, leading the rebels, being the head of the Emartis.

Fuck you. I sneered.

He chuckled. *No. But I'll fuck you tonight if you want.*

You swear you didn't know Arianna was the traitor?

Am I not the one who told you of the elixir's existence? he asked. *Am I not the one fighting to liberate the enslaved? I hate everyone who uses our vorakh against us. I hate everyone who enslaves our kind, steals from us, rules us. I've done nothing but try to help you. And yet you question me?*

You've kept secrets before.

We all keep secrets.

I turned on my side, facing away from him, thinking of the secret he'd shared with me, the one I'd guarded more closely from both my sisters than any other.

When vorakh hunters arrested my kind—those with the vorakh of mind reading—we weren't taken to Lethea like the others. We weren't stripped of our magic or killed. Mind-readers had a special fate.

Why get rid of us when we could be used to further the positions of the Empire's rulers, to command them greater power? Why kill us and destroy our magic when our magic could be siphoned from us, drained from us until we were dead? The elixir created from our magic provided a mental shield to those who drank it, allowing the Emperor and all those in his favor to continue with their backroom dealings and maintain their illicit and illegal affairs without fear of discovery. Vorakh like us were the Empire's most expensive and heavily guarded secret.

The elixirs worked beautifully—too beautifully. I'd only just begun to recognize when they were in use, but I didn't know how to get around them. Not yet.

The mattress dipped behind me, and a warm, calloused hand slid up my leg, gathering my dress around my ankles and shifting the material higher and higher until he reached my hip. Small shivers ran through me, his touch igniting me with heat, like my body knew it was about to get relief. His fingers pressed into me, drawing me against an already impressive erection as he glided his palm over my ass.

I am sorry for your loss, he thought. *Did I tell you that yet?*

Yes. I'm already sick of hearing it. Are you here out of pity? I asked. *Or did you learn anything new?*

We'd used each other like this for a year. He only ever came when he had news. He didn't make social calls.

His hand lingered a moment against my ass, rolling and squeezing my flesh. Then, slowly, more slowly than he knew I liked, he slid his hand down my backside, pushed aside my undergarment, moved between my legs, and buried his fingers in my folds.

Nothing new, he thought, beginning to work me from behind.

If you're here out of pity, I don't want it. Despite my angered thoughts, I was shamelessly rubbing back against him, urging him to the place where I wanted him, needed him.

I don't do pity, he thought, as the pad of his finger found its way to my core. He pressed down before drawing a circle around it. *You know that well.*

I gasped, rocking my hips back and forth, seeking more friction as my arousal coated his fingers. Even then, tears brimmed in my eyes, the grief for Father suddenly hitting me. Alongside the betrayal of Arianna. And the truth of the Afeya. And Lyr's true identity.

I felt like my heart was squeezing in on itself.

Not now, kitten. No crying. You've had too many thoughts in your head tonight. And there's been far too many in mine. Tomorrow, we'll look for more answers. Tonight, we relish in the darkness, the silence. Tonight is for peace.

The sound of his belt unbuckling and clattering to the ground beside the bed fought against the distant voices running in the back of my mind: Rhyan and Lyr talking in her room; Meera falling into a dream; a Bamarian sentry on patrol grumbling about the cold.

"Shhhh," he said, a rare moment of speaking out loud. *No more thoughts.* His thumb circled my core as one finger thrust inside, then two.

He groaned audibly at my wetness, pulling out his fingers to untie the strings of my underwear and tug the material away from me.

But I wasn't ready to succumb. I wasn't ready to stop talking—or whatever the hell this was. My questions were circling my mind unceasingly. I rolled off the bed onto my feet and looked down at him, as my dress fell back around my legs.

A cocky smile spread across his lips. *I thought you said no games tonight.* He reached forward, pulling aside what remained of my gown, exposing my breasts.

I'm not playing a game.

You never look at me. He raised an eyebrow in question, cupping me as his thumb brushed over my nipple. *What exactly do you want?* He squeezed until I gasped from the mix of pleasure and pain.

Heat pooled between my legs, but I pulled back from his touch.

It's not about what I want, I thought. *But what I need. What I need to know. How could she have gotten this past me, gotten hold of the elixir without my knowing? How could I have been blind to my father's murderer being right under my nose? To not have been tipped off to the plan even once? She didn't work alone, she hasn't for decades, and yet not one person thought this in front of me.*

I knew many had wanted my father dead. I'd been forced to the point of sickness to listen to idiots fantasize about all sorts of cruelty, all manners of ending his life and even taking mine and my sisters. But these thoughts had been merely fantasies. Nothing more. Blaming the arkasva for daily inconveniences and taking out one's anger and frustrations by thinking about killing the arkasva was very different from forming a coherent plan and having the means to see it through.

Tell me, I demanded.

He rose from the bed, stalking toward me. In one swift motion, he was upon me, spinning me against him, his cock straining through his clothes and pushing against my backside.

Morgana, I came here tonight for one thing and one thing only. Now stop this. I already told you I suspected. Now I don't suspect. His fingers pressed into my hips. *Now I have confirmation. Now we know. We have more information than we did yesterday which we can use to our advantage. And now, if you want to have any chance of getting more done here, we move on.* His thoughts hardened, growling in my mind like a dark shadow. *How do you want me?*

I want you, answering my Godsdamned questions!

I'm seconds away from finding another tonight. He pulled up my chin, his lips smashing against mine. He tasted like wine, and already I was dizzy, barely able to keep my body from responding. *But tonight, I want you.* He tightened his grip on me. *No more games. Now tell me, how do you want me?* This time, the thought was demanding, desperate. His need pulsed through his thoughts, and his aura wrapped like a blanket around us.

My own need was answering his. I was finished holding back, finished prolonging my suffering without reward. I was finished listening, finished seeing, finished thinking.

Hard. I closed my eyes. *Rough.*

Good. He pulled his hand back, and the room was silent save for the sound of his clothes being removed—fabric being untied, loosened, and shucked off. Then his full body was pressed against me, all broad, defined muscle, warm, almost god-like in strength and build. He grabbed hold of my dress straps and pulled them off my shoulders.

There was a sudden tug, and I gasped over the sound of ripping fabric. My dress fell in two pieces to my feet as cold air hit my spine and shivers danced between my legs.

You weren't going to wear that again, were you? He laughed the thought, his warm body covering mine, his calloused hands running down my arms, the hair on his legs tickling the backs of mine.

The dress I wore to name my father's killer as his heir? No. I'll burn it.

He was so hard and thick against my backside, the feeling of desire and anticipation warred with the remaining thoughts dancing at the edges of my mind until his mouth found a pressure point on my neck, sucking while he returned to fondling my breasts.

Need to clean this place up.

Shekar arkasva! Drink up!

Where the hell is she now?

I writhed back against him, as he rolled and pinched my nipples between his fingers, his mouth hot on my neck, biting and licking.

I pushed my ass back at him, angling myself just right for him to enter, for him to stroke me in the exact way I needed.

His erection slid between my folds from behind, back and forth, the head of his cock brushing against my center until he was slick with my arousal. *Ready to make the noise stop?*

Yes, I thought. *Please.*

One hand stretched beneath me while his other slid from my breast to my neck, fingers hard against my skin. *Tell me you want me.* He squeezed.

I want you.

Good kitten. Roughened fingers slid down my leg, gripping beneath my thigh, and in one swift movement, his arm wrenched behind my knee, widening my legs, arching my back further, as he thrust up and inside me.

I gasped, my hands slamming into the wall, fingernails scraping for purchase. His movement forced me to my toes, the pleasure of him piercing the pain I felt everywhere else. I was so full I couldn't hear, couldn't feel anything else. My legs were already shaking with exhaustion.

He moved faster, his hands sliding up my arms. The backs of his hands slammed against mine, pressing me into the wall as he thrust harder.

And then, at last, there was silence but for the sound of his body pounding into mine and our gasps mingling with our moans. Both our minds were quiet. Not a single thought from anyone in the fortress could penetrate the walls in my mind—it was mine again. Mine alone. Not the Council's. Not Meera's. Not Lyr's. The bliss of the quiet, the peace...I almost came from the relief alone. No one could ever understand. No one but him.

At last, I could think and voice to myself the thought I'd feared Lyr would land on if she ever knew what I knew. It was the one secret I could only safely dwell on when he was inside me.

Since I'd learned the Emperor could siphon off the magic of mind-readers, I'd had no doubt he was using every vorakh for the same purpose.

All of the spies we'd sent so far had come back empty-handed from the capitol. We couldn't yet prove there were elixirs for traveling or elixirs for visions. We hadn't yet been able to prove the other vorakh-wielders were being held, enslaved, and abused. But our spies had seen enough. They'd seen enough Lumerians with vorakh transported from Lethea after their tests. They'd seen the empty graves on the island. They'd seen the captives arrive in the capitol in chains with black rope binding their power, keeping them from vanishing, from seeing, from listening.

Tonight's revelation changed everything, and I was going to find a way to use that to my advantage. To finally finish what I'd started.

I moaned as he gripped my hips to turn me and bend me over my bed. My face smashed into the sheets, my knuckles white as I gripped them, my first orgasm exploding deep inside me.

The blood of Ka Batavia was too powerful, too strong, too desired. It wasn't the kind of Lumerian blood one spilt without using, not when that blood belonged to a noble with vorakh. This was partly why he wanted me now, why he came to me.

Our spies hadn't seen her yet, but it didn't matter. I knew it in my gut they would find her, and I'd have my proof. Proof that we'd all been lied to. Proof that we'd been deceived.

Proof that Jules was alive.

CHAPTER SEVEN

LYRIANA

I STOOD IN MY bedroom with Rhyan, silent as the wind outside howled and snow continued to fall. A sliver of moonlight streaming through my balcony doors mixed with the flames of the outer tower torches. My chest plate was laid out on my dressing table, the red stones in the center of each star glowing against the fire as I stood before the mirror, staring at myself, wondering if I looked different now, if I was different.

I felt different.

I was Asherah. The heat in my chest forbade me from forgetting. And now Morgana knew. Now Rhyan knew.

Somehow, their knowledge made it more real. Made it settle into my body in a way it hadn't when Mercurial had told me or even when I'd had my first vision of myself as her and gone from standing in Ramia's tent to an ancient beach from just a touch of the golden stars against my skin.

Rhyan's jaw hadn't untensed since he'd heard the news. His emerald eyes had flashed with such an unbridled intensity, I'd felt weak looking at him. The worry and concern raging inside his body were written all over his face. I watched him, standing behind me, through my mirror. Already I could see his mind working, trying to decipher how much danger I was in because of this revelation. I could see him agonizing over what to do next to protect me.

He was still missing key information, information I was trying to find the courage to say out loud without bursting into tears, without falling to pieces. Hating Arianna for what she'd done, for the role she'd played, was still at odds with the part of me that had loved her my entire life—that still loved her and wanted this all to be untrue.

"Are you okay to be here?" I met Rhyan's gaze in the reflection. The bells were ringing, and small blue lights lit up the sky. He was skipping out on patrol duties, and without my father, I wasn't sure how much protection he'd still have if he were to get in trouble.

He sighed loudly, stepping closer behind me. His hands glided down my arms until his calloused fingers entwined with mine.

I closed my eyes and leaned back against him, feeling his warmth, his strength, and his sturdiness. Alone in my room with him, I finally felt safe again after all I'd seen downstairs.

Rhyan took my weight, supporting me as he always did, but he remained silent.

When he still hadn't answered after a minute, I opened my eyes, meeting his gaze again through the mirror's reflection. That same look of worry painted through his expression.

"Rhyan, don't you have guard duty?"

His mouth tightened. "You called," he said simply. "I came."

When Meera's vision had become violent, I hadn't had the strength to fight back. It had happened again—her voice had changed, becoming something monstrous, something inhuman. Her eyes had turned black. She'd called me *Asherah* again in a voice completely foreign to her own—a voice that had left me terrified.

The moment she'd spoken the words, she'd touched me, her hands on my shoulders, and my heart had felt like it was aflame. The contract with Mercurial, the Valalumir, had begun to pulse, the heat so intense, I hadn't been able to breathe or fight her off of me.

I'd always been able to handle Meera, to fight back, to hold her down. I'd been getting better and better at it over the years. And with my training, I was stronger than ever. I should have been able to handle her. To protect her. To protect myself.

But tonight...somehow, her words had activated the contract. My chest had been on fire, and she'd pushed me off the bed in my weakened state. I'd been desperate. Morgana had been on the floor, fighting her own battles. I had been in so much pain, and Meera had been screaming so loudly, I'd barely managed to get Rhyan's vadati out from beneath my armor before she'd knocked me unconscious. I'd scrambled away from her just in time to shout his name.

He'd come instantly despite having been on duty and put himself between her and me, helping me, restraining her until the vision had passed.

But he had soturion duty now. I'd heard Aemon order him back to his post in the Seating Room.

"Rhyan, you can't get in trouble for me."

"Yes, I can." He wrapped his arms around my waist, hugging me to him. "I'm right where I'm supposed to be." His scent flooded my senses, his aura and warmth cocooning me.

"We shouldn't be doing this. We said we weren't going to."

"I know. But I can't...." He groaned, tightening his hold on me. "I can't stay away."

The wind howled, banging against my balcony doors. A torch flamed out, smoke hissing in a corner. I closed my eyes and leaned against him, as I breathed him in.

"Are you alright?" he asked, his breath warm against my neck.

I snuggled deeper into his embrace. "No. Not even close."

"Lyr." He bent his head, kissing my shoulder. Shivers ran down my body. He squeezed me tighter in his arms, pulling me back into him. His nose pressed against the curve of my neck, inhaling, before he kissed me where his breath had been. "Sorry." He started to pull away, to loosen his grip.

But I turned my head, capturing his lips with mine. His kiss was soft and tender with the worry and concern plaguing him. For a moment, the kiss seemed to exist in its own world, a world where it was just me and him and our lips moving against the others. Our bodies pressed together but didn't seek friction, didn't escalate this into something more. This kiss existed for the sake of itself.

Then he groaned, his mouth opening to me. The kiss deepened as his tongue moved against mine with such a slow sensuality that heat coursed through my belly, sliding lower and lower.

His hips lifted so his arousal pressed into my backside. He released my hands, his palms scraping my ribs. I arched against him, writhing and urging his hands higher and higher. Groaning into his mouth, I reached behind him and tangled my fingers in his soft curls. I gripped the nape of his neck as we kissed and kissed. My breasts swelled in his hands as he kneaded them, and my breath hitched as he gripped my dress straps and slid them off my shoulders, forcing my arms down.

I gasped as the cold air hit my bared skin. His kisses trailed down my neck, but his eyes remained on my breasts in the mirror, on the star between them. His hands slid over my curves, searing my skin. My nipples hardened in his palms, as his fingers pressed down over my heart. His lips found mine again.

And then, just like during Meera's vision, my heart beat too fast. It was thumping with my blood, pounding with the pulse of the Valalumir—with Mercurial's soul.

You're the fire.

I cried out, "Gods!" I was burning alive. Flames were firing inside my chest.

Rhyan's eyes flew open. He broke the kiss at once and spun me to face him. I stared down, gasping and sweating as the seven-pointed Valalumir between my breasts glowed with blinding golden light. It had never been this bright before, not even when Mercurial had forced the star into my heart.

Rhyan pushed the vadati stone around my neck out of the way, his hand sliding over the mark. "Here?" He sounded desperate, terrified. "What's wrong? What happened?"

"It's burning," I cried, gripping his shoulders, my knees buckling from the pain.

Rhyan's hand went taut over my skin, his nostrils flaring, anger and fear pulsing in his aura. "Shit. I feel it." He let out a grunt of pain as if I'd burned him, too, but he held on. He closed his eyes, breathing deeply. With a low growl, steam hissed between our skin. His hand against me was no longer warm. He was growing colder against my burning flesh, sending all of the ice of his aura to me.

My chest heaved, my breath short. Rhyan also looked out of breath, but within seconds, the pain stopped. The flames calmed. Rhyan had taken the fire from me.

"Lyr?" It was all he seemed able to say after the effort he'd just used. He looked pale, ready to fall over.

"I'm okay," I panted, dizzy. "It stopped. It's not burning anymore."

He pulled his hand back, and I took it, half afraid I'd branded him with the star, but his skin was untouched, only roughened by his usual callouses.

Now I was shivering, my teeth chattering. Ice prickled over my skin, and every limb shook with cold.

Rhyan pulled the straps of my dress up to cover my exposed breasts. Goosebumps sprung up across my arms. Every inch of me was freezing like I'd stumbled naked into a storm. A sudden wave of nausea hit me in the stomach. I wanted out of this dress. I wanted out of what it meant—the memories I had now from wearing it. I never wanted to wear it, see it, touch it again.

"No," I sobbed, fighting against him. "No. Get it off. Get it off me."

Rhyan nodded, his jaw tensed, pulling back down the straps, working quickly at untying my laces, unbuckling my belt, and pushing the remaining skirt past my hips until the entire ensemble pooled on the floor around my legs. I was left only in a pair of underwear and my black leather boots, shivering.

"You're freezing," Rhyan said, running his knuckles down my arm. "Your skin's like ice."

I hugged myself, as he unstrapped his armor, removed the leather from across his chest, unbuckled his belt, and let his weapons clatter to the floor. De-armored, he was able to unwrap his soturion cloak from around his shoulder and waist and wrap me up in it like a blanket. He pulled me toward him, pressing me flush against him and offering me what body heat he had left through the black tunic he wore beneath his uniform.

He rubbed my back, the cloak wrapped around our shoulders. But it wasn't enough. "Keep this on," he said, "and climb into bed. You need to get warm." He pulled the cloak off of him, draping the remaining material around me.

I started across the room for my bed, crawled on top of the covers, collapsed, and burrowed into the heat clinging to his cloak. I closed my eyes, inhaling deeply. I was still freezing but soothed by the scent of musk and pine, the scent that was so uniquely Rhyan's.

There was a popping sound and a hiss as flames crackled in my fireplace.

"Hang on," Rhyan said.

My closet door scraped against the floor, and I peeked one eye open to find Rhyan searching through my array of dresses.

"Dresser," I muttered. "Warm clothes are in there."

He grunted in confirmation and moved to my drawers, opening and closing them until he found a pair of sleeping pants and a long-sleeved shirt made from a heavy cloth.

He sat beside me on the bed and peeled back his cloak. My teeth were still chattering, the cold clinging to me.

"Arms up, partner," he said then rolled the shirt over my head and pulled my arms through each sleeve. He stood and moved toward the edge of my bed, pulling his cloak back just enough to expose my boots. He unlaced and tugged them off one by one then slipped the sleep pants over my legs, his hands vanishing beneath the cloak that still covered me, fingers scraping my bared thighs and hips.

He checked that the fire was strong in my fireplace then crawled onto the bed. I opened his cloak, motioning for him to join me.

The corner of his mouth tugged up, but he shifted, drawing the cloak over our heads and cradling me against his chest, his hands slipping inside my shirt.

"Sorry," he whispered, stroking my back. "I went too hard with the cold."

"It's okay," I said. "It helped."

He rested his chin on top of my head and pulled me completely on top of him, arms wrapping tight around me. "Are you feeling any warmer?"

Lying flush against him and feeling my body mold to his was helping. So was the sensation of his arms across my back and the comforting feel of his skin on mine. "Getting there," I said.

A muscle in his jaw tightened. "What the hell happened?"

"I don't know."

Rhyan's nostrils flared. "I'm going to kill him. Was it like this when he...when the star entered you?" His voice shook.

I squeezed my eyes shut. I'd been hoping to keep that from him. I knew it'd upset him. It would have upset me had the roles been reversed. But lying now seemed useless. "It was. I passed out after. It felt like I was on fire."

Rhyan growled. "Bastard. Moriel fucking bastard."

"It didn't hurt after that though. It just felt...warm. More annoying than painful because I couldn't forget about it, couldn't ignore it. Then during Meera's vision, she attacked me, and it flared up again. It was so hot. It almost started when Morgana took my armor. This was the third time it's felt like I was on fire." This had been the worst.

"I don't think it should be doing that," he said. "I've never heard of Afeyan marks acting this way."

"Maybe it's settling or something."

"I don't think that's it."

I shrugged. "I've never made a deal before, so I can't say."

"If that Afeyan bastard has done anything to mess with it, to make this worse for you, I swear to the Gods, I will kill him."

"I'll go with you," I said weakly.

"You can have first punch. As long as I get second."

I tried to laugh but felt too weak. "Deal."

Rhyan sighed, kissing my forehead and snuggling me against him, hands resuming their massage over my back, attempting to warm me up.

We lay there for several moments, our breathing synchronized, my body slowly returning to its normal temperature.

"Lyr?" Rhyan said, his voice so low, I wasn't sure he'd spoken at first. "Can I see?"

"Hmmm?"

"Can I see? Please." His fingers danced uneasily against my spine.

"See the star?" I lifted onto my elbows.

"If that's all right? I just, I don't know." He tensed beneath me. "I need to see it. When you're not in pain."

I pressed myself up, meeting his eyes in the bit of light that seeped through his cloak. "Are you just trying to steal another look at my breasts?" I teased.

"Every man needs a reason to get up in the morning."

I laughed.

Rhyan's eyes crinkled at my response then narrowed. "If we're going to fight this, I need to understand it better. I need to see it when it's not burning."

Sucking in a breath, I pulled back his cloak and rolled to the side, sitting all the way up. Rhyan sat up as well, turning toward me, one eyebrow furrowed.

"You're warm enough?" He squeezed my knee.

I nodded.

"And it doesn't hurt now?" he asked, sounding like his heart was breaking.

I squeezed his hand. "No."

"It still should have been me," he said fiercely, inching closer.

I shook my head. "Rhyan, you know there's nothing you could have done."

Gripping the hem of the shirt, I pulled it up the center of my torso to my collarbone, exposing only the middle patch of my skin with the star. Rhyan sucked in a shaky breath then trailed his fingers up my belly to the star.

"Is this okay?" he asked.

"Yes."

His fingers paused. "Does it hurt?"

"No."

His touch was light, his finger tracing the shape carefully while he frowned in concern. "You feel warm," he said. "Soft." He pressed his hand over the star again, holding his breath as if he expected it to flare up or for me to go cold again, but the star seemed to be dormant now.

I slid my hand down over his, holding it in place. My shirt fell like a blanket over our arms.

"Lyr, if he wants you to claim your magic, there's a reason. And not a good one. He wants to use you. And he's not the only one. There's," his jaw worked, "there's something I need to tell you."

I searched his eyes. "What is it?"

His shoulders tensed as his fingers pressed into my skin. "Three years ago, when I was here with my father, he said something to me. Something about you that I never understood, not until tonight."

I narrowed my eyes. "Your father?"

Tears were wetting his thick lashes, his gaze distant. "He was trying that summer to force your father into signing a marriage contract for you."

My heart pounded. "With you?"

His eyes darkened. "No. With our warlord. Arkturion Kane. He, um, well...." Rhyan's mouth tightened. "He makes the Bastardmaker look like a gentleman."

My mouth fell open. I'd never known about this. That summer, I'd had such a crush on Rhyan. I was always trying to catch his eye at Court or dinner, to find something to say to him to get to know him, to make him open up. But he'd been cold. He'd ignored me and all my attempts at friendship for weeks. I'd felt this undeniable pull towards him all summer, even while thinking he'd hated me, until the night of solstice. That night, he'd taken my hand, and we'd danced and stolen away into the trees where we'd kissed, and kissed. And then the next day, he'd been cold and distant again. And then he was gone. I had been heartbroken until I'd forced myself to forget him, to move on.

Then he'd returned, scarred and forsworn.

"Was this why...?" I searched his eyes. "Was this why you ignored me that summer?"

He nodded, his expression miserable. "I thought...." He ran his fingers through his hair. It had curled when he'd been fighting earlier in the snow but now fell into loose waves. "I thought my father was using you to get to me. It was around the time he was starting to lose control—he was less able to manipulate me with just pain. He introduced other tactics. And I believed you were one of them at the time, a way for him to control me, a way for him to have leverage and ensure I did his bidding and kept his, our, secrets—what he was doing to me, to my mother, and that I was...that I was vorakh. But it didn't matter in the end. Not much. He knew immediately how I felt about you. I tried to hide it. To bury it. To protect you. I tried all summer to stay away."

I squeezed his hand tucked beneath my shirt, pressed between my heart and my hand. "Rhyan."

"But on solstice, I couldn't." His eyes burned emerald. "We danced. And...Gods. We kissed, and it was all over. He knew. He'd known. And I had to...had to do some *negotiating* to force him to end the marriage discussions."

The way he said *negotiating*, his voice strained, made me wonder just how much he'd sacrificed, how much he'd secretly given up to protect me years before I'd had any idea.

"And when he was convinced," he swallowed, "he said I'd made a huge mistake. That I'd regret what I'd done. I never did. It was the right thing to do, and I'd do it again to keep you safe. But the words he used always haunted me, as if you'd been more than just a way to get to me."

My heart pounded. "What words?"

"He said you had 'the potential to unleash more power and destruction than anyone in the Empire ever has.' And now, I think I might know what he meant. That you have magic we don't know about and that the Afeya want to use. Somehow, because of who you are. Because you're...." He trailed off, not ready to say it. To say I was Asherah.

My eyes searched his. "Does he know?"

Rhyan shrugged helplessly. "He never told me anything more. He might know who you are, what you can do. Or maybe not the specifics. I'm not sure what information he has—or how in Lumeria he got it—but to be safe, we need to act as if he does. We have to expect every arkasva to know the truth about you. Every arkasva, Imperator, and the Emperor himself. Every single one of them is now a direct threat."

Shit.

I bit my lip, knowing I couldn't wait any longer. Knowing I was only adding to the lists of dangers we faced. "This threat, it now includes our newest arkasva," I said, tears beginning to stream down my face.

"What?"

I stared down at my lap, my lip quivering. Saying it out loud almost felt like I was betraying her, spoiling the façade she had so carefully created—that I had so desperately bought into.

But she didn't deserve my protection or my love. I needed to get rid of it, to burn these feelings away.

I took a deep breath. "It was Arianna. Arianna killed my father. She led the Emartis."

Rhyan's eyes widened. "Lyr, how do you know? Morgana?"

"No. As far as I can tell, Morgs didn't even know until she read my mind." Gods, the look in her eyes, the feel of her aura....

"You're sure?" he asked.

"After Mercurial tonight, I saw her. I saw her outside, surrounded by the Soturi of Ka Kormac. They were protecting her. Guarding her. She was preparing to go back inside for the announcement, and she readjusted her arm cuff—it was irritating her or something. I was around a corner, so she didn't see me. But I could see her clearly. And I saw a tattoo she'd been hiding beneath the cuff. A silver moon above black seraphim wings."

"Emartis," he whispered. "Fuck. Lyr if this is true, and she knows...." His entire body was brimming with tension as his aura pulsed. "We can't stay here. We need to go."

"Go where?" I asked.

"Anywhere. You say the word, and we're gone. We don't have to live within the Empire. My vorakh can get us out. Get us beyond Lumeria."

"We can't do that."

"If your life is in danger, yes, we fucking can."

"And my sisters? My people? Yours? We can't abandon them to this. Can't let her get away with it." I sniffled. "I can't let my father's memory—his life—I can't let this go without justice. Not when I know." My shoulders shook. "I know you want to protect me. And I want to protect you, too, more than anything, and I will if it comes down to it. But you and I, we're not made for this, for running away. It's like you said, we live in a world forcing us to make horrible choices. And I know what these choices have done to you. What they're doing to me." Haleika's face flashed in my mind: her eyes red, her teeth sharpening into fangs. Because of me, because of my actions, one of my best friends had been turned into a monster, and I'd had to kill her. I'd had to end her life.

"Lyr." Rhyan's eyes searched mine. "Please."

"Rhyan, the fact that you're still here tells me everything I need to know. I remember when you didn't swear to my father. My blood runs through your veins, as yours does in mine. But you are still part of Ka Hart. And I know you still want justice. You still care about Glemaria."

His eyes squeezed shut. "You're right. I don't want to run away. I have little left to my name but my word. My oath. And I know what I said before about us—about what we need. I don't take any of it back. I meant everything. We need time. I'm scared. Scared of what my feelings for you can make me do. Can make me become. I wanted to give us time. But not when you're in danger. Not like this. Not when I can't stay away from you. Not when I can't fucking bear to be parted."

"Then we stay together. And...we stay."

He pulled his hand from mine, drawing me onto his lap. "Okay. Okay." He hugged me to him. "We'll stay. But if Arianna finds out you know, if I catch one whiff of a threat to you from her, from anyone—I don't want to run. But I will, for you. The plan hasn't changed." These were the same words he'd said to me before I'd entered the arena to fight Haleika. He pulled back, cupping my face, and said fiercely, "I won't lose you."

"And I won't lose you."

"So what in Lumeria do we do now?"

"I need to get through tomorrow. Put my game face on. Stand before the people of Bamaria. Allow my aunt to be named arkasva by Meera. Clap when she's announced as High Lady. Convince everyone I support this, that I'm not a threat. And then

I'm going to find the map Mercurial spoke of. I'm going to find my power and claim it. It's the only way."

"How?"

"Mercurial wants this to happen. Something tells me it won't be long before he returns with some instructions on what to do next."

"Which makes me not want this to happen," he growled.

"I know, but what choice do I have? I know I've gotten this far with training—thanks to you—but now, without my station, the Emperor's promise doesn't mean as much. I could still be forced out of Bamaria because I have no power. I could still be refused a role as a soturion. And if I'm going to fight my aunt, I need to claim my magic. I have to."

Rhyan exhaled. "What if," he said slowly, "what if you could find your magic without the Afeya?"

"I didn't find a way before," I said, but I hadn't had much time to look either.

"You didn't know there was a way before."

Frowning, I exhaled sharply.

"Sleep on it," he said. "We'll figure this out. I promise."

I nodded, and we both fell silent.

My heart pinched. A wave of grief came out of nowhere. I remembered this feeling—it was what I'd felt after Jules had been discovered as vorakh. I'd be living my life, experiencing a rare moment of peace, and then without warning, the tears would fall. The grief would rise. The panic and fear would appear like sudden rainstorms on a sunny day. The constant reminders that she was gone and the sensation of losing her all over again had plagued me for months.

"Partner?" Rhyan's eyes searched mine.

"My father died," I cried out, bursting into tears.

Rhyan's face fell. "I know," he said. "Shhhh. I know." He laid us back down and held me against him. I was shaking and thrashing with the grief, overcome and overwhelmed in a way I hadn't been allowed to feel since it happened. Rhyan shifted my blankets out from underneath me, momentarily breaking us apart, and I rolled onto my side, turning away from him.

"It's okay, Lyr. Come here to me."

But I couldn't turn. I closed in on myself, pulled my knees into a fetal position. My body shook.

He pulled the blankets up to my shoulders and closed the distance between us, pulling my back against him. One arm slid under me from behind, his palm tucking beneath my shirt to lay flat against my belly, while his other arm wrapped over me, that hand pressing to my chest. "It's okay. I've got you. You can let go. I've got you."

I squeezed my eyes shut, as Rhyan held me tightly through every sob until I was cried out. My breathing slowed, and my face felt damp and swollen. My head ached from crying.

"Can you sit up?" he whispered, after my body had gone still for several moments. "Just to drink some water?"

I remained curled in a ball, my eyes still squeezed shut.

"Lyr? Please?"

"Okay," I croaked, letting him pull me to a seat. A decanter of water had been placed across the room on a small table.

"One second," he said. He vanished, appearing at the table, grabbing a glass, and filling it. He was back at my side a second later, forcing the glass into my hand. "Drink this."

I stared dully at the water, knowing I was dehydrated from crying so hard.

"Drink that for me? Come on, partner."

I gulped it down and handed the glass back to him.

"Good girl." He laid me back down and stroked my back. "Why don't you try to sleep so you can be ready for tomorrow?"

I sniffled. "Do you need to go?" I felt pathetic, needing him, not wanting him to leave me. I wasn't sure how much time had passed or how much trouble he might be in if caught away from his post.

"No."

"What about patrol?" I asked.

"Before I came, I traveled to, um, see Uncle Sean. He's covering my post for me. It's okay. I just killed an akadim. They won't exile me for this. Worst case is a lash. I don't care. I'm where I'm supposed to be right now. I'll stay until you fall asleep."

"Rhyan." I shook my head. He had to be exhausted. Even if Sean was at his post, he was risking a lot.

"It's fine. I swear."

I curled my knees back into my chest, starting to shake again, to feel that familiar sensation of panic rise inside me. My hands were cold and my fingers going numb, the ceiling was caving in, my heart was pounding too hard, too fast, too loud.

Rhyan wrapped himself tightly around me, one knee sliding between my legs.

"Deep breaths, partner. Can you do that for me? Give me a few deep breaths?"

His chest, pressed to my back, rose and fell, and I breathed with him, my eyes swollen and heavy. His hand slid back inside my shirt, his fingers wrapping around the golden charm hanging from my neck, his vadati stone hidden inside it.

"Call me." He gave the chain a light tug. "If you need me again. I don't care what hour. I'll be here."

I nodded. "Even after I fall asleep," I said, my voice small. "Will you still hold me a little longer?"

He kissed my shoulder again. "I'll hold you until you're dreaming."

I stood in the arena, dressed in my soturion uniform. The Valalumir stars on the straps of my belt all shined. I reached down, trying to pull off one of the seven-pointed stars. I needed it. There was an enemy. And I needed to kill. To protect.

But the star cut me. I hissed, blood gushing from my finger. I sucked it into my mouth, feeling cold. Snow was falling. But it didn't feel like snow. It was thick and heavy and wet.

I gazed around the arena. The snowflakes were red. Blood red.

An akadim growled, its teeth gnashing, and I spun, trying to find it.

"Asherah," Haleika growled.

I threw my star, watching in horror as Haleika jumped to the side. The star hummed, spinning past her. Rhyan was there, bound and tied up.

"No!"

The star flew past him, flying back at me, piercing my heart. I screamed as my chest exploded with a bang.

I sat straight up in my bed, a terrified cry on the edge of my lips. My balcony door had flown open, the sound of it crashing into the wall having woken me. Wind howled, and a gust of winter air burst into my room. I turned to the side, my hands sliding against empty sheets. Still warm. Rhyan couldn't have been gone long.

I slid out of the bed, taking a blanket with me around my shoulders to close the balcony.

Before I could reach it, I stumbled over a black leather case on the center of my floor. It didn't belong to me—nor to Rhyan. I'd never seen it before.

I checked my door. It was still closed. Locked.

Had someone thrown this in through the balcony? I ran out, searching the horizon. No one was there. No one was below, no one was in the sky, not a single ashvan or seraphim was in sight.

I came back inside and closed and locked the balcony door, shivering and pulling the blanket closer.

I picked up the case and unhooked the lid. Parchment fell into my hand. Unfamiliar handwriting was inked across the small scroll.

Your Grace,

Now the phrase "shekar arkasva" has true meaning. Not all support the illegitimate black seraphim. You're not alone.

131189114141

I read the number sequence twice, trying to understand, to find a pattern. But the signature didn't make any sense—it was just a meaningless group of numbers. I rolled up the parchment as tightly as I could, sliding it into my cuff where I kept Meera's vision log.

I crawled back into bed, shifting to where Rhyan had been, inhaling what lingered of his heat and scent as I wrapped the blankets around me.

You're not alone.

I closed my eyes. At least I knew one thing. There weren't just traitors on the Council of Bamaria or supporters of the Emartis around me.

Someone supported me, too.

CHAPTER EIGHT

A LOUD KNOCK RAPPING against my door made me jump.

I turned from the mirror above my dressing table. It was morning, but the skies were gray and full of the promise of snow.

"Just a minute," I called. I was supposed to be downstairs at the end of the hour, ready to face Bamaria for the public announcement of Arianna's ascent to the Seat.

The knock sounded again, harder, more urgent this time.

"Morgs, what?"

"You're decent?" Markan, my ever-present shadow and guard, growled from the hall.

Without permission, he swung the door open.

"I did not—" I shouted, but he cut me off, walking into my room without invitation. He slammed the door behind him, his burly arms crossed over his golden armor, his face screwed into a scowl. I was so caught off guard by his appearance, by his brazenness, I was speechless. Markan hadn't been up here in years. Not since Jules.

I stared back at him. The blatant disregard for my orders, for my permission, took me right back to the temple, to the moment he had chased me down, drugged me. My fingers clenched.

"Get out," I seethed.

"Your reputation for being a morning person persists, your grace," he said, his head shining in the light of the torches on my walls. "Much as I wish to oblige, these are the Imperator's orders."

I willed myself to calm down, to stay present, to breathe. It was only Markan. As much as I hated him, he was the least of my problems. "I thought you answered to the Arkasva. Your new High Lady," I practically spat the words.

He shrugged. "Call it her orders then. They're the same. You just tend to skip faster for the Imperator. Either way—downstairs."

I stood there, my feet frozen to the ground. Arianna's orders were the same as the Imperator's. Shit. "I'm not ready."

He looked me up and down, rolling his eyes. "You look ready."

"And you're the judge?"

"Your grace," Markan mumbled. "Come."

Turning my back on him, I faced the mirror once more.

Snow coated my balcony, and winter frosted my windows. The air was frigid, and the last thing I wanted to do today was step outside. I wore a long black dress with my soturion-issued boots beneath for warmth. In the daylight, my Valalumir mark had faded, blending into my skin, but it was just visible enough for someone standing close to me to notice. Asherah's armor covered it. At least it wasn't burning me now, though from the cold I'd felt since I'd crawled out of bed, I could have used its heat.

I'd restrung the charm holding Rhyan's vadati stone around a belly chain and wore it discreetly around my waist beneath my dress. A long velvet cloak—Batavia red—kept my arms warm. And for what was perhaps the last time, I'd pinned my diadem in place, the ends concealed beneath my hair, which would show no signs of red as the sun had been obscured by the snow. I smoothed my hair over the pins again—my hands had shaken the whole time I'd arranged the diadem in my hair.

I'd tried to line my eyes, to look presentable as Lady Lyriana, but they were still so red and puffy from crying all night, I'd settled for mascara only.

"Your grace," Markan said again. I could hear the impatience in his voice.

Himself to Moriel. This was my last morning like this, but he didn't care. So long as my heart was beating, he kept his job.

"Fine," I snapped. "I'm coming. No need to drug me this time." I marched past him for the door, slamming it open and passing through without turning my head back or looking down as I made my way through the winding halls of the fortress down the stairs to the Great Hall.

Painted columns full of the deeds of past arkasvim—my ancestors, the rulers I'd wanted to emulate, the women I wanted to become—stared back at me. When I was younger, I'd come down here when I couldn't sleep and stare at their pictures, wondering what was meant for me—how I might find my own place, my own destiny, in such a long and powerful bloodline.

I felt like I was being cut from this bloodline today.

I found Morgana and Meera at the base of the steps, their bodies stiff, backs straight. They wore similar dresses to mine, black, with velvet coats to guard against the chill and snow.

Meera looked pale as a ghost, her mouth half open, her eyes wide with shock.

She knew. Morgana must have told her first thing this morning. Both of my sisters' eyes caught on my armor, my connection to Asherah. Their escorts stood close, looking sour-faced, as Markan tried to herd me into place.

The Imperator stood at the other end of the hall. Behind him were six soturi, all wolves loyal to him and him alone.

"Good morning, ladies." His mouth curled into a sneer. He blinked slowly, tracking our curtsies with predatory eyes.

I noted the slight as I straightened. None of us had been referred to as "your grace." We were still heirs, but he hadn't wasted one second in stripping us of our titles.

Footsteps echoed down the hall from the Seating Room. Arianna and Naria approached. Neither wore black to mourn my father, but red. Batavia red. Our color. Our symbol of power.

"Good morning, my dears." Arianna's steps slowed as she neared. "How are you all feeling today?" She paused, offering a curtsey to the Imperator. "Your highness."

I managed a blank expression, nodding and noting Meera and Morgana were also offering lukewarm acknowledgements.

A cough from the Imperator caught my attention. His eyes slanted toward me, chin upturned, nostrils flaring as he frowned. A look of utter disdain and impatience was written across his wolfish features. "Do the ladies of Ka Batavia not bow before their arkasva?"

I blinked, my mouth going dry as I realized we were meant to bow before Arianna now. And Naria.

Small tremors in my legs kept me from following through at first. Something red and hot and full of rage burned through my blood at just the thought of giving them this courtesy. But the Imperator's aura was striking, biting, and I had no choice.

I gripped the skirt of my gown once more, sinking into a perfectly practiced curtsey beside my sisters.

Arianna waved us off as if this were unnecessary, but I caught the smallest hint of a smile forming on the corner of her lips. I saw the lie clearly now.

"It's a historic morning. Changing the line of succession in Bamaria. Are you three ready?" the Imperator asked, his eyes roving back to me.

I rolled my shoulders back. I hadn't left my room until now—hadn't had breakfast—and I was starting to feel a mix of hunger and nausea. Stepping forward, I offered a nod. I was ready to get this over with.

But a commotion came at the front doors, and I caught the end of an argument taking place between two men. Euston strode in looking flustered, a mage at his heels. "Mage Bellamy, private escort to Lord Tristan Grey," he announced. "For the Lady Lyriana."

I froze. I'd been paying Bellamy for months to keep from Tristan my movements. He'd even helped me escape from Days of Shadows with Meera in my arms, in the thrall of a vision—though he didn't know what was going on—only that I needed to leave with her. What in Lumeria was he doing here now?

"We're busy," the Imperator said. "Did no one inform his lord of the morning's events? Come back later."

Bellamy bowed quickly to the Imperator and then turned, bowing before Arianna. He did not bow to Naria, but he gave her a long look, his eyes narrowed. "Your highness. Your...your grace," he said, as if unsure of Arianna's current title. "I apologize for the intrusion. I was tasked with delivering a message to the Lady Lyriana before the morning's event. Not after."

I stepped forward, heart pounding. Had he truly come with a message from Tristan? Or was he coming personally to warn me of something else, something about the arrangement I had with him? Had Tristan found out?

I lifted my chin, taking another step forward. Whatever this was, it was important. "I will hear it."

"You will not," said the Imperator. "Lord Tristan may approach the lady at the conclusion of our announcement."

Bellamy persisted. "My lord said not to return without delivering."

"You will not return at all unless you leave now. We have a schedule. In mere minutes, the Lady Lyriana Batavia will not be an heir anymore. And these urgent matters between her and his lord will cease."

Naria giggled, the sound grating in my ears.

At the jerk of the Imperator's head, a rather frog-faced soturion standing behind him sprang forward, sneering.

Bellamy looked desperately to me, his chest heaving, but even he wasn't paid enough to suffer a beating from a Kormac soturion. I nodded for him to go.

I eyed Morgana. *Did you hear?*

She blinked, looking away from me, her eyes fixed with venom on Naria before she shook her head.

Morgs?

Her eyes found mine, and she shook her head again, her message clear. Not now.

What the hell else in Lumeria was going on?

Naria laughed while adjusting her red velvet gloves. "Don't worry, Lyr. You'll find out."

"And how would you know Lord Tristan's personal business?" I snapped.

A wide yet and sinister grin spread across Naria's face as she stalked toward me. "Cousin," she said, her eyes flicking up and down my body, "you forgot to say, 'your grace.'"

"I believe that was you," I said under my breath. "I still wear the diadem. I am still Heir to the Arkasva."

"Heir to the Arkasva, High Lord of Bamaria," she crooned. "But we don't have a High Lord, do we? He's—"

"Shut your fucking face," Morgana snapped.

"What did you say to me?" There was glee in Naria's voice. She was getting pleasure from this.

I stood between my sister and cousin, feeling the Imperator's attention closing in on us. "She said she won't address you as her grace until you wear a diadem. You're not an heir yet. Don't expect to be treated like one."

"And yet you've already bowed to me." She reached forward, brushing her hand against my forehead, her velvet-clad fingers on the golden circlet centered over my forehead. "Hmmm. It was pretty." She pulled her hand back, waggling her fingers in my face. "Shame it will be destroyed." She moved toward the double doors with such a lift in her step, she looked like she was skipping—the way she'd walked through these halls as a girl. She tossed her blonde hair over her shoulder, batting an eye at the Soturi of Ka Kormac.

I looked to Arianna. Naria taunting us over Father's death left me feeling sick but didn't surprise me. Naria had turned on Jules before I'd processed what had happened at her Revelation Ceremony.

But for her to touch my diadem—it wasn't an offense written down anywhere I could cite because it was not something ever done. Such a breach in protocol was unfathomable. Even without a specific law forbidding such a thing, we both knew she'd deeply insulted me and my station.

And nothing was going to be done about it. Arianna taking power last night was also unheard of. Every breach of protocol, every change and transition away from tradition, put me in danger. I was standing in the room with my father's killer, trusting civility because of custom. I realized how much I was relying on my safety to come from Arianna's desire to be legitimate. But I was feeling less sure of that game by the second. How far was this going to go? How quickly was I going to have to act, to find my power?

How soon would it be before Rhyan determined the danger too great and demanded we run?

"I'm so sorry, Lyr," Arianna said, looking truly embarrassed. "I will speak to her. She will be punished for her rudeness."

I stared down at my boots. My aunt was lying—I knew that now. So much of their relationship was becoming clear. My aunt had trained and groomed Naria to act this exact way. Of course, she had. The woman was a master at appearances, at controlling society's perception of her every move. Someone like her didn't have a wild, uncultured daughter. Every word out of Naria's mouth had always been carefully calculated. Naria, her loyal servant, had acted out and played with treason purely so Arianna had a constant excuse to remind others of her position. Thanks to Naria's antics, Arianna had been given a daily excuse to separate herself from the one person who looked just like Tarek—the man who'd been blamed for the entire treasonous rebellion. All while Naria attracted those who shared her viewpoint, finding a safe place to exercise their treason.

Another set of soturi entered Cresthaven. Ka Kormac. Armed.

"Your escort," drawled the Imperator.

"Arkturion Aemon's in charge of our escort," I blurted.

The Imperator grinned. "He is. But not this morning. Crowd control has become an issue once more."

Meera stepped forward. "Then perhaps this is not the right moment for such an announcement to be made. I will show my support for this transition of power—but not at the risk of my life, or my sisters."

Father's warnings about crowds had never felt more important than in that moment.

Arianna's mouth tightened. "Perhaps my niece is right."

"No. I have an entire legion dedicated to your safety this morning. While I remain in Bamaria, no harm shall come to a single member of Ka Batavia."

The words were spoken with honor, but I was shivering from their threat. We wouldn't be harmed only because we were needed. But when Arianna was legitimized and when the Imperator left for the capitol....

The soturi sneered, and within seconds, we were surrounded. I was separated from my sisters, forced to walk with soturi on either side of me while Meera and Morgana were marched in front of me down the icy glass of the waterway and into separate seraphim carriages.

Markan joined me along with three soturi belonging to Ka Kormac.

I remained silent, refusing to look at any of them, even the one who sat behind the partition as was custom. It was becoming clearer by the second. They were not my escorts. They were my jailers.

My sisters and I had been taken prisoner the moment Meera had abdicated, but no one could see our chains or bonds.

We landed in the Urtavian port, yells and chants pounding through the carriage walls.

I peeled back the velvet winter curtains to look at the city, shaking a little as our bird settled onto the ground. "I thought we were going to the temple."

One of my guards raised an eyebrow. He'd unevenly shaved his face, and random blonde whiskers stood out as he sneered. "We are."

The carriage door opened.

"Then explain to me why we are not before it," I said carefully. We were about a mile away.

"Because we're not," he said, his eyes dipping down my body and landing on my soturion boots peeking out from the hem of my gown. "Lucky you wore your boots today."

I was tugged to my feet and ushered out of the seraphim before I could protest. Roughened hands gripped my arm, pulling me forward until my boots hit the ground. The badly shaved soturion's fingers dug into my bicep, and he growled, hitting the arm cuff I wore.

"What in the—!" He squeezed my arm, fingers wrapping around the imprint of the metal through my sleeve.

I froze. "Take your hands off me," I demanded.

He poked around, sliding his hand around the cuff. "Why wear jewelry no one can see?"

"Who gave you permission to ask me questions?" I snarled.

"You're only heir a few more minutes, princess."

"Even if not heir, I am and always will be a Lady of Ka Batavia. Daughter of two arkasvim. And now I'm niece to the coming High Lady. My blood is ancient, and nothing your Imperator does will change that, you dog." I sneered. "Do not call me princess again."

The soturion growled, his fingers tightening, but Markan pushed between us.

"Myself to Moriel," he snarled. "You can't ever make my job easy?" He pulled the soturion off me. "Remember your orders from my High Lady and your Arkasva and Imperator. She's to remain unharmed and untouched."

"And remember yours." The whiskered soturion took hold of my arm again, and Markan moved to stand directly in front of me.

"I don't leave her side." Markan glared.

I willed myself calm. My arm cuff was safe. Meera's secrets were safe. My message of support was safe. I couldn't touch the vadati stone chained to my waist, but as long as my guards didn't become too handsy, then my secret with Rhyan was also safe.

"*Shekar arkasva! Shekar arkasva!*" The chants began at once, and my soturi surrounded me.

The streets had been cleared, and within seconds, I was marched out toward them, the Imperator's guards still closely surrounding me. The air was so cold and the wind frigid I began to shiver. My cloak wasn't enough. My fingers were growing numb. I stared straight ahead at the empty street, keeping my head high, refusing to meet the eyes of the audience crowded on either side of me.

I thought we'd arrive at the Temple of Dawn, say the words, lose our diadems while watched by the nobles, the Council, and the few members of Bamarian society who could get to the temple, and be done.

The Imperator's plans had been far grander. He'd meant for us to parade about, to be seen by as many Bamarians as possible. It wasn't enough that our father had been murdered, that we were to hand over our power and publicly acknowledge his murderer—we were meant to be humiliated on our way to doing so.

I squeezed my eyes shut. Once again, the Imperator had out-maneuvered us and made it clear that Korteria was conquering Bamaria. His show of support for Arianna was just part of the game. We were losing more than our status and position.

We were losing our country.

I swallowed, sensing Morgana and Meera lined up beside me. I had to remain composed for them. To protect them.

The shouts kept coming, louder and louder, until soturi wearing silver and gold appeared on the edge of the street, using their bodies to hold back the crowd.

Minutes passed during which we just stood there in the freezing cold, shivering and being gawked at. I bit my lip, tapped my fingers against my sides, pressed my palms into my hips—anything to keep from going completely numb. I had to keep my wits about me, to stay alert, to fight back if possible.

At last, three more seraphim arrived. The one carrying the Imperator featured a banner of his sigil, a snarling wolf. The next carriage to land showed off a flag of the sigil of Ka Batavia, and Arianna and Naria emerged from it. The third seraphim to land waved a gray flag; a silver moon above silver seraphim wings blew back and forth in the wind. It was the sigil of Ka Grey.

Tristan, along with his grandmother and grandfather, emerged, surrounded by a full escort of mages. Including Bellamy.

What?

Lady Grey looked smugger than I'd ever seen her as she stepped out of the carriage. She quickly joined Arianna's side, and her eyes found mine. She offered a quick lift of her eyebrows in acknowledgement, her wine-colored mouth tight. She wore a cloak of silver velvet with silver satin on its borders and white fur at the collar. At least half a dozen of their mage escorts had been waiting in the crowd for her arrival and immediately surrounded her.

I eyed Tristan as his boots touched the ground, his blue velvet mage robes blowing in the wind behind him. His mouth was tight, his hand on his stave, his entire expression alert and ready for a fight. The moment his eyes met mine, his face fell with an unusual amount of emotion: sorrow, grief...and guilt. The over-sized silver sigil ring on his finger caught a flash of torchlight, shining like a small beacon before he covered it with his hand.

His lips quivered before he mouthed from the distance, *Lyr, are you okay?*

My gut twisted. I shook my head.

He closed his eyes and frowned, his head cocked to the side and red rising up his neck, before he looked back at me.

I'm sorry, he mouthed. He shifted and glared toward the Imperator. For once, he seemed as angry with him as I was. His hand slid to the hilt of his stave tucked into its silver holster. There was a fierceness in his stance, a fury, before he looked to me once again. *I am so sorry.*

I couldn't hear him, but I could imagine the anguish in his voice, and my heart began to pound in response.

Lord Trajan stepped down from the carriage with every finger dripping in silver rings and silver arm cuffs that pushed back the sleeves of his blue robe. At once, everyone began moving toward the street to join the Imperator, who was standing in the center of the entire commotion. Before I could signal anything back to Tristan, the Imperator's voice amplified, drowning out the noise of the crowd.

"Greetings, Bamaria. Greetings to all my fellow Lumerians who have come here to study, to live, to work." The Imperator's voice boomed as he stepped into the street, slowly strolling past us as if we didn't exist. "And a belated happy Valyati to you all if I were not able to personally wish you so before."

I was only reassured when several boos and shouts of protest at his presence rose above the rest of the noise. There may have been those who disliked my father—there had been many—but most Bamarians hated the Imperator more and resented his presence in our country. Half of the complaints about my father's rule was that it had seemed to coincide with the Imperator's increase in power. Bamaria was the only country that allowed a foreign soturi to defend its borders, and this foreign soturi had left us under attack. It had allowed akadim inside its borders and the beasts to kill our own.

Not all support the illegitimate black seraphim. You're not alone.

I touched my arm, my fingers gliding across the velvet of my sleeve to press down on the cuff of golden seraphim wings. Still there. Still safe.

The Imperator began a speech formally announcing my father's death, reiterating his plans to deal with the akadim problem, and announcing Lady Arianna as the new Arkasva Batavia, High Lady of Bamaria. She had been offered the silver laurel last night, but now she was to formally receive it before the public outside the Temple of Dawn. There, Meera would announce her abdication. And there, our diadems would be removed and destroyed.

My head already hurt from the screams—I couldn't imagine how Morgana was feeling. She'd definitely smoked this morning, but still.... I caught her eye, watching her dark eyebrows form a V as she winced. Meera was swaying slightly from side to side. Her diadem hung loose against her forehead, the center banging against her as she moved.

My hands and arms shook, though I was no longer sure if it was from the cold or my nerves and the shock of what was happening.

Several mages wearing the colors and sigil of Ka Kormac began to march down the street toward us in two rows. It took me a moment to realize they were all carrying litters on their shoulders. The litters were missing the usual walls that offered their riders privacy from the outside world. Instead, each one had four poles holding up its silver roof, revealing the single couch each contained. I'd never seen any litters like this before, and didn't like the idea that I'd be exposed to the crowds of Bamarians as I was taken down the street.

"We shall now ride to the Temple of Dawn," the Imperator announced, "where Lady Meera will formally abdicate to Lady Arianna Batavia, your new High Lady."

The crowd yelled as the mages lowered the litters to the ground. The mention of power going to Arianna seemed to unify them. They had no idea we'd already fallen into chaos.

Meera was directed into the first litter with Arianna—the pure picture of a power transfer. I felt sick looking at them, knowing the truth. Last night, I'd been barely able to stomach seeing Arianna. Now, Meera had to sit beside her, talk to her, look happy.

The second litter was taken by Naria and her sentry, the next by Lord Trajan and Lady Romula.

Why was Ka Grey here, riding on a litter to attend a transfer of power? They were on the Council, but no other nobles had been given this role, this prestige.

Bellamy's message....

"Lyr," Tristan yelled, heading for me. One of his escorts followed close behind looking annoyed. Tristan's arm was outstretched like he was trying to get to me as quickly as he could. He seemed desperate, almost wildly so, to reach my side.

"Lord Tristan," the Imperator admonished. "We have a seat for you. Up here." He pointed toward Naria's litter, but Tristan ignored the command, continuing to move my way.

"Tristan," Lady Romula hissed.

His mouth tightened, but still he progressed until one of the Imperator's mages stood before him.

Tristan froze, his brown eyes widening. He recognized the mage the moment I did. It was the one he'd fought and punched at my Revelation Ceremony. He'd beat this man in order to bind me himself, and from the way the mage was leaning forward, his stave pointed toward Tristan's neck and his knuckles white and shaking, he remembered just as well as we did.

"Let me pass," Tristan seethed, his voice dripping with the kind of command only nobles ever achieved.

"Lord Tristan," shouted the Imperator, his voice magically amplified. "Come." He laughed as if this were all some big joke, some misunderstanding. "It's not proper on this occasion for you to sit with your fiancée's," he paused, his black eyes watching me, "cousin."

My stomach dropped.

Fiancée's *cousin*. I was the cousin.

Which meant....

Myself to Moriel. That was why he'd sent Bellamy.

"Lyr," Tristan said, sounding hopeless, his eyes red and watery.

"We have so much to celebrate today!" said the Imperator. "Our new Arkasva, our High Lady. The restoration of power in Bamaria to a woman, to Ka Batavia. And the announcement of our new Heir Apparent and her engagement. Such a happy occasion to bring joy after our recent tragedies. Please, everyone, let's cheer for Lady Naria Batavia, Heir Apparent to the Arkasva, High Lady of Bamaria, and her new fiancé, Lord Tristan Grey."

CHAPTER NINE

EVERYTHING NUMBED—MY BODY, MY mind. I felt like I was barely myself anymore, barely able to keep track of time or what was happening around me. Of Naria's litter being lifted with Tristan beside her. Of the cheers and congratulations erupting from the crowd alongside shouts of, *"Tovayah maischa,"* as she stood from her seat and took Tristan's arm. Of the way she removed the velvet gloves she wore to reveal a large silver ring on her finger.

Even at a distance, I knew that the sigil of Ka Grey adorned her now. I'd missed it before, when Tristan had covered his hand, that he also had a ring. A golden one. A ring of Ka Batavia.

I wondered if the seraphim feathers were black.

I was going to be sick. Two years. Two Godsdamned years. All the endless nights, the kissing and touching and smiling and dancing...for nothing. For absolutely fucking nothing.

Even though I knew we weren't right, weren't destined for each other, even though my heart belonged to another, it still hurt, losing this future. Losing his protection. Losing the status I'd fought so hard for to keep my family safe.

I'd thought Tristan loved me in his own way. I'd thought, at least, even if he never fully accepted me, he was my friend. But this...I never would have imagined he'd betray me like this, humiliate me this way before all of Bamaria. I'd thought I'd been more to him, at least worth being spared this shit show.

And I'd thought I at least had the loyalty of Bamaria, who knew Godsdamned well Tristan was mine for two years, but I didn't, not based on their cheers and shouts of congratulations. As if they'd forgotten me completely. As if Tristan and I had never been together. As if I'd never been Bamaria's heir. As if he weren't now sitting right beside my own flesh and blood, my cousin.

My vision blurred, and I found myself being led to the very back of the line of litters and placed into a seat. I closed my eyes, my cheeks red and my heart hurting, until I felt someone climb onto the litter beside me.

"My lady," drawled the Imperator.

I jolted. He was sitting on the bench beside me. There was barely an inch of space between us.

"Your...your highness," I managed. "Have I...?" I turned desperately around the litter, looking everywhere but at him. "Have I sat in the wrong seat?"

"Not at all," he said, voice low. "I requested this."

My throat went dry. "That hardly seems proper. I'll no longer be an heir when this litter comes to a stop." I willed my heart to slow, to stop beating so loudly. "I do not deserve to sit with the Imperator."

He smiled, an actual smile that lifted his eyes—eyes that were black, wolfish, predatory. He leaned toward me. "How about we let Imperators decide who does and does not deserve to sit beside them?"

I felt my lip trembling with fear but tamped it down. "Of course, your highness."

"You disparage yourself, my lady," he said. "You know, I think sometimes me and you got off on the wrong foot. Years ago. I'm not sure what I may have done to cause such offense, but I do hope we can mend our relationship moving forward."

You rapist piece of shit. You murdered my cousin...and Gods know what else.

I schooled my face, forcing a smile across my lips. "Your highness, I would enjoy a mending of our relationship. And I meant no offense now. I was simply confused," I said sweetly and glanced beyond him. "When does Arkturion Aemon take control of our security?"

His lip curled, and he leaned toward me. "Do you doubt my ability to protect you, my lady? Do you believe only the Ready capable?"

"No," I said. "Simply that I know he is...." My heart was pounding too hard, beating too loudly. For a second, terror gripped me. Would my contract with Mercurial heat again? I still didn't know what caused it. The Imperator couldn't know, couldn't ask why. "He's," I continued, feeling that there was no extra warmth in my chest, "supposed to be in charge."

The Imperator nodded. "Your life was in danger back in the arena. And believe it or not, I do care about your safety as much as the Ready and your aunt."

My fingers squeezed, knotting into the folds of my dress at my lap.

"Which is why, my lady, I am making it my personal mission to keep you safe. Ka Batavia's favor is not with Bamaria right now. It is particularly not with you." He grinned and waved to the crowd. "Not after they all witnessed you killing one of their own."

She was my friend. And you and your Gods-damned-Moriel-bastard uncle forced me to.

I nodded.

"I am sure it cannot be easy to see Lord Tristan with Lady Naria. But you must remember, the people now see you as his cousin's killer. I know you care for your Ka. This is for the best. And my sitting with you here now as we ascend to the temple and turn over power to Bamaria's rightful ruler sends a statement. A powerful one."

"Oh," I said carefully. "What statement is that?"

"That you are protected. That you are welcome."

I swallowed, my throat still painfully dry. He was speaking in this strangely sweet way I'd never heard from him before.

"I thank you," I said, praying my voice wasn't shaking as terribly as my hands were. "I am grateful for the protection."

"Perhaps, in this short time we are together, we might begin to mend this rift between us."

"I...." I swallowed again, feeling thousands of eyes on me, acutely aware of Tristan and his new fiancée up ahead and the fact that I was helpless, sitting on this litter with a wolf. "I would like that."

He nodded, smiling even wider, a cold gust of wind breezing through his blonde hair. "Good. Because I think it's important for you to see the possibilities of such a relationship. After all, you are still without magic. And while you were impressive in the arena, I think we both know you may not be so lucky next time. I would not place my bets there."

"Can any soturion bet on luck, your highness?" I asked. The litter lifted, and we began to glide forward, the crowd yelling at us—a mix of cheers and protests. I was no longer able to tell who supported my family and who was angry with us. It was one huge blur of noise.

"No," the Imperator said. "None can. Which is why it's important to know your options. I mentioned this at the ball. And my offer still stands. I could find a place for you. One that doesn't involve such...pain to your body." His eyes dipped down to my waist and back to my breasts, one hand lifting with a finger pointing, tracing my curves in the air. "Other options might call for pleasure instead."

I shuddered involuntarily. I was fully clothed, covered in my dress and armor and cloak. He hadn't touched me this time, and still, his gaze made my skin crawl, made me remember the torture he'd inflicted on my back, the feel of his phantom fingers pressing in, poking....

"I do intend to continue my studies," I said sweetly. "Soturion training has grown on me."

"Many would offer you marriage," he continued, completely ignoring my statement. "You are of age, and while lacking in power and soon status, you are still from a well-respected bloodline in the Empire. And you will not mind my saying, you are rather pleasant to look upon. Many of the arkasvim up north have expressed interest in such a contract with you."

Rhyan's admission that his father had tried to marry me to his arkturion ran through my mind. Deciding with Rhyan that we needed to approach every ruler of Lumeria as a threat had felt smart last night. Assuming they all might want me because they might know of my true identity had made sense. That they would use it against me, turn me into a pawn in their game before I could take control of my power, claim it, master it. It had all seemed so hypothetical, what we'd discussed while I was in Rhyan's arms, tucked into my bed.

Now, I could feel how dire the threat was. What did the rulers of Lumeria know?

I needed answers. And I needed off this Gods-forsaken litter. Away from the wolves. Away from my enemies.

The Imperator's eyebrows raised, clearly waiting for me to respond.

"I should think," I said, "that Arianna was the most desired woman now."

His lips curled. "One would think. Just know that I am fully prepared to make your life much more comfortable than it has recently become. Life isn't always easy for women in the Empire. Especially women without power. Many problems can arise for women without men to protect them."

"Some women protect themselves," I said before I could think better of it.

The Imperator laughed. "Some do." His gaze narrowed. "Some don't. You know," he said casually, "I used to spend time with the Lady Julianna before, well," he winked, "you know."

My breath hitched. *Control what they see. Control what they see.*

"Is that so," I said.

"We used to have chats, her and I, on my visits to Bamaria. Quite intimately."

I had to keep breathing. I knew this. I knew he'd often cornered her at dinners and parties and acted improperly on multiple occasions. Often, she'd find an excuse to get away, or her guard would come to her rescue. I'd watched her guard seething in the corner on dozens of occasions, waiting for the right moment to step between Jules and the Imperator in such a way that he would not lose his position. Her guard had to protect her, but he could not offend the Imperator or make things worse. I even recalled Rhyan intervening on his visit that summer, coming between her and the Imperator and taking her out of the ballroom.

But after her arrest, I hadn't been able to think about those times. I'd blocked so many memories of her, just so I could survive. I couldn't go there. I couldn't allow those thoughts in my head, or I'd lose every ounce of sanity I'd clawed my way toward after the Bastardmaker had grabbed her. I could feel it even now, the panic, the terror—how desperately I missed her—all rising to the surface at once. Threatening to ruin me, to destroy me.

"And because of those intimate conversations," he drawled, "I was able to pull some strings for her after her arrest."

"Intimate conversations?" I seethed.

Smiling, he nodded. "We'd spoken together many, many times before. I am not the monster you seem to think I am. I made sure she was as comfortable as she could be."

"Comfortable!" My voice shook. He'd had her dragged to Lethea and murdered and...Gods. No. I couldn't allow myself to imagine anything else she had suffered under his *care*.

His eyebrows lifted in admonishment, the look so predatory I nearly sank to the ground of the litter to avoid his stare.

My mask had fallen. I took a deep breath, affecting my voice to be controlled and sweet once again. "I'm sorry, I wasn't aware any strings could be pulled for someone like her. Vorakh is vorakh." Sweat beaded at my neck.

"True. But sometimes I like to show some kindness to those about to...be stripped."

Breathing was becoming difficult.

"You said she was a fighter," I snarled.

"I did say that."

Wind blew harshly against my cheeks. The crowd watching us cheered as we passed.

"If she was so comfortable," I said, my voice rising, "I'm unsure what she was fighting against."

He laughed. "I see so much of her spark in you. I do wish to keep you safe. And your sisters."

"I had no idea our safety was of such importance to you."

Beyond him, the crowd was surging, trying to push their way into the streets as the soturi linked arms, forming a wall, holding them back.

"My concerns have always been for those in the south of Lumeria. For all in the south. And that especially includes you."

"Then we are in alignment," I said, willing my hands to remain steady in my lap, to not curl into fists, to not swing at his face.

Breathe. Just breathe.

"Should any other offers come your way," he continued, "I do hope you'll come to me first. I can make a better one, one with the Emperor's approval. Keep it in mind," he jerked his chin ahead, his wolf eyes landing on Naria and Tristan, "now that you are suddenly on the market."

I stared ahead. Naria was rubbing her hand up Tristan's back, her fingers snaking their way up his neck and into his hair.

"My lady, I know you think Korterians to be very different from Bamarians." The Imperator leaned back on the couch, stroking the hilt of his sword. He widened his legs until one pressed into mine. "But we are not so different. I know you are smart and you like to read. It may surprise you, but I've done some reading, too. In your very own Great Library."

"Is that so?" I asked. I'd spotted Rhyan in the crowd, his green eyes burning into mine. His mouth was tight, and he was moving quickly, keeping pace with the progress of the litter, sliding in and out of open spaces, pushing through closely knit groups who stood in his way.

My leg began to itch beneath my dress. I wanted to move it away from the Imperator and his disgusting warmth.

"Have you ever studied the history of the sekhium?" he asked.

"Ritualistic transfers of power in Lumeria Matavia," I replied dully.

"Yes. Quite out of style in Bamaria. But did you know they are still practiced up north? You'll have to ask your apprentice, I'm sure he knows all about them. With the infighting amongst the northern Kavim, they've proven necessary." He turned his head in that moment to look right at Rhyan and then back to me.

I stared straight ahead again. Had the Imperator known Rhyan was there? Or had his look been a coincidence? And why was he bringing up the practice of sekhium now? They were brutal, humiliating, uncivilized, and not performed in Bamaria.

"Fascinating history," he crooned. "You see, when a Ka or country is conquered, it is important for the people to know and to see that power has transferred completely. It is also important for them to understand their new ruler is strong. The ritual is designed to change their allegiance. Did you know that before the Drowning, the conquerors would take the conquered and tie them to wagons before all of their people?" He mimicked tying a rope. "Their homes would be ransacked for valuables and possessions. These would be displayed on the wagon-tops, free for the people to take. Those conquered were to lose all signs of their status." He reached for my hair, and his fingers curled around a strand, tugging and twisting and knocking the pin holding my diadem out of place. The gold circlet slipped down my forehead, banging into my nose. "Diadems, of course, were taken." His hand moved down my neck and shoulder. "Fine jewelry, armor," his eyes flicked to mine again, "and clothing."

"Sounds barbaric," I said, barely able to breathe.

"Quite so," he agreed, his smile friendly again. He reached for my hair again and pinned my diadem back into place as if he proving to me that he had the ability to take and return it. "Can you imagine? Being stripped naked in public, marched through the streets, while the people you ruled and cared for pillaged your belongings. And sometimes, if the soturi weren't careful to hold the mob back...they pillaged your body."

Rhyan's eyes caught mine from a distance. He was frowning, his shoulders tensed. I could feel the fury of his aura from here.

"We can be grateful we live in more civilized times," I said, unable to stop my voice from shaking.

"Of course. Though there is a sort of beautiful simplicity to it. Is there not?"

Feeling the Imperator's eyes heavy on me as he awaited a response, I shrugged.

"I am very happy that you and your sisters are falling into line and supporting your aunt. The Empire needs Bamaria to be stable. If you or your sisters were to revolt or put forth a separate claim, it might take going all the way back to the traditions of Lumeria Matavia to bring your people into line. Don't you agree?"

He was threatening a sekhium. Threatening to march me naked through the streets if I rebelled or if I claimed Arianna false.

"I would not entertain such a possibility," I said. "No one has any intention of putting forth such a claim." Sweat beaded at my neck despite the cold. Did he know I knew Arianna was a murderer?

"I am so happy to have had this conversation with you, my lady," he said. "Please do pass it on to any other...supporters of such an idea."

Not all support the illegitimate black seraphim. You're not alone.

I breathed through my mouth, my exhales in the air before me.

"Should Lord Eathan or the Ready try to stir up any trouble, we would have to act swiftly for the good of Bamaria." His thigh pressed into mine with such pressure, I felt sure I'd bruise.

"I am dedicated to the good of Bamaria, your highness," I said, my voice barely rising above a whisper. I raised a hand in salute.

The Imperator laughed. "You remind me so of the Lady Julianna," he said. "Ah, the temple is before us. I hardly noticed we finished our ride." He winked again. "I found my present company so entertaining." He sat back up, leaning in closer than before, his leg now pushing mine back. "You?"

I nodded. "Yes."

"What a good little daughter of the Empire. And, my lady, if you change your mind about wanting marriage, I am to be the first to know. Your sisters' safety will be tied up in your match." He glanced over at Tristan and Naria then back to me, smirking. "You can tell me. You never really wanted Lord Tristan, did you?"

The backs of my eyes burned as our litter was lowered to the ground. The Imperator stood at once, extending his hand for me to take.

I stared at it, my chest heaving with nervous, panicked breaths, and he waggled his fingers impatiently in my face. When was it going to end? When was he going to finally leave me alone? I didn't want to touch him, to feel him on me for one second. I didn't want to accept his help, not even for this. But I'd been given no choices today. Spared no humiliation.

I took his hand as I stood. His grip was painfully tight and his skin sickeningly soft, reminding me of his fingers on my back, within my torn tunic, my torn bandages, my torn wounds. My stomach roiled, and my skin crawled.

A field of snow-covered grass stood before me, the Temple of Dawn in the center. Resembling a seven-pointed star from above, it was made of seven distinct rays—each one assigned a color relating to the shards of the Valalumir. We stood before the Red Ray and its door which, until recently, had always been private to Ka Batavia.

Arkmage Kolaya stepped outside it just then, her white robes contrasting against the red door, her face solemn.

I suspected the remainder of the ritual was meant to take place inside—nearly all of our ceremonies did. But it had only been three days since the akadim attack. The sanctuary had been all but destroyed from the fight and carnage. With magic, it would be fully restored, but the sanctuary was huge, and with all the chaos of losing an arkasva, it was probably still a few days from complete restoration.

"You will not mind me walking you there, will you?" the Imperator asked.

The backs of my eyes burned with tears. "Not at all."

"Shall we then, my lady?" He released my hand, fitting it into the crook of his arm as if he were a gentleman. He was still acting sweet, like he thought he might actually convince me he wasn't a monster. His hand swept across my back, and my spine stiffened.

I caught his expression from my periphery. He frowned at my sudden discomfort, a look of sympathy in his eyes. His fingers began to dance between my shoulder blades, poking and prodding the way they had months ago, searching for my wounds, opening them, torturing me.

I was clothed. I wasn't injured. He couldn't hurt me. He couldn't hurt me. He couldn't....

"Your highness," said a voice like death.

I looked up into the dark eyes of the Ready. His red arkturion cloak flew behind him, and his golden armor shined.

"Arkturion Aemon."

"I'll take the lady from here," he snarled.

The Imperator patted my back, and I jumped, unable to help myself.

"Of course, Aemon." He winked, releasing me at once.

I practically stumbled out of the Imperator's arms, my entire body shaking.

"You're okay," Aemon said, extending his elbow for me to take. "It's almost over. I'm taking over your protection detail now. He has no reason to come near you after this." There was a violent undertone to his words.

I was grateful and desperate for the relief, but I didn't believe anyone could protect me. Not anymore.

"Thank you," I said, my voice small.

Aemon walked me forward, calling off the soturi who walked with Morgana with such violence that for a second, I thought he'd leave me to slit both of their throats. Morgana instantly took his other arm, a dark look in her eyes. All it took was a look from the Ready for Meera to be released.

"You're Heir Apparent still, Lady Meera," Aemon said. "Walk before us."

He escorted me and my sisters to the front of the temple to stand before Arianna and Kolaya. Naria stood behind her mother and Tristan behind her.

I couldn't look at him. I was going to be sick if I did.

Instead, I tried to find Rhyan again. A crowd was gathering on the grass, the field filling with more and more bodies, boots crushing and melting the remaining snow. He was out there somewhere, watching me, waiting.

Kolaya began speaking, but I couldn't hear her words. Everything was foggy. My mind was reeling with all that had happened, all I'd learned.

At some point, I was made to bow before Arianna. My skin crawled with my newfound hatred for her, the sensation tingling over the parts of me that still clung to and wanted her love—the parts of me I needed to die.

With all the care of an actual mother, of a blood relative, of an aunt who loved me, Arianna removed my diadem from my hair. Her fingers carefully unpinned it, gingerly brushing my locks back, and my head instinctively pushed into her touch.

The moment I sought her comfort, my stomach turned.

I sank back to my knees. Cold, wet grass seeped into my dress. I felt like the cold was beginning to seep into my bones. I'd never felt more naked in my life, never more stripped of my sense of self. My diadem glittered as it dangled in her hand, the golden circle in its center fiery as it reflected the glow of the torches around us.

Morgana's diadem joined mine next, hanging between Arianna's long fingers, and then she had Meera's, the symbol of the Heir Apparent. Arianna's knuckles whitened, her grip tightening over the chains, her sigil ring standing out in stark contrast. A small shake of her hand had the diadems tangling, lightly jingling as they swayed and twisted around each other.

We'd had those for nearly our entire lives.

Words were spoken in High Lumerian, words I could no longer hear as Arianna used her stave to produce a small fire, and then one by one, our diadems—the symbols of our stations, the gifts we had been given as young girls by our father and our mother—were tossed into the rising flames. For a moment, they all lay there, immobile in the fire, and then it began. The flames licked the cold air, hissing and crackling as the diadems slowly heated, lost shape, lost purpose, and melted, losing all semblance of form. Becoming nothing.

"Time to stand and step back, my lady," said a soturion behind me.

I came to, startled at my new title. It hadn't been the first I'd heard it, but it was the first time it'd been uttered with my station stripped: my lady. I was no longer your grace. No longer heir to Ka Batavia. No longer third to the Seat. And despite how many times I'd gone without my diadem, my forehead felt unbelievably bare, just like my soul.

Even when I'd been found without magic, I'd still been an heir. I'd still had my station. I'd thought I'd felt vulnerable before, but I'd been a fool. I'd never realized just how reliant I was on my title to protect me, and just how exposed and in danger I would feel without it.

If Aemon thought the Imperator would leave me alone now, he was so wrong. The Imperator was going to come for me—if Arianna didn't get to me first.

And now, almost nothing could protect me. Staying here, remaining without power, was never going to be anything other than a constant threat on my life.

Somehow, I made it to my feet, pulling my cloak tightly around me, every inch of my body shivering with cold.

My head felt heavy as Naria approached Arianna. A golden diadem, gleaming with its newness, was placed against her head and pinned into her golden blonde hair as Arkmage Kolaya chanted. The crowd cheered and yelled with encouragement. They yelled at Tristan and Naria as if we were already at their wedding feast, as if they'd sworn their oaths to each other, as if I'd never been. The cheers grew with excitement and fervor. Tristan's eyes found mine, deep and sorrowful, his mouth tight. He looked like he was on the verge of tears, and then he took Naria in his arms and kissed her.

My stomach twisted the moment their lips touched. I was going to be sick. But I couldn't be. Not here. Not now.

His hands slid up her arms to cup her face, and she pulled him closer, their bodies pressing together in a way that was almost unseemly, considering their stations and the fact that they were in public. But the ease with which they came together, the closeness....

This was no first kiss.

Tristan had confessed he'd once been with Naria years ago on the solstice—the same night I'd first kissed Rhyan. But over three years had passed since then. From here, it looked like no time had passed at all.

The Imperator clapped, and the entire audience behind me roared in approval.

I looked away. I couldn't stand to see their mouths moving against each other, his tongue swiping past her lips in a pattern

I knew far too intimately. I knew the way he smelled, the way he tasted, the exact pressure he used with his hands. He'd been touching me only the other night at the ball. Before Rhyan...before everything else had happened.

Lady Romula caught my eye. Someone had brought her a glass of wine in a silver goblet. I could see the mage beside her who'd done it—his stave pointed at the tray floating past and offering its service to every member of Ka Grey standing behind them. Her dried, cracked lips widened, as she lifted her glass to me.

Bitch.

She'd finally gotten what she wanted. Her grandson was not going to marry a Lady of Ka Batavia, third from the Seat. He was finally marrying the Heir Apparent.

If the old crone lived long enough for Naria to become High Lady, Lady Romula would be the Arkasva in truth. Tristan would bow to anything she wanted. And I didn't believe Naria to have any agenda other than what was fed to her by the most powerful influence nearby.

I wasn't sure whom I wanted to lose more in that moment, Arianna or Romula.

Tristan broke free of the kiss first, his cheeks red as he looked out at the audience—the mob—toasting and applauding. I could see the guilt and sorrow all over his face, but I didn't want to see him or for him to see me. I looked away.

More words were spoken. Congratulations. Announcements for the official consecration and anointment. Announcements of the invitation of the other eleven arkasvim of the Empire and the return of Emperor Theotis in one month. With each statement made, Arkmage Kolaya stamped her stave against the ground, the crystal on top emitting rainbows of light over the crowded field.

"Congratulations, Lady Arianna, Bamaria's future Arkasva and High Lady. And to Lady Naria Batavia, your new Heir Apparent."

The crowd clapped. Finally, it was over. Many of the noble Kavim who'd been present in the field for the finale, surrounded by their personal escorts and the soturi who kept the regular crowd back, began to disperse. Ka Shavo's representatives slowly vanished into the edges of the field. Senator Janvi of Ka Elys and her niece Lady Pavi rushed forward to congratulate Naria and admire her ring.

Tristan looked up at me then, and I stumbled back. I had to get away. I couldn't face him. I turned, trying to bolt, and ran right into Aemon's arms.

"Lyriana," he said, startled, his hands on my shoulders. "Are you...?"

Shit. Tears welled in my eyes. It was happening.

My chest—my heart—was on fire. I was burning up from the inside.

"Lyr," Aemon asked again, concern growing in his voice. "What is it? What happened?" The more concerned he grew, the harder he grasped me, and the more pain I was in.

"I...I...."

Morgana's aura swept around us as she saw me, her eyes instantly registering what was happening.

I couldn't admit to Aemon I'd fallen prey to the Afeya. It would only lead to questions. I wouldn't be able to get out of telling him why I'd done it, what the Afeyan messenger was holding over me: that I had broken my oath with Rhyan. As much as I trusted Aemon, he could never know that. It was the one law he'd punish severely whether he was like my uncle or not.

Morgana vanished from the crowd.

I stumbled backward, trying to think of a way to escape from Aemon, to keep my secret.

Pine and musk enveloped me. An aura of cool wrapped around my body.

"Arkturion," Rhyan said, his voice stiff. "I'll take Soturion Lyriana home. I assume, despite the shift in status, my job remains?"

Aemon gave me a hard look, still trying to understand what was wrong with me.

I was going to faint. The burning was getting worse, crackling and popping inside my skin, my muscles aflame like they were being pulled and twisted. It felt like the fire was spreading across my body until every inch of my skin was lighting and sparking with it. It took all I had not to scream.

Rhyan's hand reached for my back.

"Yes," Aemon said. "She needs protection now, more than ever. At least until consecration when things are settled." His dark eyes returned to me.

Sweat was dripping down my face. I was going to faint. Gods. I was going to pass out from the pain.

"Don't underestimate the Emartis just because they got their way," he said.

I nodded, but it felt more like my head was rolling around, my neck too weak to hold myself upright. "Bathroom," I cried. "Bathroom, now."

Aemon stepped back with a curt nod. "Go."

I leaned back, feeling Rhyan's hands wrap around my arms, sure and steady. We were just outside the entrance to the Red Ray.

I made eye contact with Kolaya. She seemed to understand and opened the door. I rushed inside, practically tripping over my dress, Rhyan right behind me. The moment the doors closed, he swept his arm beneath my knees and lifted me to his chest.

"Mercurial?" he seethed. He pulled open my cloak, his hand sliding between my breasts and over my heart. "Lyr?"

It was too much. Even as the cold began to gather in his palm, pushing against my burning skin from his calloused fingers, the pain overtook me.

I fainted.

CHAPTER TEN

HALEIKA STOOD BEFORE ME, her brown hair bouncy and full of curls. "He's really handsome, isn't he?" she asked.

Leander walked across the arena, his hair golden in the sun, a warm smile across his face.

I nodded, eyeing his muscular stature. "He is. Hoping to get him?" I asked, my voice echoing across the Katurium's rounded walls.

Haleika giggled. "Not as my apprentice since, you know, it's forbidden."

I shook my head, an odd sense of déjà vu settling over me. I'd been here before. I'd said those words another day, another time.

She raised her eyebrows, twirling a brown curl between her fingers. The color was exactly like Tristan's, and seeing it made my heart ache for some reason. Her lips curved into a mischievous grin. "You're in love with him, aren't you?"

I narrowed my eyes, about to refuse, when I realized I wasn't looking at Leander but Rhyan sinking into a stretch, his back bare. He wore only a half-tunic, his belt tightened around his waist, his muscles flexing and tensing, causing the ink of his gryphon tattoo to appear as if it were coming to life.

Haleika giggled again. "Careful. That can kill you."

"What?" I asked.

Her eyes glowed red, her fingers elongating into claws as she snarled and revealed sharpened teeth. Akadim.

She reached for me, and I jumped back.

"You can't," I said. "I'm Asherah."

She laughed. "You were." Her claws wrapped around my throat. I stared down. My armor was gone. "But you're human now."

"I won't be for long."

"That's what you think, you powerless, false heir." She squeezed my neck until I coughed.

"Haleika, don't do this," I croaked, my toes lifting off the ground.

Rhyan began moving through the 108 poses of the Valya, sweat dripping down his back as he sank to his knees. I kept expecting him to turn, to notice me, to sense I was in danger, but he only flowed, moving from pose to pose.

"Haleika!" I gasped, barely able to breathe. "Don't."

"Why not?" She threw me against the wall. I rolled onto my back as she stalked toward me, her body elongating and stretching into the full size of an akadim. "Why shouldn't I kill you? You killed me."

The entire arena shook with a bang.

I woke with a start, my heart pounding. I clutched my chest, the sound still reverberating in my ears, the noise amplified as if by magic.

But then it sounded again and was followed by a male grunt of pain.

"Naughty, naughty, my not-lord. You didn't say please."

I squeezed my eyes shut. I was going to be sick. My room was pitch black with not a single torch lit, but when I opened my eyes, I could see a golden glow emanating from my chest.

The events from earlier resurfaced as I cleared my mind of the dream. My heart had heated again after losing my diadem. I'd grown too hot. Rhyan had ushered me into the temple, had been holding me in his arms, and I'd fainted from the pain.

I felt my heart, the skin between my breasts. It was not warm now, but my stomach felt wrong, full and heavy and twisting. I was sore everywhere, my legs feeling like they'd gone for a run without stretching before or after, even though I'd barely walked all day. Even my back was sore.

I clutched at my belly, my insides rolling and tightening, trying to blink the sleep from my eyes, to get my bearings.

The curtains were dark against the windows. Hardly any light came through, save some distant torchlight. It was night. I must have been out for hours.

Then I noticed the position of the window and the bed and the scent of pine and musk. I wasn't in Cresthaven or my apartment. I was in Rhyan's bed.

His bedroom door slammed open, and Mercurial stood there, his skin blue and glowing. Black whorls with diamond centers glittered across his nearly naked body. His black hair was flowing in a wind that didn't exist, and his lips curled into a sneer.

I sat up in the bed and gasped. My stomach now felt like it was splitting in two. I couldn't get up. I couldn't move.

"What have you done to me?" I asked.

"Ah, my lady—for that is your mortal title now, is it not?"

I tried to sit up but could only manage to lean forward. "What have you done?"

"Exactly as you asked. I've kept my mouth quiet about you and your little tryst with the not-Lord."

"With our bargain!" I seethed. "You expect me to claim my power, and yet at every turn, your little contract is trying to kill me."

Mercurial laughed. "It's a standard Afeyan contract. Trust me. It'll take far more than a little fire to kill you, Goddess."

"Why is it doing this? Why does it keep heating up?"

Mercurial shrugged. "The meetings of light and souls...one can never be sure of the outcome of any such combinations." He snaked his head from side to side. "Not my secrets to tell. And you don't have enough in you to bargain for a second deal."

"I'd never bargain for a second."

He laughed, the sound musical and haunting. "You swore you wouldn't bargain for a first. And yet, here you are." He stalked toward the bed, his finger tracing the shape of the star shining brightly between my breasts.

"Fine," I said. "Are you here to tell me what to do? How to claim my power? That's what you want, isn't it?"

His hands clamped down on the bed, fisting the blanket on either side of me, his face just inches from mine. He was hovering over me like a lover, but there was nothing loving in his eyes. He was a predator, and I was his trapped and helpless prey.

"Not yet. There are some...details I must put in order. Invitations I must send out. Guests we need to arrive. And only when the sun and moon are in alignment with the stars might you act. But not one second before."

I shook my head. His words made no sense.

"What does that mean? My aunt has already been named acting Arkasva and High Lady. She'll be consecrated in less than a month. When will the sun and moon be in alignment with the stars?"

He smirked, his face alight in the glow of my star. "When they accept their invitations to a party." He stiffened and lifted one hand, making a fist.

There was another crash from the living room.

"Bastard!" Rhyan growled in pain from outside.

"Stop hurting him!" I yelled, realizing only now that he had Rhyan imprisoned somehow in order to speak to me. I tried to sit up, but my stomach left me frozen on the bed.

"But the not-Lord is always getting in my way." Mercurial pouted.

"Leave him alone, or I will do everything in my power to make your end of the bargain miserable," I bluffed.

"You can't even stomach our contract, my lady," he said, voice deep and rumbling. "Might I remind you that I am the one who holds power now. Not you." He held his palm up to me, and with a turn of his wrist, my star was on actual fire.

I shrieked in terror at seeing the flames on my chest. But there was no pain, at least, not there. My stomach though—Gods. The cramps were getting so intense, tears were springing to my eyes.

"LYR!" Rhyan roared from the other room. "Don't touch her!"

"I'm okay!" I called back, though I still felt panicked. It only looked like I was on fire. "Mercurial," I said. "Mercurial, please, stop."

The Afeya rolled his eyes, but the flames vanished.

I exhaled in relief, gripping my chest, pulling Rhyan's blankets up to cover me.

"The not-Lord is oh so protective of you. But his blankets are no shield from me." Mercurial stepped back and begun playing with his hair, which was long and silky and splayed across his shoulder. Small golden stars appeared, weaving their way through the strands, pulling and twisting the locks into intricate braids. "I told you. No harm would come to you by my hand. Not as long as you fulfill your end of the bargain. I didn't come to you sooner because the stars were not yet aligned, my remembered Goddess. I only came now to warn you, to tell you. I have a plan. Wait." The final word was like a knife, sharp and cutting.

"Wait for what?"

"For me, you simple girl. I am the one you bargained with. No one else. So do not get the idea in your little mortal mind that you can do this alone, without my help. Because you cannot."

"Are you spying on me?" I seethed. This was exactly the conversation I'd had last night with Morgana and Rhyan.

"Such a mortal concept. You think after centuries bound to this Earth, I haven't learned a thing or two of how minds work? Especially desperate ones? You think I can't predict the pattern of thought of a Lumerian who is running scared? Or those with the right knowledge now seeking to take advantage?" He shook his head, the movement so inhuman, so ethereal, so threatening. "Try, and there will be consequences."

"Like I'll burn from the inside?" I sat forward, hands fisted in Rhyan's blankets, my knuckles turning white.

Moonlight gleamed across Mercurial's black hair, and his eyes sparkled. "Like you don't want to know." His head snapped to the side, his gaze narrowing, before he looked back to me, a feline grin spreading across his lips. Then the room darkened, and Mercurial's anger burst, leaving me gasping. It felt like little flames, dancing, and pricking at my skin. "Some bastards never learn their lessons." He snarled, almost animal-like in his rage. "I'll be back soon. Looks like another wants to play with me—someone very naughty. Say goodbye to the not-Lord for me. Give him a kiss." He winked. "Won't you?"

Rhyan stumbled into the room, cursing as he walked through the black shadows of Mercurial's silhouette. He grasped at Mercurial's arms, trying to pull him back, to overpower him, but the Afeya was gone.

I groaned, clutching my belly. My head was now heavy with a dull ache.

"Bastard! I'm going to—" Hearing me in pain, Rhyan lit a candle and immediately crouched beside the bed. "Lyr? Did he do it again? Is it burning?" He held out his palm before me, his aura filling with cold that left goosebumps on my flesh. An icy breeze swirled around us.

I shook my head and moaned. My stomach felt like it was punching me from the inside. I made another noise of pain, gritting my teeth.

Rhyan's eyes narrowed on my waist. Frowning he pulled the blanket back, his mouth falling open in shock. "You're bleeding!"

"What?" I looked down in horror and then absolute embarrassment. This was what had caused the cramps and the soreness. "Oh. Fuck."

Rhyan's eyes raced between my hands clutched to my belly and the blood staining his sheets.

"What the hell happened?" He looked frantic and scared, breathing quickly.

I shook my head again, my cheeks heating with shame. "I'm not hurt."

He was still frantic, trying to search for the source of injury. "But you're bleeding."

"I know," I moaned. "It's...time."

His eyes widened, and then softened with understanding. "Oh."

I squeezed my eyes shut.

"Lyr. It's okay," he said quickly. "Come here." He stood, reaching around me and pulling me into his arms.

"Wait, Rhyan, I'm sorry. You don't have to—"

"Shhh," he said. "It's alright. Let's get you cleaned up and feeling better."

I squeezed my eyes shut, tears forming within them from my humiliation. "I didn't mean to. I'm sorry, this doesn't usually happen." I gestured helplessly at the bed. "I ruined your sheets."

"No, you didn't. Hey, Lyr...Lyr look at me." He stood, cradling me against him while I desperately tried to move my hips away, sure I was going to get blood on his tunic. "Come on, partner. It's okay. I promise. Are you in pain?"

I opened my eyes, met his gaze in the darkness of his room, and burst into tears. "I just...I hate everything right now," I sobbed.

As if witnessing my father's murder, handing over power to my aunt, being forced into a deal with Mercurial, losing Tristan to Naria, and having had to kill my friend who'd become a monster wasn't fucking enough...I was now on my cycle and having one of those months where it was bad. I had bled completely through my dress and all over Rhyan's sheets. The pain in my stomach wasn't relenting. I'd been so focused on Mercurial, I hadn't registered the sensation of blood between my legs. But I could feel it dripping now.

"Gods. I'm so sorry," I said.

"Hey now, no apologies. It's not a big deal," Rhyan whispered in my ear. As if to prove his point, he tightened his grip on me, pulling me closer. "Come on, Lyr," he crooned. "It's not like I haven't cleaned your blood off my sheets before. I didn't mind then, and I don't mind now. To be honest, I much prefer having to do it for this reason."

"Rhyan," I protested.

He shook his head. "I mean it. Last time, you were hurt. This time...." He offered a soft smile and shrugged. "This time, it's just your body doing what it's supposed to. It's natural. No big deal."

He carried me into his bathroom where a small candle was already lit. Holding me with one arm, he lifted it to the torch, allowing the entire room to be bathed in a soft, fiery glow.

"Can you stand?" he asked.

"I'm fine," I said, as my toes touched the ground. He started running the water in the shower while I stared at his bloodied bed in the mirror. "This doesn't normally happen," I said, feeling defensive.

Rhyan ran his hand under the water, testing the temperature. "Hmmm. It might be from stress."

"Maybe." I bit my bottom lip. "I'll clean your sheets up for you."

"No, you won't. I've got it. Now I want you to get in the shower and relax. I'll take care of everything else, make you some tea and something to eat. Unless...." He frowned, one eyebrow furrowed as he looked back at me. "Do you need any help in there?" He sounded uncertain, like he really wasn't sure if he should have asked.

I folded my arms across my chest, staring at my bare feet on the ground. "No. I've done this before."

He turned toward me, reaching for my hand. I recoiled, seeing some of my blood on him. Why didn't he care? Why wasn't he upset?

Rhyan nodded. "I know you have. And I know," he squeezed my fingers in his, "I know we're not...defined right now...or, um, not quite where we're seeing each other naked." His lips quirked. "At least, not completely naked. But I can stay and help, you know, or go out there." He sounded nervous. "I just," he exhaled sharply, "I just wanted you to know—whatever you need, whatever you want, I'll do it."

"My dress," I said pathetically.

"I'll clean it, too," he offered quickly then gave me a piercing look. "Or if you don't want it...?"

"I don't want it." I didn't want anything associated with Arianna taking power or the memory of the Imperator pressing his leg into mine.

"Consider it gone. Should I...?" He gestured at the door.

I nodded. "I'll be okay. Thank you."

"Take your time." He squeezed my hand again and leaned forward, kissing me on the cheek before he closed the door behind him.

I tore open the dress, let it slide to the ground, threw off my undergarments until I was naked, and stepped inside the hot spray of the shower.

The relief I felt at washing the blood from my legs was palpable, as was the sensation of heat against the cramps in my stomach. I let the water blast against me, soothing my belly. I felt the tension I hadn't realized I was carrying in my shoulders soften. But after standing there a few minutes with my mind no longer occupied, the day began to catch up to me.

I touched my scalp, feeling the grooves where my pins had gone, tracing the line of the chain of my destroyed diadem to the center of my forehead.

I felt the Imperator pressing his thigh against mine and remembered Tristan kissing and holding Naria, the look on Arianna's face as she wore the laurel, and the sight of my father falling....

I slid against the wall to the floor and curled my knees to my chest while the water sprayed down on my head. Then I cried. Heaving, sobbing wails shook my entire body. I clutched my knees, watching the water droplets slide down my legs and pool at my feet before slipping down the drain. More droplets fell, slipping down the wall, some keeping their perfect teardrop shapes, others stretching into rivers. Each descending droplet gave me something to concentrate on until my fingers pruned.

I sat there several more minutes, letting the water soothe my belly, my skin flushing red from the hot water, before I stood. I used Rhyan's shampoo, which smelled like pine, to wash my hair, then scrubbed his soap over my body until I was raw.

I didn't want to get out of the shower. It seemed like one of the few places I could safely fall apart. Grieve. Acknowledge the nightmare that had happened before I had to put my mask back on, become Lady Lyriana who was okay, who was fine, who supported this regime change.

But the water was getting cold.

As I turned off the shower, I realized I was going to need some supplies.

There was a knock on the bathroom door at once, like Rhyan had been ready and waiting for me to turn off the water. "Lyr?"

"I'm done," I called out. "But I need clothes and something to catch the blood."

He opened the door a crack. "I have clothes for you," he said, thrusting forth a pile of folded sweats. There was a pair of gray sleep pants, a white long-sleeved shirt, and something very small and black folded neatly on top. He shifted inside, averting his gaze and carefully laying the clothing on a shelf before backing to the doorway again. "What else do you need?"

I remained in the shower behind the curtain. "There's pads that...."

He nodded vigorously. "Are they at your apartment?"

"In my bathroom. Under the sink basin."

He nodded again, and before I could offer any more instructions, he said, "One second," and vanished.

Half a minute passed before he reappeared in the doorway, breathing heavily, looking slightly pale and winded. He clutched a black bag full of the pads I needed.

"Um," I bit my lip, still feeling embarrassed. "Underwear?"

Now he looked embarrassed, coughed, and cleared his throat. "Those are yours." He pointed to the pile of clothing. "You...um...left them. Last time. They're clean."

My cheeks reddened. The morning we'd kissed, I'd lost my underwear in his sheets. By the Gods. He still had them. He'd washed them!

"Okay," I said, voice high.

He set the bag beside my clothes and closed the door.

A moment later, I was dressed in Rhyan's sleep clothes. I padded out of the bathroom, noting the bed had already been stripped and remade, the old sheets in a hamper he kept inside his closet.

In the living room, Rhyan had lit several candles. Two steaming mugs sat on the center of his coffee table. He was in the kitchen preparing a plate of pita bread with hummus and nuts.

He'd already put out a bowl of hardboiled eggs and another containing a mix of chocolates and fruit.

"Chocolate helps, right?" he asked.

"Right."

"How are you feeling?" He grabbed the plates and bowls and balanced them on his arm on his way to the table. He stumbled, looking like he was about to drop the plate hanging the most precariously against his elbow. He vanished and reappeared at the coffee table, dropping everything on top of it. The plates somehow landed exactly where they needed to go.

"Smooth," I said.

He laughed. "Sometimes the vorakh comes in handy." He collapsed onto the couch, patting the cushion beside him. "Sit?"

I moved to his side, curling my knees under me. My arm rested on the back of the headrest, allowing me to stroke my fingers down his neck.

He leaned into my touch, a small sigh escaping his lips before he shifted in his seat, inching closer to me, his eyes hooded as I massaged up his neck to his hair.

"Do you want to try the tea?" He shifted again until his head rested in my hand then straightened as if remembering he was taking care of me now. "I know it's not coffee, but it is midnight, so...."

"I'll try it." I smiled shyly. "No one's ever taken care of me like this before. No one who wasn't being paid to work in the fortress."

"Oh." He made an exaggerated frown. "I didn't tell you about my new job?"

"Rhyan!" I smacked his shoulder.

"Ow!" He rubbed his shoulder.

"Come on," I scoffed. "There's no way that hurt."

He grinned at me. "You forget, you're a trained warrior now."

"So are you."

"Yes, but I'm a mere mortal. I was just assaulted by a goddess. I call foul play."

I wanted to laugh but froze instead, the weight of his words pressing down on me. "Right." I exhaled sharply.

I was a goddess, but I couldn't touch any of her power—my power—not without Mercurial's help.

"Sorry," he said. "Probably shouldn't joke about that."

"I'm still figuring it out," I said, settling back against the cushions. Rhyan reached behind me for a blanket and laid it over my lap. A fresh tear fell down my cheek.

"Lyr." His thumb brushed it away, his eyes staring into mine.

"I'm not sure what to do. There aren't guidelines for," I waved my hands around, "anything I've experienced the last few days."

Rhyan reached for my belly and laid his palm flat against it, heavy and soothing. "No, but this...this you've dealt with before. This we can manage. Are you feeling better?" The moonlight cut across his face, making his curls bronze and his scar appear more silvery and pinker than its usual red.

I shrugged. "I'm probably going to feel like shit for at least two more days. Or forever."

"Hmmm. I better buy a lot more chocolate then." He nodded thoughtfully, his thumb stroking my stomach.

I sniffled, and after a moment, we both began taking slow sips of tea and snacking on the food.

"I'm really sorry," he said after a few minutes. "About today."

"Which part? The part where my diadem was taken? Destroyed? The part where the Imperator threatened me? The part where Tristan showed off his engagement to my fucking enemy in front of the entire country?" I practically choked on the last words, my mouth tasting as bitter as I felt.

Rhyan's eyes darkened. "That's what you're upset about? Lord Grey?"

"I just...." I closed my eyes, realizing how awkward this was and how much I'd hate it if our roles were reversed, if I had to console Rhyan over a past lover that wasn't me. I hated the idea of him ever having kissed anyone else. Hated the idea of anyone else ever having had their hands on him. But...if he needed to talk to me about it, I'd do it. Because he was my friend.

Rhyan was watching me carefully, his nostrils flared, his hands fisting, a flash of anger in his aura as he sat straighter, shifting his body back from mine.

"Yes," I gritted through my teeth. My heart felt like it was sinking as I recalled Tristan's hands on Naria, the silver ring on her finger, the golden ring on his. "Okay? I am."

Something dark flashed in his aura. "You still want to be with him?" Rhyan looked away from me, the hurt so clear in his voice, it felt like a punch to the gut.

"No."

"Really," he said, voice dull.

"No! Look, I'm not going to force you to believe anything. I'm not going to try and convince you that I don't want to be with him if you don't take me at my word."

The hurt in Rhyan's aura pulsed. "Sounds like you do." He cracked his knuckles in his lap then reached for some pita bread and jammed it into the hummus.

"Well, I don't! And I haven't for a long time. Gods, Rhyan. Since the moment I laid eyes on you in the street. A part of me.... It's just complicated. I'm sorry. I'm really sorry. I don't want him. I want you. I told you I loved you, and I meant it. But seeing him with Naria just fucking hurts. And seeing everyone cheer. Everyone celebrating her and not me. I know it's stupid, but it feels like, like a judgment on me. Like I was never worthy of him, and so I was never worthy of Bamaria, I'm not worthy of being here now. It just feels like...like I've lost everything."

"That's not true," he said, but he wasn't looking at me.

"Yes, it is. I don't want to be with him. I never loved him the way I was supposed to. I don't think I could have. But I can't help but feel what it means that he's not with me."

Rhyan's eyes softened. "What do you mean by that?"

"Do you know how it feels to realize you're only as loveable as what you can do for someone, as loveable as the position you hold, how you look to the public or how you make them look, but not ever for who you are? Not because you are actually deserving of love, or worthy, or enough—never for just being...for being yourself. I tried so hard to be good." My voice broke into a sob. "For years. I tried to prove I was smart enough, pretty enough, talented enough, kind enough, good enough. Now I have to prove I'm strong enough, and I'm not. No matter what I do, it's never ever been enough." I was crying now.

Rhyan rested his hand on my knee.

I shook my head, hysterical with all I'd done, all I sacrificed. "I followed all the rules. I did what they told me—what I thought I had to do. I was who I was expected to be. And I have never been enough. Even when I made strides, even when I got stronger, I still fell short. I still failed. I lost Jules. I lost my father. I lost Haleika. I lost my station. I lost Tristan. And now I'm terrified. What else is going to go wrong? What will I lose next? What if I lose you? I'm...I'm weak. And I'm worthless. The way they all cheered—"

"Stop. Lyr, stop!" Rhyan pulled me against him. "I know how hard today was for you. And if I could do anything to take the burden from you, to spare you the pain, I would. In a heartbeat. And I'm sorry I said anything. I didn't mean to upset you more, he's just such a shit—" He groaned. "My problem. I was—I got jealous. He got to be with you—openly. He got to...got to be with you in a way I haven't. But you need to know, you're not losing me, not ever. And you are enough, Lyr. You are so enough. You're fucking everything to me."

"I don't deserve this. Any of this."

"Yes, you do." Rhyan stroked the back of my hair, still damp from the shower. "He never did any of this for you," he said slowly, "did he?"

"What?"

"Did this ever happen before with him? The bleeding?" He practically growled despite the tenderness of his fingers in my hair.

I stared down at my hands. "Once." It had been right after soturion training had started, and Tristan had nearly lost it. Luckily, he'd been in my bed. He'd gone home, though, in the middle of the night. "He can't...he can't handle blood. Because of his parents."

Rhyan groaned but didn't say anything, just continued to lightly massage my scalp and smooth my hair down my neck. "I'm not going to pretend I know the right answers or all of what you're feeling. But just know I want to be here with you. I want to take care of you. And clean your dirty sheets and feed you and touch you." His free hand found mine, threading our fingers together. "Because I love you. I love *you*. Not because of anything you've done, or how you look. I just...I love you, Lyr."

I sniffled. "I love you, too. But I'm scared. Scared you're going to see how imperfect I really am. I just keep losing things. I can't lose you."

"You won't." He looked away for a moment then took a deep breath. His eyes found mine again, and he looked shy. "Do you remember the day we read together in the library?"

"The Great Library?" I asked. I vaguely remembered taking him and his father on a tour for his last visit—back when we still had celebrations and made spectacles to show off to the visiting arkasvim. We'd done tours of the temple, the Katurium, the Great Library—whatever place we'd thought they'd be most impressed with. But I didn't remember reading with Rhyan. Not on his last visit.

"No," he said. "It was in the small one, in the heir's wing at Cresthaven. Um, it had red velvet couches and a balcony opening toward the ocean."

I knew exactly what room Rhyan meant, but he'd never been in there before. "When?"

"It was the first time I'd ever come to Bamaria. You were seven." His throat bobbed. "I was ten."

I shook my head, still not recalling.

He bit his lip, looking even more embarrassed, his gaze distant. "I was in trouble," he said quietly, "with my father. I was...always in trouble. And I ran away, well, I ran through the halls of the fortress. And I found your wing by accident. I was hungry. And I smelled your lemon cake, and so I walked into the library, and you were sitting there alone, reading."

A hazy image formed in my mind—just the vaguest recollection of what he described.

"Did I...?" I closed my eyes, trying to remember. It was like a foggy dream I could barely grasp. "I told you to read the same scroll as me."

Rhyan exhaled, his eyes watery as he laughed. "You did. You had a second copy. We didn't talk much. But you invited me in, let me stay, let me be." He swallowed hard, blinking a few times. "I didn't think you'd remember. You were kind and open. I always guessed for you, it would have been a small thing. But to me, it was...." He stared down at our joined hands. "I never really had friends before, wasn't included by the other nobles on state visits, and you let me come in and share a scroll. You shared your cake, too, and you asked a servant to bring me water, and...." He pulled his gaze up to mine. "I was just a kid, but I think part of me loved you then."

I stared at him, seeing the young boy he'd been, conjuring those old memories in my mind. I'd thought he was so handsome at the time, but he was always angry and rude. I'd been intimidated by him. A little scared he'd be mean in conversation even though I was inexplicably drawn to him. I could understand now why he'd acted the way he had and wished I could go back in time and do so much more than just allow him to sit with me and share a dessert I'd already bitten into. I wished I could hug him. Tell him not to listen to his asshole father. Tell him he was also worthy of love. So I did the only thing I could do—I hugged Rhyan now.

"I wish I remembered more," I said. "I wish I'd done more."

"You've done everything," he said, pulling me onto his lap, his arms around my back. He took the blanket from my lap and wrapped it around us. "That's actually how I knew you liked lemon cake. I was embarrassed to admit the real reason I knew that day in the fall, but you'd eaten it at least once in the hall, so I figured I had an excuse for knowing." He leaned forward, pulling me closer. "You didn't do anything special that day. You didn't have to do anything special at all. You were just being you. And I loved you. And that's not going to change."

I sank into him. "What are we going to do?" I asked, holding the ends of the blanket behind his neck, cocooning us inside it the way we had been last night in his cloak. "The Imperator was threatening me today," I said, voice barely above a whisper, as if the Imperator could hear.

Rhyan stiffened. "What did he say?"

"That I was now the most eligible lady for marriage in the Empire. And he wanted to be the one to arrange my contract."

"Fuck." His breath was uneven. "I don't know what game my father's playing, but I'd bet anything, he still wants you. Wants your power."

"Funny. The one thing I've always wanted for myself...I had no idea everyone else valued it, too."

"We can't let any of them have it." Rhyan's eyes darkened. "I don't trust Mercurial. Or any Afeya. And I think," he grinded his jaw in frustration, "I don't like it, but I think we might need to start searching tomorrow. Finding a way you can claim it yourself."

"But Mercurial."

"Fuck Mercurial. Unless he wants to present his solution, his true motivations, we're not waiting. We're doing this on our own."

I nodded, knowing he was right. It was time to stop listening to what others wanted, to stop following the rules made for me. It was time to make my own. "We still have a few days of the winter holiday before soturion training starts again."

"With the Imperator's new task force, I can almost guarantee I'm going to be called away. Aemon's already informed me. The vorakh hunting, it's going to increase. It's going to be necessary."

I hated when he left for those. Hated that he put himself in danger.

"But not for a few days, I think. And I don't think I'll be sent far when you need additional protection. We'll go to the library tomorrow, see what we can find to start. First, I want to know more about this deal, why the Valalumir is heating up like it does. I want to know if Mercurial's done anything he shouldn't have with you." His palm pressed against my heart, over his sweatshirt. "I want to know everything about Afeyan contracts."

"I should probably go back home...to my bed. In case I...." I looked to his bedroom and back to him, my cheeks heating. "In case it happens again."

"Stay with me," he said urgently, brushing my hair from my face.

"But I'm—"

"I don't care." He gripped my hips.

"You're sure?"

"Yes. Please. Lyr, I...." His good eyebrow furrowed, leaving a pained expression on his face. "I don't sleep well when you're not in my arms."

We'd only really slept together—beside each other—once, after one of his nightmares. The few other nights Rhyan had been with me through the night had been because of bodyguard duties or because he had been caring for my injuries. He'd stayed awake each time, keeping watch while I'd slept, afraid he'd disturb me with his nightmares. I knew they plagued him. I knew he hated to acknowledge they were happening, hated to show weakness. So I knew what it cost him to admit this now.

I leaned forward, kissing him slowly, softly. "I don't either." I sat back, staring into his eyes.

He let out a shaky breath, staring back at me. "You'll stay?" he asked, sounding unsure.

"I'll stay." I frowned. "What are we doing? What are we?" Not just friends. Not quite lovers. Still completely forbidden. Everything had changed between us—and yet, everything was the same. The reasons keeping us apart still remained.

He pushed a wild and loosened wave behind my ear, his finger tracing the slope of my ear and running down the length of my neck until I shivered.

"We're us," he said definitively. "And it's enough for now. Let's go to bed."

His hands slid around my thighs to my ass, and he lifted me against him as he stood. I gripped the edges of the blanket around his neck and wrapped my legs around his hips, locking my ankles behind him, as he blew out the candles in the living room and kitchen and carried me back into the bedroom.

He gently laid me on my back and crawled beside me beneath the blanket. Our arms and legs tangled. I waited for his breaths to even and slow. He'd been the one to stand guard and watch over me last night. Tonight was my turn.

Sleepily, his hand grazed my hip, seeking the warmth inside my shirt. Skin to skin. His palm rested on my belly, fingertips just beneath my breasts, beneath my Valalumir. His hand twitched.

A soft glow began to emit from beneath my shirt. A golden seven-pointed star.

I held my breath, waiting for the pain, waiting for the fire. But no heat came.

Rhyan made a small noise, his eyebrow furrowed, and he pulled me toward him, his hand sliding onto my back. I smoothed the crease between his eyebrows with my thumb until he relaxed.

The glow faded from my chest. The room covered in darkness. I finally closed my eyes.

CHAPTER ELEVEN

MORGANA

THE CLOCKTOWERS WERE SHOUTING midnight. My head was pounding. I'd gotten Meera to calm down and sleep after this gryphon-shit nightmare of a day, after having to tell her the mistake she'd made in naming Arianna as arkasva. The mistake I'd made in not knowing she'd betrayed us.

Like Lyr, Meera had been too upset to question me much. She'd been more focused on her own role in this Moriel-damned thing. It was only a matter of time, though, before she'd ask. Before she'd demand to know.

Why hadn't I known?

I was going to find out.

Arianna was in the Arkasva's rooms. Too close. I wasn't sure yet if it was a curse or a blessing that she was so exhausted from the day she was already asleep. At night, when she was alone in her room, I had an opportunity to listen in and try and hear her secrets. And I was waiting to see whom she'd invite into her bed first. My money was on the Imperator. He wanted her.

Not as much as he wanted Lyr and had lusted for her the past year. Now I knew why. His obsession with her made so much more sense even though I still could barely believe the reason for it—that she was Asherah.

I'd heard him speaking to her on the litter earlier, discussing marriage.

Over my dead body.

I rounded a corner in the fortress, bombarded with thoughts too loud for the hour.

She needs to add more salt to her cooking. I keep telling her.

Where the fuck is he? It's midnight. Change of the fucking guards.

Lord Eathan's sure licking his wounds.

I narrowed my eyes, ready to approach the guard disparaging Eathan, when another thought caught my attention.

Can't believe they left me behind. As if I'm so dispensable? The Emperor can go fuck himself.

It was coming from down the hall on the first floor.

I turned and listened for more.

It's going to cost me a month's worth of earnings to book transport. The akadim are dead anyway—not like his majesty was in any actual danger. But no, he has to run. And leave the rest of us commoners behind. And Gods know, I'll be punished for missing work.

I followed the voice into the dining hall, arranged with tables full of food for all the guests currently walking through the fortress.

A female mage stood in the corner, slamming back a glass of red wine. She had black hair braided down her back, cat-like eyes, and full, pouty lips dyed red from her wine.

Blood began to rush through my body. I'd meant to get in a fuck to shut down my thoughts, but if this mage was from the capitol.... I lifted my chin, heart pounding.

I tried not to get my hopes up. I'd gone through over a dozen of the Emperor's servants during his stay. Talking to them, kissing some of them. I'd only fucked one—and it had been disappointing. Not the sex—but what I'd learned. So I couldn't get my hopes up. They'd been dashed too many times before. But since Father's fall, I felt like I was on the brink, like I was getting closer. My heart was racing as I took my next step.

"We have better in the kitchen," I said.

She turned abruptly, eyes widening as she took in my appearance. "Lady Morgana." She sounded startled.

I pulled her name easily from her mind. She wasn't noble, but she did seem to have a rather close servitude to the Emperor in the capitol—just not close enough to warrant a ride home. I'd seen him do that before, leave some of his servants behind.

Some made their way back. Some stayed and found work here in the city.

"I'm very sorry about your father," she said.

"Everyone's sorry." I slid my fingers over hers, taking the glass from her hands and sipping what remained. It was a rather good bottle, actually, but I needed to soften her up. "We can definitely do better than this."

Her aura pulsed lightly with fear that she'd offended me. "I think it's fine wine, Lady Morgana." A blush crept across her cheeks.

She was nervous. I outranked her. And she was lonely and liked the slope of my waist, the soft curve of my breasts. She was wondering if being noble made my skin softer than hers. She wanted to know if my hair felt as silky as it was shiny. She liked that it was nearly the same color as hers.

She wasn't too proud, but she was the sort who was a touch vain, the sort who was attracted to qualities of herself in others.

She was perfect. And if I was lucky, and I prayed I was, she'd serve more than one purpose.

"I'm not insulted," I said. "Simply in need of a drink. You don't have to be nervous around me. I am, after all, the one who offered. And," I wet my lips, looking up at her through my lashes, "I'd love some company. I could use a friend. It's not easy right now. I was going to drown my sorrow, but maybe...." I twirled a lock of my hair in my fingers. "Would you honor me by sharing a glass? And maybe...by sharing your name?"

"Namtaya, your grace." *Shit!* She internally cursed, remembering my new title. "Sorry. My lady."

I set down the wine glass and threaded my fingers through hers. "Have a drink with me, Namtaya."

Nerves exploded in her aura like butterfly wings, as a shy yet eager smile appeared across her lips. I led her through the hall into the kitchens, showing off our vast store, then retreated to an unused sitting room off a library, one I knew was empty. We popped open the bottle I'd chosen.

An hour later, Namtaya was three glasses into Ka Batavia's finest red, the red we reserved for the Emperor himself.

I was, for once, a drink behind. I needed to keep my senses intact until I got all I needed from her—if there was anything to get. I was still trying to decide.

The rulers of the Empire all had shields, magic stolen from vorakh to keep their secrets, to conceal their true thoughts. But we were a limited resource. Not all of us had fallen into their hands. And those who did only had so much magic, meaning we were very expensive. Someone like Namtaya would never be offered the elixir. Nor knowledge of its existence. Which meant she'd never be offered any true secrets to keep.

But servants had eyes and information, if one knew the right questions to ask.

I asked about her childhood and where she had grown up to get her started, watching as she relaxed on the chaise next to me. Her cheeks flushed with wine as she told me how she came to be in the service of the Emperor. I learned from some gentle coaxing how many nobles she had met. How many servants she was friends with. I was given the layout of her bedroom in the palace. Her favorite breakfast food. The way she took her coffee. With every piece of information I gleaned, I inched closer to her, allowing her to trust me more. My hand rested on her knee, then above it. My fingers slid up her thigh as my body angled toward her.

Her eyes zeroed in on my palm's placement. Her stomach tightened. She'd had no idea that the Lady Morgana was so forward. Or so beautiful up close. I'd seemed so shy before, it was endearing how interested I was in her life. I was such a good listener.

It was almost flattering to hear. She clearly hadn't been made aware of the rumors of my promiscuity.

I kept talking to her, looking into her eyes—a pretty blue—smiling at each piece of the puzzle she offered, asking for more details, letting her visualize all of her thoughts, strengthening them so that they offered me more information.

She was nervous with me. My fingers danced across her inner thigh. Our eyes met—we both knew where this was going. Namtaya was not really one to do this with complete strangers and certainly not with nobles. At home, servants gossiped too easily, sharing intimate details with the staff immediately after. And nobility rarely looked her way. But I kept asking her questions, and her guard kept going down. Her eyes did, as well, taking in my cleavage, dipping to the slits of my skirt which I had positioned just so to reveal the full expanse of my bared thigh.

The more she talked, the more clearly she visualized her life, her home, her day to day in the Emperor's palace. In her thoughts, I saw the servants who kept to themselves, who didn't interact with the others, who didn't dine with Namtaya or her friends.

They were known in the palace as the chayatim, the cloaked. They were secret servants. I'd heard of them before. Most assumed they were prostitutes, and some were.

But more often than not, chayatim were vorakh. Vorakh walking about in broad daylight, forced to offer their power to the Emperor and whomever he deemed worthy. I'd seen these chayatim in the memories of our spies—servants who looked broken, who winced with every noise, who had permanent frown lines on their foreheads from migraines. Several of the servants I'd encountered in the last week had chayatim in their memories—even if they all didn't know what they were.

I had not yet seen one that I knew to be having a vision, but I'd seen some with the haunted look of vorakh who'd recently had an episode.

"We're friends, Namtaya, aren't we?" I asked sweetly.

She smiled shyly and laughed. "I've never been friends with a noble before."

I gripped her skirt in my fingers, playing with the fabric, lifting and pulling it back, exposing her ankle and then covering it again. I was being playful. Flirtatious. Keeping it light and fun. She was vain, but a full-on seduction would have scared her. "I'm honored to be your first." I giggled. "I mean, your first noble friend." I tilted my head to the side, exposing my neck, brushing my hair past my shoulders. On instinct, I reached to adjust my diadem, only to remember at the last second it had been melted into nothing.

My hand fisted with my fury and embarrassment at forgetting. But I recovered quickly.

"Have you ever...?" I stared down at my lap, pretending I was shy. Pretending I didn't do this every day. "Have you ever been with a noble before?" I asked.

Namtaya was glowing with her arousal. She'd wanted me the moment she'd laid eyes on me. She'd wanted me days ago. She'd seen me at the Valyati ball. She'd fantasized about me then. Had been jealous when I gave my attention to others. She could barely believe her luck to be here with me now. But she was a little shy, and, there was an insecurity there—a hurt. She was tender in her heart. She'd fallen in love with someone else and felt rejected.

Ah. I saw it now. She'd fallen for someone who was off-limits to her.

Namtaya was in love with a chayatim. She was beautiful in Namtaya's mind, which was suddenly full of thoughts of her.

Gods. She's so graceful. I love her body. She's lean, but those curves—just the right amount. How? How is she so curvy when she's a servant to the Emperor?

I danced my fingers against her legs, trying to bring her into a more sensual mood—to not just think of this person but see her.

And then she did. In her mind was an image of the exact body her thoughts had described. And there was more details taking form. Her hair was wild and loose, a dark brown that curled and waved from her scalp like a lion's mane.

By the Gods.

I clutched at my heart. I couldn't breathe. I was going to faint. Shit! Shit! I was actually going to faint. No. That was Lyr's gryphon-shit, not mine. I had to stay alert. Focused. Awake.

But Namtaya's mind had already moved on. She was picturing me in very vivid detail—helped by the fact that I was right before her, touching her, breathing against her. The room was warm from the torches and crackling fireplace. She was wondering what color my nipples were. Wondering how I tasted. She imagined spreading my legs and laying me back on the chaise—this royal chaise that cost more than she made in a year. She was lost in the idea of showing me how good it could be with someone who wasn't noble. She would prove that even if her skin wasn't as soft as mine, her callouses would bring me pleasure.

"I want you," I said, voice hoarse.

Her eyes darkened, hooded with desire.

"But," I said, still needing more, needing confirmation of what I'd barely dared to believe I'd seen. "I have to be honest with you. Because I like you. I'm a little sad right now. Not just because of my father. Of course, I'm sad about him." I squeezed my eyes shut, and, horrifyingly, a tear fell. Shit. "But I also had my heart broken recently. There was this girl, a noblewoman, her hair wild like a lion's mane." I sighed. "I thought we had a connection, but...." I shrugged in defeat.

Smiling sympathetically, she took my hand in hers, the image of the girl she loved, of the chayatim, returning to her thoughts.

I barely dared to breathe, afraid I'd break the spell, afraid her thoughts wouldn't be clear. I needed to be absolutely certain.

She had spoken to the chayatim a few times and recounted those conversations in her mind now. She was absolutely taken with the girl's beauty but also her kindness. She saw something in the girl, a kind of spark, an inner fight. It was something she saw in—

Namtaya froze, looking at me now, blue eyes wide. She was thinking we shared something in common—the girl and me. Something in the defiance and shape of our eyes, the curve of our lips, the color of our skin, darker and tanner, marking us from the south. From Bamaria.

My heart was going to pound out of my chest.

My soul wasn't in my body. Gods. I was farther than fucking Lethea. My head was going to split.

I started to breathe heavily, barely able to remember my role now, who I was pretending to be, what I was here to do. The images in her mind was drumming into me, branding me with their truth.

Then, suddenly, Namtaya was kissing me, her lips savage against mine—wholly unexpected after how shyly and innocently she'd spoken the last hour.

She closed her eyes, licking the seam of my lips, as she crawled onto my lap. Her hands were hot on my waist, rising up my torso, caressing the sides of my breasts as her tongue brushed against mine.

We kissed until we were breathless, and she gripped my chin, licking my ear.

"Can I fuck you, Lady Morgana?" she asked coyly.

My eyes widened. When had the roles reversed? I'd misread her, so intent on playing my role, on finding what I wanted. It didn't matter. We were all getting what we wanted now—in more ways than one. I bit her bottom lip. "Yes, Namtaya. Please."

She cupped my breasts through my dress, finding my pebbled nipples beneath the fabric, and squeezed, eliciting a moan.

I wasn't in control. I was always in control. I tried desperately to catch my breath, but I was spiraling with what I'd seen.

Namtaya was still thinking, imagining the chayatim, fantasizing about her, using me. I was close enough. I was sweet, and I was noble, and my face reminded her of the chayatim's. Eerily so.

She pushed me onto my back. My shoulders hit the top of the armrest, as she slid down my body and between my legs and pushed what remained of the fabric of my dress aside, kissing my shaking knees and then my thighs. I started to tremble as she kissed me just above my core, sliding my underwear down. I was feeling too much too soon.

She gripped my thighs, pulling them apart. And right as her tongue licked right up the center of me, my mind went blank.

Peace. Quiet. Silence that usually only he could bring.

In some ways, he had. He was here. I could sense him now. I always could—even when my mind shut off. His presence, his darkness, it was overwhelming at times.

Namtaya parted me with her fingers, and I found his dark eyes—the eyes I hardly ever looked into—watching from the shadows in the corner. His gaze was like fire, glued to me, his aura pulsing with desire.

I looked away, but he knew I'd seen him.

Fuck. I wasn't going to last long if he was watching, if he was secretly going to find his pleasure as I received mine. And I wanted to last. I wanted to savor this—the silence.

Tears welled in my eyes as I closed them, seeing what Namtaya had showed me—a girl who looked like me but not quite. We could have been related. She could have been my cousin.

She was thinner than when I'd last seen her. So much thinner despite Namtaya admiring her curves. Namtaya didn't know—hadn't seen her before, hadn't known her—how curvy she could be. Her skin was paler. Her eyes hollower, cheeks sunken in. The light from her eyes was gone.

But I'd know that face, that walk, that crinkle of her nose anywhere, even after two years without it. Jules.

Namtaya had seen Jules in the Emperor's palace with the other vorakh he'd enslaved.

My hips bucked under Namtaya's tongue as she circled my center, sucking on me until I squirmed. My emotions were so high, I was already riding the wave of an orgasm, losing control, losing myself, my eyes burning with tears.

But all I could think was one thought, again and again and again as the pleasure rolled through my body, my hips rising with each proclamation.

I was right.
I was right.
I was fucking right.
Jules had survived.

THE SECOND SCROLL:

ME SHA, ME KA

CHAPTER TWELVE

LYRIANA

AFTER RETURNING TO MY apartment the following morning in Rhyan's sweats, I showered again and dressed in a fresh pair of long riding pants and a long-sleeved tunic. Morgana had called first thing in the morning using Meera's vadati. She'd spoken to Rhyan the day before—when I'd been passed out for hours. I'd told her of my plan with Rhyan to see what we could find out about my bargain, and to my surprise, she'd wanted to come.

Morgana had never been one for research. She was too impatient. She hadn't liked to sit before scrolls any longer than absolutely necessary for her studies. But she had researched while seeking a way to release herself from the blood oath Father had forced on us; I'd never known until the night she'd admitted it just how deeply she'd resented her scars.

We'd agreed to meet in the port of Scholar's Harbor. Rhyan was also coming but would be arriving separately.

Aemon had taken over all of our security detail as he'd planned. From what I'd gathered after speaking to Morgana and receiving a grunt of acknowledgment from Rhyan, Aemon wasn't changing anything about my guards' protocol. After I'd been admitted to the Soturion Academy, I'd been under Aemon's care, and since the Emartis had made me their target months ago, I had been on constant watch, so I was used to high security.

Meera and Morgana, however, were about to experience an increase in the presence of their escorts. Aemon wanted my sisters to have constant protection starting at once, especially since they'd be moving out of the fortress's main keep after Arianna's consecration. Meera, as Heir Apparent, had always been assigned the most soturi for protection, but because she'd rarely ventured out of the fortress, her escorts had been mostly relegated to guards standing idly by inside Cresthaven.

Rhyan was to remain as my bodyguard, but his station would be kept a secret from all except the others on my detail and Arianna. Which meant the Imperator knew Rhyan was my guard, too.

But Rhyan wasn't on duty today, so to keep suspicions at bay, this meant traveling separately to Scholar's Harbor.

The snow was beginning to melt as I fed my seraphim a treat and climbed into the carriage. Markan climbed aboard with me, looking as surly and annoyed as ever. But I, for once, was grateful he was coming. Markan hated visiting the Great Library so much, he always sat up front, annoying the lead librarian until I was ready to leave. At least this would allow me the ability to do some actual research and keep him from seeing Rhyan arrive.

Though everyone on my security team knew Rhyan was part of the detail, I worried one would soon suspect something more between us. I wasn't sure anymore how much we were giving away with simple looks or small touches. We had to be more careful than ever. Haleika had known something was going on between us. Tani had suspected. And I'd gotten enough crude comments from Lord Viktor and the wolves of Ka Kormac to know that if they weren't suspicious of me and Rhyan, they were certainly fantasizing about the possibility, drooling over the idea of me naked with him and imagining reporting us to his father.

A deal with Mercurial wasn't going to save us twice.

Haleika knowing had been the worst. It had put a strain on my relationship with her, as I'd feared she'd betray me to Tristan, just as she'd feared I'd betray her. I'd been keeping her secret, too.

I'd dreamed of her again last night, tucked safely in Rhyan's arms, burrowed beneath his scent and covers. He'd pushed back my hair in the morning and kissed me on the forehead with his face scrunched up in worry.

"You were thrashing just before you woke. Did you dream of the arena?" he'd asked, voice still full of sleep.

I'd nodded.

"Me, too," he'd said and rolled onto his back to stare at the ceiling. His aura had felt like it was shimmering with unease.

I'd watched the sunlight shift behind a cloud, staring at the patterns the rays made on his ceiling that early in the morning, not knowing what to say to Rhyan, who'd been breathing heavily.

He'd been in the arena, too. He'd helped kill Haleika, too.

I'd been the one to take her past the point of no return. I'd stabbed her with a flaming stake. I'd set her on fire. But it hadn't been enough. She had been suffering, dying too slowly from the fire after I'd missed her heart, so Rhyan had cut off her head. The killing blow had been an act of mercy, but nothing could change the fact that she was dead by both our hands. And so was Leander.

Those memories, my role...they were going to haunt me for the rest of my life, as I knew they would Rhyan. Even if those nightmares faded, I knew I'd be plagued with night-mares of what had happened the night before, when I'd faced down two akadim and watched Rhyan slay one before escaping the second. That was the one that had killed Leander then eaten Haleika's soul.

Rhyan and I knew this had the potential to tear us apart. There was too much happening right now, too much diverting our attention for us to stand still long enough to feel it. But if we were both having nightmares, both afraid to talk about it, both afraid to touch each other....

In bed that morning, Rhyan's finger had tapped the sheet, stretching toward mine. Our pinkies had touched, the sudden contact like a blast rushing through me, but he'd pulled away.

A small blue light had emanated from my waist, from the vadati stone Rhyan had given me. It had been Morgana, checking in.

Rhyan had slid out of bed, not looking at me. He'd gone into the kitchen and brewed coffee for us. I'd come out after speaking to Morgana to tell him she'd be joining us at the library, and he'd only nodded and drank his coffee in silence, looking haunted.

He'd asked how I was feeling, if my cramps were better—but otherwise, he'd shut down, and was impossible to engage with.

An hour later, as I sat in the seraphim carriage, I still felt uneasy about his change in demeanor.

I stared out the windows, watching the shining rooftops of the city give way to fields of grass and snowcapped forests before we flew past the bay into the desert of Scholar's Harbor. The air was dry as ever, but it wasn't plagued with its usual stifling heat.

I loosened the soturion cloak wrapped around me, allowing a small breeze to hit my neck, as Morgana's seraphim descended, her talons causing a dust cloud to burst.

Markan lifted an eyebrow at Morgana's appearance, aware of her lack of interest in the Great Library as well.

How's Meera? I asked.

Morgana rolled her eyes, marching through the sand to my side, her bodyguards following close behind.

"Hello to you, too. Yes, I'm fine."

She didn't look fine. Her hair was wild and unkempt in a way I'd have never allowed if I was at the fortress. And her eyes were red, like she'd been crying recently. She stiffened as she saw me, like she was afraid of me for some reason.

I cleared my mind, knowing she'd be angered by my observations.

"You know I care how you're doing," I said quietly. "More than I care for myself." But I hadn't seen Meera since she'd had her last vision and learned the news of Arianna's betrayal, and sometimes asking about Meera was easier than asking Morgana about her own feelings.

"I know," Morgana snapped. "She's about as well as I am. As well as you. You *can* ask how I'm doing, you know. I'm going to bite your head off either way. *Everything* sucks. But your situation is more important right now. So I'm here. Let's find some Godsdamned answers."

She paused, wincing from pain, then shrugged her shoulders back like she was coming out of it. Her hands moved automatically to her temples, fingers searching for a diadem that wasn't there.

I looked away, embarrassed for her. I'd done the same thing three times this morning.

"Shut up," she muttered under her breath.

"My lady?" asked a guard. "Are you unwell?"

Morgana spun around. "My lady!" she scoffed. "I guess that is my fucking title now. And no, I'm not. My father was murdered. Any other stupid questions?"

"Lady Morgana," Markan warned.

"Soturion Markan?" Morgana stepped forward, pressing a finger against his golden armor. "I may have lost my station, but you're just a poor soturion born beneath the dregs of Urtavia."

Markan stilled.

"I still outrank you. No more questions." She backed up, eyeing our entire team of escorts. "From any of you. I'm here to read, and I need quiet to do so. I want silence."

I took her arm in mine, leading her down the path to the three pyramids looming before us. My last few visits had been in the smallest pyramid, the one that housed all of the scrolls on ancient Lumeria written in High Lumerian.

Today, we were going to the middle pyramid, larger and newer. It housed all of the scrolls on Afeya—their history, their writings. If I was going to find answers about the Valalumir in my chest and why it kept burning me, this was the place.

Two soturi stood guard. I hadn't been to this library in quite some time, preferring the collection under Nabula's care in the smallest pyramid. But the soturi recognized me at once, uncrossed their swords, and stepped aside for us to enter.

The entrance was full of Valalumir stars hanging from the sloped ceiling. Each one was carved from amethyst and alight. Zenoya, the head librarian who was also half-Afeya, lounged on a black velvet chaise surrounded by piles of scrolls laying at the feet of her chair. She lazily pointed her stave to a floating pair of golden seraphim wings, which flapped back and forth, fanning her as she read. The violet light from the amethyst stars shined against her tanned skin and vanished as the shadows of the wings fell upon her.

"Ah, your graces, yes?" Zenoya lifted her head from her scroll, letting the parchment roll up and drop to the floor with the others. She tucked in her stave, the seraphim feathers stilling, as she rose from her chaise, revealing a matching black velvet dress. "Welcome. It has been some time."

She spoke with a light accent, reminiscent of Ramia's though not as pronounced. Zenoya had been born in Bamaria from what I'd gathered, though she'd spent many years in the Courts and kept to herself in the library. Ramia had been raised primarily in the Afeyan Courts until a decade ago. The question I should have asked a long time ago ran through my mind. Why had Ramia come here?

For me.

The answer came instantly. Ramia was here for me under the orders of Mercurial.

I stepped forward. "It has been a while, Zenoya," I said. "And it is just 'my lady' now."

She lifted a dark eyebrow, her lips pouting, and then she shrugged.

"It has been some time, my ladies." She nodded at the escort behind us. "Gentleman. What can I do for you today?"

I eyed Morgana. *They can't know.* I was trying to think of some lie about what we wanted to read when Markan groaned in annoyance.

"How long will our ladies be?" he asked, leaning against a wall and drumming his fingers against his belt buckle.

"Their lives were threatened days ago. And you think you can lean against a wall?" growled Jace. Morgana's personal escort, who had been with her for two years was the youngest on any of our teams—with the exception of Rhyan. Jace had this incredibly deep voice that brimmed with power. He was tall and thin, but his lean body was deceiving. I'd seen him knock a soturion twice his size to the ground with a single slap.

"You're new," Markan drawled. "I've accompanied the lady here hundreds of times. They call it a library, but it's more like a tomb. No one's here. No one gets in but through these doors. The perimeter's been checked. You want to go read? Go. I'm staying right here."

The rest of the escort with us looked ready to find a seat on the long benches lining the entrance hall. One of Morgana's escorts had his eyes on Zenoya. But Jace stepped forward, looking determined to stay by our side.

He can't. He'll see Rhyan.

Morgana pushed out her bottom lip, walking back to Jace. "We won't be far," she said in a seductive tone I'd never heard her use before. "Markan's right. Plus, we have soturi outside. You can come, but I worry that you'll be completely bored."

Jace gripped the leather strap across his armor. "I won't be."

Morgana smiled. "Lies. I'll tell you everything I read on the flight home if you're that interested."

Frowning, Jace looked ready to push the issue but said, "I'll wait for you, my lady. But not out here. I'll be inside the main doors."

I nodded at Morgana. Good enough.

"Thank the Gods," droned Markan. "If we're cut down, Jace is our last defense."

"Hmmm," Zenoya hummed. "I see now I must find some ways to entertain you all." She turned to me and Morgana and snapped her fingers. "Come. We'll get you set up with some reading material."

She reached up on her toes, her elegant arms stretching to reach two golden lamps that she passed to me and Morgana. Jace stepped up to the shelf and pulled down two amethyst stars, hooking them onto the lamps that Morgana brought to life.

"Right this way," Zenoya said, pulling open the set of double doors behind her.

I nearly gasped at the sight inside. I'd forgotten just how big this pyramid was, how high the ceiling went, how many scrolls were stuffed into the walls. The markings of Ka Scholar and their sigil peppered Nabula's pyramid, but this one featured paintings of the original seven Guardians of the Valalumir on the diagonal ceiling high above the shelves.

I spotted Asherah right away, her flaming red hair and silk gown painted Batavia red. She was painted as if she were flying through the sky, her arms outstretched toward the Valalumir, a bright golden light painted at the pyramid's point. I couldn't see paintings move without magic, but some other kind of spell had been used on the star above me. It glowed with such ferocity, it nearly made our lamps null. Beside Asherah was Auriel, his arms reaching for the light it was his duty to protect but his eyes were on her and her alone.

For him, she's brighter than the brightest star in Heaven.

Rhyan had said that about Asherah and Auriel months earlier. And with this painting, I could truly see it—how he only had eyes for her, how she seemed to glow where his eyes focused.

I scanned quickly over the other goddesses. There was Ereshya, a goddess with raven hair and an orange dress symbolizing her connection to the orange ray and shard. It was said she had been the most loyal to Asherah, Guardian of the red ray, but after the banishment, Ereshya had turned on Asherah.

In the paintings, Moriel flew beside Ereshya, his eyes black and vicious, his robes indigo. Cassarya was easy to spot next, painted with the largest eyes of all the Guardians, the same blue as the magic Lumerians possessed. She was said to be the most observant, and so she was always painted with eyes too big for her face. She was pale, with silvery-white hair, and wearing blue, depicted as flying toward the light on the opposite side of the pyramid. Beside her was the fourth goddess chosen to protect the Valalumir, Hava, in a flowing violet gown. Her golden mane fell in loose waves down her back, and there was a fierce look in her eyes.

And, finally, the third male god set to guard the light, wearing yellow robes, was Shiviel. One of the last to have been banished from Heaven, Shiviel was supposed to have become Moriel's Second in command, a monster like his arkturion. He was the one who seemed to be talked about the least, though I'd heard cults devoted to him had formed in the north.

I turned my attention back to Asherah, as Zenoya led us farther into the cavernous pyramid, which was full of mazes of shelves that seemed to rise up an endless number of floors to the paintings above.

"I assume you are here for Afeya research?" Zenoya asked.

"I want to read about Afeyan contracts," I said. "Pull every scroll regarding them. How they're formed. How they're broken. What happens after one is made. Side effects. Links between the Lumerian and the Afeya."

Zenoya tilted her head, her dark eyes flickering to my chest. She straightened, her neck undulating like a snake as I'd seen Mercurial's do so many times. She struck quickly, her fingers gripping the top of my tunic and pulling it down just enough to reveal the top point of the Valalumir.

Morgana's stave pressed into Zenoya's neck. "Hands off my sister."

Zenoya held up her hands and stepped back. "Mercurial's handiwork, I see. What do you want to know?"

"Everything," I said. "How he did this, to start."

"You didn't know the basics?" she asked. "You don't know that every Afeya gives you a piece of their soul?"

"And the Valalumir?" I asked. "Mercurial said it was part of the original light and his soul mixed together."

"The light is gone. It's all in shards now. And those have been lost for ages. Except for one piece of light. One ounce of pure energy from Heaven. Every Afeya brags that they are using the original Valalumir. Most are just copies."

My mouth fell open, remembering all I knew about Asherah and all I'd read in the last few months. "When Auriel stole the light and fell, it started to become a crystal. But he was able to put some of the light into Asherah."

Morgana watched me carefully, her eyebrows furrowed in concentration.

"Everyone knows that," Zenoya said.

"So Mercurial is just pretending it's the light from Asherah?" I asked.

"I do not question the First Messenger of Her Royal Highness. That would not serve me."

"So the light that Auriel put into Asherah's heart—that's not inside me now?"

Zenoya shrugged. "I'll get you scrolls." She turned on her heels, pointing her stave at an empty cart, which began to follow her into the stacks.

"Lyriana. Morgana." A northern lilt wrapped around me. Rhyan approached from behind a shelf in the opposite direction. "Sorry I'm late."

He was dressed in his full soturion uniform, his extra sword strapped to his back, his Valalumirs shined and sharpened. A camping pack was on his back like he was about to ship off to battle.

"Are you on duty?" I asked.

Rhyan shook his head, his good eyebrow furrowed.

"Again?" Morgana asked.

With a pained sigh, Rhyan nodded in response.

"What's wrong?" I asked, searching his eyes, which had darkened.

"I'm being called away," he said, voice low. "They found two more nests. At least two dozen akadim in each, they believe. The Elyrian border."

"Two dozen?" A month ago, it had been unheard of for akadim to be even a dozen strong in our territory. Forget a dozen working together. These nests were new and frightening enough, but it felt like overnight, that number had doubled. And

Elyria was far too close. Gods, how many more akadim could have ransacked Bamaria if we hadn't stopped the threat?

"The Imperator called a meeting. Just after," Rhyan eyed our surroundings, looking suspiciously at Morgana before turning back to me, "after you left."

"Shit." I wanted to reach forward and take his hand. I wanted to hug him. To hold him. To squeeze him in my arms and never let go. But I couldn't. Not in public. And not when things felt so unsettled between us. We hadn't touched each other since his finger had inched toward mine this morning. For the first time, he hadn't taken me back to my apartment, instead saying goodbye at his door. "When do you have to go?"

"In an hour," he said. "We're expected at the Katurium. We're heading out on seraphim and ashvan."

"An hour?" I asked, my heart sinking.

"I'm here," he said. "I'm packed. I'll research with you until it's time."

I was breathing heavily, my stomach roiling at the thought of him out there hunting akadim. It always left me anxious, even if he was one of the most accomplished soturi at killing them. Leander had also been a powerful soturion. There were no guarantees when these demons were involved.

"I'm going to be okay," he said. "I'll stay in touch as often as I can."

My chest felt tight. "You make it sound like you're going for a long time."

He shrugged. "The other nests were empty. And there was only one before. The akadim scattered quickly. They're guessing we'll be gone longer. And this time, the Imperator wants us to keep hunting. Wants, I guess, some credit for his new task force. We might have to go beyond the Empire. Track them into human lands."

Zenoya returned with a cart full of scrolls a moment later, her stave out to roll the cart wheels forward. "Sit," she said, gesturing at an open table. She eyed Rhyan. "Guards are waiting out front. Unless you actually like to read."

"I do," Rhyan said coolly. He sat in the first open seat, pushing his bag against the table's leg. He began sliding scrolls from the cart onto the table, passing them to me and Morgana as we sat across from him. Though he kept a suspicious eye on the half-Afeyan.

"Hmmm." Zenoya looked him up and down. "I better go keep an eye on the men out front. When they get bored, they start to make messes, and I hate to clean. My librarians are all available to you, my lady." She bowed to Morgana. "My lady," she said again, bowing to me. Then she looked to Rhyan, a question in her eyes.

"Not 'my lady,'" he said. "Also, not 'my lord.'"

"Soturion, then." Zenoya turned and strutted back toward Jace who was standing watch before the pyramid's entry hall.

When we were alone, Morgana leaned forward and asked in a low voice, "When was the last time the Valalumir heated up?"

"Yesterday." I closed my eyes, remembering. "After we lost the diadems."

"And not since?" she asked.

I was acutely aware of Rhyan's worried gaze on me. We'd both thought it'd happen again when Mercurial had come to visit. And Rhyan didn't know about the moment it had lit up in my sleep, seeming to stir with his touch, but it hadn't heated, only glowed. "No. Not since."

"So there was the moment the star entered you. Then during Meera's vision." Morgana's dark eyebrows formed a V, her fingers ticking off each incident. "After Meera's vision in your bedroom," she said, voice sly. Rhyan coughed, unraveling a scroll. My cheeks heated, knowing full well where Rhyan's hands had been when it had happened. "And then after the power transfer at the temple. Do any of those events have anything in common?"

I shrugged. I had been scared for some of them. With Rhyan, I had been turned on. And in the temple, I'd been sad. But I didn't think my emotional levels were equal or similar to be the common factor.

Morgana watched me carefully, reading my thoughts, and I shook my head. "No. I don't think any of those have anything in common. Other than that they all took place within the first twenty-four hours." There wasn't even a connection between the times—like every four hours or so. I'd tracked Meera's visions long enough that I'd have seen a pattern if there was one.

"It does look like it's settled," Morgana said.

"But we don't know that," Rhyan said. "And I want to make sure."

So the three of us got to reading. The hour passed quickly. Every scroll seemed to say the same thing. The contract was shaped like the Valalumir. It was embedded with a piece of the Afeya's soul. It marked the person, though often the star was too faint to be seen. Some recorded the star lighting up at first but fading into something unseen unless carefully scrutinized—or unless the person failed to fulfill their end of the bargain.

Some said it hurt when it entered, but others felt nothing.

Most said the contract was created with a piece of the original Valalumir. But that only seemed to be true part of the time.

"It does seem like Mercurial has some piece of the original light," I said. "Why else would it be acting this way?"

Morgana shook her head. "I don't know. It's plausible that he's telling the truth. Some of the Afeya must have had access. And it seems like when a contract ends—when a deal is fulfilled—their star and soul return to them, which would mean the light also returns. But no one else is reporting that it heats up or glows. Father made a deal."

My stomach sank as I recalled that detail. Father had made a deal with Mercurial, a deal that had led to his death, because I'd broken my blood oath.

"Not your fault," Rhyan said quickly as if reading my mind.

"I know," I said.

"The point is," Morgana said, "I saw Father right after, I read his mind. And I saw him the next day—his Valalumir acted nothing like yours."

"So we're right where we started." Rhyan groaned in frustration. "Mercurial's lying and did something to the contract, and we have no answers." His eyes met mine, pained.

"I know you don't trust him. Neither do I." I reached my hand across the table. Rhyan watched it but didn't move to take it. "It really might be that he has the light. He's old enough to have been there at the Drowning, and, I don't know, maybe that's why I reacted...because of who I am. Or maybe it was because of the kashonim. Maybe it's not the contract at all."

We were clearly dancing around the fact that I was the reincarnation of Asherah, a Guardian of the light, and now, possibly, that a small piece of that light was inside me.

Rhyan exhaled sharply. "It hasn't bothered you since yesterday morning?"

"No." It hadn't bothered me. It had only glowed last night at his touch.

"Enough, we're officially going in circles. If we're not going to get answers about that, then we need to move on to how Lyr's going to find her power," Morgana said.

I plucked at another scroll and unrolled it. It featured a rendering of a craggy mountain with decorative flames.

"What's that?" Morgana asked, grabbing the scroll from me.

"Hey," I snapped. "You have to be gentle with these."

She squinted. "This looks exactly like the scene from Meera's vision. There was fire and snow on mountains that had this exact shape. And I saw Lyr—or Meera saw Lyr. She was Asherah, and she was holding part of the Valalumir. The red shard."

I looked up at the painting of Asherah again. Asherah was the Guardian of the red ray of the light, and then, when it had crystalized, she was the Guardian of the red shard.

"That was in her vision?" I asked, voice low. I eyed Jace, who was still standing at the doors to the entrance hall and looking, despite his earlier promises, rather bored.

"This looks just like it." Morgana scanned the scroll again before looking at the painting. "It doesn't offer a location though. Or a description of where this is."

"Can I see?" Rhyan asked.

Morgana slid the scroll across the table to him.

His green eyes widened. "This was in Meera's vision?"

Morgana nodded.

Rhyan's jaw tightened. "I know these mountains. I know them like the back of my hand. They're almost always covered in snow back home. This is Gryphon's Mount."

"Gryphon's Mount, isn't that...." I squinted, recalling something Rhyan had told me a month ago. "That's where the seraphim statue is, right? The one made of moonstone."

Rhyan nodded. "Meera's never been to Glemaria."

"No," Morgana confirmed.

The bells began to ring from the clocktower.

Rhyan had to go. It was too soon for us to be parted. Too soon for him to be running right back into danger.

He was still focused on the scroll. "Do you think it's significant?" he asked Morgana. "The vision?"

"After what just happened with the black seraphim, I do. But I'm not sure what that means yet."

Rhyan stood, his eyes averted from me, grabbed his bag, and slung it over his shoulder. "I'm going to," he looked around the library, noting the movement of every librarian and patron in the distance and Morgana's escort, "go behind some shelves and...go." His chest heaved. "If anyone asks, I'm reading on my own." His eyes flicked to Jace.

"Rhyan?" My heart was hammering. Why wouldn't he look at me?

He turned to me, his eyes rimmed with red. "Partner."

"Be safe."

He nodded.

"And...come back," I said. "Promise." My voice was barely above a whisper.

"I will," he said, his voice heavy. He reached forward as if to take my hand, but then he dropped his hand back down.

My arms were aching for him. I needed to hug him, especially if I was about to go days without him. But we couldn't be seen touching. Even him coming here and sitting across the table from me had been a risk.

He nodded at Morgana, hoisted his shoulder strap higher across his chest, and turned without looking back, heading into the shelves.

Tears sprang to my eyes.

"He's gone," Morgana said. She looked me up and down. "Calm down. He'll be back. He's nearly as good a fighter as the Ready. It'll be okay."

Dizziness rolled over me, the amethyst lights of the library suddenly too bright. Morgana was right, but my stomach was twisting. Rhyan always swore oaths to me, and the fact that he hadn't.... I recalled how uneasy he'd looked this morning. He'd dreamt of the arena and seemed hesitant to touch me ever since but for one sleepy forehead kiss. Something had changed overnight. Something was wrong. And now he was too far away for me to reach him.

"Lyr," Morgana said, a warning in her voice, "he doesn't have to swear every single time."

"I know, but...." I had a sinking feeling in my gut. He'd left to do this so many times before, and I trusted his strength more than I trusted myself, but—

This time was different. This time, he had something to prove. He wasn't just going because he was forsworn or because of his skill. His honor was on the line—honor he felt he'd broken by putting me first. If Rhyan couldn't be a noble, he was going to act noble. And in the quiet moments he wasn't reaching out to comfort me, he was flailing. I could see that now. His admission to me last night should have been a bigger warning. How vulnerable he was feeling. Instead, he'd been convincing me that I was enough.

"He's trying to redeem himself for Leander and Haleika." My voice shook. "Isn't he?"

Morgana nodded slowly, pressing her lips together, and I knew she'd known his plan all along.

"Fuck!"

Morgana took my arm. "Listen, he'll be fine. Focus for a second. I don't know why, but I think Glemaria is important. I'm not sure how yet. It was in Meera's vision, and I saw you there. And the fact that his father was interested in a marriage for you, a marriage that would let him control you, only furthers my suspicions. And if Imperator Kormac is interested in arranging a marriage for you, too, but not one for Meera or for me, then he might know more than he's letting on. He wants his hand in it to keep you out of the north. Out of Glemaria."

I wrapped my arms around myself, cold with this realization.

"Morgana," I said, suddenly going cold. Something I should have known a long time ago was becoming clear.

She stiffened, her skin paling. "Yes."

"Why was my courtship with Tristan pushed, but no negotiations were ever made for Meera?"

I could be wrong, but Morgana looked relieved at my question, then frowned. "After Rhyan's father attempted negotiations, Father said he wouldn't entertain anymore proposals for you until Meera and I were betrothed. He never took a single meeting for either of us."

He'd been protecting me from Rhyan's father. And any other Imperator who knew the truth. All this time—and Meera and Morgana had been kept on the sidelines.

Morgana held up her hand. "Do not get emotional or feel guilty about this. Please. Neither of us have any interest in marriage anytime soon. But I think Tristan was always encouraged for you, because he was known, and he was here. So he was safe."

"And now both Imperators are going to try and control me—and no one will stop them."

Morgana continued, "I think we've done enough today. Go home. Rest. You need it. And so do I."

"I can't," I said. "I need to figure this out. And I need...I need a distraction. Is he going to be okay?"

Morgana squeezed my hand. "Lyr, go home. Rest."

"Is he?"

She sighed, rolling her shoulders back like they ached from all of our research. Her eyes met mine, and they filled with a rare show of kindness. "I'm not the one who sees the future. But I think if anyone is guaranteed to come home after facing akadim, it's him."

I watched her go before returning to read until Markan finally stormed in and escorted me back to the port.

CHAPTER THIRTEEN

TRISTAN WAS WAITING FOR me outside my apartment door when I returned. It had been hours after I'd set out for the library.

Bellamy stood off to the side, shadowed in a corner of the hall, his eyes downcast. I tensed as I passed him, not wanting to make eye contact or hint at any other interaction between us. The silver sigil on his blue tunic was a stark reminder of where his loyalties truly lay and what a betrayal it had been for me to pay him to keep secrets from Tristan.

I found it hard to look at Tristan, too. My skin was crawling with nerves, his aura escaping from his body. The sensation should have been familiar, yet there was something so unfamiliar and off about it. Like I was approaching a stranger.

Tristan's usually handsome face was drawn and pale. His brown eyes appeared distant even as he watched me approach. Dark circles below his eyes unlike any I'd seen on him before made it look like he hadn't slept in days.

My stomach tightened with each step, the utter mess of everything between us dragging me down, making me feel weak. I didn't want to see him. I didn't want to talk to him. I didn't want to have this conversation. It already felt too intense, and neither of us had said a word.

I stopped before him, trying to meet his eyes, my stomach hollowing. But he gazed beyond me, his lips pursed tightly together.

He was looking for Rhyan.

I squeezed my eyes shut, inhaling through my nose, my hands fisted at my side until he finally spoke.

"Lyr." His throat bobbed as he said my name. "Gods, Lyr. I've been trying to talk to you since yesterday."

Hearing his voice made my heart ache. Despite how well I knew him and as long as I had, despite the countless hours I'd spent listening to him speak, despite the intimacy with which I knew his rhythms and specific Tristan idioms, Gods, he even sounded like a stranger.

And I felt like one, too. Like I didn't even know who I was anymore.

I didn't have it in me to talk to him, to hear him out, not after he'd hurt me. Not after Rhyan had left, barely having said goodbye, to hunt akadim again. My eyes were burning. I saw Tristan kissing Naria and heard the crowd's cheers, and, like a punch to my gut,   I remembered that Tristan was going to marry the daughter of my father's killer. He had put a ring on her finger before he'd spoken to me to end things between us. He'd gotten engaged without ever closing things with me.

"Sorry," I said curtly. "Bellamy didn't get to me in time to speak *for* you." I pushed my key into the lock, angling my body away from him.

"Lyr, I tried. I tried to get to you first, I did. And then I...but it was too late. I went to Cresthaven—you weren't there. And I've been here, waiting outside your door for hours. I did the same yesterday—right after the announcement. But you never came home. Or sent word." He looked miserable. Broken. "Where were you?"

My hand shook as I tried to turn the key, but it was stuck. "You don't get to ask me that anymore."

"Lyr, stop."

I cursed under my breath, still focused on the lock and key, turning it back to unstick it.

Tristan took a step forward, his shadow against my door. "My feelings for you—they didn't just vanish. I can't just make them go away. And I don't want to."

"Tristan, stop." I slammed my hand against the door. "It's over. You're engaged. To Naria." I spit her name. "To my cousin! To the girl who went after you behind my back while I was sitting alone and scared in fucking prison."

"I know. I know. I know how fucked up this is. But I need you to listen. I need you to believe me. I didn't want it. And I didn't want it to be like this."

"But this is how it is!" My chest heaved. I was caught between fury and guilt. I may not have been innocent in this situation. Maybe I was the villain. I didn't know. I was too tired and confused to process it. But at the very least, if our situations had been reversed, I wouldn't have been parading Rhyan around all of Bamaria. I wouldn't have been parading him in front of Tristan and kissing him. I wouldn't have been allowing half the country to remind Tristan of how worthless he was. How replaceable.

I turned the key again, this time hearing the small click of the lock, and pushed open the door just enough for me to slide through.

"Lyr, listen to me." He gripped the doorframe. "This isn't what I wanted."

I turned on my heel, grasping the doorknob. "You didn't want what? To be engaged to the girl you almost fucked three years ago? To be engaged to my cousin who never stopped openly lusting for you? The girl who's finally going to give your grandmother the prestige she's always wanted?"

"No!" he yelled.

"I saw you yesterday! The way you were kissing her! You can't pretend with me. Because I know. I could see it. That wasn't the first time you'd kissed in three years."

He squeezed his eyes shut. "No."

I felt like an idiot. What the hell had I been playing at for two years? "When?"

"Let me come in, please. Let me talk to you."

"I don't want to talk to you right now," I cried. "My father is dead! And you—"

"My cousin's dead! And I had to watch you kill her!"

My hand flew to my forehead. I opened my mouth, but no words came. What could I say? He was right. I had killed her. In more ways than one. And who was I kidding? I was no better than him. I'd been in another man's bed last night, in his arms. His lips on mine, on my body. And it hadn't been the first time. The same night he'd been with Naria, I had been with Rhyan. Three years ago, even, on solstice.

I released the doorknob, letting the door fly open. His escort moved forward from the periphery. Bellamy drew closer, and two more mages shifted position. Their silver sigils glowed in the hall's torchlight.

"Only you," I said, eyeing the men behind Tristan.

Tristan signaled for his mages to stand down and stepped forward. I backed away just enough to allow him inside then slammed the door shut.

His arms were around me a second later, his face buried into my neck, his eyes wet with tears. I expected his embrace to feel natural, familiar. I expected my body to fall right into its old patterns of wanting to please him, to make things better, to seek out the breadcrumbs of comfort I'd allowed myself from him over the years.

But I felt nothing. I didn't want him to touch me. Everything about him wasn't Rhyan, and that made everything about him feel wrong.

"I still love you," he said.

My eyes watered. "It doesn't matter. It's not enough."

He sucked in a breath, his arms stiff around me. "Would it be enough if I turned myself forsworn?"

I pushed away from him. "Tristan." My eyes widened, my body seizing up, ready to fight, to protect Rhyan. "What?"

He shook his head. "I don't know what I'm doing." His voice had gone low, turning into something dark and dangerous. "I...I look at you, and I want to kiss you so fucking badly. I see the girl I loved, the girl who was my friend for my entire life. And I look at you, and I see you killing Haleika." He pinched the bridge of his nose, practically hissing in anger. "And I want to fall at your feet and say I'm sorry. That I don't love Naria. That I had no choice. That this was decided for me. Like so much fucking has been. And I want to fight for you—and forswear myself." He pushed his fingers through his hair. "And then I see every instance of the way *he* looked at you. And how *you* looked back at him."

My heart pounded too fast. "Him?" My chest was rising and falling.

"Rhyan," Tristan snarled, stepping forward.

My mouth fell open, desperate to deny it.

Tristan stepped forward again, crowding me, the veins in his arms popping. "I saw it, Lyr." His neck reddened, his head cocked to the side, and his fingers danced on his belt over his scabbard. "I saw the way his eyes followed you. The lust. The desire. He wanted you—three years ago. And the moment you picked him up off the street—that look was still there." His voice shook. "I could see it. And I wanted to kill him for it. But then I looked at you, and I saw...." He gritted his teeth. "I saw you wouldn't admit it even to yourself."

I blinked back tears, gasping. "Admit what?"

His nostrils flared as he stared down at me. "Admit that you were looking at him the same way."

I couldn't breathe. This couldn't be happening. "Tristan." I shook my head. "I...I loved you." Oh Gods, I was going to be sick.

"Maybe," he sneered, staring up at the ceiling, "maybe I did it to get back at you."

I reached for his blue robes, tugged him toward me. "For a look?" I shouted, half enraged and half praying he didn't suspect anything more. "You did all this, betrayed me, for a fucking look?"

He stepped out of my hold, pushing his robes over his shoulder and circling behind my couch. His hands slammed down on the edge. "For a look you never once had for me. For a look you never gave me in two years."

"So that's it?" I asked, circling toward him. "I didn't look at you the right way, so I deserved to be humiliated?"

"You know it's Godsdamned more than that. You know I know you better than that. You know I knew what it meant."

I picked up a pillow and threw it at him, but he caught it with ease. "You don't know! A look! A fucking look! I was always with you, always." I bit back a sob. I didn't even know what I was fighting against because he was right. I was equal parts sorry and terrified. I just wanted him to go. I wanted to crawl into bed, erase his touch, call Rhyan, and hear his voice. But I couldn't. I couldn't let Tristan keep believing what he did.

He squeezed the pillow between his fingers, his knuckles whitening, before he threw it violently back on the couch, his brown eyes rising to meet mine.

"Kiss me," he demanded.

"What?" My stomach twisted.

"Kiss me, then! Go on. Prove it."

I stepped back. "Tristan."

"Am I wrong?" he asked, voice low and dangerous. "Am I? Have I been imagining this? We were almost engaged the other day. My feelings didn't just stop for you. So, if you feel the same, then come on, I'm right here." He pounded his chest. "Prove me wrong. Show me that look." He gripped the couch's armrest, leaning forward. "Show me how much you want me."

The old me would have fallen into his arms in a heartbeat, would have used everything I had to prove him wrong, would have finally given in and invited him to my bed. The old me would have sacrificed my soul to keep the status quo.

The old me would have never let it get this far.

But that Lyr was gone. She'd died in the arena. Nothing was going to bring her back.

I closed my eyes, trying to catch my breath. "I can't."

His nostrils flared. "I know." He released the couch and stepped back, brushing his fingers through his hair as if trying to compose himself.

"I didn't mean to," I said, my voice barely above a whisper. "I didn't mean for it to happen. I fell out of love with you."

"I know," he said and took a seat, his elbows resting on his knees, his shoulders slumped in defeat. "I knew you did."

"I'm sorry."

His fingers flexed and fisted. "I am, too."

I took a tentative step forward and sat on the armrest on the opposite side of the couch. "But I did love you. For a time." Just...not the way I loved Rhyan.

The muscle in his jaw flexed as he sat up, turning his head to me. "I loved you, too."

"When did you become engaged?"

He blew out a breath. "An hour after Meera abdicated."

My bottom lip quivered, but I bit down on it, squeezing back my tears. What did it matter? I had been in my room at that time, alone with Rhyan.

"So what is this, Tristan? Goodbye?"

He scoffed. "You think so little of me?" He raised his voice, his entire body angled toward me now. "You think I'd do something like this to you if it were up to me? If I had any choice in the matter?" He threw his arms up. "I didn't! It wasn't up to me!" I stood again. "It never is!"

"And how much did you choose?" He practically jumped to his feet, stepping toward me again. "How much of your life is exactly what you want it to be?" He was breathing heavily, his aura hot and angry and pulsing around him. "You always do this, you know? You follow the rules as well as I do. You know that, right? I see you." He pointed at me. "I see the masks you wear. The smiles. The feigned looks of interest. The false words. The—" His voice broke, nostrils flaring, neck reddening further. "The false kisses. It took me longer than I'd like to admit because I loved you so fucking much. And I wanted it. Wanted you. Even though it wasn't beneficial. Even though she didn't want me with you. I didn't care." He pressed his finger to his heart. "I wanted you. But you were always just dancing for your supper—performing—even for me. Why?"

I stepped back, barely able to breathe. Because he was too close—too close to the secret, too close to sniffing out the truth. The vorakh hunter who was so near his prey. "I don't know," I lied. "I was scared."

"Of me?" He fisted his hands at his sides, helpless, vulnerable. "I don't know."

"You've always held me to a different standard, you know? We're alike, you and I. We grew up in the same world. We had the same privilege. The same shackles. The same expectations. I've watched you cave to them again and again. And I've never said anything. But when I do," he grimaced, "you look at me like I'm a monster."

He was right. I squeezed my eyes shut. "I'm sorry."

"Me, too."

"So this is it? We're over just like that? You're marrying her?"

He shrugged. "It's what has to be."

My heart squeezed. I was surprised at how much this hurt and, at the same time, how relieved I was to be free. "I am sorry I hurt you," I whispered, my voice shaking.

"That's why I came here. If I thought for one second you felt different, that this was—that you felt something more—I would have fought for you. I want you to know that. And not like last time. I would have thought it through. I would have seen it through. But I had to know. And now I do." He ran his fingers through his hair again. "I never thought I'd...fuck.I never thought I'd lose both of you. Two of my best friends. Not like this." He pressed his fingers to the bridge of his nose, squeezing.

Two of his best friends. Me and Haleika.

He went to the door and had his hand on the doorknob before he froze, his back stiff. "Lyr? Was this how it felt?"

"How what felt?"

His shoulders drooped, as sorrow and guilt permeated his aura, sweeping toward me until I felt weighed down and nauseated by it. "When you lost Jules? This sorrow and anger and...hopelessness. This sense of injustice and...." He shook his head.

I sniffled, knowing exactly what he meant—knowing all the feelings and emotions he hadn't named. "Yes." The word came out a whisper.

"I told you she was supposed to die," he said, his voice breaking.

"You did."

He shook his head again, and then he was gone, the door closing softly behind him.

I stared at the door, seething. Afraid. Guilty.

I wanted to fight. I wanted to hit something. Or yell and scream. I was filled with such fury over the situation, over how helpless I felt, over my role in everything, over the way that no matter how hard I tried, I was still a pawn. The wards protecting my apartment hummed, buzzing with magic. It was a constant sound that I'd grown accustomed to these past months, ever since Arianna had put up new protections and enchantments to protect me from the Emartis.

Now the sound was driving me farther than Lethea. It was full of her essence. Her magic. Her touch. Her evil. I felt like she was watching me, sitting in here with me, spying. Laughing.

I needed to get out. I needed to do something before I burst.

Night had fallen. I headed out of my apartment building, walking listlessly through the streets of Urtavia. I knew Markan and at least three other escorts were following close behind. It was reckless. But I couldn't stay still. Couldn't lay in my bed and fall apart—I wasn't sure if I could be put back together. I stopped at a restaurant I'd gone to once before with Tristan and Haleika.

The owner knew me at once and offered a table. But a whisper of *shekar arkasva* and a table full of patrons recognizing and staring at me had me heading back for the door. I didn't know if they were Emartis, if they'd been there, if they'd killed my father.

I didn't want to know.

I walked out. There wasn't one place safe for me. Nowhere I could go unrecognized or without fear of meeting my father's killers or facing memories of Tristan or Haleika.

I ended up at the Katurium, my appetite gone and a nervous energy running through me. I just wanted to run, for once. I wanted to feel the cold on my face, the wind in my hair. The ground as my feet slammed into it. But one step into the arena, and I was pulled back into that night.

Haleika's screams. Her body burning. Rhyan's sword swinging. The thud of her head hitting the ground. The cheers and cries in the arena. My father falling. The sickening sound. His body broken and twisted. His eyes wide and filled with horror and finding me. The cold on my skin. The knowledge that he was dead, saying goodbye with that one look before he closed his eyes forever.

I slammed the door of the Katurium shut and ran through the halls until I was in our training room. It was empty because Rhyan was gone.

The room carried a light scent—his scent. I could feel him all over as I locked the door and sank down onto a mat, my back against the wall, knees drawn up to my chest. I pulled the vadati stone from my waistlet, letting it roll against my palm, cool and nearly translucent white. I closed my eyes, listening for sounds of anyone beyond my guard in the building. But I was alone.

I lifted the stone to my mouth.

"Rhyan," I whispered, my voice desperate. Immediately, the stone began to glow, blue light surging from within. It warmed in my hand, and I waited, holding my breath.

But a moment passed, and the light faded, no longer swirling with the glow of Lumerian magic. The stone filled instead with a milky white and then cleared, cooling against my palm.

I released a sob, squeezing the stone in my fist and burying my face into my knees.

And then it warmed, blue light escaping in tiny slivers from between my fingers.

"Lyr?" Rhyan's voice was low and muffled in my hand.

"Rhyan?" I opened my palm, seeing the full blue of the vadati return as I lifted it to my face again.

"Partner, what's wrong?" he asked, his words urgent and worried.

"What's wrong?" I squeezed my eyes shut, shoulders shaking. "You're not here."

"I know." He spoke the words almost coldly. "Are you okay? Is your...is the Valalumir doing anything it shouldn't?"

I glanced down at my chest. "Not since last time."

"Good. Good." He sounded relieved. "If it does, tell me."

"Okay." I shifted.

There was a long pause on his end before he asked, "Did you find anything else out with Morgana?"

A torchlight in the corner crackled and hissed, tiny billows of smoke blackening toward the ceiling. "No."

"Are you back home?" he asked, still keeping his voice low. "In your apartment?"

I sighed, running my hands through my hair, my temples dull with the start of a headache. "I was, but now I'm sitting here in our training room." I looked around at the empty space, at the unused mats, at the place where we'd have coffee, at the drawer in the armory where he'd stashed snacks for me. He'd only been gone a few hours, and already I missed him like I'd lost a limb.

"Training room?" he asked.

"I—" I took a deep breath before he could continue, knowing I needed to get this part out. Knowing he needed to know. "I spoke to Tristan. It's over. It's all over."

There was another long silence on his end, the light fading from the stone before it swirled to life again, full of blue light.

"You don't have to...." He trailed off, his voice full of frustration. "You don't owe me an explanation."

"Yes, I do!" My hand shook, the stone rolling over my fingers. I clutched at it and stared at the light glowing against my skin. "Rhyan, come on. Of course, I do."

"Okay," he said slowly. "Truly?" He sounded anxious. "It's completely over?"

Now I was quiet. It felt strange to discuss this with him, especially through the vadati. I needed to see his face, his eyes. I needed to touch him. I could detect the note of insecurity in his voice, the jealousy, the fear.

I pulled my knees closer to my chest and wrapped one arm around my legs, watching the stone in my palm as I held it to my face. "Yes. It's completely over."

"Okay," he said again. There was a small noise on his end like he was shifting around. "I am sorry about it. All of it."

"I know," I said. "But, Rhyan, you need to know, that hasn't affected how I feel about you. What I had with him, it was something else completely. And it hasn't been a factor for me, for my feelings for you, not in a long time."

There was a pause before he asked, "Are you alright? Why are you at the Katurium? It's late."

"I just needed to get out of there, out of my apartment. I was going to—I wanted to run the track. Try to use up some of my energy. But—" My voice broke. "I couldn't go out there. Couldn't go where...where...."

"It's okay, it's okay, Lyr, don't go out to the arena yet. I'll be back before training starts again. Alright? Wait for me."

I shook my head. "I hate this. I should be able to walk out. It's just a track. But I...I just kept.... I couldn't do it. So here I am. Hiding in our room."

"No one expects you to go right back out there." Beyond his voice, I could hear him strapping on his leathers and buckling his belt.

"I'm pretty sure the Imperator has other ideas," I said.

"Fuck him," he growled.

"If only," I sniffled.

"He's not there now. So get him out of your head for the time being."

I stood up and paced around the room, imagining him preparing to hunt in his full uniform, his swords strapped to his sides and the spares behind his back. "I'll try."

"How long are you staying there?" he asked.

"I don't know." I continued pacing. "I don't want to walk past the arena again or be trapped in my apartment. But I don't feel like I can go anywhere. I don't want to see anyone."

"Partner, I need to know, are you safe? Your security detail is with you, right?"

My hand fisted, and I kicked the stack of mats before me. "You're worried about that, but you're not here to be on the detail?" My voice rose.

"Lyr, please. Of course, I'm worried. I'm never not. They're with you, right? In the hall, I assume?"

I exhaled sharply. "Lined up and down it."

"Good. Let them do their job."

"Like I've ever had a choice."

He sighed loudly through the stone. "The Emartis are still out there! And you're still their target, especially...especially now."

"I know."

"You should expect those who were arrested the other night to be released soon if they haven't been yet."

When I reached the wall, I hit it. Above my hand was a small hole Rhyan had punched into the wall after my lashing. I traced the rough edges with my fingers.

"Knowing what we know," he continued, "that's going to be your aunt's next likely play."

"I know." I found a loose piece of panel and picked at it until it broke off.

"Lyr, we need you to stay safe. I...." There was a long pause. "I need you to stay safe."

I turned, leaned back against the wall, and slid back to the floor with my head in my hand. I wanted to tell him to stay safe, too, that I needed him safe, too, but I couldn't get out the words.

"How are you feeling otherwise?" he asked. "How are your, um, your cramps?"

I clutched my belly. "Not as bad as yesterday."

"That's good. Listen, if you're alright, I can't...." His voice shook. "I can't really talk long. We just arrived at the border and have our assignments." Metal sang in the background like he'd just sheathed his sword. "I'm in the first hunting party."

"Is that the most dangerous?" I asked.

There was a long pause. The light faded from the stone before it flared back, and blue filled my palm. "Yes."

"And you're part of this party because you volunteered or were assigned?"

"What's the difference?"

"Rhyan. Don't try to do word play with me now. Assigned or volunteered?" I demanded.

"Volunteered," he said, voice clipped.

"Like you volunteered to go in the first place." My voice was shaking.

"I had to go."

Just like that, I was back on my feet, pacing again. "No, you didn't. You didn't have to."

"I am the only soturion to have killed two akadim within the span of a few months. Three akadim, if you count...if you count Haleika. I couldn't not volunteer."

I squeezed the stone in my palm. "Haleika doesn't count," I yelled. "And I don't buy that for a second. Rhyan, you're playing the fucking hero."

"No, I'm not. I signed up for this, remember? I made a deal with your father, and I keep my promises. I'm doing my duty as a soturion."

"Gryphon-shit! There's an entire legion of soturi here doing nothing. You're not working for my father anymore. He's—" The backs of my eyes burned, and I pressed my free hand against them, blinking back tears.

"Lyr?"

I pushed my fingers through my hair. "You're on the Imperator's task force now. And you can't be doing this. You're still an apprentice."

"An apprentice who has been making these trips for months! I'm the most experienced soturion here. And you know Ka Kormac doesn't do shit. I couldn't suddenly say no."

"Why? Afraid you'd look weak? Scared? I know what you've been doing, and I know what you're capable of, but I also saw the look on your face when you left—and the way you barely looked at me this morning. Stop trying to use logic to defend this. I know you. And I know what you're really doing there."

"My duty!"

"Your duty is here!"

"My duty began before I ever came to Bamaria. We already had akadim reach the border, get close to you. Did you think I'd let that happen again?" There was another long pause. The only sound that came from the stone was his breathing and a thud like he'd set it down somewhere. "What else can I do?" he growled, his voice louder. "Huh? Tell me, Lyr! Tell me! You're not the only one having nightmares. Not the only one seeing Haleika and Leander's faces when you close your eyes. They're dead. Murdered! Because of me. Because of my failure."

"Rhyan, that's not true. They're not dead because of you. You didn't kill them."

"I might as well have. I didn't stop the threat. I let my feelings for you get in the way of it. I told you, I don't know what I'm capable of doing, what lengths, what depravity I might—"

"Rhyan! Gods, do you even hear yourself? So what? You were forced to make a choice, and now, because it wasn't perfect, you're going to get yourself killed?"

"No! That's not going to happen. That's not what I'm trying to do here. I just...I need to find a way to fix this, to somehow even the score, I don't know."

I grabbed the nape of my neck, and squeezed. "You said you'd choose me again."

"I am choosing you. This protects you, too."

"You're not protecting me by leaving me here alone. And you're not evening the score like this. Auriel's bane, Rhyan. You'll never even the score. The akadim that killed Haleika, that killed Leander, is dead."

"And I killed Haleika."

"I KILLED HALEIKA!" I roared, my voice breaking.

There was a noise on his side, something between a sob and a groan of frustration.

"Lyr. Partner." Rhyan's voice was strained. "Come on. This isn't you."

"And you want me to believe this is you? Scared? Running away? Throwing yourself into danger because you're not the most perfect soturion in the world? I know you're better than this."

He grunted.

"I know you're scared," I said. "And I wish—Rhyan, if you were feeling like this, you should have talked to me before you left."

"I did talk to you." His voice darkened.

"No, you didn't. You didn't tell me you were feeling all of this. I know your word is your oath. I know how seriously you take that, how much honor means to you. And I know what happened is horrible and a mess. But you barely talked to me. I didn't know that you were feeling this guilty, this responsible."

"How else could I possibly be feeling? And I tried at first. But then, how could I? With all you're going through?"

"I don't care! It doesn't matter what I'm going through."

"Yes, it does," he growled.

"No, it doesn't! Not when it's this important. Don't you get it, *partner*? We're in this together. We take turns. And I want to be there for you. Even now, even with everything that happened, that I lost. Look, I understand why you felt the need to go, I do. But you have to swear to me you're coming back, that you won't let this become something it's not. Swear. I know how you feel. I know because I feel it, too. But this doesn't change anything. Rhyan, swear to me you'll come back. If there is any threat to your life, I don't care what it is, you come back home to me. I can't...I can't lose you, too."

"Lyr, I...I...." He went quiet, and there seemed to be some commotion happening around him. "I have to go," he said, voice low.

The light left the stone.

I yelled and threw the stone on the mats, sinking to my knees and burying my head in my hands.

It was the second time he'd refused me his oath.

CHAPTER FOURTEEN

MORGANA

THE WEEK FOLLOWING THE murder of my father passed by slowly. Painfully. Meera kept herself up in her room, crying and only rousing herself to make any necessary public appearances. We were to appear at breakfast and dinner. And we were expected to look put together, like everything was fine. Aunt Arianna demanded it.

The amount of soturi within the fortress had nearly doubled overnight, a mix of Ka Batavia soldiers and Ka Kormac. Cresthaven was becoming so unpleasant to be around that I found myself joining Lyr at the library for research every day, which was annoying and frustrating.

But keeping my secret from her—keeping the knowledge I had about Jules—left me riddled with guilt, so I sat with Lyr reading and rereading the same Godsdamned boring information. I couldn't find anything new about her contract with Mercurial, and neither could she. But the more I read, the more I was convinced that he really had put a piece of the actual light inside her and that it had reacted to the part of her that was Asherah. Asherah had part of the light in her, too—Auriel had placed it there just before the Valalumir had crystalized. If Mercurial had been holding onto Asherah's chest plate for a millennium after her death, it made sense he'd found a way to recapture the light as well.

But even knowing that—so what? The information was use-less. It didn't get her out of the contract, and it didn't tell her what to do next. We were both completely stumped. The Afeya hadn't offered anything useful beyond his last appearance. In fact, Mercurial had been mysteriously quiet for days. Lyr said he'd vanished from their last meeting, claiming he'd been an-gered by someone else, and had gone to take care it. But he never resurfaced, or gave Lyr any hint of when he'd return.

When all of our Afeyan contract research led to our hun-dredth dead end, I urged Lyr to return to researching the history of Asherah, looking again for clues into Asherah's loss of power and how it might connect to finding Lyr's own. Much of it, she'd read before, but now, as she poured over the scrolls, she was acting possessed. Every scroll had to be read from start to finish, no detail miscounted. Every little thing she could find, she'd obsess over and then cross-reference with her earlier notes.

I was so fucking bored, having to read this all and then hear Lyr repeat it again in her mind. I'd known the story—every Lumerian child did—but never to this extent. If my old teachers could see me now....

Canturiel created the light in Heaven. Akadim tried to steal it. A war was fought in the Celestial Realms, and the demons lost and were banished to Lumeria on Earth. The gods and goddesses of the realm were materializing as well, playing with taking physical form. Some came and went as they pleased, incarnating into fully grown bodies and abandoning them at will.

Then one day, they got stuck. Their bodies were permanent. They began to age—far more slowly than we did—yet they were mortal. New Lumerians weren't simply falling from the sky, or magically appearing, they were being born. Wars were fought to drive back the akadim, and Lumerians were dying.

In Heaven, four goddesses and three gods sacrificed their lives to protect the light, forswearing all other duties—until Auriel saw Asherah and Asherah saw Auriel. And after years of denying their attraction, they broke their oaths.

The affair discovered, Asherah was banished to Lumeria. Au-riel stole the light to come to her aid, and the Council in turn punished every god and goddess who'd failed to stop him.

Moriel, who had first reported the affair, was the most furi-ous. He led the akadim forces. The goddess Ereshya, Asherah's most loyal companion, defected to Moriel, and the god Shiviel became Moriel's Second. Three of the Guardians battled the remaining four until Lumeria Matavia sank to the bottom of the ocean, and the Valalumir shattered into seven pieces, and knowledge of their location vanished.

By the end of the week, I was near tears, largely from frustration. Lyr was going in circles. She had no idea how to find her power or what anything meant. And Mercurial was nowhere to be found. I could see the toll it was all taking on her.

And I was near tears also because of boredom. I'd been avoiding going outside as much as I could—still reeling from what I'd learned about Jules—and I knew the streets were full of people talking about the transition of power, yelling in support of Arianna, or gossiping about Tristan and his new beautiful, talented bride. Disgusting.

Lyr was more hurt by that than I'd expected. Tristan had always been a piece of shit in my eyes, but Lyr had really loved him—or somehow convinced herself she had. The way her heart raced when thinking of Rhyan was an entire universe away from how she'd always felt around Tristan.

I couldn't get her to talk about it or about Rhyan. He was still gone, still hunting, and apparently barely speaking to her. He called her vadati once a day under the guise of checking in and assuring her he was alive. I'd been around the forsworn long enough to know the truth—he was reassuring himself that she was alive.

By the end of the week, we were expected to appear at dinner at Cresthaven, a formal banquet with the entire Council to show support for Arianna and celebrate Tristan and Naria's engagement. We still had not even had a funeral for father.

All week long, when I hadn't been with Lyr, I'd been trying to listen—to be near Arianna as much as I could stomach, to hear her slip-up and forget to use the elixir and leave her thoughts unshielded. But she never did, not once.

I'd spent another night with Namtaya, torturing myself with her memories of Jules, piecing them together with my own.

Just before the banquet began that evening, I felt his presence outside my bedroom.

Are you coming in? I asked.

Are you inviting me?

I rolled my eyes. *Oh, now you're waiting for permission.*

I have always waited for permission.

Who gave you permission to watch me the other day? I could still feel his eyes on me, the darkness and intensity of his gaze watching me writhe beneath Namtaya, watching me come undone by her tongue and her fingers and the truth I'd learned—and come undone by knowing he'd watched in the shadows.

Now, now, kitten. You and I both know you've always enjoyed that.

My core tightened at the truth of his words. I always expected him to be watching. The darkest part of me loved it. Wanted more.

I opened the door to my bedroom and stepped back, returning to my dresser to...not fix my diadem, but arrange my hair for dinner.

Were you going to share with me your news? He stood behind me, his body warm against my back, his calloused hands caressing my arms.

I shivered as I reached for oil.

Allow me, he thought, taking the bottle from me and pouring oil into his hand. He rubbed his palms together, and the scent of jasmine permeated the room. His fingers ran gently through my hair, his touch now so unlike the rough touches he used to bring me to orgasm, so unlike the touches I knew he possessed when he fought, when he killed.

I leaned back into his touch.

Well? When were you going to tell me? he asked.

You were there—you mean to tell me you only found us after my mind turned off?

When one's been reading minds as long as I have, sometimes it's a pleasure to be told the information directly.

Like you told me about Arianna?

He wrapped my hair around his fingers and tugged my head back—lightly, but enough to impart the message that I shouldn't question him. I gasped, and he pulled harder, to the point of pain.

I told you what I knew. His thoughts felt like a snarl, his aura bursting across my skin heavy and dark. *Mind-reading doesn't allow you to know everything.*

I met his gaze in the mirror. *Jules is alive.*

Then you know what that means.

Yes.

His hand wrapped around my throat, and his lips pressed to my cheek, teeth grazing my skin. *It's time. Time to begin putting our plans into action. Things are already in motion.*

I nodded.

We need to move quick. Now that you know, the secret isn't safe.

I'm aware.

His lips quirked. *Good. Be ready.*

I will be.

I was beyond ready to take action, to get revenge, to get Jules the hell out of the Emperor's service, to bring her back. And to bring the Empire down.

CHAPTER FIFTEEN

LYRIANA

I'D STEPPED INSIDE OF Cresthaven hundreds of thousands of times over the course of my life. It had always felt comforting. It had always felt like home.

Until tonight. Nothing was different, nothing I could point my finger at. The décor appeared the same, and much of the staff was recognizable. But there was a coldness in the air, one I'd never felt before.

I sat in the ballroom with my sisters on either side of me, our escorts standing against the wall behind us.

Arianna announced that the Imperator's task force was currently doing well. They were hunting at the Elyrian borders. And, according to the report, a soturion from Damara had killed an akadim.

I stiffened. Rhyan hadn't mentioned any of this in our brief calls all week. He'd offered me no details at all, only calling me once a day to know I was okay and to assure me he was fine. Once that was established, he always found an excuse to end the call. And I'd watch the stone turn white, feel its heat leave my palm.

Going to bed at night was getting harder.

I could feel Arianna's magic protecting my apartment, hear her essence in the buzzing of the wards. I slept in Rhyan's clothes each night, rewearing what I'd borrowed, but his scent had become so faint, I could barely feel him. I had found the only way to fall asleep was to wrap my arms around myself and pretend they were his.

And then the dreams came. The nightmares. I was back in the arena. Watching my father die. Watching Haleika die.

Watching Rhyan die.

I woke up crying every time, hand clutched to the vadati against my waist, wanting to call him. I didn't know what to do, how to get through to him. He'd done this before—shut me out when he was scared—when he'd thought it would protect me. But this time felt different. The hurts between us far greater than they'd ever been. This time was leaving a hole in my chest.

"That is good news," Aemon said, breaking me from my thoughts. He sat across the room from us, close to Arianna. I suspected he was trying to maintain his position as arkturion. Morgana had confirmed as much. Arianna was within every right to replace him, but so far, thank the Gods, no announcements had been made.

I had a feeling she was dying to put one of her lackeys in his role, but despite the years of turmoil, the Ready remained a beloved warlord, and replacing the man who'd ended the first Emartis rebellion immediately following a second uprising was going to look bad in ways even Arianna couldn't control or rectify. Not yet, anyway.

"The Soturi of Damara have always been talented fighters," Turion Dairen said. "That's two akadim kills for...." He trailed off. "Well, I'm glad to hear it. May we slay many more in the coming months."

Aemon's eyes fell on me. Two akadim kills for Damara. The first had been Leander—the kill we didn't acknowledge, that didn't count because Leander had broken his oath, because Haleika had become forsaken.

Because Rhyan and I had let that monster go.

This was why Rhyan was risking his life to hunt these monsters. Why he'd left me alone.

"He's alive," Morgana said quietly. "Calm down."

I nodded, staring ahead as Lady Sila stood, her camouflaged robes making her body invisible. And just like Rhyan had predicted, she announced that the suspected members of the Emartis, arrested the night of my father's murder, had all been released. There hadn't been enough evidence to hold them.

My stomach dropped.

Arianna looked genuinely disappointed at this news, frowning with slanted eyes. "Then we must do better. We must find more evidence from the guilty party. We must find those responsible for taking our Arkasva from us too soon."

There was a round of applause, and servants emerged with fresh bottles of wine. Eathan sat in a corner by himself, looking stoic, his face drawn and eyes downcast. There was a clear air of sadness in his aura, gray and clouding around him. When a servant offered him a fresh glass, he declined.

I was not in the mood for anything to drink. Tristan was in my line of sight, and Naria had her hands all over him. Her fingers traced the lines of his chest and teased their way to his belt. Her engagement ring flashed with every turn of her hand as she played with his hair.

We hadn't spoken since that night in my apartment. He'd given me a nod and a look of sympathy when I'd entered the hall. His brown eyes had lingered on me for a long moment before Naria had taken his hand. And I'd felt a pang in my chest. Missing him—not as he'd been for me—but as my friend. The boy I'd once trusted and grown up with. We had a unique bond, so much history, but we had also been torn apart, and nothing more than a nod would be allowed for some time.

The usual gossip began to stir—discussion of the Emartis's next move, how the Imperator's task force was doing, possible picks from Arianna to become the next Master of Education on the Council, and, of course, when Tristan and Naria would formally become husband and wife. Every mention of dress designs and cake flavors made me sick.

"Almost done," Morgana said quietly.

Meera reached behind her chair to squeeze my hand. She was looking a little better than she had after she'd first learned the truth about Aunt Arianna. But she never truly looked like herself, not with her vorakh ravaging her.

"Soturion Lyriana," Aemon said, "training begins again in a few days."

I nodded. "Yes." There was a lump in my throat. I couldn't go back to training. Not in the arena. Not where it had happened. Not without Rhyan. Not without any answers. I hadn't been back to the Katurium since that first call to him. Every time I thought about running the track in the place where I'd killed Haleika and where my father's body had fallen, I wanted to vomit.

"Are you ready to return?" he asked, folding his arms across his chest. He leaned toward me, his armor gleaming with firelight. But there were also bags under his eyes, clear signs of exhaustion. I'd imagined he was working every hour he could to maintain order, and keep the additional legion of Ka Kormac soturi under control.

"Do you want the honest answer?" I asked, voice low. "Or the one I'm expected to give?"

He smiled grimly. "That is answer enough. You appear to be without an apprentice at the moment." His eyes roved beyond me, no doubt picking out the members of my security detail still present. Then his darkened gaze was back on me. "I do expect him to return soon, but in the meantime, as a precaution, I'm going to pair you with Soturion Galen and his apprentice for training."

My heart sank. I hadn't seen Galen since the arena. I had no idea how he was doing after losing Haleika, after learning she'd loved someone else. I should have reached out to him, but I'd been too afraid.

"I don't need to remind you," Aemon said, "of what's at stake. You know I am sympathetic to all that's happened. I support you, and I'd give you far more time to recover were I in charge. But, just as before, we cannot afford to make any mistakes. The Imperator and now the Emperor are still watching your every move. Closer than before in some ways," he added darkly. "Understood?"

"Understood." I was to be Soturion Lyriana again. To suck it up. To prove I was strong even without magic. To expect no special favors. It was all I could do to maintain my position, to keep Imperators from negotiating marriage.

"I'm making a call to the Imperator," Aemon said, "to bring Hart back at once. By now, he should have shared all the knowledge he has and led enough of the hunts—especially considering his age—that he has done enough. I believe his services here are required. Especially now that the *rebels* have been freed." His hands fisted at his sides, his eyes moving to Morgana and then Meera.

Morgana stiffened at his words, her aura tense and pulsing. I turned, seeing Meera looking faint, but then she straightened and reached for a glass of water.

Gods, I was never going to be able to relax with them.

I smiled back at Aemon, schooling my face to appear calm. "I would like that," I said, praying I sounded neutral. It was taking all I had to keep myself from demanding he be the Ready and march straight to the border himself to drag Rhyan back.

Aemon pulled a small flask from his belt. "This is for you, Lady Lyriana. I can't do much for your situation at the moment, but you look like you could use this." He pressed the cool silver metal into my palm.

"What is that?" Morgana asked.

"Fine wine for the *soturion*," Aemon said. His eyes pierced Morgana. "I dare say, my lady, you have had enough already?"

Morgana rolled her eyes. "If you say so, Arkturion."

"Drink up," he said quietly. "Try to relax tonight. Because after the weekend passes, everything must return to order."

I nodded, watching him walk away. I felt the chain around my waist and itched to touch the stone, to call Rhyan right then. But instead, I drank Aemon's flask, surprised at how sweet and how strong it tasted.

The night carried on with more inane gossip and chatter and Morgana continuing to drink until I had no choice but to help her up to bed, bringing Meera along as well.

We curtsied before Arianna on our way up, my skin crawling as she touched my hand.

"Have a good night, my dears. You must be exhausted." She squeezed my hand, and I felt the eyes of every noble in the room on us.

How many supported her?

How many supported me?

Now the phrase "shekar arkasva" has true meaning. Not all support the illegitimate black seraphim. You're not alone.

No other messages had come to Cresthaven or my apartment, and I was no closer to solving the riddle of the signature.

131189114141

Arianna released my hand, her blue eyes assessing. I lowered my chin.

"Good night," I said, making one last sweep of the room for clues. Attention had returned to the small talk happening at each table.

I got Meera to her room first despite feeling slightly drunk from all I'd had downstairs. I'd finished Aemon's drink when Naria had begun kissing Tristan in the middle of the room and then I'd borrowed what remained in Morgana's cup while they'd danced across the floor. Lady Sila had sent over a glass to me, worried I was upset at the news of the Emartis's release. She'd been right. I'd downed the entire thing.

When we reached Morgana's bedroom, she gripped my arms, her fingers cutting into my skin.

"Morgs—"

"Shut up," she snapped.

I froze. "What?" *Did you hear something?*

Her eyes widened, as her grip on me tightened.

Morgs? Ow!

She shook her head, true fear in her eyes.

I tried to empty my thoughts to let her hear while I strained my ears, listening for whatever or whoever was nearby. But I couldn't sense a thing.

Morgana's chest heaved, her dark eyes searching mine.

Is it Meera? I'd never seen her like this—so scared, so vulnerable looking. Not in years. *Morgs?*

She had that look she got when she was focusing, when she was purposely trying to open her mind to hear something distant or private.

Was it Arianna? Or someone else who'd conspired against us?

"Lyr?" she asked, her fingernails cutting into my flesh.

"Ouch!"

"How drunk are you?" she asked.

I shook my head. "Not enough." I was still coherent, still thinking of Rhyan, still seeing Naria rub her body against Tristan's as they approached Turion Dairen's seat.

"Lyr," she said again, this time truly sounding terrified. Like something was wrong with me or something terrible was happening to me.

I looked down—was I bleeding? Nothing. No injury I could detect, no mark.

She pushed me all the way into her bedroom, slammed the door shut, and locked it before she was on me again.

"By the Gods." Morgana cursed under her breath.

"Morgs! What's going on?"

She ignored me, pushing at my dress and turning my necklace to expose the Valalumir mark. It had been a faint gold but was now glowing brightly again, almost as bright as it had been that first night it'd marked me. I braced myself, gritting my teeth, waiting for the fire to burn inside me.

But nothing happened. It only glowed.

Was that what had upset her?

"When's the last time it did this?" she asked.

"Last week," I told her. "With Rhyan. But it hasn't glowed or warmed since."

"Something's wrong," she said. "I think it's done something to you."

I swallowed, looking down at my chest again. "I don't feel anything." I pressed my palm to my heart and shook my head. "What are you talking about?"

"I can't...." Her neck strained as she leaned forward. When she looked at me, her eyes widened, and her face paled. "I can't hear your thoughts anymore." Her eyebrows furrowed, and she waited a long moment, like she was listening. She frowned, looking like she was on the verge of tears. "I can't read your mind. I can't...I can't get anything off of you. Not a single thought or feeling. It's like there's a wall around you."

"What?"

"Do you feel any different?"

"No."

"Fuck," she cried. "Lyr, your mind has gone silent."

CHAPTER SIXTEEN

ALL WEEK I'D BEEN at the Afeya library, reading, researching, coming up empty. Trying to find some answers, trying to find a way to understand what was happening to me. But after what had happened with Morgana, I was done reading. I was done playing nice.

I'd dealt with feeling like my insides were on fire and my star glowing at random with no explanation for why or how to navigate this. I'd received no word from Mercurial and no advice from Zenoya or any of the scrolls I'd reviewed.

And now, Morgana couldn't read my mind. We'd tried to go back over the events of the night, to figure out the moment it had happened, but the dinner had been so loud, and she'd been drinking so much, she hadn't noticed the silence of my mind until we were alone. Morgana's vorakh was still well intact with everyone else she'd encountered, so we were sure it was just me.

Before there were any more unwarranted effects, I needed answers.

I marched straight up to Zenoya the next morning, realizing what I'd been missing all week long. I'd been so focused on Mercurial's absence, I hadn't realized another signifanct member of the Afeya had been mysteriously quiet.

"Where is she?" I asked.

"My lady," Zenoya said coyly. "Where is who?"

"Ramia," I snarled. "Where is Ramia?"

Nearly every time I'd been to the library these past few months, she'd been waiting for me, teasing me with a clue or some scroll I needed but couldn't have or couldn't read. But for the last week, I'd been sitting here like fresh bait with Mercurial's Valalumir inside me, and she hadn't appeared once.

"Her office," she said.

"Where is her office?"

Zenoya stretched her neck from side to side, undulating like a snake about to bite, her eyes watching me like a viper's. Blinking slowly, she said, "She's been away, now she's catching up on work, and she does not want to be disturbed."

"You realize whom you are speaking to?" I demanded.

"A former Heir to the Arkasva?"

"A lady of Ka Batavia," I hissed. "Heir or no, I still belong to the Ka who rules over you, still carry the blood of the arkasvim in my veins."

"Good." Zenoya smirked. "I hate to see a woman downplay herself."

I was going to punch her. The last thing I needed were Afeyan mind games in which she tried to convince me her cruelty and dismissiveness were favors. She was just getting on my nerves now.

"Ramia's office? Where is it?"

"Second floor," Zenoya said then sank back onto her chaise and unraveled a scroll she had chained to her waist.

I turned back, signaling to Markan to wait, and marched through the main doors without a light.

My feet seemed to carry me on their own, running as if suddenly remembering what they'd done every day for months. I climbed the stairs and raced through the stacks until I found her door. I burst through it and found Ramia lounging on her own red chaise, twirling an aging scroll in her hand.

"My lady," she said, startled. "You come. For once I was not expecting, I have no scroll pulled for you. But I do have new jewelry."   I slammed the door behind me, marched straight for her, and pushed her shoulders back against the armrest. "What do you know?"

"My lady? Know?" She tilted her head to the side. "Know what? I know many things. What you want to ask?"

"My contract with Mercurial," I said. "Don't pretend you didn't have a hand in it, don't pretend you don't know about this. It's not behaving normally. Why?"

Ramia's lips tightened. "That I do not speak of. Contract between you and him. You want answer? You ask him."

"And where is he?" I asked.

She snarled, "I do not know. For once, I cannot find him."

I searched her eyes for some semblance of the truth. "What do you mean, you can't find him?"

"I mean what I say. He missing." She lifted her chin, her eyebrows narrowed and defiant, her lips pursed together. "I could ask you same question."

I stepped back. Ramia had revealed so little to me of her relationship with Mercurial over the years that this felt like a huge piece of information. She'd never told me how often they spoke or saw each other—she'd barely admitted she knew him, and now she was openly admitting she couldn't find him.

"How do you know he is missing?" I asked. "Was he supposed to meet you?"

Her eyes searched mine. "He was. And he not show. The First Messenger is many things, but he is Afeya of his word. He say he come, he come." She shrugged. "He say he come, he not...something wrong."

I'd found it so odd he'd been silent on my end, too. Had something gone wrong with whoever he'd left me to go see?

"Are you sure?" My heart was sinking. Something felt wrong to me. And yet, no person or Lumerian could overpower or compel him. He was immortal.

"You his focus now," she said. "When Afeya have focus, they not relent. He missing? Bad. For everyone." And for the first time in the years I'd known Ramia, she was showing real signs of emotion. She'd dropped her persona, her jewelry-seller façade. She was genuinely worried.

"Did his queen call him back?" I asked, sure there was some explanation. "Or could he be at one of the other courts?"

Ramia shook her head. "No. I visit Sun and Moon Court. Why you don't see me for days? Why you think I know already? He missing."

Maybe this was a good thing. Maybe this was why the Valalumir had stopped heating. But it was still glowing and was most likely the reason Morgana couldn't hear me.

"Are you sure he's not just...busy?" I asked.

"Yes. But I know what he working on. He not busy with that."

My heart pounded. "What he's working on?"

Ramia's hand reached for my heart but stopped just before she touched me. "How necklace working for you?"

I stepped back. Did she know what it was? What it meant? She worked with Mercurial. She had given me the armor in the first place.

I swallowed. "It worked very well."

She lifted an eyebrow, her lips quirked. "Keep wearing. Be careful." She paused, something dark in her eyes. "My lady in grave danger if he is gone. Only one thing powerful enough to overcome Afeya."

"Akadim?" I asked.

She shrugged. "Maybe. Maybe not." She pointed at my heart again. "Maybe a god."

"A god?"

"We have goddess now among us. You think she walk alone?"

Did you really think that Asherah could just die, and her part in this was done? She's only getting started.

Mercurial's words came back to me. My vision went in and out of focus. I stumbled backwards, and my hip hit Ramia's desk. I turned and grabbed hold of the edge to balance myself, the movements causing a small crash of scrolls. Rubbing my hip, I realized I'd knocked a stack onto the floor. Each one had a tag full of numbers.

79114141

12085141251

I reached for the leather cases, rolling across Ramia's floor as she scowled.

"Lumerian mess!" she hissed.

The numbers...they were just like the signature on the noted I'd received. Ramia began to gather the scrolls, as I reached for more—scanning each tag, reading through every number sequence I could find.

And then I saw it. A brown leather case sat in the center of the pile. It was tied shut with black leather cord, attached to which was a faded parchment tag that read, 131189114141.

The signature.

Your Grace,

Now the phrase "shekar arkasva" has true meaning. Not all support the illegitimate black seraphim. You're not alone.
131189114141

I grabbed the case. "What is this? What are all of these?"

Ramia's eyes slanted into narrow, snake-like slits as she sat back. "Not for you."

"I think it is," I said, pushing her back against the chaise. "I've seen these numbers before."

She grunted, straining against me. "How exciting," she snarled. "Congratulations. You see same numbers two time."

"What are they?"

"Mess I clean up. Someone take out—leave in office."

She hadn't meant for them to be here.

I pressed harder, my hand snaking its way to her throat.

"You not strong enough," she said.

"No," I said and touched my armor with my free hand. "But *we* are. If a god can overpower a full Afeya, what can a reincarnated goddess do to a half one?"

Ramia rolled her eyes. "Numbers mean nothing. Filing numbers."

"Filing for where?" I demanded.

Ramia's lips pressed together.

"For where?" I asked again.

"Journal records."

"Records for who?"

"Nobility," Ramia spat.

"And whose journal is this?" I asked, clutching it to my chest.

"If they want you to know, they tell you."

"They did! I received a note with this exact sequence."

Ramia shook her head. "No. Not possible."

"Yes, I—" Something in Ramia's eyes made me pause.

"Not from author," she said. "I promise. Not unless they send ages ago."

I'd only had the note for a week. Was it possible it had been written a long time ago and someone else had shared it? What if the note hadn't even been written to me? It had been addressed to *Your Grace*, not to Lady Lyriana.

"How do you know?"

Ramia smiled. "Because journal only go into our archive when complete—when no more to write. We only acquire when author dead."

My throat went dry as I clutched the case to me. "Ramia? Who wrote this journal?"

Lowering her chin, she said at last, "Your mother."

I released her at once, taking a step back.

"I'm borrowing this," I said.

"Journals are not for public to borrow."

"I am not the public. I am Lady Lyriana—"

"*Former* Heir to the Arkasva."

My nostrils flared. "And as her daughter and a current lady of Ka Batavia, I am borrowing this."

Ramia shrugged. "I cannot fight you without losing. Do what you will. But know this. You making big mistake."

"By reading a journal?"

"I not pull these out. Someone else. Someone did this when I away." Ramia smoothed out her dress and stood, clearing her throat as she fixed her necklace. "You making big mistake not finding him first."

My heart was pounding too loudly for my chest, and I inched back, partly fearful she'd come for me and retrieve the scroll.

I turned the scroll in my hand, my grip tightening over the leather ties as I pulled it to my chest. "If you see the ambassador," I said, "tell him I'm looking for him."

"And he see you first," she said, her tone full of disapproval, "tell him I did same. And tell him I tell you not to read journal."

I narrowed my eyes, placed the scroll in the bag attached to my belt, and walked silently out of the library, past Markan, and back into my seraphim carriage, barely daring to breathe as we took flight over the pyramids.

Back in my apartment, I opened the scroll slowly, checking the tag against the note I still kept in my arm cuff, confirming the numbers were a match despite having memorized them. I unraveled the scroll on my kitchen table and gingerly ran my finger over the scripted text. My mother's handwriting stared back at me, elegant and full of lean loops. I'd only ever seen it before on signed documents framed in Cresthaven.

Shaking, I touched the parchment again. She had touched this. She had written these words. I wanted to run my hand over all of it, but I didn't want to ruin the ink or damage the text. I didn't have a glass reader or gloves in my apartment, so I grabbed a golden reading stick and secured the scroll's end under a clip.

Sitting back and taking another deep breath, I began to read. The scroll opened with my mother describing her first day as High Lady and the feel of the weight of the Laurel of the Arkasva on her head. She described how much heavier it weighed than her diadem, which she had put aside for her first daughter.

Meera's diadem. I saw it swinging in Arianna's hand. Melting into the fire. Gone forever. I turned the scroll, sliding more of it through the clip, my reading stick moving quickly over the words. Hours passed as I read of my mother's day-to-day tasks: sitting in Council meetings; visiting the city; and having conversations with my father, some of which I didn't need to know about it. Finally, buried within the daily moments of her life as a ruler, I came upon this:

Our first daughter is here. Meera. She is so beautiful and precious. I didn't know I could love like this before. Harren did. But I feel full to bursting. She is special. I know it. Not in the way all mothers believe their babies special. But I wouldn't be surprised if upon her Revelation...a deep power is revealed.

I can't stop looking at her. Poor Gianna. My Second has been working overtime to run Bamaria while I lay here with my girl. She should be on bedrest, too. She's nearly ready to give birth as well. We sure timed this poorly, didn't we?

I froze. My aunt Gianna. She had been my mother's Second. I'd never known that. I bit back tears. My mother was talking about when Aunt Gianna had been pregnant with Jules.

If only she'd known.

I swallowed roughly, reading on about Meera's first days, which consisted mostly of sleeping and eating. The notes grew sparser over the first year of her motherhood. There were more pages about ruling Bamaria: attending Council meetings; becoming pregnant again, this time with Morgana; and detailing her visions for the future of the country as well as a reoccurring dream she experienced in her third trimester.

I had the dream, she wrote. *It's come again, so I suppose that means I ought to write it down. I stand on mountains, sharp and craggy, full of snow—the same mountains every time. A goddess lies at my feet. She's so still I'm unsure if she's dead or simply sleeping. Even when I sense I've seen this before, I always remain unsure of her condition. What I am certain of is that she's beautiful, her hair a vibrant, fiery red, and somehow, she seems familiar to me in some inexplicable way. I know it sounds farther than Lethea, but I never have the sensation that so often occurs when we look at the gods and goddesses—we see them powerful and mighty. Above us. Like mothers, fathers, rulers. Absolute power.*

Not in my dream. There I watch the sleeping goddess, her hair full of fire, red like mine. Batavia red. And each time, I think to myself, daughter. My daughter.

I don't want to worship her. I fiercely want to protect her.

A goddess with red hair sleeping on a craggy, snowy mountain. Meera's vision.

My heart pounded as I read on, the sun setting early and wind howling outside my window, banging against the glass.

Morgana was born, and my mother had been disappointed for a second when she'd seen the shock of her raven hair.

Nine months I've been imagining my red-haired babe. I'm not sure where Morgana came from—almost as if she swooped in and took her sister's place. I already feel certain there is another daughter coming to me. But I love her. So much. It doesn't matter her hair color. It's only...I had thought the dream a symbol or sign.

During Morgana's first months, the dreams stopped. But once my mother was pregnant with me, the dream came again and again. More intense. More vivid. The same goddess, always asleep. The same feeling of motherly tenderness.

Then she wrote:

I'm in labor. Contractions have started. She'll arrive quickly, I am sure. Before sunrise I expect. Auriel's Feast Day.

I let out a shaky breath. My mother had been writing about me. My birth. I'd never heard anything about it before. I'd never even known what time I'd been born. All talk had always been of her death not long after. Of my father coming into power. I squeezed my eyes shut, inhaling through my nose, and continued.

I think we will find the day to be fitting, if all I believe is correct. The pains...but I must write this down first. The dream that's come to me so many times now, came again. But this time was different. I saw her sleeping at my feet, snow beneath us. I wanted to reach down and stroke her hair. I knew she was glowing, full of warmth and light. But naturally, as a mother, I worried she was cold. And for the first time ever, her eyes opened. Beautiful. Hazel. A little bit of green and sparks of gold. She looked right at me, a knowing in her eyes, and then she vanished.

She reappeared, standing before me, full of so much light, glowing and vibrating with warmth and power. Beautiful.

I never had to describe awe before, but I felt it looking at her, and I knew.

Asherah.

Asherah came to me. I've been gifted with a vision of the Goddess Asherah, it is she who has been visiting me all these months.

The journal cut off, and her next entry was after my birth.

It's her. I gave birth to her. The vision of my dream. Her hair upon birth was a bright, fiery red. Like the goddess. And then after the nurses cleaned her up and brought her to my breast, the color left, replaced by a dark, beautiful brown. Like Harren's hair.

I think it's a sign—though I'm afraid to say of what.

A few days passed. She wrote of sitting in the Council meetings with a pillow behind her back on the Seat of Power as she held Court and nursed me at the same time. She'd done the same with Meera and Morgana, and whenever they'd finished, they'd slept in her arms as most babies did after feeding.

According to her journal, I was like any other baby except in Council meetings. After I fed, I sat up, alert. She said I looked like I was listening, my eyes following the flow of conversation and debates. Like I was preparing to rule. She saw me as High Lady and Arkasva even though I was third.

Then she took me outside and discovered my hair was still red but only in the direct light of the sun.

Then Gianna died. She didn't write much. The pen seemed to fall across the parchment as if she were too sad to complete her script. She dated the parchment a few times, like she had an intention of writing something more but couldn't.

Then I came upon a single entry.

I no longer trust her.

My gut twisted as I read the words again.

Arianna. It had to be Arianna.

There was not another word about it or whom she was referring to. The parchment continued with more daily tasks—Morgana taking her first steps, Meera sleeping through the night in her own bedroom in the Heir's wing.

There had been a visit from the Imperator, whom she'd intensely disliked. Apparently, that had been rare in those days.

And then....

I haven't spoken to anyone. But the dreams won't stop. You'd almost think I have vorakh with these visions. Gods. I shouldn't write such things. I am not afflicted. But they are constant. And now I've been invited up north, to visit with Imperator Hart. A rare opportunity. I have yet to cross the northern border of the Empire, to see his country.

In my condition, the healer does not advise it. I'm still nursing Lyriana. But I must.

The snow. The mountains. I have to see for myself. Is this the place?

By the Gods.... I started reading faster.

My mother left me behind with my father and our nursemaids and traveled by ashvan, flying out into the night with her guard, including Aemon, surrounding her. Motivated to get there and return, they flew nearly non-stop for three consecutive days and arrived in the early hours of the fourth.

The Imperator's son is quite adorable. The greenest eyes I've ever seen, and beautiful dark curls. He clings to his mother in the hall, always reaching his tiny little hand to hold hers. It's so sweet to see. I think I would like a son.

Fingers tightening over the reading stick, I bit my lip, the backs of my eyes burning.

She'd met Rhyan when he was a child. And she'd adored him, the little Rhyan who was lonely, who only wanted a pet gryphon to care for and be his friend. My chest tightened. I felt simultaneously touched by her words and sick over her initial observation of him—clinging to his mother. Already fearing his father. He would have just turned four. Poor Rhyan.

Imperator Hart has interest in a marriage with Lyr. I assumed with the young Lord Rhyan, but he is far more interested in her marrying one of his nobles when she comes of age.

I can see no reason why we would agree to this. I would never arrange a marriage for my daughter before she could speak and decide if she wanted this for herself or not. I simply would not arrange a marriage. These things have never been done in Bamaria. But the Empire's ways of men keep trying to creep their way in.

I stretched my neck side to side, feeling a cramp after having sat and read so long, but my mind was racing. Rhyan's father had been trying to win my hand in marriage far longer than I'd ever suspected. He'd asked my mother for my hand and tried to take control of me when I was a baby. Had he known about me? How could he have, when my mother had barely suspected it?

I kept reading, my eyes moving more quickly across the parchment.

Then my mother gave me the answer I'd needed for days, for months.

It's Glemaria. My vision, my dream. It's Gryphon's Mount. The shape of the mountains, the fall of the snow.

A seraphim of white moonstone lays atop the mountain, partially covered in layers of snow that's frozen over. The seraphim was sculpted much in the way of the Guardian, resting on its belly, but its head lifted and alert, looking out toward the Lumerian Ocean.

My guard accompanied me on my walk up the mountain pass in the morning.

And I touched the statue. And I saw her. I saw the goddess as if she were standing right before me.

Her hair was dark, unlike any depiction I'd seen. It was the color of Lyr's hair. Her eyes were closed. And when she opened them, they were Lyr's eyes. And then beneath the sun, her hair was red.

She was weak, though, couldn't stand. She fell against the statue.

Again, I thought, my daughter, and I reached out to grab her. Aemon said I looked like I was in a trance. That I'd reached for nothing. No one else could see what I saw.

But when I touched the statue a second time, she stood before me in all her power, holding the red shard of the Valalumir in her hands.

We were called back to the keep for breakfast and a meeting of the Glemarian Council. I didn't hear a word. I kept thinking of the mountain and the snow. And Asherah.

I snuck out again at night. Unable to sleep. Possessed.

Under the moonlight, I saw something that was not visible before in the sun. Writing. It was faint, scripted in very old-fashioned High Lumerian letters as such:

Ha zan aviskan me shyatim, cain ani chaya tha o ha yara.

I squinted, absorbing my mother's old-fashioned handwriting. I'd read many scrolls like this before, but it always took me a moment to adjust to the style. Slowly, the translation came to me.

The sun revealed my secrets, so I hid them with the moon.

The statue held a message that could only be read in moonlight.

Imperator Hart interrupted me then. Beneath the message, embedded into the moonstone, was the shape of a star—a Valalumir. But it was unusual in its shape. The rays curved, reminding me of a sun. And under the moonlight I could see there were creases along the edge of the moonstone, an opening.

"It takes a key," he said. His voice was nonchalant. Off-putting.

I'd turned to him, startled, and asked, "A key, your highness?"

He smiled back at me, but there was something strange about it. Like he was hiding a grave secret. "It takes a key to understand this puzzle." Those were his words. And he laughed. "No one yet has understood this. Looks like she belongs more in your country than mine."

I nodded in agreement. "We have our own mysterious out-of-place statue. The Guardian, a great gryphon." My heart was pounding so fast as I spoke.

He'd nodded in agreement. There was a knowing in his eyes I didn't like, that made me sick to my stomach, but then he grinned easily at me, inviting me back inside, offering to take me away from the cold.

I may be High Lady, absolute ruler of Bamaria. But I dared not refuse the request of this Imperator.

I came inside. But not before I looked one more time. Not before I saw the tiniest inscription alongside the star.

Aniam aviska sol lyrotz, ka, e clavix. Shukroya mishverach, o tha trium.

Had I not been diligent in my studies, I'd never have memorized it so quickly. Luckily, I did.

And then only inside did I notice the hilt of his sword for the first time. A red star in the same exact shape and size of the

Valalumir I'd just seen engraved into stone. And his star was not just red. But Batavia red. Red as the red shard of the Valalumir. Of my visions. Of Asherah.

He doesn't know I figured it out.

Maybe he isn't fully aware himself of what he holds. I don't know. He's hard to read. He is very sweet and accommodating. But he makes me uncomfortable. He is hiding his true self.

But my reservations about the Imperator aside, I know now beyond a shadow of a doubt what this means—the answer to the questions I've researched my whole life.

My visions, my dreams, the seraphim and the color red, all things that relate to her. To Bamaria. The shard I saw.

If I were to share this with someone, they might call me farther than Lethea. And they might be right. But I believe with whole heart that at least this one mystery may have been solved.

One of the lost shards of the Valalumir has been found.

And it's in Glemaria.

I could barely breathe. I sat back in my chair, rereading her words.

Aniam aviska sol lyrotz, ka, e clavix. Shukroya mishverach, o tha trium.

I translated it easily, and instantly, sweat beaded at the nape of my neck despite the growing chill in the air as the night rolled on.

We unlock for blood, soul, and key. Power is restored, with these three.

Blood. Soul. Key. If my mother was right, then the red shard was in Glemaria inside their seraphim statue. To open the statue, I needed three ingredients. My blood, Asherah's blood. Something of my soul...was it the light that Mercurial had put inside me, a fraction of the original Valalumir that Auriel stored inside Asherah's heart?

That was two. I was sure of it. And with the third, according to the inscription, I'd have my power. Accessing the red shard. Asherah's shard.

The only problem—Rhyan's father possessed the key.

CHAPTER SEVENTEEN

I PACED MY APARTMENT, unsure what to do. My entire body was shaking with everything I had learned.

It was dark outside, the moon faint. I'd been reading the whole day, the whole night, obsessed, and now with all I'd learned, I couldn't stop moving, couldn't stop thinking. I felt like I was leaving my body, my soul hovering above me.

I shut myself in my bedroom, trying to calm down. There was a path to my power. One I could take without Mercurial. One that put me and Rhyan directly in danger of his father.

He held the key. Of course, he did. One of the lost shards of the Valalumir was right under his very nose. How he must have hated that he couldn't get to it himself. Not without me.

He sure fucking tried though. First with my mother when I was barely crawling. And then again with my father, when I had no idea what was happening.

Who else had known about this? Who had taken the journals out? Eathan? No, why wouldn't he just tell me? But someone did—someone who wanted me to have my power. Someone who supported me ruling in Bamaria. And it wasn't Mercurial.

Lying down in my bed, I took out the vadati. Only one person would calm me now, would understand. Could offer advice on what to do.

"Rhyan?" I spoke into the stone. "Rhyan?" I said again when nothing happened. The stone was cold and clear. Another minute passed. It had been a full day since we'd spoken. I was about to give up when Rhyan's voice came through, the vadati glowing with his words.

"Lyr, you okay?" he asked.

"Yes. But I—"

"I'm sorry," he cut me off. "I can't talk. I'm on patrol."

"Oh," I said. "Okay."

The stone cleared. My throat tightened. Right. Of course. He was busy.

I stared at the stone, debating whether or not to call Meera and Morgana. Meera had had the same vision as our mother, and Morgana had experienced it alongside her. Morgana had already confirmed that the picture of Gryphon's Mount was identical to Meera's vision. But with everything I'd just learned, I was too tired to tell them now. The enormity of what I'd just read seemed to crash down on me, and I slipped out of my clothes and pulled on Rhyan's pants and shirt as I'd done every night since he'd been gone. I closed my eyes, thinking through what my mother had written.

The red shard was the answer to my power.

And Rhyan's father, that fucking bastard, he was the key.

We unlock for blood, soul, and key. Power is restored, with these three.

I repeated the phrase again and again until I lost consciousness.

"Lyr? Are you asleep? Partner?"

Haleika was screaming. She was burning alive. But she was human. I'd stabbed her with a wooden stake. Set her on fire. No. No. No.

Then Rhyan was there. A sword came for him, for his neck.

I opened my eyes, sitting up straight, nauseated from the dream. My room was dark except for the slivers of blue light pouring from my palm. Trying to catch my breath, I opened my hand. The vadati was glowing. I'd fallen asleep clutching it. My chest heaved, sweat beading behind my neck, my mind still halfway in the nightmare.

I clutched the stone to my heart.

"Lyr?" Rhyan spoke again. "I know it's late. Or early, depending on how you look at it. I hope you're asleep. And having a good dream. I hope at least one of us is getting rest." He sounded miserable. "I miss you." There was a loud sigh, and I was about to respond when he continued, "I'm sorry for earlier. I'm sorry for this whole week. I shouldn't have left. You were right. I ran away. Like a coward. And I'm sorry." There was a long pause. "I'm so sorry. I've been miserable here. Not sleeping. Worrying about you. Feeling so fucking guilty. Stupid." He groaned. "I know what gryphon-shit it was to even think I could even the score. Or make amends. I know that's not possible. It will never be even, it will never be enough. I left because...because I was scared." His voice broke. "I failed. I didn't keep them safe. Like I didn't keep my mother safe. Or...Garrett."

Garrett? He'd never spoken that name before.

"And I just kept thinking, what if I'm not strong enough for you? What if I fail you? Lyriana," he sobbed my name.

"Rhyan," I said. "I'm here."

"Partner?"

"I'm here."

"Did—" There was a slight rustling that echoed beyond his voice like he was shifting in his blankets. "Did you hear everything?"

"I did."

There was a long pause and then, "I'm sorry."

"It's okay. Just come back. Please?"

"I am. I'm coming home to you tomorrow. First thing. I swear."

"Thank the Gods." I breathed a sigh of relief, lying back against my pillows. "What happened?" All week he'd barely spoken to me, refused to give me his oath that he'd return. I'd seen him like this before, going down a self-destructive path. He'd tried to convince me he was bad, unworthy. He'd allowed his past failures and father's words to mess with his mind. But the last time this had happened, I'd been with him and able to talk him down, bring him back to me. I couldn't help him when he was away, not when he was shutting me out.

He was silent.

"Rhyan? Please. You barely spoke to me all week. Did something happen tonight? What changed?"

I could hear him shifting again. "Nothing. Everything. We had a close call. Me and an akadim. I killed it. Add it to the list," he said with a laugh, though I could tell he was covering a deeper emotion.

Three akadim kills for him. I wouldn't count Haleika. That was mine. And it was one I'd never brag about.

I pulled my blankets up to my chest. "Are you okay? Are you hurt?"

He let out a heavy breath. "No. A little bruised. Not hurt."

"Do you swear?"

"I swear. I'm not hurt. Just had a close call. The beast came up behind me, caught me off guard. It's dead now."

"Auriel's bane." I clutched my chest, taking my own deep breath. "And that changed things for you?" I tried to control my breathing, hating how worried and fearful I felt knowing he'd come so close to one of the monsters, knowing it had bruised him.

Only a bruise was miraculous. But still.

"It, well, I wouldn't say it clarified anything. Shit, Lyr, the moment I left, I regretted it. And I missed you so fucking much. But I was so messed up. I just, I don't know, I needed some time to get myself together. The nightmares...they were so bad. You were having them, tossing and turning in my arms, crying, and I was having them with you, and I felt so helpless, and I just...I panicked. I'm sorry. And then tonight, when there was a moment, and—" His breathing grew heavy. I was having trouble understanding his words, he seemed so overcome with emotion. "I thought, fuck. What if I never see you again? I couldn't bear it. Couldn't bear the thought. Fucking tore me apart."

"You will see me again."

"Gods, I just want to hold you."

"I want that, too."

"Tomorrow," he said.

"Yes. Tomorrow. Are you coming home the traditional way?"

"I have to. I'm traveling with the task force. They'd notice."

"So not until tomorrow evening?"

"Most likely. I'll come to you first. The moment I'm back. Wherever you are, I'll find you."

"Good."

"Be careful until then, partner."

"I will."

"Swear," he demanded.

"I swear."

"Okay." He paused. "It's almost morning. I, um, I should—"

"Wait," I said. "Don't go yet. I'm awake, and I don't want to stop talking to you."

There was a sigh of relief on his end. The vadati swelled with blue light as if it were his breath. "Good. I needed to hear your voice."

"You could have, you know?" I said. "All week."

"I know. Sorry. How are you feeling?"

I shook my head. "About the same. Sad. This...this hurts less at some point, right?"

"At some point," he said softly. "Have you made any progress on the contract?"

"The only thing that makes sense right now because of my being Asherah is that Mercurial really did put some of the original light into me. But otherwise, no. And I haven't seen him. But I saw Ramia today in the library. I think she was away until now."

"She's the one who gave you the necklace—I mean, the armor?"

"Yes. And she said something strange about Mercurial." I pulled my knees to my chest, hearing the bells in the distance. The faint light of the ashvan on patrol flew past my window.

"Strange how?" Rhyan asked.

"She said he was missing."

"Missing? An Afeya?" Rhyan grunted. "They vanish all the time. We just saw him last week. I wish he was actually missing, finally leaving you alone."

"No, she really seemed genuinely concerned. I've never seen her show emotion before. I don't know, I believe her. And when he left your place, it seemed like something had gone wrong."

"Maybe. But I wouldn't be worried about the bastard. He'd be protected under Afeyan law from any misconduct as a First Messenger. Unless his Royal Highness, Queen Ishtara, decided to take him out, my guess is he's off tormenting someone else in between visits to you."

"Ramia had a different theory of what might have happened to him." I bit my lip. "You said that Lumerian power doesn't come close to an Afeya's. And Mercurial wants mine. What could he need it for? What if he needs me to fight someone more powerful?"

"Like who?"

"Like a god."

There was a long pause on Rhyan's end before he said, "Lyr, I don't like this."

"Me neither."

I ran my hand through my hair, knowing I needed to tell him all of what I'd learned about the shard and Asherah in my mother's journal. He'd want to know. He needed to. But it involved his father, and I wasn't sure if now was the time to bring that up. He was already upset, and it was the middle of the night. He'd just calmed down after losing it for a week. He'd faced an akadim and nearly died, just a week after having to fight for his life and mine.

I couldn't tell him now that his father was involved more than he'd already suspected. I'd tell him as soon as he was back. For now, it was enough to know he was safe—bruised, lonely, but safe. And it was enough to know he was coming home and to hear his northern lilt again.

"Don't do anything else until I'm back. Lyr, promise me. As much as I hate the bastard, him being gone...I don't know what trouble that spells for you. Shit. As if I wasn't having enough nightmares about the past, now I have them about the future."

"Were you having nightmares all week?" I asked.

"Yes," he admitted. "Luckily, it's snowing here. Or someone might have noticed."

I'd once seen Rhyan's full-blown nightmare in action. He had caused a blizzard in his apartment, had been freezing until I'd woken him from it. "Are you warm enough, despite?"

He gave a small laugh. "Don't worry," he said, his accent comically exaggerated. "We northerners have ice in our blood."

I laughed. "Be that as it may, when you come back, I'm staying with you. In your bed. Every night from now on."

I'd meant it to sound practical. We slept better together, keeping each other from nightmares, the cold of winter, and our pasts. And if we were both having nightmares, we could take turns. But the moment the words were out of my mouth, my skin flushed.

There was a long pause, and then he said, voice scratchy, "Are you now?"

I chewed the corner of my lip. "I mean, um, if that's okay? Just because of, you know, nightmares and sleeping and—"

"Partner, I know. It's okay." I could tell he was smiling. It made me smile, too. "It's more than okay. I like that idea a lot."

"You do?"

His voice deepened. "Do you have any idea how much I want you in my bed?"

Heat spread through me. "So I can protect you from bad dreams?" I asked, my heart beating faster.

"Well, there's that," he said slyly. "But also the fact that I," he lowered his voice, the sound echoing like he was cupping the stone against his mouth, "I desperately want to bed you."

The heat pooled in my stomach then moved lower. My breath caught, and I licked my lips.

"Have you been thinking about that?" I squeezed my legs together.

"I'm thinking about it now." He coughed, and there were more shifting sounds—fabric against fabric.

"You're moving around a lot," I said, realizing I was also moving on my bed, sinking deeper beneath my blankets, lying back.

"Had to, um, make an adjustment."

I grinned. "An adjustment?" I tried to affect my most proper heir voice. "Why, whatever do you mean by an adjustment?"

"You want to play that game?" he asked, a low growl in his voice.

I made some sort of noise halfway between a breath and a moan and involuntarily lifted my hips, my legs still pressed as tightly together as I could manage.

"What I mean, partner, is that my cock is so fucking hard for you right now my pants are too tight."

My breath caught. I could see him in my mind, lying under the blankets on his small cot in his tent. Probably in soft gray pants, a matching pair to the ones I was wearing. I held the vadati with my left hand and ran my right down my legs, down his pants, the thick material soft and worn after so many nights of wearing it. "Your pants are loose on me," I teased.

"My—wait, you're wearing my pants right now?"

"And your shirt. I've worn them every night this week."

"Lyr," he groaned. "Hearing that, you're making it worse."

My hand slid up and down my thigh. "I'm so sorry. You must be so terribly uncomfortable right now."

"Do we need to have a discussion, you and me, about the word 'sorry'? Because from your tone of voice, I don't think you're sorry at all." There was a threatening edge to his words, something feral and hungry that made my toes curl.

"And what are you going to do about that?"

"Only thing I can do. Start considering the proper punishment."

"I suppose we can discuss such things if you want," I said, surprised by how hungry my own voice sounded. "But I wouldn't worry so much about me in this moment. I think you're in quite a predicament right now. Maybe you should take care of your little problem."

There was a cocky laugh on his end. "I assure you, at this very moment, it is anything but little."

Gods. "Really?" I said, pulse racing. "Well, then," I swallowed roughly, "what are you going to do about it?"

"No, Lyr. What are *you* going to do about it? It's your fault. I think you should be the one to fix the problem."

I blushed, squirming on the bed beneath the blankets. "Maybe tomorrow I can."

"I won't survive until then." His breaths grew louder, more erratic, more intense. "I think you're going to have to help me out, partner, right now."

I gasped. "Rhyan, what? Are you—are you going to travel?" I whispered.

"Would be worth it." He groaned. "So fucking worth it. But I'm staying right where I am. And so are you."

"Then how am I—?"

"Where's your hand?" he asked.

"What?"

"You heard me, Lyr. Where is your hand? Tell me."

Oh. *Oh!* I felt my eyes widen. He was.... Gods. I'd never thought of this before. My heart started pounding so hard I wouldn't have been surprised if he could hear it.

"Lyr," he said, a warning in his voice.

"On your pants," I said, voice high.

"Where on my pants?" His accent curled around his words, low and hoarse.

"On my thigh."

"Put your hand inside," he commanded.

Exhaling sharply, I slid my hand up to the waistband and then inside his pants, settling my palm back against my leg. My thighs clenched together. "I did."

"Where's your hand now?" he asked, voice somehow even lower.

"My leg," I said.

"Hmmm. What if you put it between your legs?" He shifted again, and a groan filled the vadati. "What if you imagine it's my hand there? My fingers teasing you, touching you?"

The image was so clear in my mind and so clearly felt between my legs I almost gasped out loud. Trying to compose myself, I said slowly, "I might do that. If you tell me where your hand is."

"Already there."

"Are you...?" Fuck. I couldn't ask this. I threw my head back, squeezing my eyes shut, and pulled the rest of the blanket up over my face as if he or anyone else could see, as if anyone would know. I'd never done anything like this with Tristan. Not that either of us had vadati stones, but even in person, we'd never been very vocal together. Our intimate encounters had been mainly silent with a few compliments thrown in. Nothing like...nothing like this.

"Am I what, partner?" he teased.

I shook my head. "I can't say it."

"Yes, you can," he said, his voice full of mischief. "Use your words. I know you have them. So, so many of them."

"Rhyan, I...I don't know."

"Is this too much? Do you want to stop?" he asked, his voice suddenly serious. "We can."

"No, I don't. I just...." I needed a moment to compose myself, to make my desire, my brain, and my mouth somehow work together. I exhaled sharply. Breathlessly, I asked, "Are you touching yourself—now—under your pants?"

"Not under my pants," he said. "I had to pull those down...take myself out."

My chest was rising and falling in rapid succession. "You're doing that now? Stroking it?"

His breathing grew heavier. "Yes."

By the Gods. I slid my hand inside my underwear and down my center. I was soaked.

"Are you?" he asked.

"Yes."

"You're so wet now, aren't you?" he crooned.

"Rhyan!"

"Come on, partner. I know how you can get. I knew when I found your underwear in my bed."

"Gods," I moaned, my entire body heating.

"Hmmmm," he said. "I thought about that morning so many times."

"I did, too." My hand pressed harder against my center.

"I thought about you in the shower right after. Had to relieve myself twice. And every morning after that."

Twice? "What did you think about when you did that?"

"I thought about the way you looked underneath me, the sounds you made as we kissed, the way you gripped my ass and pulled me closer, grinding against me, driving me farther than fucking Lethea. Gods, Lyr. I wanted you so much, your hair in my hands, your tongue in my mouth, your soft skin filling all my senses."

I lifted my hips into my hand, my heels pressing down onto the bed as I began to rock, rolling my hips up and down, pretending my hand was his hand, then his cock. It felt so good.

"Did you ever think about me?" he asked.

"All the time." I rolled against myself, my fingers rubbing right over my core, circling. A moan escaped my lips before I could stop myself.

"Fuck, Lyr. Do that again."

"Do what?"

"Make that sound. Please. I want to hear you."

I made a small sound of surprise and pleasure. Then I breathed through my mouth, so turned on, my inner walls clamped together. Gods, the way he described that morning....

For a second, my embarrassment kicked in. Was I really doing this?

Yes. Yes, I was. This was Rhyan. Rhyan, who made me feel safer than anyone else ever had. Remembering that gave me the courage to let loose. To thrust against myself, to coat my fingers with my wetness and moan again, louder that time. And then again, even louder.

"Lyr, yes. Just like that." Rhyan fell silent, his breaths heavy through the stone, and then I could hear the sounds one made when rubbing...when fisting a cock. I could hear his movements, hear them increasing in speed, hear the rustling of his blankets beneath him with every thrust into his hand. He was quiet otherwise, and I realized I didn't want that. I didn't want that at all.

"I want to hear you," I said, and before I could stop myself, the words were spilling out. "I want to hear you moan. I want to hear you growl—hear the sounds you make as you take your pleasure and know that it's all for me."

"Fuck," he groaned.

"Fair's fair," I teased breathlessly.

"You were the one who owed me," he said. His breaths grew heavier, louder, like he wasn't controlling them anymore. And then, at last, he growled.

I moaned in response, circling my center again, gasping, my hips lifting and falling, my muscles tightening. I could feel a crescendo building, my pleasure increasing in a way it never had before—not even close. It had never felt this good before by myself or with anyone else. Anyone but Rhyan. He'd almost gotten me to this place that morning, and then in the temple, in the cave....

Every time, I had been so turned on by him, I could feel myself getting closer and closer to the edge. And every time, we'd been interrupted.

For the first time, we were going to finish. Gods, this was really happening. The sensations I felt as I listened to him move, breathe, and moan were intoxicating. We weren't even in the same country, and yet I'd never felt closer to him, never more vulnerable. That alone was going to make me explode.

I gasped and gave a strangled cry as I hit another wave of pleasure.

He groaned. "Are you close, Lyr?" His breathing was rapid and shallow. "You sound so fucking close."

"Yes," I cried, moving faster. "Yes."

"Move the stone down between your legs," he barked.

"What?"

"Put it between your legs. I want to hear it. I want to hear how fucking wet you are. I want to hear the sound your fingers make as they slide through your cunt."

By the Gods, I was going to come right then and there. For a second, I hesitated, nervous. Then I pulled down my underwear and Rhyan's pants, slid them off my legs, and placed the vadati on the bed right between them.

Staring down my body, I could see my bared skin, Rhyan's sweatshirt pushed up against my exposed belly, the golden chain across my waist where the stone had been, my hand working furiously over my center, and my hips thrusting into my palm...all glowing in the blue light of the vadati.

"Gods, Lyr. So good."

I threw my head back, adding a second hand, sliding a finger inside myself, moaning and gasping and thrusting until...until....

I cried out. My feet slid out, and my knees shook, as my hips lifted one more time before I collapsed on the bed, my legs splayed.

"Rhyan," I gasped, chest heaving.

"Fuck, you sound pretty when you come."

I reached down for the stone and laid it between my breasts, watching it rise and fall with my breaths, imagining him on the other side, his eyes hooded, sweat curling his hair, his biceps flexing, hips thrusting. "Now you. Come for me, Rhyan. I want to hear you come undone. I want to hear you moan as you take your pleasure. And I want to hear my name on your lips when you explode."

"Fuck, where did you learn to—" He gasped. "FUCK!" he roared. "Lyr! Lyr!" I could hear every stroke, every forceful huff of his breath. "LYR!"

I swallowed, my core tightening again. I was still trying to collect myself, to catch my breath.

We were both silent for a moment, the sounds of our heavy breathing coming through the stone as we settled back down.

"Partner, you okay?" he asked.

"Just remembering how to breathe. You?"

"Same," Rhyan said, laughing. "Gods. That was...you were...I mean, I knew you had a mouth on you, partner, but Auriel's fucking bane."

"That was okay?" I asked, unsure.

"That was the best thing I've ever heard. You have nothing to be embarrassed about. I loved it." He took another deep breath and laughed again. "Shit, Lyr, you're not even here, and you still managed to get my sheets all dirty again."

"Oh, Gods," I said, biting my lip, half ashamed, half...absolutely loving the effect I had on him. I never would have expected to say all the things I'd just said or to do...this. My chest felt so warm, and for the first time in a week, it was warm in a good way—not from the Valalumir or my contract. It was warm from Rhyan.

"Good thing I'm coming home tomorrow," he teased. "Too cold to do laundry out here."

"Good thing," I said, unable to stop myself from grinning.

"Do me a favor, partner?"

"What?" I whispered.

"Wear my pants the rest of the night." His voice was gruff. "Just the pants. No underwear."

I flushed, still unable to breathe normally.

"Why?"

"I just like the idea. A lot."

I licked my lips and reached for his pants, pushing my feet through the leg holes and sliding them back up my heated skin. I kicked my underwear and what remained of my blanket off the bed—I was still hot. I ran my hand over my center, now covered in his clothes. "They're on. Exactly as requested."

"Good girl."

I was still blushing. "Did we really just do that?"

"The mess I made says yes."

I laughed.

"But seriously, Lyr, are you okay? Was that...too much?"

"No. I needed this. Needed you. I love you," I said.

"I love you, too," he whispered. "Thank you."

"For what?"

"I needed this. More than you know." He sighed. "And now I might actually get some sleep."

"Will you fall asleep with me?" I asked. "I like knowing you're there, hearing you breathe. Even if it's just through a stone."

"It's taking all my willpower to stay in place, to not travel and wrap you up in my arms. I want to hold you."

"Me, too. I wish you were here."

"I will be soon. I swear. *Me sha, me ka,* Lyriana. Close your eyes and know I'm coming home to you. Tomorrow night, you'll be falling asleep where you belong. In my arms." His breathing deepened the way it did when he was trying to calm me, to pull me from a panic attack.

And for the first time in days, I wasn't afraid to fall asleep.

Someone was pounding on my door. I rolled over in my bed. Sunlight I hadn't seen in days was streaming through the window, blinding. The vadati was by my side, silent now.

Auriel's bane. My cheeks were completely heated as I remembered what I'd done with the stone the night before. Gods...Rhyan and I had...and said....

The pounding grew more intense, pulling me back to reality. I slid the stone back onto its chain, tucked it into my pants—Rhyan's pants—pulled my hair into a quick bun, and headed for the door, my pulse quickening as I swung it open.

Markan stood on the other side, and I prayed he didn't look too closely at my clothes.

"Now they have me playing fucking messenger," he snarled.

"It's customary to begin a conversation at this hour with good morning."

"Good morning. Here's a message for you. My lady." He shoved a scroll into my hand, a tiny piece of parchment sealed with the sigil of Ka Batavia. It was from my aunt.

Sweat beaded at the base of my neck as I broke the seal, the wax splitting between the full moon and the seraphim wings.

Dear Lyriana,

Please come to dinner tonight at Cresthaven. Imperator Hart of Glemaria arrived just this morning for the consecration. Formal attire as usual. A seraphim will be waiting at the Urtavian port to bring you at 6PM.

Love,

Aunt Arianna

I was having dinner with Rhyan's father.

CHAPTER EIGHTEEN

I STEPPED ONTO THE waterway within the fortress walls, the sky, full of stars, glittering on the glass below me. The air was frigid with the winds of winter, but the waterway flowed swiftly. the water no longer frozen beneath my feet.

"Your grace." One of the port attendants bowed then quickly straightened and coughed. A dash of embarrassment in his aura swept across my arms. "Lady," he corrected.

I waved him off and walked forward, my fingers twisting in the skirt of my gown as I approached the promenade, every nerve in my body alert.

I'd been praying all day Rhyan would have returned by now. I'd waited for him at my apartment until the last possible second before venturing out to reach my seraphim at Arianna's appointed time. I needed to talk to him. In all that had happened between us last night, he still didn't know what I'd learned—that the answer to finding my power was in Glemaria, and that his father had the key.

He also didn't know I wanted to speak to his father to find out what I could, which he would definitely be upset about. I'd wanted to brace him by telling him about my plan first.

And I'd wanted to see him after our...I didn't know what to call it. The conversation between us had been so intense, so intimate, I still felt a strange mix of elation and vulnerability hours later. My cheeks blushing, my heart racing everytime I replayed his words in my head.

But there was no sign of him, and there'd been no calls on the vadati all day. Most likely he was traveling, surrounded by others. I just hoped he got back soon.

A litter with green velvet curtains and silver threading depicting a gryphon was surrounded by a dozen mages outside the fortress walls just left of the promenade. My stomach dropped. This was Imperator Hart's litter. I remembered it from his last visit with Rhyan.

The front doors opened, and Euston and Rhodes both greeted me, their faces drawn as I stepped inside the Great Hall.

There was a change in the feel of the Cresthaven that I noticed immediately. A colder, more brutal aura overlaid what I'd grown up experiencing. I barely recognized my own home. It was full of Glemarians, all Imperator Hart's men. His soturi wore black leathered armor like Rhyan and heavy soturion-issued boots. Thick leather straps across their chests. Their eyes followed me as I walked through the hall, tracking and assessing my progress, but no one reacted otherwise to my presence, and I couldn't tell if that was from their training or because without my diadem, they had no idea who I was.

A guard from Ka Batavia stood outside the dining hall, though not one I was familiar with. Perhaps it was someone new who had proven her loyalty to Arianna. I eyed her suspiciously even after she nodded at Markan and opened the door for us, calling out my name to formally announce my entrance.

I stepped inside, finding myself face to face with Tristan and Naria. Shit. All of Ka Grey was apparently in attendance tonight. It was as if the two kavim had already merged despite the wedding date not even having been set yet—unless I'd missed the announcement. Which was entirely possible considering how distracted I was. The remaining members of the Bamarian Council along with their significant others filled the room, everyone decked out in fine velvets and satins. We were still in our mourning period, but hardly anyone wore black. Most had returned to wearing the colors and symbols of their Ka.

At a head table in the center, sitting on golden chairs, were Arianna, and Rhyan's father, Arkasva Hart, High Lord of Glemaria, Imperator to the North.

My body stiffened.

I felt the cold the moment his eyes landed on me. It was nothing like Rhyan's aura. Rhyan brought forth the soft side of

winter, the calm cold I needed to soothe me when I was too
fired up or anxious.

Devon Hart's coldness was strangling and oppressive, giving me the sensation of being lost in a desolate wasteland. It
was frigid and biting, an endless darkness I wanted to take
cover from.

Imperator Hart had a similar height and build to Rhyan. He
was certainly older, but like many soturi, clearly in robust
health, his body one of thick muscle. His hair was shorn
short, a mix of black and gray, as was his closely trimmed
beard. His hairline receded a little at his temples, but otherwise it appeared thick. I recognized the distinct shape of
Rhyan's eyebrows though Imperator Hart didn't carry a scar.
And that detail alone evoked a sudden rage within me.

I'd told Rhyan I'd wanted to kill his father for what he'd
done to him—what he still did to him—and I could feel that
anger burning now. My fingers clenched into fists, as the
dagger sheathed at my thigh began to feel heavy.

Imperator Hart's eyes were on me, cruel and calculated, as
he lowered his chin and bowed in respect. He straightened
with a false smile on his lips and with a flick of his finger,
beckoned me forward.

I gritted my teeth. I may have lost my status, but I was
not one to be beckoned. I did not come when called. And
certainly not to this monster.

*We unlock for blood, soul, and key. Power is restored, with
these three.*

I exhaled sharply. I had to put back on my mask. Be Lady
Lyriana. Be pliant and pleasant. He had the key, and I needed
it. My personal feelings didn't matter.

I started to nod, but then Morgana appeared at my side and
grabbed my arm, dragging me to the table where she sat with
Meera and a few of the daughters and sons of Council members. Nobles I'd been acquainted with my entire life—but had
grown apart from after we lost Jules.

"Were you just about to go speak to Imperator Hart?"
Morgana's eyebrows lifted in surprise.

Morgana didn't know about our mother's journal. Or the
key.

"Lyr," she hissed. "What in Moriel? I can't read your mind,
remember?"

"I found something out. About Meera's vision," I said. "I think Rhyan was right. It was definitely Glemaria, and I think—"

Before I could say more, the herald announced, "Arkturion Aemon Melvik, Warlord of Bamaria, and Turion Dairen Melvik, Second." The Ready was here.

Aemon entered the room dressed in his full armor. His eyes immediately fell on Rhyan's father, and his aura darkened as a sneer fell across his lips while he crossed the room.

Auras of the nobles around me began to crackle, filling with palpable tension. Everyone felt alert, expectant, as if preparing for a fight. Their postures remained proper while their necks strained and their eyes watched, eager to bear witness to this new development.

"Are they all reacting to Aemon?" I asked under my breath, knowing Morgana felt the change in auras, too.

She nodded solemnly. "Everyone is remembering the rebellion, how he got his nickname. I think some are wondering if he'll do something else. Earn some new title in the process." Morgana rolled her eyes. "Not likely. For that to happen, there'd need to an open declaration of war. But the snakes are in the shadows."

"Anything new there?" I asked, voice low. "Have you learned anything else?"

Morgana narrowed her eyes. "This is so strange. I'm so used to hearing you."

I remained silent. Even though any unexplained change to my body or to Morgana's vorakh was concerning, I didn't mind this one side effect of the Valalumir in my heart. For once, I didn't have to review all my thoughts in front of Morgana to make sure I wouldn't upset or offend her. And it was comforting to know my *conversation* with Rhyan last night would remain a secret between the two of us. She'd been privy to too many of our intimate moments already, and that one...no one needed access to that one. It was ours, for us alone.

"Let's sit," she said. "Arianna's about to start talking."

I let Morgana lead me to my chair, aware of Imperator Hart's eyes still on me. I'd selected a green dress for the night, and my armor covered the star over my chest. I wore my usual arm cuff and the golden chain around my waist with the vadati. A silver belt lay on top—I'd chosen silver to impress Rhyan's father, not Ka Grey, for once.

Arianna stood up, holding out a glass of wine. She toasted to us, her three nieces—the nieces she grieved with for the death of our father.

Gryphon-shit.

Then more congratulations were offered to Naria and Tristan. There was a lump in my throat as they stood together, hand in hand. Sorrow filled Tristan's brown eyes, but I no longer felt anything toward him.

At last, Arianna welcomed Rhyan's father.

"Your highness, Imperator Hart," she said. "Welcome back to Bamaria."

He stood, a wide smile on his face as he turned toward my sisters and I and lifted his cup. "It's good to be back. I have missed this country and her people. And while I am saddened for your loss, I am looking forward to the next steps in the development of our relationship. To the future of Glemaria's continued friendship with Bamaria." He spoke in the formal, educated way of the nobility, the way I had perfected and that Rhyan spoke when needed. Not once did I hear the lilt of Glemaria escape his lips. The perfection of his tone somehow made him feel even colder, like there was something completely unnatural about his entire person.

Imperator Hart turned, his black cloak sliding behind his shoulder to reveal the belt at his waist and the hilt of his sword. The handle was thick, covered in shining black leather like the armor of Ka Hart, but right in the center was the exact symbol my mother had drawn into her journal—a Batavia-red star with seven points, each one curved like the rays of the sun. The key.

He gulped down his wine, finishing his glass in one go, before he delicately wiped his mouth with the back of his hand and grinned.

Several of the nobles cheered, but most of the amusement in the room came from the soturi, as if they respected him for this. Despite how formal and cold he was, he seemed like he truly wanted to please the soturi in the room, to be considered one of them.

His eyes found me again, and he lifted his empty glass to me then sat down, as Arianna called for the feast to begin.

I sat with my shoulders tensed, my back straight, slowly eating and wondering what to do. Maybe I didn't need to talk to him. Maybe I only needed to find a way to steal the key from his sword. A theft would be simpler, and if done properly, I'd have no interaction with him.

"What are you plotting?" Morgana asked, as the musicians used a volume-enhancing spell on their instruments. They'd stopped playing the slower, quieter music used for dinners and had begun to play a dance. Drums beat in the corners of the hall, their rhythms quickening. I recognized the music at once, a popular water dance. One I used to perform, and as if on cue, water dancers in gold and red silk costumes with blue ribbons tied to their ankles streamed into the room, their hips shimmying to the drums.

We hadn't had water dancers perform in Cresthaven for more than two years. My heart panged.

I took a deep breath, knowing we had the cover of the music to speak. It was time to fill in Morgana on what I'd learned and to start plotting a way to get the key.

But Turion Dairen and Aemon appeared before us.

I barely held back my sneer as Dairen bowed to me and my sisters. He'd never showed such respect in the Katurium.

Aemon's eyes were on me, dark and shadowy. "The Imperator's task force has just returned," he said. "Your security team will be back in full force very shortly."

I felt a weight lift off my shoulders. He meant Rhyan. Rhyan would be back.

But I carefully schooled my face to remain neutral. I couldn't let on what it meant to me or how excited I was after a week apart to see him.

I lifted my glass. "Considering the volume of guests now entering the country, I suppose that's a good thing."

Aemon smirked. "I do have some concerns I'd like to discuss." He turned toward Meera and held out a hand. "Will you dance with me, my lady?"

Meera elegantly nodded and stuck out her hand for Aemon to take. It was so like what would have happened without thought for the last few years if we hadn't been cursed, but Father had rarely held such fancy dinners since Meera's visions had started. Now, I could almost see what would have been—all of us regularly dressed up for parties, carefree, dancing with the nobles of Bamaria, not constantly hiding. Courting freely, openly who we wanted.

Noticing Arianna's eyes narrowing as Aemon took Meera into his arms shattered the illusion at once. A pit formed in my stomach as reality returned. We'd been cursed. Our father had been murdered.

Dairen held out his hand to Morgana, and though she grimaced—no fonder of the Ready's Second than I was—she accepted and stood, holding his hand as she walked out from behind the table with the folds of her dress shimmering beneath the torchlight.

That left me sitting alone, suddenly acutely aware of Naria's icy glare and her hands crawling over Tristan's shoulders and chest. She pointed her engagement ring toward me, the movement forcing her hand into an awkward position that startled him. Tristan's eyes met mine, then immediately, he looked away. I reached for my wine, my arm prickling with goosebumps.

A shadow loomed over me as I swallowed and practically crashed my cup against the table.

"My lady," said Imperator Hart.

I looked up. "Your highness." I began to push back my chair so I might stand and curtsy, but he shook his head, clicking his tongue lightly.

"Stay," he said, sitting informally on the edge of my table. "No need to bow. Up in the north, we don't require such formalities."

I willed my stomach to settle as his aura struck out at me. "How was your journey to Bamaria?"

"Cold. Unlike the last time." He shrugged, his eyes narrowing down on me. His hand rested on the table before reaching for my wine glass, the rim of which his finger traced in slow circles. "I hear you and my...offspring have formed a *kashonim*."

My throat went dry. "Upon our arkmage and arkturion's assessment, yes," I said, my eyes zeroing in on his sword hilt, on the red star—the key. It was so close, within an arm's reach.

"Hmmm," he said, sounding amused. "For your sake, I do hope he is doing his job."

"He is, your highness. He's an excellent teacher."

"Is he now?" He picked up my goblet, his forefinger stained from the rim, and brought it to his nose. He swished the wine inside then sniffed it. "May I?"

"Of course," I said, sitting straighter.

His eyes remained on me, as he tipped the glass back, his throat working as he swallowed all I hadn't yet drunk. "Hmmm.

I remember Bamarian wine from my last visit." His lips lifted in amusement. "I am sorry about your father, of course," he said, voice suddenly solemn. "*Bar Ka Mokan.*"

"His soul freed. I thank you, your highness."

"Shame. Being arkasva...." He shook his head. "Not what it used to be." His hand struck out across the table, grabbing hold of mine.

Only through years of training, of having been raised by Arianna to please disgusting, entitled noblemen, was I able to keep my fingers delicate against his.

Leaning forward, he added, "If I can do anything to help you, Lady Lyriana, please let me know."

As he pressed his palm against mine, I willed myself not to pull away in disgust. All I could think about was breaking every one of his hateful fingers, every finger that had touched Rhyan in violence, that had hurt him. I wanted to shatter their bones and rip them from his hand one by one, slice them into little pieces that I'd shove down his throat.

"I am also sorry to hear," he continued, "about the loss of your engagement. Or is it more accurate to say the loss of the engagement to become engaged?" He smirked again, and again, I found it odd that not once did his accent convey even the slightest hint of the northern lilt Rhyan and Sean favored. "News from the south sometimes reaches the north in a very slow manner."

"Yes, I imagine with the whole Empire standing between us."

"You must be in want of a new engagement, my lady. Perhaps one that includes...a ring this time?" He turned his head toward Tristan and back to me, the pad of his thumb tracing a line across my ring finger. "Mayhap, someone more mature?"

I shuddered. "First, I plan to grieve my father after my aunt Arianna is consecrated and then complete my studies. It will be years before I think of such things."

"Wise," he said. "I remember now, you're a smart girl. My last visit, you gave a wonderful tour of the Great Library. You were so young, enthusiastic."

"It's one of Bamaria's treasures," I said carefully. "Offering a tour of the ancient scrolls is an honor."

"I must admit, I did not pay so much attention to the scrolls as I did to you."

I exhaled sharply. I didn't want to be nice. I didn't want to give this man one second of satisfaction. But I needed something from him.

I swallowed back the bile rising in my throat and looked up at him through my lashes. "You flatter me, your highness."

My gaze darted to the key. It looked like it had been sewn into the leather. Getting it wasn't going to be as simple as stealing it. The entire hilt's design would need to be taken apart.

"You are quite bold, my lady," he said with a seductive laugh.

Startled, I looked up. "Your highness?"

"My eyes are up here."

I bit the inside of my cheek. It was time to bet. "I apologize," I said, acting embarrassed. "I was simply admiring the hilt of your sword. That red star, it's unlike any I've seen before. Not part of the sigil for Ka Hart."

Imperator Hart's eyes narrowed quickly on me, then he laughed, the corners of his eyes crinkling. "No, it is quite unique. A rare find. It has been passed down for generations in my Ka. An heirloom of Lumeria Matavia."

"Fascinating," I said. "Most heirlooms of Ka Hart are green, are they not?"

"Ah." His eyes were alight with mischief. "Are you accusing me of stealing a possession of Ka Batavia's simply because it is red?"

I forced a laugh. I hadn't said anything even close to that. For him to have suggested such a thing on his own—his words felt like a confession. "I would never even insinuate. Merely curious. I have an interest in ancient artifacts. Perhaps, because it is red, I am drawn to it."

"You would be," he said, voice suddenly filled with a deadly edge.

I sat back, my veins rippling with his unspoken threat.

Before I could hide my discomfort, he gave me a conspiratorial wink. "I hear you slayed an akadim."

"Yes."

"Thanks to your...tutoring?" He squeezed my hand in his too tightly. Enough to bruise. Enough to make it so I'd be unable to pick up a sword for a day. Tears burned behind my eyes, but I blinked them back.

"My apprentice has well prepared me for the Emperor's task."

He looked me up and down, bringing his other hand forward and sandwiching mine between his. The pressure was temporarily relieved, but now there was no escape from his touch. Every inch of my hand was against one of his. I'd have to boil my skin after this to get the smell and feel of him off me.

"Despite his many shortcomings and failures," Imperator Hart continued, "he is a good fighter. But, of course, he has to be. It was destined. I made him, after all. And I taught him everything he knows."

My blood was boiling.

You taught him nothing but fear and hatred. You taught him to second-guess himself, to see himself as unworthy, when it's you who's unworthy, you sick fuck.

I managed a polite nod. "I know that you are yourself a most accomplished soturion."

"Were I not destined to be Arkasva Hart and Imperator to the north, I would have been an arkturion," he said proudly.

"Would you have preferred that?" I asked. My hand was growing sweaty inside his. Disgust rolled through me. I wasn't sure how much more I could take. Instinct was going to override my social cues soon, and I was either going to pull away my trapped hand or slap him with my free one.

His eyes darkened, his aura swirling with that hurricane-like force that had terrified me as a child.

"It is treason in Glemaria to suggest I could be anything other than Arkasva."

My shoulders tensed. "I apologize, your highness. I meant no offense."

"Dance with me," he said suddenly. He released my hand so violently it fell on the table, and with one swift move, he stood, his posture expectant as he waited. There was no doubt on his end I'd follow his orders.

The Moriel-fucking bastard was right. I walked to his side.

He took my hand again, leading me onto the dance floor past Meera dancing formally with Aemon, past Morgana being twirled by Dairen, and past Tristan and Naria, their bodies pressed close.

I averted my gaze, barely noticing when Rhyan's father took both of my hands. He placed one on his broad shoulder, and the other, he squeezed between his fingers, his hold far too tight.

Tears sprang again to my eyes.

"Your highness," I said. "Your grip is...a bit tight."

"Too tight for an Imperator?" he asked. "Tight enough for an arkturion?" His grip was unrelenting as he pushed me back.

I stumbled, trying to remember the steps amidst the pain. "Please," I said, nearly stepping on my gown. "You would have been stellar in any role. That's why you're Arkasva of Glemaria," I winced, "Imperator of the North."

He softened at once and laughed as if it had all been a silly game. "My lady. I was testing you." He poked my nose with his finger, something a father might do to a child. "You killed an akadim. Surely, some hand holding wouldn't bother you."

I breathed through my nose, my stomach knotting with panic. Gods. Was this what Rhyan had faced growing up? Constantly shifting moods? A second-by-second change of humor to violence? Not knowing how his father would react, not being able to predict the correct way to respond? My heart was racing at just minutes of this.

"Back to my query," he said, serious again. "You are in a predicament, my lady. No longer heir and without power."

My eyes flicked back to his hilt as he spoke. I could feel the moment his eyes tracked mine, and I looked down at my dress, pretending to inspect the folds of my gown. I removed my hand from his shoulder to adjust the material. But anger was vibrating off of him, and I knew he'd noticed where my gaze had been, that he wasn't buying my game.

"I seem to have something you want," he said. "Perhaps, it is," he grabbed my chin, lifting my face toward his, "something you need?"

"Your highness," I said, keeping my voice light.

"I hear Imperator Kormac was inquiring about a marriage contract for you. But you should know, my lady, that I once spoke to your mother about such a thing. And your father upon my last visit. I know you would like to honor their wishes and both felt strongly you were a match for the north."

"Oh," I said, feigning ignorance.

"I would grant you what you seek if you were to agree to a Glemarian union."

There was only one Glemarian I'd ever marry, and I knew he'd never suggest it.

"A union with whom, your highness?"

His nostrils flared as he watched me, a knowing look in his expression, before he looked away. "You could have your say amongst the eligible suitors. And I'll make you a wedding present. The star you so fancy on my sword."

"I shall think on it," I said. "But as I mentioned, I'm not really looking to marry soon."

"You have less time than you think. You no longer have your title to keep you safe—to push off contracts for the sake of politics. Nor will the excuse of your eldest's sister singleness protect you. You will be married sooner than you think. What kept you safe will now be used against you. Your new arkasva must secure alliances. It is simply the way. I, at least, offer you something in return."

"I still would like to think about it."

"You'll need to be quick about it. You're not safe here, you know? Not from them. And not from me. Unfortunately, you no longer have your little protector to keep you safe."

"My protector?" I asked.

"Rhyan," he said, his voice a cold threat.

His father spun me across the floor, his movements picking up speed, my feet tripping to keep up as I danced backwards and in circles.

"Did he never tell you?" he asked.

"Tell me what, your highness?" I was starting to feel nauseated by the whole conversation and dance.

"Your father was about to have you married to our warlord, a most honorable man. But your apprentice did not like this. He threw quite a fit before me."

And I had to...had to do some negotiating to force him to end the marriage discussions.

My stomach twisted. "What did you do to him?" I asked, unable to stop my voice from going low.

"He had his Birth Bind put back in place—there was a need to quell his power. But that wasn't enough for his defiance. So he was bound again. Black ropes all across his body, his arms and legs. No one could see, of course, but him and me. He wore them for months, his skin heated and itchy, his power contained. Nearly drove him farther than Lethea."

Black spots appeared in my vision. The horror of Rhyan in ropes made me sick. I remembered now our final meeting years before. I'd dropped scrolls before him, and he'd been cold as he'd helped me pick them up. Distancing himself from me, from our kiss at solstice. Had he been bound then? Had he been covered, being tortured by the thing he hated, all so he could protect me? I'd been crushed, heartbroken. I had no idea what he'd been suffering at the time.

"I'm sorry," I said, my eyes burning. "I'm feeling dizzy."

I couldn't catch my breath. Rhyan had been protecting me for years, long before I'd had any idea he'd felt anything for me. He had been sacrificing, submitting to this monster, for so much longer than I'd known.

All for me.

"You look touched by his gesture," his father said, his hold tightening again. His fingers dug into my waist, and just as I was about to cry out in pain, he shook his head. "Now, now. You slayed an akadim. You need to show me you're strong. Or else the vultures will descend, and you'll be married before you know it to someone far worse with much less to offer."

My entire body was shaking. I wasn't going to play this game any longer.

"Ah. There she is. The mask comes off at last. Never forget, little slayer. You're one step above a forsworn. Powerless in more ways than you know right now. Your name no longer protects you with this new line of succession. And your lack of magic, it doesn't help. But I can make you whole. I can provide power, give you what you seek, if you give me what I want."

"And what is that?" I asked through gritted teeth.

"You and him. Back under my roof, my rules, my command."

"You exiled him. He's not in Glemaria because of you. That's your fault."

"He murdered his mother."

"He did not, and you Godsdamned well know it!"

"I won't even entertain what I believe you're suggesting. I am forgiving. I will forgive him for the crimes he committed out of fatherly love. He is strong, he doesn't know his strength sometimes. Mistakes happen. But this clemency comes under one condition—you come to me willingly, marry whom I choose, and bring him along."

"I would never do that to him."

He grinned. "You return his feelings for you. Interesting."

I snarled.

His head wobbled from side to side as if he was deliberating a decision. With an overly exasperated sigh, he said, "Then my pretty little heirloom remains at my waist. And if Rhyan ever steps foot outside of Bamaria again, I will have him. And this time, there will be no bargain. No negotiating. And even his little...ability to move around will not save him."

His hand shot to his belt, opening a green velvet pouch at his waist. A hissing sound emerged, one I'd heard before.

My body went cold.

"Go on," he commanded, squeezing me tighter. I almost bowed over.

"Your h-highness," I stuttered through the pain.

"Put your hand in my pocket," he ordered.

He'd danced us into a corner of the room that was dark and secluded. No one could see what he was doing. See that he was hurting me, threatening me.

Morgana wasn't far. She could come. She could stop it. But she couldn't hear me. My mind was closed to hers.

I watched Rhyan's father smile cruelly through his trim beard. "Please," I begged. "No."

"I didn't ask if you wanted to, my lady. I said, do it."

His hand snapped around my wrist like a viper and shoved my hand inside the pouch.

I clenched my fist, swallowing back a cry as something scaly and hot as fire slid up my palm.

Nahashim.

CHAPTER NINETEEN

I WAS SUDDENLY BACK in the Shadow Stronghold, lying on the bed before the examiner, nearly naked, vulnerable, and terrified. I'd been imprisoned for a week, hadn't seen my sisters or Tristan, and hadn't known why I was powerless. Two of the nahashim had slipped inside my body, searching me, violating me, slithering and sliding through my every inner wall, bone, and muscle, while the Imperator and Bastardmaker had stood outside, waiting for the results and delighting in my torment.

Rhyan's father leered at me in the present and made a shushing sound, his hand covering mine in the pouch hanging from his belt. His palm slid down the back of my hand, pushing the nahashim down. He closed the pouch and took my fingers between his, bringing them to his mouth. "There, there, my lady. It's all over. Hush now."

"What do you want?" I asked.

"I told you. For you to come to me in Glemaria. For you to bring him back."

"Why?"

A look of pure derision spilled across his features. Instead of answering my question, he twirled me in a circle before pulling me close. His breath was on my ear as he spoke, his tone now jovial and lighthearted. "Have you ever been to Lethea, the place where he should have ended up? I went there, but not to see criminals or watch the strippings. I had a different purpose."

I didn't respond. I simply stared ahead, willing my pounding heart to calm.

He continued, "We're up to our ears in gryphons. I was curious about the breeding and raising of other ancient beasts. Of nahashim. You see, my son has a habit of moving a little too quickly, staying out of my grasp. I doubt that's news to you. As soon as I learned this, I visited a farm, and I selected two of the snakes to bring back home. One male, one female. Have you ever seen nahashim mate?" He paused expectantly then frowned at my silence. "Oh, come now, my lady. It's a simple yes-or-no question. You can answer."

"No."

"It's quite violent, actually. At least, that's how it looked to me. A lot of thrashing. And you'd think they hiss—they hiss during everything else they do. But they don't hiss while they mate. They scream." He grinned.

I stared ahead, trying to get Morgana's or Meera's attention. Fuck, even Tristan would be able to read my face now.

"Not interested in the mating habits of nahashim?" he asked. "That's okay. The point is, I'd selected quite a virile male and a rather fertile female."

"Good for you," I seethed.

"Yes. Very good. Not good for Rhyan though."

I pulled back, meeting his gaze. "In what way?"

"Nahashim don't just find whatever you're looking for. They retrieve it. And I'm sure you saw the way their bodies expanded and retracted before they entered yours. I heard the ones they used on you were rather small. Necessary for fitting into," he licked his lips, "tight spaces. Mine, however, they can grow to over ten feet long. We keep our gryphons controlled by confining them. By tying them down with ropes before they know their strength. Letheans control their snakes the same way. They keep them inside little boxes, show them that this is all the space they have to take up. So they do. When my nahashim were born, I took the opposite approach. I gave them all the space they needed to grow and expand. And they did so beautifully. And now, I've trained them to find one thing: him. Since he left, every single nahashim has been born and raised to bring him back."

When Rhyan had revealed his vorakh to me, he'd said his father had beaten him every time he'd traveled—that, somehow, no matter where he'd travelled in the fortress, his father had always known. This was how. He'd trained the snakes to find vorakh, and then he'd beaten Rhyan for using it.

"If you touch him ever again—"

"Oh, I certainly will touch him," Imperator Hart said. "And there's nothing you can do to stop me, my lady, especially if you refuse my offer. Now, perhaps, I will have my snakes bring him to me. In which case, you will get nothing. Or," he pulled my hand back to his belt, this time forcing my fingers over the star embedded in the leather of his hilt.

For a second, my vision went out of focus. A male's voice sounded in my ear. Ancient, familiar. "Asherah." He was crying.

And then I was back on the dance floor with Rhyan's father, my hand pressed against the key.

"You come, too." He pushed harder, to the point where I knew there'd be a star-shaped mark on my skin. "You come, and you get this."

A dark shadow fell over us, and Rhyan's father stiffened. The Ready stood before us, his dark eyes ablaze with fury. "Your highness," he snarled, "I think you've kept the lady long enough. Release her."

"Release her? She's no prisoner. We're simply dancing. I'm getting to know the novice that my former heir has bound himself to," replied Imperator Hart, unclenching my hand from around his sword. "Your choice for this match I hear?"

"It was my choice, and it's worked well in the lady's favor as you well know. Your dance is over," the Ready said.

"I am free to dance with her as long as I wish. She's no longer heir. Do you understand how you're overstepping?" Imperator Hart asked, a challenge in his eyes. Were it to come down to it, I'd put my money on the Ready winning a battle against him. But Imperator Hart far outranked the Arkturion of Bamaria.

Aemon leaned forward. "Heir or not, the lady is still under my care and protection. Hands off my student."

Rhyan's father spun me to face Aemon before pulling my back against the black leather covering his chest. "Tell him you're fine, little slayer," he whispered into my ear. "Or I tell him you're in love with my son."

Black spots clouded my vision before I blinked them away. "I'm fine, Aemon. Thank you for the concern. I was, um—" And then I saw him. Rhyan. He was back, standing in the door to the ballroom, his green eyes wide, his hair dark and wild, his face pale as he took in the sight of me wrapped in his father's arms. His hands shook visibly, reaching for his sword, while a blazing fury spread across his face. "Aemon," I said desperately, jerking my chin at the door.

"Fuck," Aemon mouthed, taking off for the door and intercepting Rhyan before he could charge into the ballroom.

Rhyan's father released me. "You've told me all I need to know." I felt him move from behind me, but I didn't look back. I could barely move. I was too worried about Rhyan and what his father had revealed to me—that he had another weapon to use against us.

As the music slowed and servants entered the room with fresh goblets and decanters full of wine, Morgana appeared beside me and grabbed my arm. "Lyr, are you okay?"

"I need to talk to him. Now," I said, not taking my eyes off Rhyan, who was still raging at the door, his face turning red as he yelled at Aemon.

"Get him out of here," Morgana said. "Go to the door. Tell Aemon you want to go home. Too much wine. He'll believe it. He wants Rhyan out before he causes a scene with his father. I'll cover for you with Arianna."

"Thank you," I said and rushed for the door. I walked right up to Aemon and said the exact words Morgana had given me.

Aemon kept his hand on Rhyan's armored shoulder, literally holding him back from charging. "You're on duty then, Hart. Immediately."

Huffs of breath came from Rhyan's mouth, his expression feral. "I just returned from a week of hunting. I have another kill to my name," he roared, practically spitting as he spoke. His accent was so strong, so full of rage, it was hard to understand him. I'd never seen him this angry before. I had to get him out of here and calm him down.

"Yes, Hart, I'm aware. Congratulations. Add another notch to your belt. But right now, you need to calm the fuck down. Take the lady back to her apartment. Go! And I better see you on the track tomorrow morning, ready to train with your attitude in check." He turned to me. "And you, too, Soturion Lyriana."

I nodded.

Shivers ran down my spine. I felt that utterly familiar sensation of being watched from behind. I turned toward the dinner party and immediately found the source of the feeling.

Rhyan's father, sitting back at his seat like he was on a throne, openly watched us both like the nahashim he was deep down inside. He had his hip turned so the hilt of his sword faced me, and his finger traced the shape of the curved star as slowly as it had the rim of my wine glass.

Behind him was Arianna, her eyes narrowed into slits, an assessing look on her face. She disapproved of my sudden departure, and looked ready to call me back.

We had to get out of here.

"Rhyan, take me home," I said.

He'd barely acknowledged me, his face still red and his green eyes blazing as he stared back at his father. I'd thought the Ready looked like a god of death on more than one occasion, but in that moment, if vengeance were a god, it would be Rhyan.

"Rhyan! Take me home," I ordered. "Now!"

"Get out of here." Aemon grabbed both of the doors to the ballroom and slammed them shut behind us.

Alone in the hall, I grabbed Rhyan's hand. His skin was ice cold, his entire body shaking and angled toward the doors like he was two seconds from breaking them down and storming inside.

"Hey," I said, standing before him. "Rhyan, look at me. Look at me." I reached for his chin and pulled his face toward mine. "Rhyan!"

His chest heaved, his breathing was erratic, and his eyes were wild, barely seeming to see me. Then his fingers tightened around mine, and his other hand gripped my waist as he walked me back into a wall.

"Rhyan?"

His eyes searched the hall, the tendons in his neck standing out. Nostrils flaring, he turned suddenly. Vanishing to the other side of the hallway. His fist slammed with such violence into the wall, a small crack appeared.

"Rhyan!" I hissed, running for him. But he was before me in an instant. His face red, his shoulders shaking as he pushed me back again.

"Take me home!" I demanded.

His eyes were roving up and down my body, his eyes full of rage and fear as he pressed his hips against me, pressing me harder into the wall. His arms wrapped around my waist. "Ready?" he asked, his accent still heavy.

I blinked before I realized what he meant. He needed to get away from his father so badly and quickly, he wasn't capable of simply walking away. We were traveling. This was risky, but it seemed like the only thing he could do.

With a nod, I wrapped my arms around him, my fingers interlacing behind his neck. His hands pressed into me, pulling me even closer to him, his chest rising and falling against my breasts. I buried my face in his neck, inhaling the familiarity of his pine scent, full of musk from his rage and a day's worth of traveling with our soturi across Bamaria.

He exhaled sharply, his breath hot against my face, as I felt my feet leave the ground. There was a sharp tug on my stomach and a dizzying sensation that left me nauseated before my feet hit the floor of his apartment. Rhyan stumbled back from me, slamming into the wall of his bedroom.

Faint torchlight came through the window, just enough for me to see him sink to his knees.

"I've got you," I said, rushing to his side and wrapping my arms tightly around him. "Rhyan, it's just me. He's not here. We're safe. We're home. You're okay now, you're okay."

A sob wracked through his chest, as he looked up at me, his forehead beaded with sweat and the skin beneath his eyes purple with exhaustion. He pressed his forehead to mine, as he grabbed my hand, pulling it against his chest.

"Lyr?" he asked, his voice so low it was almost a whisper. "Did he hurt you?" He pulled back from me, his eyes, frantic with worry, searching mine, before running his hand up my arm, pushing aside my dress straps, swiping my hair back. He was still looking for injuries. Looking for any hidden signs of harm.

I held back the tears ready to fall, and took his hand, halting his search. "Not as much as he hurt you." I brushed the curls back from his forehead, exposing the scar that ran through his left eyebrow.

Immediately, he pushed his hair back over the scar his father had given him. It had been a blood oath—one that Rhyan had broken the same night his father had murdered his mother.

Tonight had to have been the first time Rhyan had seen his father since he'd left Glemaria, exiled and forsworn. And he'd seen his father holding me. Rhyan would have known in an instant that his father was hurting me. It would have been like me seeing Arianna hurt him. I would have gone feral, too. I practically had just hearing his father speak. Piecing together the smallest understanding of what Rhyan had been through, how he'd been tortured his entire life, had left me feeling more violent than I'd ever felt before.

I took his hand in mine and brought it to my lips. Unbidden, the image of black ropes covering Rhyan's entire body filled my vision. Having been bound like that for so long would have driven him farther than Lethea. And he'd borne the punishment in silence, all so he could protect me.

"Let's get you on the bed." I sat back on my heels and stood, tugging him to his feet. Once I got him seated, I bent down to unlace his boots, slid them off, and tossed them into a corner.

Rhyan stiffened as I reached forward to unbuckle his belt. He remained still, watching me as I removed his weapons along with everything harsh and cold from his body—first his cuffs and the extra sword strapped to his back, then his armor, which I stood to unhook along with his cloak. I took everything away until he was down to his riding pants and a long-sleeved shirt.

At last, I kicked off my own boots and lifted his feet up onto the bed before crawling over him to the side closest to the wall. I laid myself back against his pillows and pulled him to me, and he rested his head against my breast and wrapped his arms around my waist.

"Tonight, you're going to breathe for me, all right?" I took a deep breath, stroking his hair, full of wild curls.

"All right," he said, closing his eyes.

"You're okay. We're together."

He nodded against my chest.

We stayed like that for several moments until his breathing calmed and the color returned to his face. I traced the edge of his ear and down the soft skin of his neck before tangling my fingers in his curls and lightly scratching his scalp with my nails. Only now that we were still could I really feel the force of his aura, how cold the room had become, how close he was to unleashing another blizzard.

As I continued to scratch, he seemed to finally return to himself. His arms around me tightened; he wasn't grasping for me but holding me in return. His aura retreated, the chill in the room fading, and he pulled the extra blanket at the edge of his bed up around us.

"Sorry for that," he mumbled.

"Don't apologize." I kissed his forehead. "You're allowed to break down. I'm not going anywhere." I squeezed my arms around him. "Feeling better?"

He pushed himself up and lay down on his side, facing me. I turned on my side as well, shimmying down and laying my head on his pillow so we were eye level.

"What did he do to you?" he asked, his voice still on edge. He reached for my hand again and turned my palm up, examining it. My wrist was reddened, full of finger marks from his father. My skin would be purple by tomorrow.

"He threatened you," I said, pulling my hand from his. I traced his eyebrow and then the scar, wanting to undo it, to fix it, to take the pain away.

Rhyan recaptured my hand. "He's always done that." He pressed a kiss to my palm, taking a shaky breath. "What did he say?"

"A lot." I swallowed, my throat dry, as I felt his father's hands on me again and remembered the nonchalant way he'd spoken of coming after Rhyan—and me. "We need to talk. There's some other things I learned that I didn't get to tell you last night."

Rhyan's eyes met mine, and for a second, they were hooded, his cheeks warming with color as if he were remembering every detail of our very intimate...conversation. Then he propped himself up on his elbow, his expression alert and mouth drawn tight. "Should I be sitting up for this?"

"Maybe."

We both shifted up, crossing our legs. Rhyan still held my hand with our fingers threaded together. His thumb soothingly stroked my skin.

I finally filled him in on what I'd learned in the last few days. I told him how my mind had suddenly closed off to Morgana's mind-reading, and so I'd confronted Ramia, and she'd admitted Mercurial was missing. I told him how I'd discovered my mother's journal. I pulled off my arm cuff, showing him the handwritten note I'd received from my anonymous supporter, signed off with the filing sequence for the scroll.

Rhyan read the tiny parchment twice. He frowned and handed it back to me.

"How do we know you can trust this person?" His jaw tensed. I shrugged. "I don't know. But it led me to the journal."

Rhyan was still frowning, one eyebrow furrowed, but he listened intently as I told him about the contents of my mother's writing, her dreams of the Goddess Asherah, her feeling that Asherah was somehow her daughter, and how much her dream was like Meera's vision. I told him about her visit to Glemaria and her meeting with his father.

"He tried to negotiate a marriage contract back then, when I was still a baby."

"He knew what you were from the start." Rhyan pushed his fingers through his hair. "How?"

"I don't know. But there's more." I took a deep breath. "She went to Gryphon's Mount and saw the seraphim statue. She said she saw a vision of Asherah there with dark hair." My eyes burned. "I think she saw me."

"Gods." He squeezed my hand.

"She said that Asherah looked weak, but then she was holding the red shard of the Valalumir and strengthened. It was exactly what Meera saw."

Rhyan chewed on the corner of his lip. "I once read a theory that the Guardian statues held the shards."

"Where?"

"In our library back home. I mean, I read a lot of theories and speculations. No scholar or historian has ever been able to confirm a thing, and for every piece of evidence to back up one theory, there are a dozen other articles of evidence that disprove it. The most plausible ones I'd read were that the statues were signs of friendship across the Empire, or that they were once end caps marking the territory of Lumeria." He shook his head. "I tended to dismiss some of the more outlandish ones, like that they held the shards. We've been searching for them for hundreds of years. If the Valalumir was simply within two statues, why haven't we excavated them?"

"Because it takes a key," I said breathlessly. I told him of my mother's second visit to the seraphim statue at night, of the words revealed to her.

The sun revealed my secrets, so I hid them with the moon.

"My mother thought she saw an opening, and your father said 'It takes a key.'"

Rhyan's eyes widened. "It's always covered in snow. And now that I think about it, we have servants all over the keep and fortress, shoveling and maintaining the grounds. My father has never once ordered the statue to be cleared or uncovered. Like he was hiding it in plain sight."

"There's more," I said. "She saw a symbol and an inscription. It was in the shape of a Valalumir, the edges curved almost like the rays of the sun."

His face paled. "Like the star on the hilt of his sword."

"Exactly."

"What else did she write?"

"She wrote the High Lumerian of what she saw. And it translates to this: *We unlock for blood, soul, and key. Power is restored, with these three.* I think I can open the statue. And I think that's how I get my power. With my blood, with the soul of Asherah part of me, and with the key that your father has."

"And he knows?"

"He told me he'd give it to me if," a pit formed in my stomach, "if I married who he wanted, and if I brought you back to him."

Rhyan put his head in his hands. "Bastard."

"You know I would never—"

"No," he said quickly, "I know. I just, I hate that he has something to hold over us. Over you. Something you need. Giving him any level of power over you—that's when he's most dangerous."

"What do we do?"

"Nothing yet. We need to think through our options first."

"I'm sorry I didn't tell you yesterday."

"It's okay. Come here." Rhyan reached for my waist, pulled me onto his lap, and wrapped his arms around me. "Anything else?"

"He's breeding nahashim."

"To find me?"

I nodded against his shoulder, my hands clasped behind his back. "He said they'd find you if you ever left Bamaria."

"At least I know my political protection here still stands."

"At least until the consecration." I frowned.

"Fuck. I hate to say it, but we need the Afeyan bastard to show himself." He breathed deeply, inhaling the scent of my hair, his hands sliding up and down my back. "But maybe not tonight. Gods, I missed holding you."

"Same," I said, squeezing him tighter.

"Do you need me to take you back to your apartment?" he asked.

I leaned back, just enough to look into his eyes. "Did you forget what I said last night?"

"I'll never forget a single word." His hand drifted down my side, fingers pausing on the chain around my waist. His fingers slid along its length until he found the vadati stone hanging just below my belly.

I held his gaze, my stomach clenching, heat coiling low from his touch. "Good. Because I'm staying."

His eyes were hooded with desire, and I knew mine were, too. Both of us were thinking of last night, of what we'd said, what we'd shared.

Gods. I'd still been wet in the morning.

But the redness in his eyes had me on guard, as did the slope of his shoulders and the way his head hung forward. He was still reeling from seeing his father. I knew he needed tonight to rest, to recover. He was exhausted. And so was I.

Tomorrow, I'd return to the arena. I'd be forced to face the track, the place where I'd killed Haleika, the place where my father had been murdered.

"Are you hungry?" I asked. "Why don't we scrounge together some food and call it a night? We need to be ready for tomorrow."

His eyes flicked up and down my body, his desire for me obvious. But as he exhaled and rolled back his shoulders, some of his tension visibly falling away, I knew I'd said the right thing.

So we did just that. Rhyan checked in with Aemon, telling him I was safe and secured in my apartment after he walked me there, just to make a show for the guards on duty. Then he made a quick trip to the Katurium's dining hall to restock on food, and picked me up. Back in his apartment, we filled our plates high with his favorites, and I stole another pair of his sleep pants and a worn-in shirt of his to sleep in.

We crawled under the covers together, kissing. But there was still a haunted look in his eyes, one I knew had come from his father.

"Only good dreams," I whispered against his lips.

"Only good dreams." He kissed me again and pulled me into his arms, his hand seeking out the warmth of my skin beneath my shirt. Soon, his breathing evened, signaling he was asleep.

I stayed awake, guarding his sleeping body as visions of him tied with black rope haunted me until morning.

I stared at the arena from the doorway of the Katurium. My stomach was in knots. My breath came in short gasps. Just like the last time I'd come here, I felt sick and terrified of stepping outside.

I searched desperately for Rhyan. We hadn't been together or even looked at each other since he'd dropped me off at my apartment this morning so we could dress separately for our first day training since the Valyati holiday. We knew we had to do our best to keep our distance in public—especially with his father in the country. Even if he didn't know any specifics, he knew enough, and Rhyan and I both knew he required very little motivation to use that knowledge against us or to attempt to manipulate me into betraying Rhyan.

I looked out on the track, quickly filling with my classmates, and realized Rhyan was already out there, standing in our usual starting point. His dagger was in the ground, and he was stretching, moving through the first few of the 108 Postures of the Valya.

A howl sounded behind me—a wolf from Ka Kormac. I stepped back, trying to become invisible, willing him to pass me by.

But that was too much to hope for. Brockton Kormac, son of the Bastardmaker and Lord Viktor's apprentice, stood before me.

"You have to step outside to run, you know," he smirked, "*Lyr.*" He elongated my name, taunting me with his informal address. I was only *Lyr* to those closest to me. Even here, if I wasn't *your grace*, I was *my lady* or, at the least, *Soturion Lyriana*.

I slid my hand to my belt, feeling the reassuring weight of my dagger sheathed at my hip.

He took a step closer, as two more wolves joined his side. "You know," he said, "now that you're free of Lord Grey, we could have some fun, me and you."

"Step aside," I ordered.   "I don't take orders from you."

Another two wolves joined him. My heart began to hammer. Aemon was nowhere in sight. Nor was Turion Dairen.

I spotted Naria passing by. Despite her engagement to Tristan, she was walking with Viktor, who cackled gleefully when he saw me surrounded by his apprentice and soturi.

"Come on, Batavia," he sneered. "Walk in with Brockton. Behave."

I eyed Naria. That bitch had betrayed me in so many ways. Was she really going to stand for this, too?

She turned up her nose and walked outside, leaving me with the pack.

Viktor stepped forward, and in that moment, I caught sight of Rhyan turning, sensing something was wrong. His face changed in an instant.

"Your aunt didn't tell you?" Viktor asked, throwing his hand against the wall, trapping me against him. "You're about to become a Kormac."

My eyes widened.

Then a dark arm shot forth, pushing through the wall Viktor had created.

"Galen!" I shouted in surprise. I hadn't seen him since...since Valyati. Since I'd killed Haleika.

"Back off, Kormac," Galen sneered. "Leave her."

"I don't think so. She belongs to us."

"Not today she doesn't," he said.

Viktor shook his head. Rhyan was nearly at the door, his face full of rage.

"Ka Scholar, right?" Viktor said. "You'll regret this."

"I don't care." Galen grabbed my arm and pushed past the wolves outside.

I froze on the spot. I could hear Haleika. I could see her body catching fire, her head falling. I could see my father....

No. *No.*

Galen squeezed my hand. "Come on, soturion. You can do this."

I took a deep breath and squeezed my eyes shut. When I opened them, Galen was watching me, his eyes filled with tears.

"Lyr, you know we've always been friends. And for that reason, I never say it. But I love you."

I nodded, feeling my own tears form. "I love you, too."

"I'm so sorry about your father."

"Thank you."

"And," he looked uncomfortable, "I'm sorry about you and Tristan."

I let out a shaky breath. "Thanks, Galen."

"I just needed to say all that. So that I could say I know you did what you had to...with Hal. I get it. I do. You had no choice. But for me, it's still too soon."

I sniffled. "For me, too."

He squeezed my hand again. "So I'll see you around. Be careful out there."

The backs of my eyes burned.

Rhyan reached my side then, replacing Galen's presence. He looked me up and down. "Partner, you alright?"

"I guess."

His eyes scanned the arena, pausing over the spots where it had happened. I knew he was thinking the same thing I was.

"Outer ring," he said. "Look to the stadium, not the field."

Roars from the stadium's seats caught both of our attentions. I realized, to my horror, that Rhyan's father, along with his entire Glemarian entourage, had come to watch the morning training—much like Ka Kormac viewed our habibellums.

Rhyan paled, his eyes zeroing in on his father.

"Rhyan," I said.

He continued to stare ahead, a look of pure horror on his face, his aura flaring, cold and explosive.

"He's just a rope," I said urgently. "Just a fucking rope. And you know what we do to those."

He squeezed his eyes shut and took a sharp breath before looking back at me. "We tear them the fuck apart."

I nodded. And then we separated, taking our spots on the track and falling into position.

CHAPTER TWENTY

MORGANA

I SAT ACROSS FROM Arianna at dinner, silently sipping my third glass of wine. She was tense, uneasy about some decision she'd just made.

What that decision was exactly, I had no clue. I'd hated and railed against my vorakh for the better part of the nearly year and a half it had afflicted me, but not being able to read someone's mind—not being privy to their thoughts when I wanted to be—was driving me farther than fucking Lethea. I also couldn't get a read on who Arianna's fellow conspirators were; I knew they were most likely using the mind-shield or had trained themselves to control their thoughts.

There were only a few people whom I felt certain were in the clear, judging from their minds and actions. I knew Eathan could be trusted, as could Aemon. Turion Dairen was out as a possible conspirator simply because he did whatever Aemon supported. Brenna was also out, which meant Bamaria's former Second and current Arkturion, Turion, and Master of Peace were all non-traitors. But the rest of the Council—the majority of them—could have been supporting Arianna.

Like silver-tongued Lady Romula. I didn't see her as being particularly loyal to Arianna, but she was one to turn her back on a losing side, and we had lost. That said—and even though she was an old bitch and I didn't trust her—she was someone I could see easily switching her loyalty back to our line of succession if she felt we'd win. And if there was something in it for her.

Then there was Lady Sila, Master of Spies. I could never read her properly. Her thoughts were as slippery as the camouflage cloak she wore. I had a suspicion she'd change allegiance depending on circumstance, too—not to be amongst the victors of the war like Lady Romula, but to join the side that would make the least work for her, the side that would cause the least chaos in the land.

Senator Janvi Elys was definitely a traitor—I didn't need to hear her thoughts to know that. Ka Elys had happily slid their way into power after the Emperor had murdered Ka Azria in Elyria. The Bamarian branch would be no different. The way Lady Pavi followed Naria like a lost little puppy and had targeted Lyr in training was evidence enough that Ka Elys could not be trusted.

Arianna adjusted the silver laurel on her head, the leaves glinting and glittering as she offered a scrutinizing look to Naria. My bitch-cousin was currently fawning all over Tristan. Could she be any more disgusting? Lyr had had to practically hypnotize herself into half-fucking him, but Naria was stone-cold sober and still wanted him. What the hell was her excuse? To top it all off, she was still fucking the son of the Imperator, Lord Viktor fuck-his-face Kormac. I certainly didn't judge her for the number of lovers she was taking, only the choice of who she was allowing into her bed. And the fact that Bamaria now saw Naria as pure, as if that mattered, but not Lyr...Gods people were stupid.

I took another sip, wanting this night to be over. The wine was doing its job, and I was looking forward to falling face forward into my pillows and closing my eyes, sinking into utter mindless oblivion.

But I couldn't leave until Arianna dismissed us.

The herald walked through the room and announced Imperator Kormac's arrival. Fuck. At least Imperator Hart was spending his evening at the Katurium, though that did not bode well for Lyr. Or Rhyan, who I assumed was with her.

I glared at his entrance. "Asshole."

You said that out loud, Meera thought, offering a staged smile to Lady Kiera across the room. The Master of Law, a cousin on Eathan's and Father's side, lifted her glass, lips pursed together.

"Oops," I said, my head swaying. I waved back at Lady Kiera. She'd never liked me. I was too loud. Ka Ezara was too prim and proper for their own good.

Morgs, pull it together.

"Fine," I said, reaching for a piece of pita and stuffing it in my mouth. "To sober up. Just for you."

It's for all of us. Meera took a dainty sip of water, somehow gracefully performing even the smallest of tasks. I swear Mother and Father passed all the qualities of a proper noble to her and left none for me. Well, no, they had some leftover, and those they gave to Lyr.

The Imperator took a seat beside Arianna, ever the predatory glint in his eyes. She immediately leaned toward him.

I still couldn't decide whether or not they were already fucking. Like daughter, like mother. Not that either truly wanted the other—this was a game. They were allies. There was no doubt about that. But even a child could see that the Imperator would screw her over if it benefited him. It was only a matter of time. He'd fuck her one way or the other.

I narrowed my eyes, watching their body language, their knees turned toward each other. I was still undecided, and my own nightly exploits were getting in the way of spying on hers.

"It is done?" the Imperator asked, his thoughts completely in line with the words coming from his mouth.

"The contract is ready. She will not like it," Arianna said. *She'll throw a fit,* she thought without voicing that concern to the Imperator. *And I'll have to pretend to care.*

I leaned forward, turning my head just so in order to listen more closely.

"What she does and does not like has never been my concern. Nor should it be yours, your grace. Securing Bamaria and her safety is what matters. That's all."

"Securing her safety." Arianna rolled her eyes. "Believe what you will. You always have."

He sneered, curling his lips, leaning even closer to sniff her. "I do. And I'm relieved to hear the ink is now dry. Especially as I hear it, Imperators are in the market for former heirs."

I pulled Meera toward my seat. "Have you heard of any contract negotiations between us and Ka Kormac? Anything in Council meetings?" I asked under my breath.

Meera shook her head, pushing herself back from me. She smiled at another noble then exhaled, her shoulders slumping as if the small gesture had been too much for her. "I was not invited today."

The hell was going on?

Several more soturi walked in, all bearing the armor of Ka Kormac, silver and full of wolf pelts and images of howling wolves. Most of them were brainless oafs not worth a second of thought.

As if to prove me right, two of their minds were open to me, their thoughts nearly identical.

Tits.

Look at her tits.

They were going to make me puke.

Then a girl I'd never seen before walked in. She was frail looking and thin—the kind of thin that appeared unnatural, like she was meant to have far more meat on her. Her pale blue eyes were wide and sunken, yet she carried herself with the confidence of a noble. She wore a long gray dress with a silver wolf threaded into the bodice. In the faint light of the room's torches, I could make out the golden Valalumir tattooed across her cheek—the sigil of the Emperor.

Her sunken eyes reached right for me, her aura striking out. There was something familiar yet sickening in her energy. It was invasive, knowing, and powerful—much too powerful for her own good.

She walked across the room with her head held high, the heels of her boots clacking against the floor. Pausing before the head table, she curtseyed for Arianna and the Imperator, then took a seat behind him like a servant. Strange. The Imperator rarely employed women.

The sigil gave her away. This was one of the Emperor's servants, like Namtaya had been, though this one was far higher in rank. She had to have been valuable to the Emperor if she carried his mark. So why wasn't she being fed properly?

I can hear you. The thought jumped into my mind, clear and loud as my own.

Vorakh. My heart hammered against my chest, as a small smile played across her lips.

She was a chayatim. One of the secret servants of the Emperor, like Jules. I'd never seen one before. I didn't think they were allowed to leave the capitol.

I couldn't let this one know what I knew; I couldn't let her into my mind. She most likely was a victim herself, had been stolen from her own country, family, and Ka on account of her magic being illegal. Her abilities had likely been villainized then used against her for profit.

But she bore the Emperor's golden mark. She could not be trusted. I could not afford for her to know anything about me or Meera.

I could only hope she lived by the same unspoken code as all vorakh did. We didn't acknowledge each other when discovered.

With the exception of him.

I stood and conjured his body—not his face, never his face—in my mind, filling my thoughts with him to hide my secrets. I pulled on a recent memory of sinking to my knees and taking him deep into my mouth. I felt heat pool between my legs. I pictured myself licking him up and down before he grabbed my head and thrusted into me, reaching the back of my throat. I remembered the taste of him with every step I took toward my aunt.

"Your grace," I curtsied before Arianna, knowing I needed her permission to leave, still thinking of the silk of his skin in my hands as I ran them up and down his length while my head bobbed. I brought my gaze to the Imperator. "Your highness."

He was instantly alert, his nostrils widening as if to sniff me out. Disgusting pig.

I returned to my memory. I thought of myself gripping his ass, feeling him twitch and moan before he pulled out of me, lifted me up, shoved me against the wall, and slid back into me.

"You look beautiful tonight, Morgana," Arianna said.

Gods, I hated her. Fucking bitch—whom I loved because she was my aunt.

"Thank you," I said. "I tried. I thought I'd feel better if I looked more like myself."

"That was a good idea." She smiled. "I'm glad to see you and Meera out tonight."

"If only Lyr were here," I said.

The Imperator lifted his chin. "She's at combat clinic where she belongs."

"Of course. I expect nothing else. However, seeing as I am also returning to my studies after...a rather eventful winter holiday, I'm finding myself a bit overtired. Would you mind if I excused myself early tonight, your grace? Might I take Meera with me?" I winked conspiratorially. "She was yawning earlier. We're not yet back to our old routine."

"Of course, my dear," Arianna said. "And you know, you can still call me Arianna."

I nodded.

"Go on." She waved, the official dismissal of an arkasva.

The Imperator's eyes dipped down my body, roaming over my breasts and waist. His aura reached out, predatory and aroused. He was sensing my own aura, my own memories that were all I had to protect me from the chayatim by his side.

I retreated again to my memories. I imagined him lifting up my legs, and my ankles locking behind his back while his cock pounded into me relentlessly.

Nice dick. Whose is it?

I stared down between my legs in the memory, watching him slide in and out of me. I watched his hips thrust and his abs flex as he pumped.

Hot. Are you trying to turn me on?

His dick slid in again and again.

I know what you're doing, she thought. *You're far too obvious.*

I swallowed. "Thank you, Arianna. Your highness. Good night, then."

I practically ran from those pale blue eyes and the thoughts invading my mind.

I'm going to figure it out. You can't hide.

I grabbed Meera's hand. "Get up and follow me, you vapid, mindless idiot. Did you really think I wouldn't notice? You stole my shoes."

Meera's eyes widened, her face paling, but then she stood. "You know I saw them first, and they're my size, not yours. Stop pretending they're your shoes."

"You know Godsdamned well they're my size. And I'm meeting him tonight. So I need those shoes back. He likes them on me. Likes when they're the only thing on me." My heart pounded. I could feel the chayatim's eyes us, as I gestured at Soturion Jace to follow us.

"Are we going to my room to get them?" Meera asked, her hands shaking at her sides.

"No," I said cruelly. The chayatim would hear us from anywhere in the fortress. There was only one place loud enough to block the sound of my thoughts.

The ocean.

I grabbed Meera's hand.

"Morgs!" she cried out. "That hurts."

I kept gripping her. We had to move. Meera understood the code, understood to keep her mind blank, to play along with whatever stupid distraction I gave her—like shoes—to focus her mind on. But she wasn't trained to control her mind like those who took the elixir. She couldn't keep this up for long. I needed to get us to the ocean.

I dragged her through the halls of Cresthaven. There was still trust in Meera's eyes, but she was losing patience. I'd never played this game with her for this long, and I'd never been this rough with her.

Morgs, you're scaring me. What is it?

"I changed my mind. I want to take a walk on the beach. Until I meet him."

"The beach?"

"Yes, the one with the ocean, the waves, the water, the caws of seraphim, the ashvan lights in the sky, sparkling and glittering over the crashing shore." I was rambling now, saying anything I could to make her think of the beach, to make her think of anything but who we were—vorakh—and what we knew—that Arianna was a traitor.

"My lady," Jace shouted. "Slow down."

"You're a soturion," I sneered. "Catch up."

"Jace!" Akillus, Meera's escort, joined our watch.

"The ladies didn't say anything," Jace said defensively. "They just took off."

Fuck. All we needed now was a team of escorts wondering what we were doing and drawing more attention to us.

I moved quicker, pulling Meera down the winding halls and out through the doors. We raced over the glass waterways and past the towers and the pools, following the path down as it sloped toward the beach. The running water beneath the glass was fading under the light of the moon, swaths of it buried beneath the sand.

Meera stumbled, and I grabbed her with both of my hands.

"Morgs! It's freezing out here!"

"Just a little farther," I said. "We won't stay long." I just needed to get our feet in the water—I had tested it out before, with him. Either the volume of noise coming from the waves or the magic in the ocean drowned out my thoughts. It had been the one place where I hadn't been able to hear him when we weren't touching. And whenever Lyr would come down here, I'd stop hearing her completely.

My feet slid through the sand, which was surprisingly loose for winter and with the constant tide. My heels were sinking into the ground, but the sand was becoming damp, and we were so close.

A seraphim squawked above us, her carriage riding low. Wind from her wings blew my hair into my eyes.

"My lady!" Jace yelled. *Something's not right. This isn't right.* His mind was turning in circles.

But I waved him off. Whatever the seraphim was doing didn't matter. The wind grew in strength, nearly pushing me back. Meera, so thin and frail, nearly fell on top of me.

Another seraphim carriage flew low.

My stomach twisted. Seraphim could fly over the shores here. Plenty spent hours lying about the beach. But it was illegal for them to fly with carriages over the fortress.

I peered up but heard nothing. No thoughts—no one inside the carriages. The rogue seraphim were probably just signs of Cresthaven falling to shit under Arianna's rule. She was already proving herself incapable of upholding basic protocol.

Water rushed over my boots, and salt filled my nose. I pulled Meera toward me as the first seraphim squawked and circled overhead, her shadow swimming through the waves and casting darkness over our forms.

"Morgs, what the fuck?" Meera yelled, her voice fighting to be heard over the wind and water. "What's going on?"

Before I could form an answer, the seraphim landed on the shore, their claws throwing gusts of wet sand into our faces.

"Fuck," I yelled, spitting the grains from my mouth. I wiped wildly at my face, trying to get the sand out of my eyes and my hair from sticking to my damp skin.

"MORGANA!" Jace screamed.

"AKADIM!" roared Akillus.

"Gods!" Meera yelled.

I bent down, cupped the water from the tide into my hand, and splashed my face, finally clearing my sight.

I stumbled back.

Two akadim towered over us, ten feet tall at least, both male. Raggedy yellow-stained cloths hung over their shoulders and around their waists. Their pale skin was corded with thick muscle and red lines—the stretch marks they'd acquired from growing into their bodies upon death.

"Stave!" I yelled, reaching for my mine at my waist.

The first akadim roared, and even at a distance I could smell its putrid breath and see its spit flying past the sharpened fangs hanging over its lips.

Jace and Akillus were both racing for the monsters with swords in their right hands and daggers in their left. Meera pulled her stave from her belt.

"What do we do?" she asked, her chest heaving.

"We stay back here. Let the soturi fight them."

The first akadim swiped its claws at Akillus, slicing him across the face. With a cry, Meera's escort fell to his knees, blood gushing from his cheek.

Come on! I pleaded, stepping back into the ocean, pulling Meera with me. *Come on! Jace, Akillus, you've got this! You've got this!*

They were seasoned soturi, picked to be our guards for a reason. They had been trained to stop Akadim. Lyr had done it. Rhyan had done it. If they could do it, our guards could, too. It was going to be fine. We were going to be okay.

But even I knew we needed backup.

Akadim! I thought desperately. He could help, too. He would know what to do. *HELP! Akadim in Cresthaven!*

There was no response from him. Only silence. Fuck.

"Where's your vadati?" I asked Meera, grabbing the collar of her dress and searching for a necklace.

I don't have it, it's in my room. Her eyes filled with tears. *I'm sorry.*

The second akadim, with red hair hanging in long tufts from its head, picked up Jace by his shoulders. It whirled around, its huge feet slamming into the sand, and sent Jace flying. He crashed face first into Akillus's golden armor. There was a loud, unnatural-sounding crack—like bone splintering. Both men collapsed in a bloody heap, their limbs tangled. They each had at least one broken arm and leg. If they woke up, they weren't going to be much help.

Shit. Shit. Shit!

How could they get in? Meera thought desperately. *How could they get this far? When did they learn to ride seraphim?*

"I don't know, and I don't care. But we need to find a way to kill them."

Meera held out her stave, glowing with blue light. I felt mine warm in my hand, the heat spreading to my wrist just as the red eyes of an akadim turned on us. It was the first one—slightly taller, with long, stringy black hair.

"Stand back!" I screamed.

"By the Gods," Meera yelled. "We became akadim in my vision." She was starting to panic.

"No!" I screamed. "Not all of your visions come true!" Someone had to be coming, had to hear us, help us. We were on the grounds of Cresthaven, our own fortress—the one place we were supposed to be safe, that was crawling with soturi trained to protect us.

But thanks to me, our soturi had no idea we were on the beach.

I screamed, and so did Meera, but the akadim was advancing on us while its partner lifted Jace into its arms.

Jace groaned, his body hanging limply, his leg twisted at the knee, as the red-haired beast used its claws to slice off the hooks of Jace's armor. His golden seraphim shoulders fell to the ground unceremoniously, and the armor protecting his torso followed with a thud.

The akadim licked its lips and threw Jace face down at its feet. Jace's moan of pain was muffled by the sand as the monster bent over and ripped off Jace's pants.

"JACE!" I screamed.

My hands were shaking, my feet were going numb. The water was freezing, rising past the tops of my boots and knees. My dress was soaking and heavy, an endless weight, threatening to pull me down into the depths of the icy waters.

I couldn't faint. I couldn't faint. But the akadim was leaning over Jace, and it was about...about to—

"NO!" roared the dark-haired akadim, its voice gravelly. It turned its head just enough to see the red-haired akadim gripping Jace's hips, pulling his ass toward it. "No time." The sound of its words was grating on my ears, and I winced, seeing Meera screw up her face in pain.

"*Glemata!*" Meera yelled. Blue sparks flew from her stave in a freezing spell—one she'd mastered. It would have been the perfect spell to stop the akadim, but it bounced off the beast. Akadim were impervious to magic.

Both of our attackers moved faster, long arms swinging at their sides. They grunted as they approached while our feet slipped and slid on the uneven terrain of the water, more of our dresses being pulled into the tide. Water and sand filled my boots.

Jace groaned in the distance. One eye opened, and he watched us in horror, unable to move, unable to cover himself or help us. "Morgana!" he mouthed desperately. Blood dripped from his forehead.

The first akadim grinned, fangs cutting its lips as it lurched toward Meera, a fresh wave rushing at its dirty feet.

"Don't!" I cried, moving in front of her, trying to shield Meera's body with my own. "Don't touch her!"

Jace stretched out his arm, his only limb that was not broken, and pulled his shattered body across the sand, his eyes wildly scanning the ground. He was searching for a vadati stone.

Akillus was still unconscious, slumped in a pile of his arms and legs, his soturion cloak bunched around his neck, the edges blowing in the wind.

I reached out with my thoughts again, trying to find *him*, even trying to find the chayatim. Imprisoned by the Emperor was better than dead—better than becoming akadim.

But my mind remained silent. No one knew we were here. We were going to die, be turned, stripped of our souls, made into akadim. Just like in Meera's vision. Tears fell down my cheeks.

"*Mageno aniam!*" I shouted, my stave burning in my palm from the force of the spell. I watched expectantly, willing the magic to come, to move faster, to work.

I shouted the spell again, sweat beading behind my neck. *Shield us! Shield us! Fucking shield us!* White light domed from my stave, splashing out around me and Meera.

The akadim held its clawed hand to its face, covering its eyes and grimacing in pain.

"*Mageno aniam!*" Meera cried, and another brighter dome of light reinforced mine, creating a barrier between us.

The red-haired demon screeched in pain.

A blue light flashed in the sand. Jace's vadati. He was calling for help.

Gods, we might be okay. My eyes focused so closely on the small blue light, I could barely breathe.

By the Gods, we were holding them off. We just needed a soturion to sound the alarm, and we'd be saved. A legion lay nearby. They'd come in seconds. We just needed to hold on, to keep our shield. We'd be alright. We'd be alright.

Then the two akadim stood side by side, roaring and gnashing their teeth, their claws ripping through our shield like it was made of water. The heat of my stave rolled back from the tip into my palm like the spell had reversed itself and burned me.

I threw myself again in front of Meera, facing the akadim. "Don't! Don't!" I yelled.

"Morgs!"

"Swim," I ordered her. "Swim until help comes."

"I'm not leaving you!" she cried.

Clawed hands grabbed my arms, hauling me into the air. With a screech, Meera was lifted next and tossed over the shoulder of the red-haired akadim. Mine held me in its arms like I was a baby, its smell so disgusting I thought I'd be sick or pass out.

"Morgana!" Jace cried. "Meera!"

"Soturion?" the vadati glowed as the head of our escort team spoke to Jace.

"Akadim!" he cried. "On the beach. Two! Come! Now! Akillus down!"

The beast cut me with its claws as it lifted me higher. I squeezed my eyes shut, my body shaking with terror. *Just please kill me first. If this is my fate—let me die first. Let me die before...the rest happens.*

"No harm," growled my akadim. It was an order to the beast carrying Meera.

Even as its putrid lips curled into a sneer, Meera's captor nodded, shaking her body over its shoulder. It opened the carriage door on its seraphim, so tall it didn't need to climb up. "Go!" it shouted, violently throwing Meera inside.

"Meera!" I yelled. There was a thud inside her carriage.

Her akadim laughed, delighted with what it'd done.

"No harm! Master's orders!" my akadim said again.

Meera's akadim stuck its neck out, its red hair standing on end as it growled and snapped its teeth. "I know!" it roared. Its eyes flicked to Jace. "Wanted to eat."

"Go!" mine ordered, clearly the one in charge.

My mind raced, as I desperately tried to piece together what I knew. Akadim didn't work together. They killed and tortured for food and pleasure. But they had been organized lately—forming nests and assigning leadership. This was what had kept Rhyan going to Elyria.

My carriage door opened, and I was tossed in. I curled into a ball, shielding my face in my arms and sliding my body across the floor and beneath the bench. Water dripped from my body, soaking the floor beneath me. I was shivering, my teeth chattering, whether from fear or cold, I couldn't tell anymore.

The floor shifted beneath me, the wood panels groaning as it accepted the akadim's weight.

I stayed curled on the floor in a ball, too afraid to move—too afraid of what might come next. Rape. Death. Losing my soul.

The seraphim squawked, and I felt the sinking feeling in my stomach that signaled liftoff.

My captor was breathing heavily, its red eyes bloodthirsty and on me. It licked its lips and reached an arm across the carriage until its clawed hand found my neck. It pressed into my skin and slid down to my belly.

I tensed.

Its eyes widened, as it pulled its hand back like I'd burned it. It reached again, but just before it made contact with me, it changed its mind, shaking its head and muttering to itself. "No. For master. *Maraak.*" It stared out the window, tapping its claws against its naked and dirty knee.

I stayed curled beneath the bench, realizing in horror I'd wet myself when it had touched me. I wouldn't have expected that would be a deterrent for it.

"For master," it said again, this time like it was trying to convince itself. "*Maraak.*"

Maraak? That was High Lumerian...it meant king.

I squeezed my eyes shut, lying in a puddle of urine, ocean grime, and tears. Fuck. Fuck. We were flying faster now, and there was no escape, no spell I could use to get off this seraphim.

I could try to crash the carriage or throw myself from the window, but I needed to live. For Meera.

And for Jules. I was the only one who knew she was alive and where to find her.

I stared from beneath the bench at the monster, who still looked like it was trying to convince itself to follow orders to deliver me unharmed. But to where? To who? And why?

I reached out to its mind, but I got nothing. My head hadn't been this quiet since before my Revelation Ceremony. Akadim were unaffected by magic, and I guessed that meant they were invincible to vorakh.

I coughed, catching its attention. Its red eyes narrowed on me.

"Who is your master?" I asked.

It reached for me again and hauled me out from beneath the bench, my soaking wet boots dragging across the floor as its nails drew blood through my sleeves.

I cried out.

Then it screamed in pain, staring at me with venom in its eyes. "Moriel," it said.

It slammed me against the wall, and my world went black.

CHAPTER TWENTY-ONE

LYRIANA

I SAT ALONE IN the stadium, listening to the fires flicker over-head and the crowd cheer for the apprentice clinic. Galen sat a few rows over, looking toward me every now and then as if reassuring himself I was there and safe. But, true to his word earlier, he didn't come sit with me.

I suddenly missed Haleika fiercely, missed the way she bounced in her seat, the way she would have been so an-noyed at the presence of Imperator Hart in the arena. The way she would have been screaming at every foul hit and punch thrown inside the rings.

Rhyan was fighting, running and attacking every soturion he faced. After seeing his father in the stands this morning, something had snapped inside of him. He'd become more focused and determined than I'd ever seen. During the run, he'd raced across the track at a speed I'd never have thought possible—even for him. His legs had been like a mirage, and a cloud of dirt had followed his tracks. I ran in his shadows, terrified he'd slip up, lose control of his emotions, and expose his vorakh. But his speed had been all him, all of his training and years of work. He hadn't traveled once, and for the rest of day, including lunch and our afternoon training, he'd been in the same intense mood. When we'd picked up our swords to spar, he'd done so with such focused vigor, we'd both ended up sweaty messes on the mats.

At dinner, I'd eyed him across the dining hall—his hair wet and curled from his second shower that day. His aura still felt cold and hard, even from across the room. He'd barely touched his food. I hadn't dared go over to him, not when Viktor Kormac and his wolves had been watching me more boldly than ever before, and certainly not when Devon Hart had stridden through the dining hall pretending he'd wanted a tour of the Katurium. Rhyan had stilled the moment he'd sensed his father's aura, his knuckles whitening and his scar reddening as if answering some unspoken call from the man who'd made it. I wished I'd had an aura so I could have sent some calming energy toward him. He'd given me one piercing look before all of the apprentices had been ushered outside to prepare for clinic.

Icy wind brushed against my cheek now, and I burrowed deeper into my soturion cloak, pulling my hood over my head. I shivered, watching Rhyan dodge an opponent, lunge to his left, and nearly sit himself on the ground before he sprang back to his feet, spinning and slamming his fist into the stomach of a wolf sneaking up from behind.

"You fuck him yet?" asked a snide voice.

I turned and found Tani Elwen sitting behind me, wearing the orange of Ka Elys, an ashvan horse on her tunic. Lady Pavi was beside her, smiling and laughing. Loyal to Naria, both of them had made it their mission to torture me since I'd started soturion training. My hatred for them ran so much deeper knowing Tani was a member of the Emartis. Because of her accusations toward me and Rhyan, I'd been forced to vouch for her in the sham trial meant to determine if she was a member. Gods. Arianna had been there, standing behind Tani. It had been right in front of my face. Arianna had been the one who'd allegedly reported Tani, but Tani had been working for her all along.

Had she been in the stands that night? Had she had some direct part to play? Arianna was the killer, but I wondered who's stave made the killing blow. Whose actions that night led directly to his fall.

"Please, Tani," Pavi said. "I don't know why you're bothering. I heard she was too frigid for Lord Tristan."

I stiffened. It was none of their business whether or not I'd slept with Tristan. No one knew what had happened between us when we'd been alone. Most assumed we had been sleeping together all along, but if Pavi was suggesting otherwise, suggesting what only Tristan and I knew, that meant....

I felt like my heart slammed into my chest. That had been private.... Fuck.

I refolded my arms across my body and turned back to the field. It didn't matter.

"Maybe she's not frigid," Tani said. "Maybe she just has her eye on someone else."

Brockton Kormac, Viktor's disgusting apprentice and the son of the Bastardmaker, charged across the field, pushing every opponent he saw out of his way. He was heading straight for Rhyan. The last time they'd met in the arena, Brockton had nearly beaten Rhyan, fighting out of bounds and brutally biting his face. He'd been exhausted after having traveled to Elyria and back within a day. But Leander had thankfully come to Rhyan's aid.

My heart panged. Leander was dead.

A wave of nausea rolled through me as Rhyan came face to face again with the son of the Bastardmaker. They were fighting so close to the spot where my father had taken his last breath. Where his eyes had closed. Where my dreams kept taking me against my will, again and again.

I tried to breathe as Rhyan missed a hit, taking a punch to his jaw. The taunts from the crowd were starting up, growing in vigor. Shouts of *mother-killer, forsworn bastard*, and *whore* echoed across the field. This had happened last time. But now with an audience full of northerners, the jeers felt louder—more intense. More vitriolic. It felt personal.

Someone sidled next to me, sitting too close; their thigh pushed against mine.

"Lady Asherah," Viktor Kormac crooned.

I stared straight ahead, crossing my legs to angle away from him. The insult he tried to give me. The way Ka Kormac all tried to make Asherah's name mean whore. He had no idea. No idea the truth of his words. What they actually meant for me now.

"I have some news for you," he said, shifting closer.

I straightened my back, determined not to let this Moriel-fucking-bastard get to me.

"I doubt it," I said curtly.

"Of course, I do. A certain...contract is in negotiation."

A marriage contract? Had the Imperator made a deal with Arianna already?

I didn't want to take the bait and give him the satisfaction of admitting I didn't know what he was referring to.

Brockton pushed Rhyan onto his back. I leaned forward, grasping my cloak in my hands.

"I promise you," Viktor continued, "what I have to tell you is far more exciting than my cousin beating your forsworn-bastard apprentice. Again."

Rhyan rolled aside, just avoiding another soturion slamming on top of him. He jumped to his feet, feinted to the right, then spun and landed a punch to Brockton's jaw. The Kormac apprentice stumbled back, and for a second Rhyan looked up into the stands, somehow finding me, meeting my gaze. Then he turned, arm swinging, anticipating the next fight.

"You were saying," I snarled.

But Viktor only laughed.

And in that moment, the bells rang. My heart jumped into my throat, and my blood ran cold as the distinctive pattern of notes beat against my ears. The pattern haunting, familiar.

A wave of dizziness washed over me.

Not the hourly bells, but the warning bells.

The akadim bells.

I jumped from my seat, my heart racing, searching for Rhyan in the chaos of the field.

I needed to get to Cresthaven. To Meera and Morgana. To see them, protect them. Know they were safe. The same horror I'd felt before was surging through me, overwhelming me, overpowering me.

All at once, I was back in the Temple of Dawn, panicking, scared, barely escaping with Rhyan from the akadim that had attacked me, that had killed Leander, killed Haleika.

Time seemed to slow.

I felt the akadim wrap its claws around me, hoist me into the air, felt its hunger for me, for my soul.

"Soturion Lyriana!" Imperator Kormac yelled. His voice was amplified and rose above the screaming of the clock towers. A dozen wolves followed behind him.

My stomach hollowed. I found Rhyan fighting his way across the field toward me. Aemon was behind the magically bound ropes of the habibellum, screaming at the Katurium mage to release the soturi, his gaze tracking me in the stands.

The Imperator yelled my name again, louder this time. Soturi were getting up from their seats, scrambling to leave the arena.

My heart hammered as the bells rang louder, and I found Galen. He frowned, standing up, horror and pain in his eyes, before brandishing his dagger in his hand, his body angling protectively in front of me.

"I'll get you to Hart," he said quietly.

"MOVE!" the Imperator yelled from down the stands. "Make a path to her."

Galen glared at the Imperator and back to me, his face full of confusion.

Akadim were attacking. Akadim had breached Bamaria again the day after the Imperator's fucking task force had returned. He was supposed to be taking his soturi to fight them and calling the task force back into action. Protocol demanded I go to Cresthaven to be with my family.

But, of course, he wasn't doing any of that. He wasn't doing one fucking thing he should have.

Why was he coming for me?

Soturi were now scrambling in every direction, climbing to higher seats or jumping to the emptied rows below. The Imperator approached with the Bastardmaker at his side, his red cloak swinging at his back as he pushed any soturion who didn't move away quickly enough.

Viktor returned to my side, his lips curled into a sneer as he grabbed my arms, pulling them behind my back.

"Hands off her, Kormac," Galen shouted.

In the distance, Rhyan was breaking free of the bindings on the field, calling my name.

"No," Viktor yelled. His fist swung, and Galen barely dodged the hit. "She's ours now."

"Back the fuck off, Kormac. There's a protocol."

"I know," Viktor said, tightening his grip on me.

"Lyr!" A yell sounded from down the field. Rhyan was racing toward the stadium's wall. He picked up speed and leapt, landing just beyond the first row of raised seats. He gripped the banister, pulling himself up.

Rhyan climbed up the wall, threw himself over it, and raced up the rows of the stands, punching out anyone who got in his way.

Aemon climbed up next, taking off behind him, both of them shouting my name.

Imperator Kormac had reached my row.

"Let her go!" Rhyan yelled, rushing for Viktor.

I shook my head. No, no. He couldn't get in trouble—not with Imperator Kormac, not with his father watching nearby. Missing a few hours of a shift and having Sean cover was one thing, but this could get him thrown out of Bamaria and right back inside his father's prison.

"Galen!" I yelled, jerking my chin at Rhyan.

He nodded once and took off, intercepting Rhyan just in time.

"Imperator, you have stepped out of line." Aemon roared, leaping past Rhyan and Galen. He stood between me and Imperator Kormac. "She needs to be transported to Cresthaven immediately."

Viktor laughed and squeezed my wrists tighter, pulling them almost to the point of breaking my arms.

"I'll be taking Lady Lyriana into custody," said the Imperator.

"Like hell you will," snarled the Ready.

Rhyan grunted, struggling against Galen, who barely had a hold on him. Rhyan was a force of nature when he wanted to be, and he wasn't calming down.

"Take your hands off her," Rhyan shouted, finally breaking free.

"I'm afraid we can't do that," the Imperator said. "See, Arkasva Batavia, High Lady of Bamaria, has just given Lady Lyriana's hand to my son, Viktor. For marriage."

"What? No!" I said.

"Your wants are not in question," the Imperator said, stalking closer. "This is between me and your High Lady."

I struggled against Viktor's hold, my stomach turning. "Why does this even matter now? There's akadim! I need to get to Cresthaven!"

"Lady Lyriana," said the Imperator, "Aemon has failed you greatly. I apologize for being the one to tell you. But as Imperator and your new father-in-law, your protection is of the utmost importance. Cresthaven is no longer a safe option for your protection."

"Because you say so!" I yelled, no longer able to keep decorum.

"Because," the Imperator screamed, "the Lady Meera and Lady Morgana were just abducted from Cresthaven. By akadim."

My vision went out of focus, the world blurry. Dark. I felt like the wind had been knocked out of me. My knees buckled, and only Viktor's grip on my wrists kept me from sinking to the ground. I opened my mouth. But there were no words. No breath. And then finally, as if someone else were speaking, I managed, "Abducted? By...akadim?"

I felt like I'd left my body and was floating above it. Everyone was yelling, but their voices were distant, like I was under water and they were on shore, and I was struggling to swim for the surface. And then I slammed back into myself, cold reality crashing into me.

"Akadim!" I cried. "Akadim you're supposed to be protecting us from! Akadim that have been breaching our borders ever since you came here!" I roared, spitting in his face. "Where are they? Who's gone after them? Why are you here and not pursuing them?" I felt like I was farther than Lethea. How were we all just standing here? Why weren't we chasing after them!

The Imperator placed his hands on his hips, his head cocked to the side. "My men are already on their trail, fighting to catch the akadim, to bring your sisters back. And I am here because I care deeply for your safety."

"By arresting me?" I screamed. "Now? Let me go! I can fight! You know I can. I'll find them! I need to find them!" I was going to lose my mind. How was this happening? How we were all just standing here! How was this even real?

"You're not under arrest, my lady," the Imperator said.

"Then take your hands off of me so I can go after them!"

"We cannot risk you being captured as well. We don't know why your sisters were abducted. Reason stands they'd take you next. Therefore, we're taking you to the most secure place available until further notice." He turned to the Bastardmaker. "She'll be safe in the Shadow Stronghold until we can transport to Korteria."

"NO!" Rhyan roared.

Aemon's aura struck out like a hammer, black and heavy. "She's not going there," he said. "Protocol demands the heirs come to my home if Cresthaven is breached."

The Imperator laughed. "She's no longer an heir. She's officially my responsibility. We'll take her back to Vrukshire Keep when its deemed safe to travel." He nodded at the Bastardmaker. "Take her to the Stronghold now." He eyed me struggling against Viktor's hold, kicking and thrashing like I was farther than Lethea. They couldn't do this. They couldn't take me like this. The Imperator glared in disgust. "The lady must be calmed." He jerked his chin, and the Kormac mage stepped forward, his blue robes blowing in the frigid wind. The mage pulled a cloth from his belt, and a familiar, sickening smell wafted toward my nose.

My breath hitched. The cloth was soaked with the same drug Markan had used to keep me from going after Jules.

I shook my head violently, struggling against my captors, squirming and desperate. I bit my lips shut and held my breath, as Rhyan shouted in the distance, screaming my name and telling them to stop. He was racing forward, a look on his face like he was about to travel. But Aemon stopped him.

Viktor's grin was the last thing I saw before the cloth covered my face and I lost consciousness.

CHAPTER TWENTY-TWO

IT WAS THE SAME cell. The same fucking cell they'd thrown me into on my birthday. The same cell I'd spent a week in, scared and terrified while I'd waited for the examiner to come for me. I knew the walls, knew the floor, knew every groove of wood, turn of stone, stain, and Godsdamned smell.

I groaned, sitting up in the same bed, the same moldy, stinking blanket covering me. I threw it off, my head pounding as I swept my feet over the edge and stood. My body swayed. Rage boiling me inside me. Anger, fear. My stomach twisted.

And I screamed.

Morgana. Meera. Akadim had taken them. Monsters had the only true family I had left. I didn't care about Arianna. I didn't care what contract she'd allegedly signed with the Imperator. I needed to find my sisters, to protect them.

If they were still alive. If the akadim hadn't—

Another scream tore through me and I slammed my fists into my thighs before rushed for the bucket and dry heaved.

"You're making a racket." Markan stood outside my cell.

I picked up the bucket and hurled it at the bars.

The surly escort grimaced. "That could have been extremely disgusting."

"Then count yourself lucky," I growled. "What do you know? Any word? What's happening? Where are they?"

"Apparently, from what we've learned, Morgana led Meera from dinner out to the beach. She went without alerting her escort. Morgana's guard Jace was with them. Soturion Akillus accompanied them as well. Akillus has not woken up yet to report more."

I squeezed my eyes shut, taking in the severity of Akillus being unconscious. "Is he...alive?"

"We're waiting for more news," Markan said quietly. "According to Soturion Jace, the akadim appeared out of nowhere, arriving on the beach in seraphim carriages. There were two. They grabbed your sisters, threw them in the carriages, and took off."

I shook my head. "Akadim don't do that. They can't fly in seraphim—seraphim won't tolerate it."

"Well, these did." Markan shrugged. "Figures. You kill one, and you think you're an expert? Their numbers aren't just growing, they're evolving. And these ones fly."

"Fuck you."

Markan's lip curled. "Do you think Jace is lying?"

My hands fisted at my sides. "I don't know what to think. No one's seen them?"

"Ashvan riders have been sent after them."

"Ka Batavia? Or Kormac?" I asked the question through gritted teeth.

"Don't ask stupid questions. Every able-bodied soturion is on their trail."

"Except me. And you, apparently." Tears ran down my face. "It doesn't matter. Akadim kill and...oh, Gods." I tried to shake the images. I was going to faint if I thought too hard about what was happening.

Markan, for once, looked uncomfortable, shifting his weight. "If it's any comfort, Jace was—" He exhaled sharply. "Jace was almost, you know," he scrunched up his nose, "by one. His clothes had been removed, but he wasn't...assaulted. The other akadim stopped him. According to Jace, one akadim told the other not to harm your sisters. Seems like they were sent to bring them back to someone else."

"Someone else?" I pushed my hands through my hair. "Who? Who could possibly have that much control over akadim?"

"No idea. Let's just hope for your sake, and theirs, that the akadim truly are under the control of this person. It buys us more time to find them."

"And me?" I asked. "Am I supposed to buy my time in here? Sitting helplessly? Doing nothing? Waiting for the Imperator to take me away?"

Markan stepped forward, his nostrils flaring. "I don't like you, *my lady*," he said. "I never have. You're spoiled, and you're a brat. And you think you're smarter than you are. But I have dedicated my life to keeping you safe because I understand what that means to Bamaria. And I do actually like my country. So yes, you're going to stay here and stay safe. Whether you like the Imperator or not, because Moriel-fucking akadim managing to not only enter Bamaria, but enter Cresthaven—that does not look good for you."

"Gryphon-shit!" I roared. Wind howled violently outside my window, and a cold breeze gusted through the ceiling. "Then why isn't Arianna here, too? Or Naria? I'm not even an heir anymore. If Cresthaven is in such danger, and this is the only place that's safe, why not bring them here? Why haven't they been evacuated?"

"That's beyond my station."

"It's because I'm a prisoner, and fuck all your allegiance to this country because you are helping a traitor by keeping me here. You're keeping me until the Imperator's ready to take me. The blood of Bamaria is in my veins and you know it."

Markan nodded. "Maybe. However, I would not dare call anyone a traitor. All I know is I am helping myself stay alive by following orders. And despite your low opinion of me, I am also keeping you alive."

I crossed my arms over my chest. "I demand an audience with Aemon."

"Demand all you want. Not up to me."

"Imperator's orders?" I snarled.

"Obviously."

"Real fucking loyal to Bamaria!" I started pacing, like I'd done the last time I'd been in this cell, trying to stay calm. I had to keep my wits about me, find a way out of here, find out what was happening, and find a way to help. I couldn't stay here. I couldn't. I'd lose my mind. I'd lose everything.

But an hour passed, and then another. It was growing late. My sisters could be dead by now, tortured, their souls eaten. Their bodies already transforming into akadim.

I squeezed my eyes shut, banishing the images of their bodies growing and lengthening, of red lines appearing all over their skin, their teeth elongating into fangs, the cries for help they would have made before it all happened, their horror hearing each other suffer, knowing they couldn't do anything because their only weapon—magic—didn't work. I brushed tears from my eyes and went to the bars, slamming my palms into them.

A door opened down the hall, and light burst into my cell as someone entered with a torch.

Arkturion Aemon. The Ready.

"Take a break, soturion," he ordered Markan. "I'll be here."

Markan nodded and headed down the hall as Aemon set the torch into a holder behind him. He met me at the bars, and he was the Ready—furious, lethal.

"What's going on?" I asked at once. "Why are you here? Why aren't you searching for them?"

"I am," he said, bowing his head in respect. "I have my best soturi out there looking for them. I'm having Aditi prepared in the stables and flying out to join the search." He held up his Empire-issued vadati. As arkturion, he was legally allowed to carry one, unlike me and Rhyan. "Ka Kormac is looking for them."

"No, they're not!" I snapped.

"Maybe not *well*, but they *are* looking."

"They let them in!" I cried.

"We don't know that yet," he said, his voice solemn. "Listen, I am trying to get you out before I leave as well, to find a way to keep them from taking you out of the country. But I need you to stay calm. I cannot free you. It's not safe. And the Imperator will have my head. But is there something else I could do to give you peace of mind? Could I bring you something of comfort?"

"Why?" I sneered. "I'm not your responsibility anymore—I'm the Imperator's."

"That's not finalized," he said. "It's not my place to get between the business of arkasvim. But you're still a student here—still a Bamarian citizen, and where I can step in, I will. Name something I can do for you. Is there a meal you want? A special blanket? Say the words, it's yours. Whatever you want."

I want Rhyan.

I put my hand on my waist. Beneath my tunic was the golden chain holding his vadati. I stifled a gasp. It hadn't occurred to me before that Ka Kormac was too fucking stupid to leave me untouched. They always underestimated women. My dagger was still at my hip. Not that it would do me any good in here. But still... I had a way out. I could call Rhyan, but only if I had privacy. No one could know I had the stone or that he was visiting. They especially couldn't know *how* he'd get to me.

"I want an hour to myself," I said. "No guards. You know Godsdamned well I can't escape. Please."

"Done," he said. "I'll give you two."

"Thank you, Aemon." Voice shaking, I stared at my feet. "They're dead, aren't they? Or worse." My vision blurred.

"No," he said. "All reports suggest this is not a normal situation."

I looked up at him, my hope hanging on by a thread.

"Are you sure?"

"Chin up, soturion. I normally wouldn't call this a plus, but akadim behavior is changing. Rapidly. Not good for the Empire, but it offers hope for Morgana and Meera. We've never seen this before. So, let's expect results unlike any we've seen before." He nodded. "Two hours. Look at me. I'm going to get them back. Next time I see you, I plan to do so with your sisters present. That's a promise." He spoke with such intensity, I almost believed him. But we both knew it was an empty oath.

Aemon turned and headed down the hall. I waited for the sound of his footsteps to fade into faint echoes beyond the hall door then listened for the sound of anyone else approaching.

I climbed back onto the bed and tugged the covers over my head, trying not to breathe. Then I pulled out the stone and held it to my lips.

"Rhyan?"

"Lyr," he replied at once, the stone lighting up in my palm. "Are you alright? What's happening?"

"I'm in the cell...same as before," I said, starting to cry.

"Shit. Did they hurt you?"

"No. Aemon got me two hours of privacy. Can you...can you come?" I asked, my voice breaking. "I need you."

The stone turned white, and I pulled back the covers. Rhyan was standing in front of me, his arms wide open. I leapt from the bed and ran into them, wrapping my arms around his back and sobbing into his armor.

"Hey, partner." His hands tightened around me, stroking my back and my hair.

Being in Rhyan's arms, I finally broke down.

"Do you know anything?" I asked through my sobs.

"No, not yet," he said softly. "I've been waiting for orders and word you were okay."

"Do you really think they're still alive?"

"I do," Rhyan said, fierce determination in his eyes.

"Aemon thinks so, too. But how? What kind of akadim don't kill immediately?"

Rhyan ran his thumb across my cheek. "I don't know. But I've been tracking them for months. They're growing in presence, and they're getting organized. Their nests...they're more sophisticated than I've ever seen. There's assigned sleeping quarters, there appears to be a hierarchy. Relationships between them. This isn't what I would have predicted, but based on what I've seen, it seems to be following their pattern. I can't deny that your sisters need to be rescued as quickly as possible, but we might have time. You've got to keep your hopes up. Anything is possible."

Footsteps sounded down the hall. My eyes widened.

"He said two hours!" It had barely been ten minutes.

"Call me when it's clear." He kissed my cheek before vanishing on the spot.

The door opened and slammed shut. I walked forward to the bars of the cell, a pit in my stomach over who might be approaching. I trusted Aemon to keep his word, which meant whoever was here now went above Aemon.

I swallowed down the bile in my throat, sure I was about to feel the dark predatory aura of the Imperator.

But no one came.

"Hello?" I called out. "Hello?"

The door had definitely opened and closed. Had someone walked down this hall by mistake? I listened more closely.

Then I heard it—a series of small thuds. The sounds were growing louder. Something was rolling down the hall, coming toward me.

I peered out. It was a small leather case, identical to the one that had been thrown in my bedroom. It was another message from my supporter, the person who'd led me to my mother's journal.

The scroll stopped dead in the middle of the hallway outside my prison bars. I reached my arm forward, but the case was too far for me to reach.

"Hello?" I yelled again. "Anyone there?"

Silence was the only response. A minute passed, and then another.

I called out to Rhyan, and he was by my side a second later.

"Can you get that for me?" I asked, pointing at the black case.

He vanished, reappeared outside the bars, and bent to pick it up. A second later, he was frowning inside my cell.

"What is this?" he asked.

"It matches the other one—the one with the note that led to my mother's journal." I slid my hand up my sleeve, gripped my arm cuff, and slid it down. Inside a compartment of the cuff was the parchment rolled up as tightly as I could manage.

Rhyan took the scroll and read through it again, as I opened the leather case. Another carefully rolled parchment fell into my hand along with a white satin purse tied with white ribbon. I gripped the purse and shook it, but it was weightless and soundless. Seemingly empty.

"Let's look at the handwriting," Rhyan said.

I reread the original note.

Your Grace,

Now the phrase "shekar arkasva" has true meaning. Not all support the illegitimate black seraphim. You're not alone.

131189114141

My eyes flicked to the new note. The handwriting was identical to the original as the case it had come in. Rhyan stood behind me, one arm wrapped around my waist and his chin on my shoulder, as I started to read.

My Lady,

I offered you all the clues you needed, and pulled the journal so you could read for yourself, knowing you're clever enough to have pieced the puzzle together. The way is clear. Claim your power. And do it now. Your sisters' lives depend on it.

Go to Glemaria. Open the seraphim. Bring what lies inside directly to me, and place it in my hands. It is of great value. I'll be waiting for you in the Allurian Pass with your sisters. You have two weeks. Come alone. Or you'll add two more akadim to your Ka.

I dropped the parchment, shaking.

"Allurian Pass?" I asked.

"It's on the western Glemarian border—a cave system leading to the human lands. It's on the other side of the country from the seraphim's location," Rhyan said, reaching for the satin purse in my hands. "Why does it feel empty?" He untied the string, opened the pouch, and dumped the contents into his hand.

My stomach turned.

There were two locks of hair. One thick and wavy, black like a raven. The other finer and ash brown.

"Cut from Morgana and Meera," I cried.

"Gods." Rhyan put the locks back into the bag before retrieving the note. "It's not signed," he said. "And the other had no signature, either, only the reference number to the journal. Do we have any idea who this could be?"

My shoulders heaved as I tried to suck in air, to not panic. Rhyan turned me in his arms.

"Shhh, partner, I know, I know. I'm sorry." He wrapped me against him. "But this is proof they're alive."

I sniffled. "How do we know we can trust them? Trust the akadim?"

"We can't," he said. "That doesn't mean we're not going to try everything to get them back."

"I don't even have everything they're asking for. I still need the key on your father's sword." I felt hopeless. "And he's not going to give it to me—not without me going to him. Not without me making another deal."

"We need Mercurial," he said.

"What?"

"We need Mercurial. This is about your power. You have a deal with him already. A deal to claim your magic."

"But Ramia said he's missing."

"MERCURIAL!" Rhyan yelled, arms out wide. "Hey! You Afeyan bastard! Where are you? Come on! Come and play! It's your favorite not-lord, I'm right here!"

"Rhyan! What in the—?"

His hands slid behind my waist and shoulder, dipping me backwards. His face leaned over mine, positioned for a kiss. "I have Lyr in my arms, in a compromising position!" he shouted. "Your favorite! Come on, interrupt, you know you want to! Look at my hand." He placed it over my heart, his fingers spreading toward the curve of my breasts. "Oh, come on, First Messenger to her Royal Highness! I know you love this!"

I held my breath, looking around the cell and hall, which remained empty.

A clap of thunder burst against the walls, so loud I cowered in Rhyan's arms.

He pulled me up at once as shadows swept through the cell. Complete and utter darkness surrounded us. Seconds passed, but my eyes couldn't adjust to the light. I couldn't see even a hint of the shape of Rhyan or the bars or anything.

But I felt it. Mercurial.

"It's him," I said. "He's responding to your call."

All at once, the cell filled with small glittering Valalumir stars. They fell slowly from the ceiling to the ground, each one spinning the way Mercurial had spun mine in his palm.

"It's his aura," Rhyan said, eyes moving slowly around the cell. "He heard us."

"But he's not here." I reached out a hand. "Mercurial?" I asked, feeling his presence, his energy imbued in every star. My chest heated, and a faint glow emerged from behind my tunic. It wasn't painful, but there was something forceful in it—something that made me positive it was Mercurial doing this, affecting me.

The stars vanished, and the light of the torches and the moon returned.

I turned on my heels, checking that every star was gone. "I think he really might be in trouble."

"Then he can't help us. I'm ready to do whatever it takes to get your sisters back. But I don't think we should just be following some stranger's orders like this. We need to tell Aemon at least," Rhyan said. "Have him send his soturi to this location immediately."

"The note said come alone."

Rhyan folded his arms across his chest, the veins in his forearms protruding. "Lyr, we don't know who this is or if this is someone who will keep their word."

"So, your solution is to alert the Ready? And then what? Aemon tries to collect the pieces? That's if he even believes me or takes this note seriously. Plus, you know your father isn't going to admit to Aemon he has the key. Or that such a thing even exists. And if by some miracle he does, do you know how long it would take to negotiate this exchange between our countries?

Think about it. Why does your father want me? Why else did he speak to my mother of marriage when I was just a baby? He knows I can open the seraphim and offer him one of the shards of the Valalumir. Imperator Kormac wants it—that's why he's forcing me into an engagement with Viktor. I was third from the Seat. I should never have been on anyone's radar. I was a spare's spare, not a prize for Imperators. Everyone is after this. And after me because I am Asherah. If we tell someone...we'll get nowhere. And I'll lose my sisters."

"But the only way to even open the seraphim, Lyr—if they're telling the truth—is to make a deal with my father, trade with him for the key."

We stared at each other, both knowing what that trade meant: Rhyan.

His chest heaved, his mouth opened in protest.

I shook my head fiercely. "You know I'd never do anything that hurts you. Especially not with him. Maybe I can offer him something else."

Rhyan's eyes narrowed. "Like what? What offer do you think he'll take, Lyr? I'm not going to let you sacrifice yourself."

"Rhyan, you don't get to decide what I'm willing to lose. I have to try. I need to get my sisters back."

"No." His aura darkened, as he took a step forward. "You're not doing that. I don't care. Lyr, you're not making a deal with my father. I swore to protect you, especially from him."

"But I—"

"NO!" Rhyan's knees bent, his hands running through his hair, before he sprung up, towering over me. "No! That's final."

"Rhyan! It's my only choice right now. Please." My voice broke. "I lost Jules, my father, my friends. I can't...I can't lose them, too."

He grabbed my shoulders. "You're not going to."

"Then get me out of here. Take me to him. Let's start. Let's figure this out."

"If you make a deal with my father," he said, voice low, "he will twist it. He will hurt you. He'll take you for all you are and more."

"You think I don't know that? You think Ka Kormac isn't already trying to do the same? I know, but I have no other choice at this point. I'm willing to risk it."

His aura exploded. "You're willing to risk it?" The room darkened. His accent was so heavy with anger, he was hard to understand. "I'm not willing to risk you. You don't know him, Lyr, you don't know what he's capable of. He'll torture you."

"I've made deals with Imperators before."

"And barely survived them."

"I *am* surviving them," I yelled. "This is about my sisters. Gods! I have to try. Please, get me out of here. Please, we'll figure something out."

Rhyan grabbed hold of my wrist, turning over my palm. "Do you see this? See his marks on you?"

I stiffened.

"That's just the start. This—" His voice broke. "This is killing me. And I know him. I know him so fucking well. This is *nothing*. Nothing compared to what he'll do. What he's capable of. Do you think I could stand it—seeing him hurt you?"

I pulled my hand from his, fighting back the tears in my eyes. "No more than I could stand to see him hurt you. But we only have two weeks to get them back—to cross the Empire and Glemaria. And if Mercurial isn't answering our calls, if he's gone or he's in trouble, we're out of options. It took me months to learn this much information." I wiped at the tears blurring my vision. "I hate this, hate that he has to be involved, but he is. Gods know why, but he has the key, and we need it."

Rhyan's eyes glazed over, his expression slack, like his mind had gone somewhere else—somewhere painful. The muscles in his jaw worked. "I can't let you do it."

"Rhyan, I have to."

"No. No deal," he growled.

"Rhyan!"

He had a strange look in his eyes. His jaw was set and his mouth firm, like he'd made some decision. His hands clenched into fists at his sides, his forearm veins straining.

"It's already decided," he said, his voice low and strange. Then he was gone. He'd traveled without even saying goodbye.

"RHYAN!" I yelled into the stone. It remained white. I yelled again and again.

But he didn't answer.

An hour passed. I nearly lost my voice screaming into the stone, trying to get Rhyan to come back, to talk to me, to work something out with me even if it wasn't a deal with his father. I couldn't think straight. I was too scared and worried, and myself to Moriel, he'd left me alone. I didn't know what to do anymore or what was right. I just knew I needed to do something. I was Asherah. My sisters had been taken to get to me because of some power I had, some leverage I was in possession of.

And I couldn't do a fucking thing.

I read the note again and again, my fingers gripping it so tightly I nearly ripped it to pieces, before I shoved it inside my cuff with the first one and returned to pacing the cell.

There was only one thing I knew for sure: whoever had done this, whoever had taken my sisters, whoever had hurt them, I would find them. And I would kill them.

"Partner," Rhyan said.

I sucked in a breath, my hands forming fists. I'd never been so angry with him in my life. Never so hurt. Or betrayed. I was shaking with it. "Now you answer!" I cried. "A fucking hour you left me here—and don't you dare call me *partner* because I'm clearly not!" I shouted into the stone. It was only afterward I realized that the stone in my palm was clear—not glowing, not blue. Not even remotely warm.

"Lyr."

I whirled around and found Rhyan standing behind me with two large bags over his shoulders. He was holding his weight unevenly, putting extra pressure on his left side, like his right leg was injured. His eyes were wet and red and had a haunted, distant look to them. Looking more carefully, I saw he also had a cut on his cheek that would turn into a black eye within a few hours. A bandage covered his hand. He grimaced as he stepped forward.

"Lyr, don't say that. You are my partner," he said softly, out of breath. "Always. I'm sorry I took so long. I had to complete a few errands first."

"You're hurt," I said, reaching for his face. He looked like he'd been punched multiple times. Red splotches on his neck signaled he'd been choked. "Who did this to you?"

He winced, shifting his face away. "Doesn't matter. A minor scuffle. Worth it." His throat worked as he swallowed, his chest rising and falling rapidly.

"Rhyan, what the hell happened to you? This doesn't look like a minor scuffle."

He gave a mirthless laugh. "Maybe minor was the wrong word. But I got you this." He reached for his belt and removed a red star with rays curved like those of the sun.

I gasped. "Gods! You went to your father?"

"Nothing like a family reunion," he joked, but his voice was shaking.

"Rhyan." I took his hand, wanting to soothe him, to tend to his wounds. "You didn't...." My eyes searched his. "You didn't make a deal, did you? Please, tell me you're not concealing a blood oath." Or ropes secretly binding and torturing him.

His jaw tightened. "No. I was old-fashioned about it. We fought." His eyes glazed over. "I'm still stronger, it turns out. But he's improved since I last saw him. Got a few hits in. And maybe a slash or two." He sucked on his upper lip, looking like he was trying not to cry.

"Shit," I said. "That bastard. I'm sorry."

He stretched his neck with a small groan. "I'll be okay."

"But he's going to—"

"Come after me?" He shrugged. "He's already after me for murder." Rhyan offered me a crooked smile. "I figured a little theft on top couldn't be too detrimental to my reputation."

"And the bags?" I asked.

He adjusted the straps over his shoulders. "I packed for our trip. One for me. One for you. Grabbed as much as I could from both our apartments—clothes, armor, food. Sorry I rushed out. Knew I had to get back before your next guard showed."

My eyes widened. "So we're going? To Glemaria? To get Morgs and Meera?"

"Of course, we are. I just, I couldn't let you entangle yourself with him. It had to be me. I couldn't live with myself otherwise. You're already entangled with the immortal. It was my turn. I had to do this one."

"But he's going to be looking for you. Rhyan, he has na-hashim."

"And I have eyes. I know how to survive out there. And we can move fast if we have to. Although," he frowned, "I hate to admit it, but I do have my limits. I can't just take us straight to Glemaria, it's too far of a jump. Too dangerous. The recovery...could be lengthy. I can't risk being unable to protect you when we get there."

"Then we won't risk it. Small jumps only," I said.

Rhyan nodded, his lips tightened into a grimace.

I sighed. "So much for us staying here." How many times had we discussed running, discussed it and then fell back on duty and staying?

"After we find your sisters and we find your power, we'll find our way back. This isn't you running away. This is you and me joining the search party."

"Okay," I said. "But what about—we're still kashonim." Anyone thinking we'd run off together would be suspicious, even if it was just to find my sisters.

"I left a note for Aemon. I told him I was taking off—that I was leaving on my own to find them. That I didn't want to waste time receiving orders and that my recent kills and hunts made me the best candidate to do so."

He could still be in so much trouble for this, but it was a believable excuse that'd hopefully be forgivable when we found my sisters. Finding them was key. I couldn't fathom a world where we didn't succeed, didn't get them back. And only in that world, could we ever come home.

"They were always going to send me on this mission anyway," he said, "But, together, we need to be careful. Avoid major cities, anywhere we could be recognized. We can't let anyone see us together."

"What if it's all a trap?" I asked, my voice small. Now that we were going, it was starting to feel like every decision was farther than Lethea. Doubts were creeping in.

"Oh, it's definitely a trap." His eyes searched mine. "But it's one I'll risk for you. And for them."

I wrapped my arms around him. "You can just get me out of here, you know, and then stay back, wait for orders, come find me later. Then you won't get in trouble or expose yourself to your father."

"Partner." Rhyan shook his head. "I'm not leaving your side. And I won't risk you out there." He pulled me closer, lifting me onto his toes. One hand snaked around my ass and hugged me against him. He breathed me in, for a long moment. Looking down at me, his lips quirked into a nervous smile, as he said, "Now, I just have to check because the last time we were here, you ordered me to keep you locked in the prison. You seemed very against breaking out, quite morally opposed. It was very proper, very law-abiding. Which," he shrugged, "as a forsworn bastard criminal, I can't say I relate to, but I respected your beliefs." He winked. "So, before we do this, I just want to know for sure that this time, you do want to break the law and all. Be a criminal on the run."

I gave a shaky, teary-eyed laugh, so grateful he had the ability to lighten things when my world felt unbelievably dark and ready to implode. I also understood he was lightening things for himself. He needed it after seeing his father. For him to have done all of this in an hour—fought his father, left a note for Aemon, and packed bags at both of our apartments—he had to be exhausted. And he'd been injured. He needed all the strength he could find for one more push, one more burst of power to get us out of here.

I tightened my arms around him. "I consent. Let's break the law."

He raised his good eyebrow and smirked. "And here I was, trying to live the straight life. Be all reformed and shit. You are such a bad influence on me."

Footsteps sounded down the hall. Someone was coming. Our opening to escape was about to close.

Rhyan's eyes widened, the green of his irises blazing as he stared at me, the weight of what we were about to do settling over us. After caging me within his arms, he made one final adjustment to his weight, his breath still uneven from his injuries. He nodded once. One final check-in. One final chance to back out.

I nodded back.

The door hinged.

"All right, partner," he whispered. "Hold on tight."

The door slammed open, and we were gone.

CHAPTER TWENTY-THREE

MY FEET TOUCHED DOWN on cold, hard grass frosted with a light coat of snow. Before I could become oriented to my new surroundings, I steadied myself, preparing to take on Rhyan's weight while he recovered.

He crashed against my body with a groan of pain.

I stumbled back, unprepared, but quickly tensed my core muscles, managing to hold him up. I felt his head resting against my shoulder in the dark and pressed my heels into the ground, tightening my arms around him.

"You okay?" I asked. I stroked the back of his neck, it was covered in sweat despite the cold.

He was still breathing heavily as he groaned. "My leg. It was bothering me before, but now it's like...like I walked across the country with it injured. It would have healed by now, but...." He sucked air in through his lips.

"I should have taken the bags."

"It wouldn't have made a difference. I still had to carry you to travel."

Gods. He'd carried me and our bags on an injured leg for who knows how many miles. "I want to look at your leg and all your other injuries. I'm going to take care of you."

His chest heaved against mine. "We need to get to safety first. Akadim are a real threat now, especially here—along with everything else."

"Where's safety?" I asked, suddenly cold despite his body heat. "And where are we?"

"Elyria. Right past the border," he groaned.

"Rhyan! That was too far."

"I know. But we had to get out of the country. They'll know you're missing by now. And the borders will have closed with the akadim attack. I needed to get us beyond them." He made a pained sound, and at my worried expression, added, "I'll recover. I've had worse."

"Here," I said, pulling his arm over my shoulder. I slid one of the bags off his back and threw it on top of mine.

There was a rumbling sound coming from behind us. Boots pounding into the ground. Marching.

Soturi.

"Against the trees," Rhyan ordered. "Now."

My breath caught, but I started moving. Holding tightly to him, I backed up, step by step, until my backside was against a large moon tree, its silver leaves glinting beneath the stars. Rhyan pushed the bags off our shoulders and loosened his soturion cloak enough to cover me in it, holding it over our heads.

His forehead pressed to mine, his body flush against me.

The marching grew louder, the soldiers moving quicker. My nerves were getting the better of me as my entire body started to shake. We were barely off the road. I knew soturion cloaks camouflaged their wearers, and we were in nature, and it was dark. I'd seen soturi vanish under far less ideal circumstances. But testing the concept now felt too risky. What if a soturion stopped to take a piss? What if the magic of the cloaks failed? What if they searched this area?

"There's no way the Batavia girl got all the way out here," came a yell. "She's probably hiding in one of the hundred rooms of the fortress."

They were close. Too close.

"Well, if she gets here, we'll be ready."

"Ready for a nap," said another with a laugh. "Did they check under her prison bed? Or in Viktor's?"

These were Ka Kormac soturi. And they weren't hunting akadim or trying to rescue my sisters—they were hunting me. Sent to bring me back to the Imperator.

My breath came in quick, and loud spurts.

Rhyan pushed his knee between my legs, pinning me in place, pressing harder against me until I stilled. "Shhh," he whispered in my ear.

I couldn't control my breathing after everything that had happened. If they spotted me, we were fucked. I'd never escape again and Rhyan would be exposed, sent back to his father. My sisters never saved.

Rhyan's hand covered my mouth, his eyes catching mine in the dark. "Breathe," he hissed under his breath. "Slow."

The soturi were running, their boots hitting the road. How many were there?

Minutes passed. The sounds of the march grew faint, as the soturi moved on.

I swallowed, staring up at Rhyan, a question in my eyes. Were we safe? Were they gone?

He loosened his hold on my mouth but kept his hand over it. "One more minute," he whispered. "To be sure."

I nodded and squeezed my eyes shut, trying to breathe as quietly as I could.

Finally, when the only sounds I could make out were the wind and the noises of creatures scurrying between the trees, Rhyan pulled his hand back.

"Fuck," he said. "Are you okay?"

"Yes," I whispered.

"Sorry about the hand."

"It's okay. I think I needed you to do that."

His eyes caught mine, and for a second, my thoughts flashed back to the last time he'd had me pressed up against a tree. His tongue darted across his bottom lip like he was remembering, too.

Then his expression hardened with determination. "We need to get inside. Fast. Akadim hunt around these parts. And more soturi will be coming through, including those who know your face."

"Where do we go?" I asked. "How are we going to avoid being seen?"

Rhyan stretched his neck, his face screwed up in pain. "There's a place nearby, safe and discreet. They, um, they cater to a certain kind of customer."

"Certain kind of customer?" I asked suspiciously.

"The sort who don't want to be seen going in there." He readjusted the cloak over our heads.

"Like us?" I wrinkled my nose in confusion.

"Not like us," he said quickly, running his hand through his hair. "But good for us. Because they won't tell anyone we're there."

"Why?"

"Because it's a brothel," he said quietly. "And I know because...I've stayed there before."

I stilled.

"Not for that," he added quickly. "Just for room and board. But they're actually, well, a very welcome alternative to the road when you're forsworn."

I nodded slowly, taking that in. "You're sure we can trust them?"

"Keep your hood up and pull an extra gold coin from your bag just in case. But yes. They've protected me in the past." He readjusted his weight, putting pressure onto his right foot. He grimaced, sucking in a breath through his teeth, but he managed to bear weight on both legs. Though he was seriously injured, he was starting to recover. His health and fitness were absolutely remarkable, but he still had a long way to go before he was at full strength again. And if we were going to survive this trip, we both needed him at full strength.

Directing us deeper into the woods, Rhyan moved slowly through the moon trees to avoid getting his foot caught or tangled in the snow-covered brambles. He kept his arm on my shoulder for support, leaning into me while I tried to keep our pace steady.

Once we made it through the clearing, I could see we were in a small village filled with simple round houses. A large rectangular building made of stone stood in the center, its sides painted with orange and purple ashvan horses. We were definitely in Elyria. The more I looked, the more I saw the sigil of Ka Elys represented on orange flags or the corners of signs. Farther down the clearing were more torches and buildings, possibly a small market. Ashvan horses depicted everywhere

"Is that it?" I pointed at the central building.

"That's check-in," he said. "There's a restaurant and kitchen inside. And it's where the employees live."

We moved forward, hearing torches crackling and popping against the wind.

"And the other homes?" I asked. They all seemed to be built around the central building. I frowned. They weren't just round, but extremely small. Smaller looking than even my apartment.

"Not homes. Rooms. That's where we stay," he said. "Like I said, it's a lot of privacy. For a brothel."

"Good, we'll need it."

"Will we?" he asked, voice low.

I bit my lip, thinking of him pushing me against the tree. "So, I can look at your leg."

He wrapped an arm around my shoulder, shuffling forward. "Come on, then."

I pulled open the front door, bracing myself for all sorts of nudity and states of undress. My cheeks were preemptively red with embarrassment at the idea of walking into a room full of people having sex. And being with Rhyan.

But it was nothing like that. We had entered a private entrance hall that reminded me more of the Great Library. In front of us was a desk, behind which a beautiful middle-aged woman poured over a scroll. Long shiny black hair, typical of Elyrians, fell in curls down her back, and she wore a long-sleeved black dress of thick woven cotton. A golden ashvan charm hung from her neck, and golden bangles chimed against her wrist. There was a fireplace off to the side for warmth, and several torches flickered against the walls, which were plain save for a few shelves holding leather scroll cases.

"Close the door, you're letting in the cold," she called without looking up.

Rhyan shifted behind me, sealing the door into place. "Evening," he said. "We'd like a room for the night if you have any available."

"Entertainment?" she asked, still not looking up. "Company?"

"Just the room, thanks," Rhyan said. "And maybe if there's any dinner left?"

At last, she looked up, and a wide grin spread across her lips. "Ah, you. Should've known."

I could see the moment she registered his injuries. But within the same moment she schooled her expression to remain neutral. Her eyes flicked to me, and I lowered my face, self-consciously pushing my hood over my forehead.

I didn't have a diadem. She'd never seen me before—she'd have no idea who I was. But her eyes betrayed her intelligence, and the fact that she recognized Rhyan made me nervous.

"Friend staying with you?" she asked.

"Yes," Rhyan said.

"We have a room. But there's only one bed. Will that be a problem for your *friend*?"

Rhyan coughed. "Not at all."

"How many nights?" she asked.

"One for now," he replied.

She turned to the wall behind her and grabbed a key hanging from a hook. She pointed her stave at it, and it glowed with blue light as she chanted a locking spell over it.

Rhyan reached into his belt pouch, but I fished through mine, producing several gold coins, and pressed them into his hand.

He looked ready to protest but then offered a curt nod.

"Room seven," she said. "Two hundred gold for the night and two dinners. We'll have two breakfasts made up for you in the morning. If you want lunch, let us know. Lunch is free. And if you need another night, we can do that, too."

Rhyan limped forward and placed three large gold coins on the desk.

She handed him the key. "Too much," she said.

"Silence is appreciated," he said slowly.

"Of course." She swiped the coins behind the desk, and tucked them into a box with a sigil I didn't recognize. The sigil was simple, a purple Valalumir before a golden sun. Her eyes tracked mine. "It's antique. We'll have those two meals to you shortly."

"Thank you," I said.

"Everyone here is discreet," she said, almost as if in warning. She offered a wide smile, looking me up and down, something pointed in her eyes before she went back to her scroll.

Rhyan leaned in toward me. "Ka Azria," he said quietly.

My eyes widened. Gods...the Ka who'd been wiped out by the Emperor. I'd never thought that some Elyrians might still be loyal to them, might not approve of Ka Elys ruling over them now. I only then realized how nearly complete their destruction had been. The Emperor wouldn't have just killed the family, but erased every last image of their sigil as well.

I hauled our bags over my shoulders, waving off Rhyan's protests, and held the door open for him before closing it behind us.

"She knew you," I said.

Rhyan stared at the ground as we walked. "Like I said, I've stayed here before."

My stomach twisted as a memory resurfaced of the word *whore* being hurled at Rhyan at the habibellum.

"Did you ever do more than just stay here?"

"No," he said, but his aura darkened, adding to the already deep chill of the night air. Elyria was considerably colder than Bamaria, and now that we'd slowed down, I was really feeling the drop in temperature, the cold seeping into my bones.

"Okay," I said.

"There it is," he said, pointing ahead at a hut painted orange with purple ashvan flying across the side. On the wooden door was the number seven. Rhyan limped past me, grunting, and unlocked the door as I followed. He lit a candle in the doorway, using it to bring flames to the fireplace and the few torches on the walls. The entire room was round like the outside and held a large bed, two nightstands, a circular dining table set for two, and a sectioned-off bathroom. The windows all had their curtains open, the glass frosted over.

I locked the door behind us and released our bags, pushing them to the side. My hands shook with the cold as I quickly shut the curtains for privacy.

Rhyan clutched his stomach with a moan. Now inside, I could feel the shift in his energy, feel just how much he'd been holding the pain in.

"Here," I said, rushing to his side. "Lean on me. I'm taking you to the bed."

He let me guide him to the edge and sit him down, and just as I had the night before, I removed his boots and weapons as he watched me.

"I never used the services here," he said quietly. "Or provided them."

I nodded, unhooking his belt. "I know. You told me. I believe you."

"You had this look on your face outside." His jaw tightened, and I sat beside him on the bed, taking his hand in mine—still loosely bandaged.

I slid off his leather arm cuffs, careful not to touch the bandage around his right hand. "In the arena, they were yelling all sorts of things at you. Including *whore*. And I guess I was just thinking about it." I set the cuffs on the nightstand with the rest of his gear.

His eyes darkened. "It's not for this." He looked away, gesturing at the room. "For something else." His hand flopped back into his lap, his fingers flexing in irritation.

"Do you want to talk about it?" I asked.

He frowned, and bit his bottom lip. "I do. And with you." His finger traced my palm. "But not tonight. I feel like shit already."

I smoothed back his hair, letting his locks run through my fingers and fall into loose waves. "I'm going to take care of you. I want you to feel better."

He cupped my cheek and stroked it with his thumb. "I should be doing that for you."

"You are, just by existing."

He scoffed.

"You are," I said again. "But you're injured. So, it's still my turn, okay? You've done more than enough tonight. I'll be careful. Let me know if anything I do hurts."

He'd always been hesitant to let his guard down with me. Hesitant to let me take care of him. I was pretty sure that was a habit he'd had for a long time. So I knew what a big deal this was for him, to be this vulnerable with me.

I looked him over. He'd been choked and punched in the face a few times—his neck was red and his cheek had dried blood over it. I needed to disinfect the cut at once and put a cold compress on his eye to keep the swelling down. I could ask the kitchen for supplies when they brought over dinner. Hopefully, he'd packed moonleaves. I could burn them to ease any pain he was in—and it probably wouldn't hurt for him to have a drink.

I took his bandaged hand in mine. "What happened here?"

"Dagger," he said, his voice rough. I unwrapped the white cloth, and he hissed. A large cut ran across the back of his hand. I'd need to disinfect and wrap that, too.

"It's okay. I'm going to take care of that. What else? Your stomach was just hurting. Anything under your armor?" I asked, reaching for his leathers.

I ran my fingers along the clasp, but he grabbed my wrist, stilling my hand.

"Rhyan?"

His green eyes were wide and blazing with tears that didn't fall. He tightened his grip on my hand.

"I'll be gentle," I said.

He took a few deep breaths, and nodded. "Sorry. This one just reminds me of when I was younger. He shouldn't have been able to do this, but he knew how to get past the armor."

"That's not your fault. And remember, you fought him off this time. You took his key. You won this fight."

He rolled his shoulders back, blowing air through his lips.

"Can I take this off?" I asked.

Exhaling again, he nodded.

I unclasped the straps and undid the leather buckles until I could ease the armor over his head. His black tunic underneath had a slash through the side, and a quick slide of the material across his torso showed a bleeding gash.

"Gods. Bastard."

"The dagger happened here, too," he said weakly. "Also, my leg."

There was a knock on the door, and we both froze. I stood and pushed my hood forward.

"Dinner," Rhyan said. "It's just dinner. I recognize the knock."

I grabbed my dagger from its sheath. "Precaution," I replied. The brothel may have been discreet—but if the Imperator pushed hard enough...I wasn't taking any chances.

Rhyan made a sound of approval before gathering up his discarded cloak and pulling it over his head as well.

Holding the blade behind my back, I blew out the nearest candle and unlocked the door.

An Elyrian woman with the long face, and golden-brown skin favored by Lady Pavi's family stood with two silver trays floating over her shoulders. "Your dinners," she said.

I eyed the expanse of land behind her, the small huts leading to the village. No sign of movement, or anyone else.

"Thank you." I stepped back into the shadow. "Can you place them on the table?"

"Of course." She pointed her stave toward our dining area, and both trays floated forward, their silver covers glinting as they landed neatly beside each other. "Anything else?"

An Elyrian man walked by, his face made up in heavy eyeliner. I tensed, but he was staring straight ahead.

"Yes," I said, and offered the woman a silver coin, running off my list of requests: clean bandages, moonleaves, sunleaf ointment, and cold compresses.

She tucked the coin into her belt. "I can gather those at once, my lady."

"Thank you. Please knock when you return. You can leave them at the door."

Once she'd agreed, I locked up. Rhyan groaned again, shifting on the bed, but I held up my hand.

"Stay there." I moved the dining chairs aside, then pushed the table across the floor toward the bed. A hot meal in Rhyan's belly might calm him down and make it easier for me to address his wounds when the supplies arrived.

"I could have sat at the table, you know," he said, his good eyebrow lifted.

"You *are* sitting at the table." I pushed the edge over his lap.

"I mean I could have walked to it—it didn't need to come to me. It's like ten feet away."

"Well, it's ten feet more than I wanted you to walk before you had to."

"Lyr, it's just a cut."

"It's multiple cuts and having had to carry me and our bags across the country plus everything else. Rhyan, you've done so much. You need to rest now and heal. I don't want you on your feet tonight."

He huffed but rolled his shoulders back and uncovered his tray. Steam rose from a large bowl of hearty stew, beside which were several thick pieces of pita bread, a mug of something that smelled sweet but alcoholic—possibly mead—chickpea salad, a side of hummus, a bowl of apples and mixed berries, and a honey-glazed cake.

It looked delicious, and my muscles relaxed as Rhyan took a spoonful of stew and sighed.

"Good?" I asked.

"Very; you should eat, too. You'd like it. Plus, you need to keep your strength up."

"I had dinner before the habibellum. And I'm not sure how much I can eat now, not knowing if they're alright." Not knowing if after all of this, I could return to Bamaria, or if I was going to be whisked away to Korteria the moment I did. Not knowing what would happen to Rhyan. Even just being out of the country—away from Cresthavan, my escorts, all I'd ever known, it was leaving knots in my stomach.

Everything was happening so quickly, I hadn't had time to sit with my fears. And they were starting to catch up with me.

"Try to eat," he said, reaching forward to lift up my dinner cover. A matching meal lay before me, but instead of digging in, I watched him take another bite, realizing he'd had this before—when he was forsworn, when he was on the run and had had nowhere to go. Unbidden, images plagued my mind of Rhyan on the run. Rhyan with nowhere to go, nowhere to stay. No safety. All because of his fucking father.

"What's that look?" he asked. "Is it because you've finally realized how ridiculous it is for me to be sitting on the bed and at the table at the same time?"

I bit my lip.

"Lyr."

Tears brimmed my eyes.

He put down his spoon. "Come here to me."

I sat beside him and let him wrap his arm around my shoulder.

"Hey," he said gently. "I know a lot's going on, but we're okay. We're together."

I rested my head against the crook of his neck. I had to be strong. For him. For them.

I swallowed, and sat up.

"How do you like it?" he asked. "Sitting on the bed-chair with the table?"

"Hmmm. I think we should get rid of chairs. Only use beds."

There was another knock on the door.

"Probably all the supplies I asked for," I said, getting back up. Holding my dagger again, I unlocked the door and found all of the medical supplies I needed for Rhyan.

He continued to eat while I arranged everything on the nightstand, urging him to drink the full contents of his mug and mine as well. Both were filled with strong mead. As he devoured his bread and drank, I poured the moonleaves into a burning bowl and allowed them to smoke and fill the tiny room with their soothing scent.

When Rhyan had cleaned out his bowl, looking full and a tiny bit drunk, I couldn't let his injuries go untreated any longer. I tugged off his tunic then had him ease back onto the bed, where he helped me slide his riding pants down his legs until he was in nothing but a pair of short-pants. My breath caught for a second at his nearly naked body. He was just so beautiful—every inch of him. The wings of his gryphon tattoo splayed across his shoulders and collarbone were the perfect adornments for his figure. He'd have been breathtaking without them, but Gods, he was fucking beautiful with them. I swallowed, imagining a later time when I could boldly touch the entire tattoo. But this was not the time for that or any of those thoughts.

I went to work carefully cleaning and disinfecting every cut. Then I applied the sunleaf paste to his leg, stomach, hand, and cheek, gently massaging it into the wounds.

He breathed evenly as I worked, seemingly relaxed under my ministrations. I continued massaging, crawling behind him to get the tension in his neck and shoulders. He closed his eyes, his head rolling forward.

Then it was time to cover his wounds. I bandaged beneath his eye first and had him lay back against a pile of pillows so I could place the cold compress on the wound. Then I bandaged everything else. He'd been kicked in the leg, close to his ankle, so I placed a pillow beneath his foot, keeping it elevated and praying it would heal come morning. It looked only slightly swollen—no doubt thanks to the healing abilities he had as a soturion.

Once he was cleaned and bandaged, I added a log to the fire to make sure he was warm. As I was about to open his bag to look for sweats for him to wear, I felt his gaze on me from across the room. I turned back to see his eyes glazed over, hooded with desire. He crooked his finger, beckoning me toward him, and gave me an equally crooked smile.

"Lyriana," he sing-songed.

"What? No *partner*? No *Lyr*?" I teased, walking back to the bed.

"I love your name," he said. "Lyriana." He was definitely tipsy if not a little drunk. "But I love calling you *Lyr*. And I love calling you *partner*."

"Do you?" I asked, unable to keep from smiling. He wasn't in pain, and as far as I could tell, we were safe for the night.

I crawled onto the bed beside him.

A cool feeling, like the calm of morning snow, filled the room, as he turned on his side, his cheeks rosy and his hair wild.

"Rhyan," I laughed and pushed him back onto his pillows. "Don't move. You need to be still and rest so your injuries heal." I readjusted his foot over the pillow, sliding my hand along his calf.

"But you know what I want to call you most?" he asked, his voice rough. His accent was heavier than usual, the lilt rolling his words together. He took my hand and brought it to his lips. "Lover."

Heat coiled deep within me. His lips were soft against my skin, and goosebumps sprung up across my arm as he kissed his way to my wrist and pulled me closer, kissing up to the crook of my elbow.

I shivered, gasping as his tongue darted across my skin.

"I want to kiss you." He turned his head on the pillow. "I know everything is crazy right now. But I haven't been able to stop thinking about you...the other night. Imagining you, doing it again, but this time...with my hands on you."

"And my hands on you." My breath hitched at the thought. We were alone, outside of Bamaria, in our own private room. Not just a room. A brothel! My body seemed hyper-aware of this fact now, aware of the activities that might be happening in the huts around us.

But over a third of Rhyan's body was bruised and cut. And he was drunk.

I brushed his hair back from his eyes, the scar through his left eye and forehead pronounced. "Trust me, I want more of that. A lot more of that. I want everything. I want it where I don't just hear you, but I can see you, touch you, taste you, and feel you. But you're hurt. Save your strength."

He pouted. "My lips aren't hurt."

I burst out laughing. "If I kiss you," I said, "you have to be gentle."

"Oh, I'll be gentle, partner. So *so* gentle." His eyes darkened, and he started to turn toward me again.

"I said no moving."

He shook his head. "I won't move," he promised. "I can be still. I can be so still."

I eyed him carefully, my face stern.

"I'm at your command, my lady," he said seriously. But he was already shifting again to reach me.

I stopped hesitating, stopped doubting. We both needed this. I straddled his waist, bringing my mouth down over his.

His hands gripped my hips before I'd even settled on him, his fingers digging into my waist in a way that was definitely not gentle but ripe with longing and a need that had been there far longer than either of us had wanted to admit. He pulled me down against him, already so hard beneath me, his length straining through his short-pants. I gasped at the contact, everything feeling heightened after so much adrenaline. He rolled up against me, hands sliding up my back and pulling me down across his chest, opening my mouth to his and swallowing my cry.

"Is this okay?" he asked.

"I should be asking you," I said, undulating against him, circling my hips until his cock stroked me exactly where I wanted him. Gods, it was taking all I had not to just grind down into him, but I was trying to keep my weight on my hands and knees.

"This is good." He nipped at the corner of my mouth and groaned. "What you're doing with your hips...so good."

I pushed back against him, my knees digging into the bed as I sought more friction. "But tell me if anything hurts."

"Nothing hurts. You feel so fucking good. And you taste good, too." He smiled against my lips. "You taste like stew."

I smiled. "So do you." I licked his bottom lip.

"Bamarian stew is better though," he conceded.

I raised my eyebrows, and sat back. "Oh really? And is that better than Glemarian stew?" I teased, bringing back our months-long debate over whose country had better food.

"Oh, no. Not even close." He circled his hips beneath me. "I still win there."

I pushed back, gasping as he seemed to thicken beneath me. "That's what you think," I said breathlessly, dragging myself forward.

He growled. "That's what I know." He rose up, rocking into me. "And when we get to Glemaria, I'm going to feed you. Prove you so, so fucking wrong."

He gripped my ass, his other hand reaching between us to undo my belt. He flung it against the wall before his fingers bunched up the bottom of my tunic and dragged it over my hips. He reached beneath it, his fingers searing my skin, moving up and up until he cupped my breast, squeezing and finding his way through the bindings I wore to training. The feeling of his bare hand against my skin was so intense—especially after a week of not seeing or touching him. He found my nipple and pinched until I cried out, bucking over him.

"Take this off," he demanded.

Bells began to ring in the distance, an unusual pattern I wasn't familiar with.

Neck flushed, Rhyan froze, his chest rising and falling in rapid succession.

"Elyrian clock tower?" I asked.

His eyes widened, as the bells rang again. "Akadim. Nearby." Jaw tensing, he gripped my hips, attempting to lift me off of him, but I squeezed my thighs together, pressing down on his chest.

"You're not getting up," I said.

"They might need my help."

"No," I said firmly. "You're in absolutely no condition to take on akadim. You can't go out there. You're not even at your post—you can't just show up in Elyria, Rhyan, out of nowhere." Even as I said the words, I could feel my own pull to go outside, my own yearning to throw myself into battle. What if it was the akadim that had Meera and Morgana? What if they were this close? What if we could save them?

But we had to stick to the plan. We had a way to get them back.

"I shouldn't have drunk anything." He rubbed his forehead and winced. The bruising around his eye was becoming more apparent.

I pulled his hand into mine. "Yes, you should have. You were in pain."

"I was weak." He looked toward the fireplace.

I turned his head back to me. "Rhyan, that's not true. Not even a little."

He laughed, but the sound was joyless. "Weak. And always going to be too late. Too late to do the right thing. Too late to save the ones I love. Even the way I got you out...I could barely walk, couldn't even handle two mugs of mead."

"Hey. Rhyan, stop that. That's your father talking. And he's a gryphon-shit liar who knows nothing about you, or strength, or love."

"And you think I know about these things? I ran before because I was so scared I wasn't going to be enough. That I was going to fail you. Does that sound like strength to you?"

"Your strength was being able to admit that. Your strength was coming back. Your strength was facing your fear. And everything you've done since has proven to me again and again that you love me. All I want to do is show you in return how much I love you." I lay carefully against his chest. "Rhyan, you've been through a lot. So much more than most people. More than anyone should. And you keep fighting, you keep coming out of it stronger and stronger. Nothing that happened has made you weak. You've experienced horrific cruelty, and you still have such a great capacity to love. So much kindness. There's nothing weak about that. I know how difficult it was for you to see him. To face him. To fight him. But you did it—you saved me tonight, and what you're doing for me, I'll be forever grateful. Don't let him in your head. Don't let him win. He's taken enough from you. He's unworthy of your presence, unworthy of the air you breathe. One day he's going to pay for all he's done. I'm going to make sure of it. And I'm going to delight in his fall."

Tears filled his eyes. "Partner." His lips were on mine again, but this kiss was slow, winding down. His drinks and exhaustion, mixed with the heavy scent of moonleaves, were catching up to him.

I kissed his forehead and both of his closed eyes. Then I threw another log in the fire, dug his sweatpants out from his pack, and carefully slipped them over his legs and hips to make sure he stayed warm.

I organized all of our things so we could leave here as quickly as possible. Once he felt no pain walking and he'd eaten again, we were moving straight toward Glemaria.

The whole room tidied and everything but our armor and essentials packed, I slipped one of Rhyan's sweatshirts over my tunic, then I slid my dagger beneath my pillow, guarding Rhyan as his breathing evened.

The bells rang again, the same pattern as before, causing my heart to pound. Akadim were still out there, and every now and then there was a faint shout. A soturion barking orders.

Rhyan shifted in his sleep, his brow furrowed until I rubbed my thumb between his eyes, and his breathing softened. I pulled the blanket higher around him. I burrowed beneath the blanket against him. The combination of his body heat and the fire made our room toasty, but I couldn't stop shivering. I couldn't stop imagining Meera and Morgana and praying to every god and goddess I could think of that they were alright, that they weren't being tortured or hurt.

I cuddled up to Rhyan. Even fast asleep, he pulled me closer to him, one hand snaking its way unconsciously beneath my shirt.

I swallowed, my heart heavy, one hand resting protectively on his chest, the other beneath my pillow, my fingers touching the hilt of my blade.

CHAPTER TWENTY-FOUR

MORGANA

I OPENED MY EYES, full of crust and dirt. Blood and sweat were dried on my cheeks, plastering chunks of my hair to my skin. I nearly gagged smelling myself—ocean water, grime, sand, sweat, and piss.

My throat was sore, and my skin felt rough and scratchy. I ran my hands over my dress, dried and stiff against my body. Darkness surrounded me. But I was on the ground—I knew that much. I was no longer in the seraphim carriage. We had landed.

But where I was—or what time it was—I had no idea. I rolled onto my side, my head aching. Yet, for once, it wasn't hurting from hearing others' thoughts. In fact, I couldn't hear any thoughts at all.

I sat up, feeling around, trying to understand my surroundings. I seemed to be on a pile of hay—a bed? Groaning, I got to my feet, my knees wobbling. My arms were exhausted just from helping me to lift. It also didn't help that they were sore as fuck, sliced open from the akadim's grip.

The air was damp, and my nostrils were assaulted with an earthy, musty smell. I reached out and felt a wall. It was soft and covered in dirt.

At least, I hoped it was dirt and not...I started to gag at just the thought, but there was no scent like that around me.

We were in a cave.

Or, rather—I was in a cave. I wasn't sure anyone else was here.

Where was Meera?

I closed my eyes but only out of habit—it was so dark, closing my eyes made little difference to my sight. Straining my ears, I listened for any sign of life. For any sign I wasn't alone.

Nothing.

I imagined the black obsidian wall of my mind—the gate keeping everyone else out—and with a groan, light began to slice through the center, the wall pulling apart and opening into two halves.

A fresh bout of a pain—coming from a thought I'd latched onto—made me wince.

In my mind's eye, I saw the face of the akadim that had attacked Meera. Its red eyes, its red tufts of hair, its cruel smile. It reached for me—for Meera—with dirty claws. I turned, diving into the ocean. But the beast turned into a fish, chasing me—Meera—through the ocean.

Tears welled in my eyes, and I clutched my chest in relief. She was dreaming. She was alive. And she was nearby. I needed to find her, wake her up, and figure out how to get the hell out of here.

"Meera?" I whispered. "Meera!" No response. With both my mind and ears, I listened for more—for any sounds of the akadim or thoughts of Lumerians. But other than the water dripping and echoing against the walls, it was silent. My eyes adjusted to the dark, and I saw what appeared to be fire somewhere in the distance, but it was so far away I couldn't hear it, and I could only make out the faintest bit of my surroundings from its fading glow.

I seemed to be in an alcove. As I stepped forward, I found another empty bed of hay on the ground. I took a few more small steps, and found another alcove. The faint light revealed the shapes of more beds across from me as well. I was in a hall. Abandoned, apparently. There was no sign of life, no movement, no sound but for the constant drip of water. It kept splattering, again and again and again.

I winced, growing irritated at the noise. It was small in comparison to what I usually experienced, but something about it was grating to my senses. I kept walking, moving farther and farther down the hall, checking every alcove for Meera.

The hall began to wind, the terrain uneven and descending. I was forced to use the walls as a guide as darkness descended on me. The glow of the fire I'd seen earlier could not reach this curve. Sucking in a breath, I tried to remain calm, open, and alert as I moved forward. Within a few more steps, the walls straightened, and the cave was lit by a close torch.

Several more darkened and dirty alcoves lined the two sides of the cave. The dripping sound had grown louder. It grew louder still as I progressed, pressing myself against the wall—

I barely had enough peace of mind to cover my mouth with both hands before I screamed. My back slammed against the wall, and my stomach twisted, nausea roiling inside me before I pushed the bile back down, choking on the taste of my sick. My whole body was shaking, and I started panting, biting down on my hand to keep from screaming again.

A mage hung in the alcove. She was nearly naked. Her clothing shredded to pieces. A black mark covered her heart. Blood was dripping onto the floor from her body—

I turned away. I had to find Meera. I had to find Meera and get us out of here.

Straining my ears again, I blinked back tears. Meera's mind had quieted, and was now empty. She'd fallen out of the dream, but she was still unconscious.

I moved farther down the hall, past another alcove and another. The section ended a few feet ahead of me. There was one final opening, and then....my heart sank. A dozen akadim, male and female, all giant, all covered in dirt and blood, were lounging ahead around a pool of water. One female jumped in, and a male followed her. He gripped her hips from behind, shoving himself inside, water splashing. She growled and bucked back against him.

Silently, I moved forward. What were the odds that they had placed Meera in the alcove closest to them and me in the one farthest away so they'd be sure we couldn't easily escape—that'd we'd have to waste precious time getting to the other—and that the noise from Meera's alcove would tip them off?

I didn't see any sign of my captor or Meera's. Was it possible the others didn't know we were here?

I stepped forward, the terrain too uneven for me to gain purchase, and my heel slid on a rock. A small echo sounded from the scuff of my foot, and I froze. No one turned toward the hall. They were still watching the akadim fucking in the water. Thankfully, their grunts and growls drowned out all other sound.

Taking another step, and another, I held my breath until I reached the farthest alcove.

Just like I'd suspected, Meera was there. She was slumped over the hay bed as if her captor hadn't been bothered to actually place her onto it properly. A gash ran across her forehead, caked with dirt and dried blood. I moved into her alcove and crouched down beside her, feeling her forehead.

She was burning hot. She definitely had an infection. If the akadim didn't rip us to pieces, they were going to sicken us to death. I had to wake her without making a sound, without speaking, and without her making any noise either.

If only she could read minds, too. I opened my mouth to whisper her name, but fear gripped my throat, and only wordless breath hit the air. A fresh set of growls came from the next room, and water splashed. Like me, Meera also reeked of urine and sweat, and my gag reflex was already at its limit. But I kept my mouth clamped shut and covered hers with my hand. Then I pressed my free hand down on her forehead—avoiding the cut—my arms shaking.

Please, please, wake up. Wake up.

A moment passed, and then she began to stir. Hazel eyes flew open and looked up, wide with fear, as tears fell instantly through the streaks of blood and dirt across her cheeks. Her aura seemed to burst to life at once like a cold, wet rain that I felt washing down on me. It was too much. She was too emotional, too afraid.

I shook my head. No time for this. We needed to run. We could cry later. Be afraid later—be afraid for fucking forever—as long as we got out of here.

Where are we? she asked in her mind.

I stood, jerking my chin at the hall.

Is it safe? she asked.

I shook my head again. But staying wasn't safe either.

Her face crumpled; her mouth opened in a silent cry. The thought she'd barely voiced in the back of her mind—she wished I hadn't woken her.

But there was no time for that. I reached for my stave, brandishing it before me.

Meera wrinkled her nose. *Magic doesn't affect them.*

I held in an exasperated sigh, pointing my stave at her bed of straw. I lifted several of the pieces up and then let them drop.

Maybe magic didn't affect akadim, but it certainly worked on everything else inside this hellhole.

She nodded and unsheathed her stave.

My heart pounded so hard against my chest I was sure it would be echoing into the hall, but the only sounds came from the akadim. I stepped beyond Meera's alcove, keeping close to the wall. Fresh grunts began behind me. The sound of flesh slapping flesh echoed against the cave walls. Whichever akadim were at it now, they were not in the water. They were close by.

Just stay occupied with each other, I prayed.

I took another step forward, turning back to see Meera behind me. We locked hands and started making our way back through the hall, around the corner to where I'd been kept. When we approached the room with the body, I pointed at Meera, signaling at her to look in the other direction. She frowned, but after I insisted, she listened and managed to pass by the forsaken without seeing her. I didn't need her to also be thinking of that image, dreaming about it. Having to see it in just my own thoughts was enough for me.

I hoped all the akadim were in the other direction and that this way would lead us out. We moved together, holding each other's hands so tightly, my arm was going numb. But I couldn't have let go or loosened my grip if I'd wanted to. I was far too afraid.

The space beyond us was dark, but as we kept moving, I could make out a faint light from a torch.

My hand shook as I lifted my stave, tears rolling down my cheeks. This had to work. This had to fucking work.

"Ani petrova lyla," I whispered under my breath.

The lights from the torches vanished. As we continued on, I called forth every approaching light until familiar sounds echoed before us—water splashing, grunts and groans of pleasure, skin against skin—the same sounds I'd heard before.

The exact same sounds.

Fuck. Fuck! We'd gone in a circle.

We had no choice. I was going to take their light and keep going. If there was a way in, there was a Godsdamned way out. It was probably on the other side of the pool. I nearly groaned. Of course, they weren't guarding us; they were guarding the fucking door. I realized we weren't being kept far from each other—we'd been placed at equal distances from them. I felt sick.

Gently, I pushed Meera into the wall, then I pushed myself against it beside her, feeling soft muck rub into my hair and dress.

I was going to get us out of here. And then I was going to scrub my skin and hair raw. For a week. And burn my clothes. Maybe even cut my hair. Whatever I had to do to get the feel and stench of this place off of me.

I sucked in a breath, pointed at the torches above the pool, and made the final incantation: *"Ani petrova lyla."*

Darkness spread across the water. The akadim started yelling and cursing, their voices grating my ears.

I wheezed, doubling over in pain, my eyes widening in shock—an akadim had punched my stomach.

I couldn't breathe. I couldn't get air. By the Gods. I opened my mouth, trying to inhale, trying to find oxygen. Meera screamed.

A light flickered to life behind the akadim. It had red tufts of hair. This was Meera's, the one who'd taken orders before.

"You thought magic would save you?"

It slapped my hand, and my stave fell and rolled across the floor.

Growling and baring its fangs, it wrapped its hand around my neck and choked me as it lifted me from the ground. My feet kicked for purchase as my back slammed into the wall.

Desperately, I clawed at its hands, pinching and striking with my nails, trying to get even one finger to pull back. I still couldn't breathe. My vision was going in and out of focus.

"Fuck it," said the akadim. "I want them." It reached forward. Its nail poked the center of my collarbone before it pushed its claw into my skin. I kicked and punched, some animal-like sound coming from me as it slid its nail down my sternum, cutting through my skin. Blood trickled down my chest. When it reached my dress, it kept cutting, slicing me, piercing through the fabric.

My voice returned, and I screamed.

It dropped me, and I slammed to the floor on my ass, scrambling to find my way to my feet. Meera was on the ground, lying on her belly, half conscious.

The akadim reached for me again and swiped its hand across my dress, touching my blood.

I lurched, about to pass out, seeing stars from the pain.

But instead of cutting me deeper, it scowled, crying out.

I'd hurt it. But how? It'd only touched my blood.

"Too much trouble," it said in disgust before it stomped toward Meera, grabbed her ankles, and dragged her onto her back while pushing her dress up her legs.

"NO!" I screamed, running at it without any thought.

It released Meera at once when I crashed into its arm. Smoke began to sizzle on its skin—right where I'd made contact with it—and the akadim made an agonized screech.

I remembered now, the akadim that had attacked Lyr had recoiled when it touched her armor—not because of the armor, but because of the blood inside it. Blood that Lyr now had inside her.

Was it possible...?

I swiped my hand across my chest, smearing it with my blood, then smashed my hand across the akadim's face.

It roared in pain, as smoke sizzled from its cheek. The scent of burning flesh filled my nostrils. Recoiling from my touch and holding its burned skin, it bolted back down the hall.

The akadim who'd kidnapped me had done something similar in the carriage. It'd grabbed my arms, making me bleed, and afterward, when it'd touched me, it'd looked like it was in pain.

A memory from over a year ago flashed in my mind as I grabbed my stave, sheathing it at my side and reaching for Meera.

That first night he'd spoken to me in my mind, he'd told me, *You're powerful. Perhaps more so than any other vorakh I've met. Your power comes from something far deeper than your bloodline and name.*

Was my power fueled by something other than my bloodline, or was it my blood itself that was powerful?

I hoisted Meera to her feet, her head falling back.

We had a short window—the majority of the akadim were distracted, and I'd scared off one, but not the one who'd captured me.

Too late, I saw it approaching, its fangs curving below its lips.

I dropped Meera and swiped my arm across my chest, covering it in blood by pushing down against my wounds to force out fresh drops. The akadim sniffed the air and growled as I held my hand forward, ready to strike it down.

It stopped too far away for me to reach it.

"Moriel will sort you out," it said. "We leave at sunset for the Allurian Pass."

Glemaria? The other fucking end of the Empire? I stepped forward, holding out my hand. "No, we don't."

The akadim snorted and pulled from its backside a rope with a loop already set. It threw the rope forward, and the hoop went over my head and fell down my body until the akadim tugged and tightened it around my waist.

It started marching, forcing me to walk along by tugging harder, tightening the rope until I could barely breathe.

We were back in my alcove.

"What about my sister?" I asked.

It shrugged. "Not worried." With that, it lifted the end of the rope and looped it through a hook in the ceiling.

"NO!" I yelled, thinking of the other girl, the one who'd been tortured and turned forsaken. She'd be an akadim soon, once night fell.

Against my protests, the akadim pulled the rope through the hook until I was on my toes, the hold across my stomach so tight I thought I was going to split in half.

It tied off the end, and I was left semi-hanging in the alcove.

"Don't do this," I cried.

"Not touching you," it said in disgust. Then, louder, it yelled, "No touching the black hair! She's blood-cursed."

Blood-cursed? Did it mean vorakh? Could it sense that?

"So's my sister," I said quickly. "She's even more blood-cursed than me."

"Shut up," it snarled and stomped out of the room, leaving my body rocking from side to side as I tried to gain purchase on the floor.

But the rope was too high and too tight, and my stave was just out of reach.

Moments later, the grunting sounds returned, echoing down the hall and into my alcove. This time, they were accompanied by chanting.

"Moriel! Moriel! Moriel!"

CHAPTER TWENTY-FIVE

LYRIANA

"MORNING, PARTNER," RHYAN SAID, his voice scratchy with sleep.

I was sitting on our bed, legs crossed, looking down as he opened his eyes. The fire was dwindling; I needed to put in a new log to keep it going for breakfast.

Rhyan lifted his arm and cupped my chin. "Did you sleep?" he asked.

"Barely."

Gingerly, he pushed himself up to a seat, the blanket revealing the warm expanse of his chest and belly. A soft light, almost white from the frosted glass, filtered through the cracks in the curtains. Rhyan reached for my waist and pulled me onto his lap.

"But you're—" I protested.

"Fine," he said. "I feel fine. Thanks to you." His arms tightened around me.

My shoulders shook, and his hands soothingly glided up my back.

"You want proof?" he asked. He pulled back the bandage on his cheek. The cut was barely there, his face hardly swollen. What should have been a black eye was only slightly discolored skin that wouldn't have been noticeable without direct light.

"And here?" I asked, grazing a finger down his abdomen.

"Here, too," he said and pulled back the bandage. The wound had been an open gash last night, but now it, too, appeared stitched up, as if he'd received it months ago.

I pushed back the bronzed, tousled curls that covered the scar running through his left eye. It seemed to be the only mark on his body that refused to heal.

"My leg also feels fine."

I nodded.

"You're worried about them," he said.

I nodded again and buried my face in the crook of his neck.

"It's okay. We're going to find them. I swear."

"I know."

He stroked my hair, and we sat like that, just breathing, until a sharp rap at the door made me stiffen.

"It's breakfast," Rhyan said. "That's all."

I crawled off his lap and moved toward the edge of the bed, but he grabbed my arm.

"I'll do it. You took care of me last night. Wait here." He grabbed his soturion cloak and hastily wrapped the green cloth around his waist and tucked it into his pants before throwing the remaining material over his shoulder to cover his chest, bracing for the cold morning air.

I watched him carefully, saw that he was walking normally, without any apparent pain, and breathed a small sigh of relief. He greeted the Elyrian woman at the door and requested as I had, that she fly our meals onto the table. He also asked if we could have two lunches packed before closing the door behind him.

I started toward the edge of the bed, but Rhyan shook his head. "Oh, no. You're staying right where you are."

"I'm not the one who—"

"I may have been slightly inebriated last night, but I do recall you saying we should have only beds instead of chairs."

Just as I had the night before, he pushed the table across the room so I could remain on the bed to eat. He took it upon himself to add the extra log to the fire—though I was pretty sure he did so more for my benefit than his. Coming from the northernmost part of the Empire, he always seemed more comfortable in the cold than I'd ever been.

"Warm enough?" he asked, uncovering the silver trays.

A tomato stew with eggs lay before me along with a heaping pile of pita bread and fruit.

"You only took a few bites last night," he said, sitting beside me. "Lyr, you've got to eat. For them. Okay?"

"Okay," I said, my voice shaky. I was hungry but also slightly nauseated. My nerves were fired up. Had been since the moment the bells rang.

"Just take a deep breath," he said. "As soon as we have some lunch packed, we'll go. We're heading straight for the north."

"Are we traveling?" I asked.

He lifted an eyebrow, a hint of mischief in his eyes. "We're running."

My mouth fell open. "You can't be serious."

"Oh, I am deadly serious. Just because we're on the run doesn't mean that I'm not still your apprentice in charge of your training."

I glared.

"Only for an hour though." He squeezed my thigh. "You've been off your schedule for too long. I have complete faith in you, but you have to keep at it, especially now. So we're going to run north, and then we'll rest and walk, and I'll travel us up ahead as far as I can before nightfall so we can find somewhere safe to stay—and hopefully find dinner."

"Where do you expect us to be tonight?" I asked.

"Cretanya by this evening."

"Is there another brothel there?"

"There's plenty," he laughed. "I could map them up and down the Empire. But that's not usually where I stayed. I became very familiar with some inns and cave systems along the way. The caves are nice. They're free and usually empty, and some have pools to bathe in—heated, too. The only problem is, well, there's a chance of running into other forsworn. Forsworn who really embody the title. But the bigger problem is the caves are being used as nests for the akadim."

"One of us probably needs to stay up all night if we're going to stay anywhere like that."

"I know an inn," he said, "in Cretanya, where we're heading. The owners' granddaughter is married to Sean. They've let me stay there before. They're kind. And discreet. Although I'll probably check in by myself and come get you, bring you straight to the room."

I knew this precaution was because even if these people were semi-family for Rhyan, we couldn't be seen together.

"After Cretanya, though, I'm going to direct us west, taking the mountain pass along Korteria. It'll keep us out of the capital."

I took a bite of my breakfast stew. "Do you think it's too dangerous for us to be in Korteria? With...my engagement?"

Rhyan practically growled. "That is not happening." He exhaled. "But I'd rather risk Korteria than Numeria. It's too risky to be close to the Emperor. After tonight, though, we'll most likely be sticking to caves. Once we're north of the capital, my face is far more recognizable. And I am far less welcome." He looked ahead, his gaze distant.

I reached for his hand and squeezed it. The north was in his heart—I hated the pain he must have felt at being rejected by what had been his home.

Rhyan gave me a small smile in return and kissed my cheek before inhaling his breakfast stew.

An hour later, our packs strapped to our backs and fully dressed in our soturion armor, Rhyan and I left our safe haven. We both kept our hoods up, planning to vanish immediately into the woods, trusting the camouflage of our cloaks to protect us from any soturi searching for me or my sisters. But a sharp gust of wind blew off my hood, exposing my braided hair.

Despite the sun having been scarce for days, it was in full force this morning, and I caught a glimpse of the edge of my braid from the corner of my eye. It was bright red. Batavia red.

Asherah's red.

A woman stepped outside of the hut next to ours, tying a large fur-lined robe around her body. It was the Elyrian woman who'd served our dinner last night. She was staring straight ahead, a focused expression on her face, her eyebrows knit together. But then she caught my gaze, and her eyes widened as she saw my red hair.

Rhyan was behind me in an instant, pulling my hood back up.

"Morning," he said politely, nodding to the woman, his hand tightening around mine. He started walking at a brisk pace, leading me away from the hut toward the woods we'd arrived in.

"She knows who I am," I hissed.

"No. She was only staring because your hair was a different color from last night."

"Exactly. I'm known for that."

He chewed the inner corner of his cheek and looked over his shoulder. "We paid for discretion," he said.

"Fuck," I muttered.

Rhyan pulled me behind a tree. "That's their job. To be quiet. Far more scandalous things have happened here."

"And how do you know these things if they're so discreet?"

"Just trust me, Lyr. You stay here enough times, you see things. Things I've never heard spoken anywhere else." He pressed his forehead to mine. "Let's just go. We have our task. We're going to stick to it. If we worry about everything, we'll get nowhere." His hands were inside my hood, his thumbs stroking my neck. "Ready?"

"Ready."

Rhyan pulled us deeper into the woods for our run. Having been through Elyria multiple times to hunt, he created the path we'd follow, keeping to the spots where the snow was lightest between the trees. He had to circle back to me a few times—I wasn't used to running in full armor or while carrying anything with me. Plus, the terrain was uneven beneath my feet. But I had to admit, I felt good after over a week of not running.

Afterwards, Rhyan led me through a couple of cool-down stretches, and when we continued on, his hand wrapped around mine, threading our fingers together.

My chest squeezed.

We'd held hands before. Many times. But this was the first time we'd ever been allowed to do so outdoors for an extended period of time. And it felt...wonderful. And helped take my mind off of everything else that was happening.

An hour passed of us walking and talking hand in hand before we stopped in a clearing to eat lunch. Rhyan traveled around the perimeter, scouting for any signs of Lumerians or animals we should be worried about. After lunch, we picked up speed, walking at a brisk and brutal pace. The days were still short, and we were toeing the line of danger. By keeping our route off the main roads, we avoided being seen by Lumerians who could report us or tip off Imperator Hart to Rhyan's whereabouts. Or tip off Imperator Kormac to mine. But the closer we got to nightfall in the wilderness, the more likely we were to be targeted by akadim.

Just when the sky had darkened enough for us to need a torch to see, Rhyan decided it was time to travel. Elyria was actually a very narrow country—nearly as wide as Bamaria but quite a short pass if traveling north—so we'd managed to cover an impressive distance even if we were nowhere near the Cretanyan border.

Rhyan pulled me into his arms and took a few deep breaths to prepare himself for the jump.

My feet lifted off the ground, and there was a sharp pain in my stomach like it was being tugged away from me. Then, with a sharp thud, my feet hit the ground. This time, I was ready for Rhyan, bracing myself to catch his weight and support him as he recovered from the jump.

Sweat beaded across his forehead, and his hair was full of curls as if he'd been sweating for hours. His cheeks were red with cold and exertion, but he was in better shape than he'd been the night before. All day, his injuries had been improving, the bruises fading. But traveling like this still took a toll on him. He wasn't only feeling the effect of running a long distance in an inhumanly short period of time—he was also feeling the effort it'd taken to carry me along. He was strong, stronger than any other soturion in the Empire. But this, this was a lot. More than he should have had to carry.

"You're doing okay?" he asked, always concerned with me first.

"I'm fine." I tightened my hold on him, urging him to lean more into me, to let me support his weight. "How are you feeling?"

He took a deep breath, steadied himself on his feet, and stepped back from me, rubbing his hand over his chin. His eyes glazed over our new surroundings. "I'm not sure I like this plan."

"Of what? Checking in by yourself?"

I started to scan, too. Taking in my first sight of Cretanya. We were on the edge of a small wood, through which torchlights and glowing amethysts blasted. Cretanya's capital city of Thene was said to put Urtavia to shame—it had the most shops and markets and was famous for its dance clubs. I'd always wanted to come here, see the lights, and hear the music that was supposedly always playing in the city at all hours of the day. The constant flow of activity and endless streams of lights made it an unpopular place for akadim to come despite the dense population. The rest of the country was mainly woods and farmlands; much of Bamaria's grain and vegetables were imported from here.

Even from behind the trees, I could hear the bustle of the city—battling musicians and the kind of loud chatter usually reserved in Urtavia for festivals. A wave of nostalgia washed through me. I'd never been here before, only read about it, but there was an energy to the city I could feel, even from this distance. It reminded me of another life. Another time. When things were simple, fun. It reminded me of Jules being alive. Nights laughing with her, running through the shops and restaurants. Dancing in the streets. She would have loved this city.

Rhyan took my hand and squeezed, leading me through the clearing.

We stepped through the remaining cluster of trees into a small park at the city's edge. The inn was just beyond the park, across the street. Rhyan pointed it out. Ruled by Ka Zarine, the building was painted gold and featured a simple golden sun.

My hood fell over my face. Rhyan's features were covered by shadows. There were people everywhere, people who didn't know us, had never seen us before, and who likely hadn't yet heard that the night before, the former Heir to the Arkasva and her apprentice had both vanished from Bamaria.

"I'll be fine." I moved my vadati stone from my waist to around my neck and tucked the chain safely under my soturion armor and Asherah's chest plate. I tapped the golden stars. "I can call in an instant if I need you. And I have this." I pulled out my dagger.

Rhyan frowned. "I'd feel better if you held your sword."

"That's not exactly subtle. We're trying to avoid being noticed."

"We're trying to stay alive."

"That, too," I agreed. "Go. It's only a few minutes, I'll be fine."

Taking a deep breath, Rhyan pulled his hood over his head then reached forward to tug mine more securely into place. "Okay. I'm going. Be careful. Stay alert. Promise me." He leaned in to kiss me, hauled both bags over his shoulder, then headed for the building's entrance.

I walked forward, not wanting to be too close to the trees. There were a few stragglers in the park, mostly couples taking romantic strolls through the city stopping to sit on the park benches.

"He took off with her." There was a gruff voice behind me. "Lady Lyriana."

I froze, dipping my chin and letting my hood fall past my forehead.

"Forsworn criminal. Poor girl. And her sisters taken by akadim?"

The first voice grunted. "I knew that whole Ka was cursed."

Shit. Shit. Word had gotten to Cretanya. I gripped the hilt of the blade in my hand, tucked behind my cloak where no one could see it.

Edging closer to the Cretanyans, I peered at them beneath my hood. They seemed to be two off-duty soturi of Ka Zarine—both wore the golden sun sigil over their tunics. Off-duty, so they weren't actively looking for me and Rhyan. But if they got wind of who I was—I was pretty sure they'd be on the job in an instant. I could only imagine the reward the Imperator would offer.

"Word is they're traveling by foot, probably just reaching Elyria, assuming he's taking her out of her country," the first soturion continued.

I exhaled sharply. My chest felt like it had been stabbed the moment they'd started talking. If the rumor was that we were in Elyria, then the women at the brothel hadn't betrayed us. Yet.

And that meant there was a still a chance that it was unconfirmed we were together.

"His father should have put him down. Murderer." My hands clenched at the second soturion's words. "Did you hear the Ready took off?"

I sucked in a breath.

The first grunted. "Some arkturion he is—lost an entire Ka's bloodline in under a month."

"What about the new arkasva?" The second soturion kicked a stone.

"The old arkasva's sister? Probably cursed, too. Like all Ka Batavia. Mark my word, it's just a matter of time. They'll all be on their knees for Ka Kormac, in more ways than one. Just like Elyria bowed to Ka Elys. Picked by Kormac. Same thing."

My heart beat faster. Ka Elys had been picked by the Imperator to replace Ka Azria?

"Heard they engaged her to the Kormac wolf."

"Wasn't the Heir Apparent fucking him? Lady Naria?"

The first soturion let out a gruff laugh. "Now she's marrying the heir of Ka Grey. Same one carrying on with Lady Lyriana. They all just swapped partners."

The second clicked his tongue. "Bamaria's a big prize. If the old bitch won't marry the Imperator, the youngest can marry his son. Sick shit in the south. Soon it's just going to be Korteria all across the border."

"Can't be that strong if they lost her. Ka Kormac had the lady safe in their lodging. The forsworn went right in and took her."

"Kormac's offering a pretty prize to anyone who can bring back his son's bride." There was a long pause as a soft hiss sliced through their chatter. The soturion asked another question, but I was no longer listening to him.

A sudden blast of heat burst through the cold of the night. And another hiss crossed the park, the eerie sound carried on the wind.

Nahashim.

CHAPTER TWENTY-SIX

I TURNED, WATCHING THE edge of the woods. A shadow moved through the trees, gliding across the ground. Two glinting orbs appeared and vanished.

I tried to remember what I knew of Cretanya's lands. I'd read mostly about the city. Like Elyria, they favored ashvan for travel. Few seraphim could be found here—no gryphons lived this far south. Nahashim were bred on the island of Lethea, but that didn't mean they didn't exist elsewhere.

Were they native to Cretanya? Or had these been sent by Rhyan's father?

My chest heated—not with the flames of the Valalumir, which had been dormant for days, but with the warmth of the vadati stone.

"Lyr," Rhyan said, voice low and muffled beneath my clothes. "Got the room. Coming for you."

I couldn't let Rhyan come where the nahashim could see him.

I fished the stone from my tunic and wrapped my cloak around me to avoid anyone seeing it. "Rhyan, I'm coming to the front of the building," I said. "Meet me there—not in the park."

"Why?" he asked, immediately on alert. "What's wrong?"

"Nahashim," I said quickly. "I think your father sent them."

"Where are you now?"

"I'm not alone. Just...meet me there. I can get there. Okay?"

The stone went white. Two sets of eyes stared at me from the woods.

A large rock lay by my feet. Without thinking, I picked it up and threw it straight at the pairs of eyes.

A loud, angry hiss was followed by the rustling of leaves and sticks as the two snakes slithered away.

"Hey!" one of the soturi yelled. "You can't just throw rocks like that! Our soldiers are out there! You could hit one!"

I stared at the ground. "Sorry. Thought I saw...red eyes."

"Akadim?" asked the soturion.

"I thought so," I said.

"Fuck. Call it in," said the second soturion. He turned to me with a frown. "You know, you're wearing your cloak all wrong." He stepped forward, peering at me with interest.

I knew I was wearing it wrong—I was wearing it over my armor, hiding any sign I was from Ka Batavia.

"I'm not a soturion," I said. "It's my boyfriend's cloak."

The soturion rolled his eyes. "Better investigate," he told his friend.

"Girl!" yelled the first. "Give your man his cloak back. You look ridiculous."

The second burst into laughter.

I didn't respond. I started walking away, praying they were satisfied with me and more concerned with the alleged akadim in the woods. I took one glance back but couldn't see or sense any more movement from the nahashim. I had to meet Rhyan and get inside at once.

The soturi were no longer looking at me, and with that knowledge, I took off, racing through the park across the street until I found Rhyan rounding a corner, nearly walking into me before the inn's doors.

"What happened?" he asked. "Are you okay?" He was looking past me, his eyes narrowed.

"They don't seem to be following me. I heard soturi talking. Word's already reached here that we're gone, but the rumor seems to be we're on foot. So they're looking for us at the Elyrian border."

Rhyan huffed out an exasperated breath. "Well, that's as good as can be expected." Still eyeing our surroundings, he added, "We should get inside."

He wrapped my hand in his and led me down a dark alleyway between the inn and the next building. Hidden in the shadows beside a wastebin, Rhyan scooped me into his arms, and we were gone. We reappeared in a room half the size of our room from last night. A bed took up most of the space with one window above it and a large chest at its foot. There was no dining table or chairs. A fireplace was just springing to life.

Rhyan set me down on my feet, looking a little embarrassed at the size of the room. "Well, we did say no chairs."

I tried to smile.

"Partner," he said. "You look pale."

"Tired," I said.

He pushed my hood off my face and smoothed my hair behind my ear, his finger wrapping around one of my stray curls. "You didn't sleep the night before."

I headed for the window. It looked out over the park, and I peered at the trees, my stomach knotting as I waited to see a nahashim appear. But the park looked clear aside from a few people walking through it.

Rhyan started toward me, but there was a sudden knock at the door. He gestured at me to go into the adjoining bathroom. Heart hammering, I scurried from the window and closed the door, trying to keep my breath even, as he unlatched the lock. The door creaked as it swung open.

"Thank you," Rhyan said. "I'll take that."

"I can set up the dinners for you," said an elderly man. "Bring you a table and two chairs. Sorry we didn't have a room with those already."

"No. That's not necessary. I'm here on such short notice, you've already done me a huge kindness. And it's only me. I'm just...very hungry. Haven't eaten all day."

The man chuckled. "Well enjoy. If you need anything else, Rhyan, you let me know. Anything at all."

Rhyan finished thanking the man. I remained hidden, waiting for the sound of the door closing, before I emerged from the bathroom.

Rather than eating on the bed, Rhyan pulled out the chest at its foot, and we sat on the floor, using the chest as a makeshift table and eating in silence.

"Why don't you take a hot shower?" Rhyan said afterward. "I think you'll feel better."

I shook my head, my nerves still on edge.

"Come on, partner. If the nahashim are out there, they have no way of getting in here through the walls. We're safe tonight.

Try to relax. Nice warm shower for you, then bed. You need it." He wrapped his arms around me. "I know it probably feels strange, like you don't deserve to or shouldn't. Not if they're not getting hot showers."

My eyes burned. He always knew me so well.

"Just remember, to get them back, we need you at full strength. Okay. This helps them, too. Go on. I'll be right out here, guarding the room."

So, I showered, letting the hot water rush over me, and washed my hair for the first time in days. It was soothing at first. My muscles ached, tense from a full day of walking and running. But alone in the silence broken only by the water falling, I was left with my grief. My father's death was still fresh. I kept seeing him fall every time I closed my eyes. And if I didn't see him, I saw Haleika. Or Leander.

Then I saw Meera and Morgana. My heart hurt. I had no idea if they were actually okay or how scared they were or if they were in pain. I doubted they were in a comfortable bed or had even been fed in the last day. My shoulders started to shake, and I turned off the faucet.

Rhyan jumped in after me, and I changed into his sleep shirt and pants again.

A few minutes later he emerged from the shower, already toweled off, and wearing his sleep pants. He looked me up and down, his eyes darkened, hooded with desire, and his chest flushed red against the black ink of his gryphon tattoo. Jaw tensed, he turned suddenly to the bed, lifted the blanket and patted the sheets next to him. But I didn't move. I was feeling stuck to that spot, overwhelmed. One look at my face and Rhyan crossed the room, scooping me into his arms.

"No," I protested, squirming. "You carried me too much today."

"No such thing." He tightened his grip, pulling me closer. "What happened between now and the shower?"

Tears fell down my face. "Everything. My father, my sisters...." I wiped at my eyes.

"Come lie down with me." He carried me to the bed and lay back with me on top of him, pulling the blanket up to my waist. "Shhh. It's okay. I've got you."

He wrapped his arms around me, his hands sliding inside the back of my shirt to run soothingly up and down my back, as I sniffled.

"Deep breaths. It's going to be okay. We're going to make it okay."

I nodded against his chest, inhaling the soothing pine scent that always clung to him. Sharpened now that he was fresh from the shower.

Bells rang in the distance—this time just the normal bells from the Cretanyan clock towers. My eyes began to close, my body still wrapped up in him. I felt his arm lift, and cold air, siphoned from his aura, gathered in his palm. He flicked it out and snuffed out all the torches in the room, leaving just the candle melting on the nightstand.

His lips pressed to my forehead, and he smoothed back my hair before his hand returned to my back, alternating between rubbing long strokes up my spine and lazy circles around my shoulders.

I couldn't sleep. My mind was racing; my heart was hurting. I closed my eyes and saw my father fall. Arianna sitting in his Seat. The guilt was like a pit in my stomach. I felt awful. My stomach twisted with guilt over the fact that I'd left Bamaria, even though I knew I'd had to. And I felt guilty that I hadn't stopped my father's death. Guilty I hadn't seen the truth sooner. Understood Meera's visions, looked beyond what was presented to me.

And I felt guilty I hadn't been at Cresthaven when Meera and Morgana had been taken—either to stop it or to be there with them.

Guilty that Rhyan and I had run that night instead of killing the akadim. Guilty Haleika and Leander had died because of it.

I shifted away from Rhyan, finding that, for once, I couldn't fall asleep curled on top of him. And I worried I was keeping him awake with all my fidgeting. He needed to sleep. He was using so much energy to move us safely through the Empire.

I rolled onto my side, my back to him, tucked my hand beneath the pillow, and squeezed my eyes shut, willing the thoughts racing through my mind to stop. To shut off. I tried counting backward then reciting old High Lumerian rhymes I'd memorized as a child, but nothing worked. I couldn't quiet my mind. I couldn't fall asleep, and the longer I lay there, the more miserable I felt.

The mattress shifted behind me, and a warm arm slid across my hip. Rhyan's hand slipped inside my shirt to rest on my belly.

His body pressed against me from behind, his knee pushing between my legs.

"You still awake?" Rhyan whispered, sweeping my hair off my shoulder and planting a kiss at the base of my neck.

"I'm sorry," I said. "Didn't want to keep you up."

"Partner." His hand returned to my stomach. "What's happening in that big beautiful brain of yours?"

"Same as before. Everything. I'm okay when we're moving, but as soon as we stop, as soon as we slow down, the thoughts come. Like a flood. And I can't turn it off. I just—I'm sad," I cried. "And scared."

"I know," he said quietly. "Gods, I wish I could take some of it from you." His thumb scraped against my hip. "Maybe to help you sleep, we need to tire out your body some more."

"What do you mean?"

He curled closer to me, his breathing slow and even against my back. "Your mind is racing, but it might stop if you're exhausted. You said it's only when we stop. It makes sense. I remember being like this in the early days, after my mother...after she was gone. The grief was so much." He traced circles over my stomach. "It weighed on me day and night. And I found that unless I took my body to the absolute brink of exhaustion, nothing else would let me sleep, not with all my thoughts. All the guilt. All the what ifs I pondered. What if I'd been faster, stronger. Made a different choice. I drove myself farther than Lethea with the thoughts. Alcohol could help, if I had enough, but I was on the run. I never wanted to risk being drunk and crossing paths with soturi trying to arrest me, or worse, akadim."

I felt hopeless. "We've been walking all day. We ran this morning. I barely sat down until now. My legs are so fucking sore, and my feet...what else can I do?"

He shrugged against me. "Even sore, we could go for another run. If it'll make you feel better, I could try and sneak us into a local arena."

Groaning, I buried my face in the pillow. "Gods, no! I don't *hate* running anymore, but you're farther than fucking Lethea if you think I'm getting out of this bed for that now."

He chuckled, running his hand up to my waist and squeezing. "Okay, no running. Push-ups?"

"No!"

"Sit-ups?"

I bucked back against him.

He coughed. "No, I didn't think so."

Sighing, I asked, "Is that what you did? Every time you couldn't sleep?"

His fingers trailed down my stomach, as I pulled my head back against the crook of his shoulder. "At first, it was. I started training day and night. I wanted to be ready for whatever came. Akadim. My father. Imperator Kormac. I wore myself out until I...did something different. I found that, uh...." He coughed again, shifting his hips back from me. "There were *other* ways to tire my body." His voice lowered. His chest rose with a sudden intake of breath while his heart pounded loudly enough for me to hear it. "Like...a release." His hand stilled on my stomach.

I sucked in a breath, my pulse quickening. "Oh."

"If you want," he rasped, "I could do that for you. Just like the other night—but with my hands this time."

"And mine?" I started to turn in his arms, but he stilled me, holding my back to his front.

"Just mine on you. For tonight. Only if you want. There's no pressure here for anything. And no need to do anything for me in return."

My core tightened, my body fully aware of how dangerously close his fingers were to my core. How easily they could slip down inside my pants, move between my legs.

I inched back, feeling his length, long and hard against my backside. Heat bloomed through me. "But what about you?"

"Don't worry about me. This is for you." He nipped at my earlobe. "Plus," he teased, "I promised to show you the real meaning of stamina, didn't I?" His thigh moved up toward my center, and I instinctively rocked against it. "I can hardly do that in a room where we both need to be silent."

"What if I swear to be quiet?" I rolled my hips.

"I don't want you quiet for that," he growled. "The first time I take you, I want you screaming. I want to hear you call my name when you explode. I want to hear all the pretty sounds I know you can make and discover the new ones I can draw from you."

At the moment, the only sounds in the room were my heaving breaths spurred on by the simmering heat between my legs. Rhyan's other hand reached beneath me, twisted up inside my shirt, and found my breast. As his fingers closed around my peaked nipple, I twisted my head back to find his lips. He squeezed his fingers, making me gasp into his mouth, as shivers danced through my body. Slanting his lips over mine, he deepened the kiss, his tongue coaxing mine into his mouth until I was breathless and writhing against him. His thumb rubbed over my nipple in the same rhythm as his tongue.

"Lyr," he whispered, sucking on my bottom lip. "Can I touch you?" He kissed his way across my cheek and bit down on my neck. "Will you let me touch your cunt?"

I undulated back against him, squeezing his thigh between my legs. "Yes."

He slid his lower hand beneath my waistband, his fingers brushing the top of my underwear and his lips licking and kissing their way back to my mouth. I reached behind me for his hair, tangling his bronzed curls between my fingers and pulling him closer. The hand in my shirt switched to my other breast, teasing me.

I gasped, wriggling onto my back to see him better. My legs spread open, as he leaned over me, and his hand paused just inches above where I was desperate to feel him.

"What are you waiting for?" I asked, undulating my body, attempting to bring his hand lower.

He exhaled sharply, watching me carefully, his hand searing as it pressed against my flesh. "I've waited for this. To touch you...here. A very long time."

"Don't wait any longer."

His eyes blazed on mine as his fingers swept inside my underwear, finally gliding through my center until he cupped me with his palm. My skin warmed even more with his touch, the heat coiling and twisting inside me.

I whimpered, then we both froze, shocked at the contact between us, at the fact that this was actually happening. I'd waited for this, too—for him to touch me so intimately, so purposefully.

"Lyr," he groaned into my mouth. "Fuck, you're so wet." He slid his fingers through my folds, exploring, teasing. He looked down to where his hand vanished beneath my pants then back to my face, watching my reaction with each new touch and stroke, as my hips rocked up against his hand, my stomach rolling in waves. He moved toward the bundle of nerves at my center, and I started to pant, reaching for his face to kiss him again. His fingers rolled back down my center with a lazy stroke before making tight circles around it.

He pressed down, squeezing, one finger stroking right through, and I bucked, mewling in response, my heels digging into the bed. His hand felt so much better than my hand had, so much better than anything.

"Like that, partner?" he said, voice hoarse. "Right there?"

I tried to say *yes* but only managed another whimper, feeling heat rush through my entire body.

"Shhhh." His lips spread into a seductive grin as his fingers slid lower, cupping me, the callouses on his palm massaging the bundle of nerves. "Remember. We have to be quiet."

My hips jerked up, rolling and pushing against him, seeking more heat, more friction.

"There you go," he crooned, pressing me back down into the bed. "Ride my hand."

I threw my head back, my back bowing off the bed as I arched. The coil of pleasure between my legs tightened and expanded with every thrust of his hand against me.

"Is this how you touched yourself?" he asked. "Is this what you did when you thought of me, when you had me so Godsdamned wild, I had to fuck my hand for you?"

"Yes. And I imagined you...just like this," I cried between breaths.

"Show me," he growled. "Show me how you made yourself come."

My core was throbbing beneath his touch, pulsing so deeply, it was almost too much. I slid my hand down over his, pressed him against me, and moved him in tight circles.

It was so good, so good. I was squirming, pushing my body closer to his, feeling his erection press into my side, his own hips thrusting forward, rocking against me.

"Are you...?" I asked, realizing he was on the edge without even having been touched.

His forehead pressed to mine, as he circled my center again and again. My hips rose and bucked. Our breath mixed. I was losing control. I was no longer guiding him but digging my fingers into his hand as he brought me closer and closer to the edge until a frenzied scream started to rip through me. His mouth clamped down on mine, swallowing my cry, as my body shook with my orgasm.

Rhyan kissed me through it, muffling the sound before he pulled back, watching me. The shivers running through my body finally stopped. My legs fell open and collapsed on the bed.

I slid my hand up his arm, holding him tightly as my heart hammered through my chest. Sweat beaded my neck and forehead.

Rhyan still cupped me, stroking me softly, his touch soothing, before he released his hand, glistening with my arousal.

He kept his eyes on me, dark with his desire, as he slid his hand down his pants, fisting himself. His eyes shut as his arm moved, his bicep flexing, stomach taut. I watched, mesmerized as he moved, his muscles glowing beneath the candlelight. His hips jerked, and I cupped his face, kissing him as his entire body tensed, swallowing his growl with my lips.

Sweat curled his hair as he lay back, his eyes still closed. He opened them, as he turned to face me on the pillow, a satisfied yet mischievous smile spreading across his lips. "Always making such a mess, partner."

A blush spread across my cheeks, but I pushed his hair back from his forehead. "I thought that was supposed to be about me."

His chest heaved. "Apparently, I like it a lot when it's about you." He shook his head, still grinning. "Give me a second to clean up," he said, hopping out of the bed for the bathroom. The faucet turned on, and by the time it was off, he was back under the covers with me, having traveled across the room.

He gathered me into his arms, pulling the blanket higher around us. "How are you feeling now?"

"Like jelly," I said. "Physically exhausted. Good."

"Good." He pushed my hair off my shoulder, dipping his fingers in the back of my shirt—or, rather, his shirt that I'd stolen. His fingers returned to making lazy circles at the nape of my neck and between my shoulder blades. "Do you need anything? Water?"

I shook my head, content to just lay there, my arms wrapped around him.

"You know something?" he said. "You look just as pretty as you sound. I think I could watch you do that every night for the rest of my life and never tire of it."

"Hmmmm." I buried my fingers in his hair, lightly scratching at his scalp. He arched into the touch. "I can say the same for you. Maybe next time, I can do the same for you."

His eyes darkened. "We can arrange that. When you're ready."

I snuggled closer to him, our legs entwining, my body more relaxed than it had been in days.

"What are you thinking?" he asked quietly.

"That you were right. This helped." I hadn't forgotten anything. There was still a pit in my stomach, but it had shrunk. Considerably so. It felt manageable for the moment. "And definitely preferable to push-ups. Why were you training before when you could have been doing this the whole time?"

He pushed a curl from my face, tucking it behind my ear and tracing my lobe with his finger. His callouses caused me to shiver.

"I couldn't," he said. "There was no one else I wanted. And for a while, the desire...." He bit his lip, the muscles in his jaw tensing. "The desire was gone. I felt nothing."

"Rhyan." I squeezed him tighter, lifting my head and finding his lips, hugging him close.

"It's okay. Clearly," he coughed, "it returned."

"How did you get through it?" I asked.

He shrugged. "I just knew I had to. I had to keep going."

"Was there anyone? Anyone who helped you? Who took care of you?" I asked.

"No. There was no one."

I sighed against him. "I wish I'd been there. I wish I could go back in time, be there beside you every step of the way. Hold you. Help you the way you're helping me."

"You are," he said. "In a way that I can't explain. I never wanted any of this for you. If I could take your pain for myself, if I could carry it for you, bear it, I'd do it. But I can't. So, I do the next best thing. And, for some reason, being able to hold you, help you, touch you, it's healing to me. Pain I've carried for months, for years, it feels lessened, it feels like it's fading when you're in my arms."

I cupped his cheek and stroked it with my thumb. "I love you."

"I love you, too."

I closed my eyes, sinking into the bed, into him, cocooned in the warmth of his body and the cool calming feel of his aura. It was the perfect combination of temperatures for sleeping.

"You still promise to show me the real meaning of stamina?" I asked drowsily.

"What do you think I was doing all that training for?"

I laughed and felt his hands sliding up my back as I lost consciousness.

I spent the following morning back on edge. We had breakfast and again ordered lunch to be packed, and then Rhyan snuck me out of the inn. He left me in the alley we'd traveled from the night before.

I was waiting for him to check out and say goodbye to the owners when I heard it again: hissing. I spun on my heels in the direction of the sound, but I saw nothing. No shadows. No snakes. My body stilled as I held my breath, my ears straining.

Only the wind, the sounds of the city it carried, and light music playing in the distance could be heard. Torches crackled outside a restaurant so patrons could dine outside and stay warm. An ashvan horse flying overhead whinnied.

Maybe all I'd heard had been the wind, the sounds of the city.

"Partner." Rhyan wrapped his arms around me from behind. "Ready to run?"

I heard it again—the hissing. Louder this time, the sound echoing. No, not echoing...doubling. Tripling.

A shadow slithered past the alleyway.

Rhyan's grip on me tightened.

"Turn around, Lyr," he whispered. "Slowly."

I started to turn, and the nahashim appeared, far larger than I'd imagined, larger than what I'd seen last night. It was at least ten feet tall—the size of an akadim.

The giant snake released a vicious hiss, more like a growl, before its scaly body retracted then expanded, its mouth open as it flung itself toward us.

"NOW!" Rhyan screamed.

I buried my face in his neck and wrapped my arms around his waist as my stomach twisted and tugged. I screamed as Rhyan took me away from the alley. My world was spinning. My back felt like it was burning.

Feet slamming into the ground, I immediately tried to get my bearings. We were in a forest. I had no idea where we were, how far we'd traveled, or how exhausted Rhyan would be.

He was shaking in my arms, trying to catch his breath, to regain his energy. "Are you okay?" I asked.

"Lyr," he said, his voice feral and commanding. "Don't. Let. Go."

"What's wrong?"

There was a hiss behind me.

I turned. The nahashim. That had been what had made my back feel so hot. The scaly, slimy creatures were hot to the touch. It had traveled with us, attached itself to me, used me as its host to follow Rhyan.

Only there wasn't just one nahashim. The snake that had struck at us had been hiding the others behind its scaly back.

There were nine.

CHAPTER TWENTY-SEVEN

"LYR. TAKE OUT YOUR sword," Rhyan said, voice low. "Stand behind me."

"But they're here for you," I said.

"Doesn't matter. I'm still your bodyguard, and trust me, if my father sent them, they'll take you, too."

"But—"

"Behind me, Lyr. Now."

He'd just traveled, and he needed to recover. But I knew this wasn't the time to argue. I followed his orders, brandishing my sword, my hand shaking as I positioned my arm the way he'd taught me. My fingers wrapped around the hilt, holding it as if it were an extension of my arm. Sweat was already coating my palm.

"Avoid their mouths. Don't let them bite you," he said quickly. "A fully grown nahashim's bite is paralyzing. That's how they transport their prey—unable to move."

I widened my stance, ignoring the growing pit in my stomach.

The nahashim's bodies undulated together, slithering, twisting, and knotting until they looked like one large snake with nine heads rolling, biting, and hissing in different directions.

Rhyan's body tensed, his sword lifted, as I took position. But it was clear there was no way to get to them—there were too many heads, too many chances to be bitten.

Then, without warning, they stilled, nine pairs of eyes glowing. One snake's head shot forward, its mouth open, its fangs dripping with venom.

For a second, all I could think was that this creature had been inside me. Two of them had slipped through my skin, stolen my secrets, invaded my flesh.

The nahashim before us hissed, and I returned to the present, lifting my sword, ready to strike.

"Hold your ground," Rhyan yelled, running forward. With a leap, he traveled, vanishing and reappearing by the nahashim's neck, his sword slicing down with a force I'd never seen him use before.

Rhyan's strike should have cleaved the snake in two, but it looked like he'd only made a scratch. The nahashim screeched, its voice grating as Rhyan's boots hit the ground. Before the snake could retaliate, he vanished again, reappearing back at my side.

He took my hand, his grip on me vicelike. "Hold on!"

In an instant, my feet touched down on the earth, nearly two dozen feet back from where we'd stood. Releasing my hand, Rhyan took off again, running, jumping, and flying past the snake, his body vanishing and reappearing again, and again, as he tried to place himself exactly where he was needed to finish the job.

But the nahashim were faster, turning their heads in quick blinks and snapping their venom-dripping jaws.

Rhyan landed behind them and called out.

He was trying to draw their attention away from me. But this wasn't like fighting an akadim. The nahashim were on a mission, and they weren't going to stop until it was complete. Only half the snakes fell for his distraction and turned toward him, their bodies unraveling from the single formation and retwisting together until there were two sets of nahashim, one with five heads, one with four. It was the five-headed monster that slithered toward Rhyan while the remaining snakes glided across the ground toward me.

I clutched the hilt of my sword in both hands, feeling the weight of it in my arm. My eyes zeroed in on the shining black scales sliding toward me. I widened my stance, heels digging into the cold hard ground, ready to fight. With a cry, I lunged forward and struck, but the sword barely cut through the scales. They were like armor, nearly impenetrable.

I stumbled back from the impact, my hand reverberating from the hit. My arms shaking out of control.

The snakes following Rhyan seemed to lose interest in him and started charging for me.

"Lyr, run!" Rhyan screamed.

I took off as he vanished and reappeared at my side, grabbing my hand, his feet moving impossibly fast; he was practically dragging me behind him.

I cried out, tripping over my feet, and yet the hissing was right behind me. "I can't keep up!"

Rhyan's hand tightened around mine, his grip like a chain around my wrist, and I knew what was coming next.

We traveled again but not just several feet away this time—we had jumped to a completely different location.

My boots sank into the ground, damp from melting snow. A close cluster of trees loomed ahead, and Rhyan headed straight for it. The weather was so much warmer than it had been in Cretanya. I wondered if Rhyan had reversed course and taken us back south.

I hadn't felt anything on my back as we'd traveled—no heat, no burning. But the hissing was still behind us, growing closer and closer. The sound intensified, as I pushed my feet to move faster. My thighs were on fire, as I tried to keep up with Rhyan's pace, to match his soturion speed. He'd stumbled when we'd arrived, and his face had been pale, but he hadn't paused to recover before taking off, his hand still clutching mine.

"Did you feel them?" Rhyan roared.

"No!"

"Fuck!" He ducked under a low tree branch.

A growling hiss sounded behind us. Hot air blew on my back. Rhyan ran faster, narrowly sliding us between two sun trees. He pulled me toward him, one hand on my back, and scooped my legs into his arms, and we were gone.

My stomach tugged, and my feet touched the ground. It was sand. Above us was more sun than I'd seen in weeks.

We seemed to be on an island—tides were crashing against the distant shore, the water so blue, and the climate was as temperate as it had been in late fall. We were in Damara? Lethea?

Rhyan stumbled, sinking to his knees.

A loud hiss came from behind me.

"FUCK!" Rhyan roared, pushing up to his feet, mud on his boots tracking in the sand. "They can travel!"

Sweat filled my palm as I tightened my grip on my sword. I'd never heard of nahashim doing this, but I should have suspected it. The snakes could find anything one asked them to. Their magic drew them to their target. If their target was a traveling Lumerian, then the nahashim would be able to travel, too. They'd be able to do whatever it took to capture their prize.

And they wouldn't stop until they succeeded.

"We can't keep traveling and running. You're nearly out of power. We need to separate them," I said.

Rhyan looked pained, his good eyebrow lowered, but he knew I was right and nodded. "Don't let their mouths get near you."

"I won't." Avoiding was one thing I was good at. Being the only powerless soturion at the academy had made me a target for months, particularly during group fights. I hadn't always been strong enough to land a hit or punch, but I knew Godsdamned well how to duck and escape them.

"Stay alert. They'll come at all angles." Rhyan's eyes searched mine, so beautifully green. The bright sun had turned his hair from dark brown to golden bronze, and my own hair was red once more.

I held his gaze, knowing he needed a moment to prepare, to recover and regain his energy. His face was drawn, his jaw tensed. The scar through his eyebrow and cheek was more pronounced, something that happened whenever he was exhausted or injured.

"We'll charge together and split in the middle," he said, "at the dune up ahead. I'll go right, you take the left flank."

"Ready," I said, taking his hand.

His thumb smoothed over my knuckle, and his knees bent, ready to sprint.

We ran, the nahashim raising their heads and snapping their nine jaws as they started, as one, toward us.

"NOW!" Rhyan screamed.

I released his hand and ran to the left, my boots fighting against the shifting sand. But the nahashim didn't break apart. All nine snakes remained twisted together in one oversized scaly body and went after Rhyan, their tails leaving tracks in the sand.

I turned immediately, nearly sliding through the dune, racing as fast as I could to get to him.

They were separating and starting to circle around Rhyan. Both of his hands were on his sword, which was raised above his head, as he turned slowly, a pained expression in his eyes. He was exhausted from all the back-to-back jumps. He looked close to burning through his entire store of power and fainting. I'd seen him do it before. He'd once jumped from Elyria to Bamaria to return to me. He'd been up the entire night hunting akadim, and had already traveled across both countries. He'd fallen flat on his face from exhaustion.

I ran faster, desperate to reach him. My hands were at my sides, as I willed my legs to move quicker. Each of the nine snakes rose on its tail, their heads bobbing before they all snapped forward at once—just as I reached Rhyan.

Our hands clutched together, and we sprinted out from the center of the snakes.

In our absence, the snakes' nine heads crashed into each other, their fangs piercing each other's faces.

"You can't keep jumping," I cried, as the snakes quickly recovered from their collision and resumed chasing us. "You're going to pass out."

"Lyr, we have no choice. We can't stop!"

His hand was shaking in mine, and to my horror, I realized I was the one leading us away—I was the one running faster. Rhyan had always been the stronger one, the faster one.

Except once—in the arena when he'd been bound and tied up, and the only thing standing between him and an akadim had been me. That instinct to protect him, to kill anyone who dared to harm him, was rising through me again just as it had in the arena that day, like a fire in my soul.

You're the fire.

The snakes picked up speed, and I ran faster, my grip tightening on Rhyan, nearly dragging him ahead.

"Where can we hide?" I asked.

He was stumbling, but he had a determined look on his face. His protectiveness over me was starting to overpower his exhaustion. I could see his mind turning, trying to figure out how to guard me against the threat. But he'd already used up so much of his strength.

"Rhyan! We need a place to hide so you can recover."

A shadow loomed over us of a giant body with nine heads. He surged forward.

"Rhyan!"

He lifted me in his arms, and the beach faded away. We were on the side of a mountain again, a fresh crop of snow on the ground. Rhyan sank to his knees.

I knew instinctively this had been the farthest jump yet. The snow and the mountains gave me a sinking feeling, as did a distant flag of a silver wolf howling. We were in Korteria. In Ka Kormac's land.

And the nahashim had still tracked us here. Already, they were surrounding us, slithering closer, their bodies expanding and retracting. When Imperator Hart had said he'd bred them to be large, he hadn't been exaggerating. The largest rose up on its tail, towering over Rhyan as he stumbled to his feet, his face red and covered with a sheen of sweat. The rest of the snakes were slithering away from the leader, spreading out and trapping us in a circle.

I turned around and pressed my back to Rhyan's. "We're surrounded."

His hand reached behind his back and clasped mine. His palm was so damp. I had no idea how far we'd traveled or how many times.

The nine nahashim were undulating their scaly bodies, towering over us.

"All things have balance," Rhyan gasped. "They have to tire, too. If I have one jump left in me, so do they!"

He leaned forward, reaching for his second sword. I unsheathed my dagger.

"Stay close to me," he said.

There was a hiss. A nahashim before me darted forward, its fangs bared. I lunged away from it, as the next nahashim struck, his teeth hitting the armor over my shoulder.

I elbowed it, throwing the snake back. It landed on top of another, and their bodies twisted together into a two-headed beast that charged forward.

I turned, my blades ready, to face both sets of eyes. My heart pounded as its doubled body slithered forward, its heads striking. I leapt out of the way, watching in horror as it flung itself to the other side of the circle.

The snakes separated from each other and charged again. I slid my dagger across one's back, drawing blood at last—but just barely. It wasn't enough to stop it.

Another snake shot forward, and I leaned back, just narrowly missing its bite. Its fangs hit Asherah's armor, and it bounced off, the snake's head shaking from the impact.

Fuck! We needed help. More strength, more power.

Kashonim. I needed to call on kashonim. Not my lineage with Rhyan—he had almost nothing left to give—but my lineage with Asherah.

Rhyan backed into me, the space between us and the nahashim shrinking. This was it. There was no way through the circle they'd created unless we traveled.

"Lyr," Rhyan said desperately. "One more. Just one more."

I squeezed his hand, my decision made. It was the only way. The only way to save him. The only way to stop this. If the snakes traveled one more time, it was over. Either they'd catch us, or Rhyan would succumb to his exhaustion.

"One more," I said. "Go!"

Tears burned in my eyes as I felt the familiar tug, the sensation of my feet lifting off the ground. My eyes locked on the red of the snakes' eyes, capturing their attention, their focus, and I bit back a sob as I let go of Rhyan. His hand vanished from mine as he traveled without me. I gasped, suddenly alone.

He was gone. It was just me and nine nahashim.

My plan had worked.

The vadati around my neck warmed instantly, and Rhyan's anguished voice cried through it: "LYR! LYR! You let go!"

"Rhyan, I'm sorry. I had to."

"Where are you?" he yelled.

"Finishing this." I held up my sword to the sky and placed one hand on my armor. A gale-force wind carrying snow blew back my hood, tossing my hair wildly across my back, where it shone red in the sun.

Asherah's red.

"LYR!"

"Ani Asherah!" I screamed. "I am Asherah. Her blood is my blood. I call upon you. *Ani petrova kashonim, me ka el lyrotz, dhame ra shukroya, aniam anam. Chayate me el ra shukroya. Ani petrova kashonim!"*

The diamond centers of the Valalumir stars around my neck began to glow at once, their light brightening with each word of the incantation. All at once, I felt it—the surge of power, the fire burning inside me. It wasn't painful but energizing, stirring my blood, filling me with power.

The sword that had been fatiguing my arm now lifted higher and I threw my hand above my head, nearly releasing the blade as I did so. Every ache, every sore in my body was gone, as were the pit in my stomach and my nerves. I felt like I'd been in a nightmare, and I was suddenly awake.

I'd only called on kashonim twice before. Once, I'd used Rhyan's, and I'd taken it slow, spreading the power out as far as I could to survive the habibellum. The second time, in the arena, I'd taken on Asherah's power without knowing it. This time, I was ready. This time, I knew what to expect.

I didn't have long.

Neither did the nahashim.

The starfire steel of my sword was alight beneath the sun with my invocation, and with a battle cry, I charged forward, almost stumbling I was moving so fast. The power was so intense, I wasn't sure how to control it, how to handle it.

I yelled out, colliding with the snake, my body nearly bouncing off its toughened body, like one giant muscle. But the thick scaly skin I'd barely been able to cut through, softened beneath my blade. I shoved the point through its body until I heard a sickening popping sound, and knew the end of my blade had pierced its back. With a grunt, I twisted, turning the sword in my hand, pushing the sword further in, pushing until the hilt pressed against its skin. I gasped. I'd had no idea I could do that, use such force.

The snake hissed in anger then fear as black blood dripped like a faucet from its wounds. Blood gushed from the front and back of its body. Its eyes went wild and feral before they closed with a dying hiss. I almost fell down with it, balancing on my feet at the last second as I pulled the sword, now covered in blood, free from its body.

The first beast collapsed into a coil on the side of the mountain, as my heart beat far too fast. I whipped my head around, seeing the remaining snakes, their hisses too loud for my newly sensitive ears, their black scales now shining too brightly. I felt like I was seeing colors for the first time, hearing my heart beat, feeling my blood pump through my veins as I watched the snakes writhe and twist, each movement more detailed than I could process. It seemed like their bodies were undulating slower and faster at the same time as my brain tried to catch up to the power rushing through my body.

The second nahashim slithered toward me, as something caught my attention in the distance. Shadowy shapes, and a strange noise. A howl?

The snake inched closer, its sharp scent of the snake over me, like rotten eggs. I held back the sudden need to gag. I'd never scented them before. Never knew they had a scent. And just like that, I could smell the grass, the cold of the snow that remained, the dried wolf feces in the distance. Everything was heightened. Overwhelming. Too much. Too intense.

I didn't think I could handle Asherah's kashonim much longer. It was going to burn through me.

I swallowed, trying to get my bearings, to control the power, to keep it focused, and I turned back to the snake, rushing toward it, both hands on the blade's hilt. I lifted my sword, and sliced forward, cutting the snake in two. Its tail waved and spun, frenzied without its head before it, too, fell. I kept running, racing through its severed body. Unable to stop myself. Unable to gain control. And before the third snake knew I was coming, I'd leapt and cut off its head in one strike. My blade sang as the nahashim hissed to its death.

Six remained.

My world shrank down to those six slippery bodies snaking along the mountainside. My breath was heavy, the burning inside my veins so intense. I needed to finish this. I needed to finish it now. I wasn't aware of anything else. I wasn't me anymore. I was the fire in my blade. I was the death coming for these monsters sent by my enemy to harm the man I loved.

And in that moment, fire burning inside of me, and a rage I hadn't known I was carrying since my own examination by these beasts, I became a goddess.

My clumsiness, my inability to control this power, this strength was gone.

It felt like Asherah was in control now.

I spun on my heels, screaming, with fire in my blood, as the next nahashim charged. It slid around my body, circling its way to my belly before I brought down my sword, slicing through every single coil and leaving the snake in pieces at my feet. My chest heaved as I spun on my heels and stared down my enemy.

Five remained.

I felt the next one coming from behind. I didn't break a sweat as I leapt from the mutilated carcass at my boots, knelt on the ground, lifted my sword above my head with two hands, and caught the belly of the nahashim before it could pounce. It let out a roar, fangs dripping with venom as it fell.

Four.

A pair came at me, twisted and tangled together, their heads swooping in opposite directions in front of their joined bodies.

With both hands still on the hilt of my sword, my arms swung, curved, and danced until the symbol for infinity was drawn in flames before me. I couldn't even see my hands, only the fire, as I ran forward, no longer scared, no longer worried.

The snakes seemed to grow taller as I approached, their bodies elongating and stretching. With the flaming fires smoking before me, I kept running, faster and faster, at a speed I'd never achieved before—a speed I hadn't even seen Rhyan reach.

A speed I knew wasn't me. It was Asherah.

The fire singed their scales, the scent of burning flesh assaulting my nose, before my blade sank through their bodies like a knife through butter. Their heads banged together before severing from their bodies, flames incinerating them on their way to the ground. Their carcasses fell amongst the rocks.   Two.

My heart was heating, the fire in my veins concentrating there—a reminder of the Valalumir, of my contract with Mercurial.

I knew I was starting to run low on fire—the kashonim would only last so much longer before it burned through me, before it claimed me. Using it like this was dangerous. Kashonim was only ever used between living Lumerians, meant only for a final push. I didn't know what calling on a goddess would do to me. Last time it had knocked me out for nearly a day. And my enemies were not yet fully conquered.

But they would be.

They must be. I wasn't going to fail. Not myself. And not Rhyan.

In the distance, I could hear his voice, still calling my name. Still keeping the connection of the vadati between us alive. So he could find me again when this was over. When he was recharged. But in this moment, I felt the anguish of our separation in my heart.

But I put that all aside as I ran for the next snake. This one was scared and retreated. My boots left dust in my trail. My calves were on fire, and sweat poured down my face. I held my blade overhead as I ran, the starfire steel flaming. The diamonds in my armor filled with Asherah's blood, lit up like rubies. The fiery red lights flashed on the nahashim's onyx-like scales.

At the last second, the snake stopped retreating and shot forward with its mouth wide open, coming at me with a speed I could barely see or process. It hissed, its fangs out, venom spitting from its mouth.

I lowered my blade, Asherah's fire running through me, and the blade sliced through the nahashim's mouth, cleaved its head in two, and severed its body down the center. I stood in the middle of the dead nahashim with black blood splattered across my armor and tunic.

One left. The final nahashim—the largest. Its body was elongated, its eyes glowing.

My vision was growing blurry, my limbs tired with the heat inside me, and I could feel the kashonim taking its toll. I'd already pushed myself to the limit. Like Rhyan had been, I was on my last jump. Either I killed this snake, or it took me to Imperator Hart. There was no in-between.

I held up my sword as the nahashim's body grew. It wasn't just elongating but expanding, too.

It stilled, taking a second of pause. It was tired, too. It fucking had to be. But then it took off, its fangs twice the size of the last snake, its tongue slipping out of its mouth, long and venomous. It was moving too fast, and I was losing my focus. I was fading, running out of time, out or energy, out of power.

My sword collided with its mouth. It should have sliced through the snake's head as it had the last one, but this nahashim clamped down on my sword. The grip of its jaw was too strong. The nahashim tore my sword from my hands, slithered away, and spat it onto the side of the mountain. Too far out of reach. The starfire flames vanquished before my eyes as the nahashim used its tail to kick the sword, which fell off the cliff we'd so dangerously neared.

My heart pounded. My fear was returning as swiftly as the strength of the goddess within me was faltering.

The nahashim seemed to know this. It charged, sliding through the grass, the ground rumbling with its approach.

I reached for the Valalumirs on the straps of my belt, ripped one off, and threw it, using everything I had left to power the throw. The star spun through the air and gashed the snake's eye. It reared back and howled, as I reached for another Valalumir. Praying I aimed true, that the goddess still supported me, I threw the second star, watching wide-eyed as it sliced just below the nahashim's head, cutting its side—enough of a wound to infuriate the snake but not to slow it down.

The ground shook, as it moved faster and faster, charging for me. Onyx scales gleaming as its body shifted.

I reached for another star, my fingers almost numb. I could barely find the grip I needed or strength to rip it from the leather, but with a grunt, I got it off, hearing the strap tear.

But I was too late. The snake was upon me, roaring and hissing and gnashing its fangs. Blood and pus oozed from the eye I'd destroyed.

I clenched the Valalumir between my fingers, knowing I had one shot.

Its breath blew hot in my face as its head came down toward me. I punched the nahashim in the throat, the Valalumir tearing through it, until there was a gurgling, strangled hiss. Black blood oozed down my arm, as a fang slipped into my exposed bicep just below the golden seraphim feathers.

I screamed in pain, my arm burning anew. Not with kashonim. Not with power. But venom.

In that exact moment, my kashonim flamed out, and I was left exhausted. Powerless, and drained.

The poison in my arm was spreading fast, as was my exhaustion. Injuries I'd barely felt before were now coming for me ten times over. Just as they had when I'd called on Rhyan's power in the arena.

The snake fell, dead, and pulled me down with it.

Sweat poured from my forehead as my arm, still inside the snake's mouth, went numb. I used my left hand to grab at the grass, at clumps of dirt, at anything I could, to pull me out of its grasp.

I just barely freed myself before its jaw closed, and my arm hung limp and useless at my side.

"LYR!"

"Rhyan!" I yelled into the stone against my neck.

"Lyr! Are you okay? What's going on?"

"I killed them. All of them. But one got me. The venom....
I'm...I...."

I couldn't speak. The paralysis was taking over. My jaw was
tightening, and my skin felt hard. I could barely move my mouth.

"I'm coming back for you! Lyr, I'm coming! Just hold on!
Cover yourself with your cloak until I get there. I'll find you, I
swear. As soon as I recharge. You hear me? I'm coming! Just hold
on!" He was frantic, his accent heavy again, his words rolling
together.

My head hit the grass. I pulled the cloak from my belt and
dragged the materials over my legs, watching as they blended
into the green of the ground. But I couldn't get to my face. Just
that one movement left me breathless.

There was a voice in my head, one I instinctively knew even
though I'd never heard it before. The first and only time I'd
called on my kashonim with Rhyan, it had bridged a connection
between us, letting me momentarily into his mind. And now, as
my kashonim was ending, I could hear Asherah speaking.

"Do not head for the stars. What you seek is with the moon."

The sun revealed my secrets, so I hid them with the moon.

The engraving hidden on the statue of the seraphim.

I know, I thought. *I'm heading there.*

But she only responded with the same words, her voice even
more urgent: "Do not head for the stars. What you seek is with
the moon."

*We unlock for blood, soul, and key. Power is restored, with
these three.*

Our soul, our blood, and the key. We had all three.

I know, I thought again.

The ground rumbled, and the wind blew, blowing back my
cloak. Ashvan horses were running across the snow—but ashvan horses didn't run on the ground, not unless they were too
old or too young to fly.

Blinking slowly, I began to understand, to remember. Korteria
was too far west, too far from the water, from the Lumerian
Ocean—the source of our magic. This was why Ka Kormac
produced so many soturi and so few mages. This far from the
Lumerian shore, with so little access to the Lumerian Ocean's
waters, even their ashvan were grounded.

I couldn't move, and between the nahashim's venom and the aftereffects of my kashonim, I could barely speak. I was fighting to keep my eyes open.

From the corner of my gaze, I could see the blue light of the vadati still in effect. A small glow came from behind my golden armor. With what I had left, I tucked it down into my tunic struggling to slide it safely between my breasts.

The ashvan approached with their riders. There were four of them, I thought. One carried a flag with the sigil of Ka Kormac—a snarling silver wolf.

"What have we here?" asked the leader, slowing his ashvan to a halt.

I knew his voice, but my brain was barely functioning, no longer making connections, no longer energized enough to bring me his name. I was on the verge of passing out, of losing all consciousness.

There was only one thing I could do.

He laughed, jumping from his horse, watching me with cruel black, beady eyes.

"Rhyan," I said, my voice raspy, exhausted. The muscles in my face were tightening. The venom was overpowering me. I knew I had one word left. And it had to count. "Wolf."

Black leather boots approached, kicking a rock out of their way. Valalumir stars at the bottom of a soturion belt shined beneath the sun.

My eyes closed as rough hands lifted me up, fingers pressing into me, an unfamiliar, unwelcome grip.

Cruel, wolfish laughter, punctuated by a howl---the howl I'd heard before. It was the last thing I heard now, before I finally paid the full price of using kashonim and lost consciousness.

CHAPTER TWENTY-EIGHT

I STOOD ON A mountaintop dressed in my soturion uniform. My belt was buckled, and the Valalumir stars on the straps were shined. I reached down and tried to pull off one of the seven-pointed stars. I needed it. There was an enemy. I needed to kill. Protect.

But the star cut me. I hissed, blood gushing from my finger. I sucked it into my mouth, feeling cold. Snow was falling from the sky.

As each snowflake hit the ground, it burst into flames. Fires were surrounding me on the mountaintop.

An akadim growled, its teeth gnashing, and I spun, trying to find it.

"Asherah," Haleika growled, walking through the flames.

I threw my star, watching in horror as she jumped to the side. The star hummed, spinning past her. Meera and Morgana were there, bound and tied up.

"You can't hurt them," I said. "I'm Asherah."

She laughed. "You were." Her claws wrapped around my throat. I stared down; my armor was gone. "But you're human now."

"I won't be for long."

"You followed the wrong path. Your enemy is closer than you think." She squeezed my neck until I coughed. Her arm elongated, wrapping around me, her pale skin filling with black, shiny scales. There was a scent in the air. A scent of death.

The nahashim hissed, its fangs bared and dripping venom, as its body squeezed mine, cutting off my circulation.

"Please!" I gasped, barely able to breathe. "Don't."

"You better be ready," the snake hissed, the sound growing into a wolf's howl.

The wolf howled in the night, the sound startling me awake.

My head was pounding. Soreness spread across the back of my neck, winding deep into the muscles behind my shoulders. With a groan, I opened my eyes, finding myself in a room darkened by night. There was a fire burning, but my vision was too blurry to see. Everything looked shadowy, hazy. I blinked, realizing I needed to wipe dirt from my eyes, push hair from my face. But my hands...I gritted my teeth. My hands were bound, tied up above my head. Rough ropes had been tightened around my wrists. And I was standing. My feet suddenly stumbling as I fully woke, trying to find my balance. I slipped, and the ropes only held me tighter as I struggled to find purchase on the floor. Tears burned behind my eyes.

I'd been asleep like this. For hours. My legs felt foreign and heavy, every muscle stiff.

A sharp pain pounded in my temples as I lifted my head up, finding through the fog of sleep that my wrists had not only been bound by rope but strung to a pole. A black pole that looked exactly like the one in the Katurium where I'd been tied and whipped by order of the Imperator.

I tried to move, to escape, but my legs were numb after standing for so long. Pins pricked the bottoms of my feet. Nausea rolled through my belly immediately followed by a pang of hunger that left me feeling even sicker.

Pressing against the ropes, I tested for any looseness in the knots, but the ropes only dug deeper into me, cutting skin that had already been rubbed raw by my body pulling down on it while I slept. I felt a trickle of blood on my forearm, and a disgusting coating to my elbow. Nahashim blood. My legs must have been desperate to sit this whole time, refusing to hold my weight, or hold me up. They were letting the ropes do their job.

My mouth was uncomfortably dry. I was so thirsty on top of my hunger, all I could do was whine. And to top it all off, I desperately needed to pee. Gods, if only I could rub the sleep and dirt from my eyes with my hands. I felt like I'd be farther than Lethea if my hands weren't freed soon. I needed to push all of the hair out of my face, I needed to scratch at the itches popping up all over my body. My skin was rolling with them.

But most of all, I needed to get out of here. Wherever I was.

I could already feel the panic rising inside of me. The fear. Now that I was fully awake, it was overwhelming.

I forced myself to take a deep breath. Rhyan would come for me. I had to cling to that. Cling to the idea that he would find me here, would travel, would save me.

But still, my heart pounded with uncertainty. With fear of where I was. With fear that Rhyan wasn't okay. Wasn't safe. What if I'd missed a snake? Or there were more? Or he was simply passed out, sick with exhaustion from too many jumps.

No.

He *was* okay. He had to be okay. And I'd be okay, too.

But if he wasn't...fuck. I'd been the one to let go of his hand. I'd been the one to let myself be captured. And now I was...

My breath hitched.

Stay calm, stay calm, stay calm. I just had to breathe. There was a way out of this. There had to be a way out of this.

Blinking several times, I managed to get some loose strands of hair out of my eyes, rubbing my face against my lifted arms. And then slowly, my surroundings beyond the pole came into focus, and I remembered exactly what I'd seen before I lost consciousness.

I was in Korteria. I'd been captured by Ka Kormac. Reason stood that I was being kept prisoner in their fortress, in Vruskhire Keep—exactly where the Imperator had threatened to take me. I'd practically handed myself over to him.

Myself to Moriel.

No. No.

Deep breath.

Swallowing roughly, I looked around, taking stock of my surroundings. I was not in a prison cell, not unless Ka Kormac treated their prisoners like kings.

Thick gray stone made up the four walls surrounding me. Across the room from me was a leather couch, a dresser, a chest, a mirror. A large bed lay in the center, full of luxurious blankets and pillows made of satin, velvet, and fur. There was also a large closet and beside it, and a wooden dummy meant for holding armor topped with a dead wolf head.

This was no prison. I was in a bedroom.

The thought made my stomach turn.

A fire crackled in the fireplace beside the closet, the flames strong like they'd been recently tended to. Somehow, I doubted the fire had been lit for my comfort or benefit. It was for whoever lived here, whoever normally occupied this room.

And whoever that was, they'd been in here recently.

I glanced down at my body. I was still dressed, my armor in place. I sucked back a shaky breath. I hadn't been violated—only captured and tied up.

Slowly, feeling was returning to my feet and legs as I shifted my weight, finding balance in my position, and I continued assessing my surroundings. Three floor-to-ceiling windows covered the wall to my right, the center one leading out onto a stone balcony faintly lit with torches. The night sky was fairly clear, and the fires of Vrukshire made the hills beyond the keep visible, snow caps reddened by flames.

I must have been asleep the entire day. I'd separated from Rhyan when it was still morning. But how deep into the night was it? Last time I'd called on Asherah's kashonim, I'd slept all night until late the following afternoon. If the same thing had happened, the same use of energy, it was probably the middle of the night, at least.

I squeezed my eyes shut, blinking back tears.

Where was Rhyan? I remembered trying to communicate to him what was happening, but I'd also hidden the vadati beneath my shift, knowing I was about to be taken. I couldn't reach it now, and the stones only worked when there was a clear connection between the speaker and the stone, a connection that only remained if one person kept talking. Silence turned its magic off.

The stone had no doubt gone silent hours ago. Rhyan might not even be conscious. And I worried he didn't know which country I was in. I'd barely known every place we'd traveled to as we tried to escape the nahashim.

A sinking feeling washed through me as I looked back at the bed, at the wolf carved into the headboard. Ka Kormac had captured me and taken me to their fortress...but instead of a prison cell, they'd locked me in someone's bedroom. Someone very high ranking in the Ka based on the room's size.

My stomach twisted. I had a bad feeling that this was a worse outcome than being locked in a Korterian prison. I knew what

Ka Kormac was—what they did to their women, to any women they encountered. And based on our last interactions, I was sure they believed they owned me now. That because of Arianna's fucking promise, they now had some legal right.

But there had to be rules, even here, some decorum that remained in place. I was still a noblewoman, still a lady of Ka Batavia legally. I was still niece to the Arkasva and High Lady.... Even if that meant shit to her, the Emperor and Imperator at least somewhat kept up appearances, wore masks of propriety. Pretended to be moral, to follow the law. I was set to be betrothed to the Heir of the Imperator. But I wasn't theirs. Not yet.

They couldn't just violate me, not without repercussions. I clung to that thought—the only possible protection I had against who was sure to walk through that door, who had no doubt been in here with me, keeping the fire going, watching me while I'd slept, tying me up while I'd been unconscious.

Just the thought of that alone left my stomach twisted. Knowing he'd seen me like this, had most likely had his hands on me. I'd been so delirious from the nahashim's venom and exhaustion of Asherah's kashonim, I hadn't been able to name him before. But I knew now. I knew whose room I was in.

This was Brockton Kormac's room. Viktor's cousin and apprentice—nephew to the Imperator and son of the Bastardmaker—he had been the one who found me.

Despite my attempts at staying calm and rational, I immediately started struggling against the ropes again, stopping only when every move I made had the rope cutting deeper into my wrists. I gritted my teeth, hissing in pain as I tried to find a comfortable position to stand in, but it was impossible.

If I couldn't relieve myself of the pain, then I needed to use it as an anchor. I would focus on the burning sting in my wrists. Focus on the discomfort only and think of how I was going to escape—not of what might happen, not of what they might do to me.

I'd spent months training with Rhyan to focus on the outcome, to see only what I wanted to happen in the end. But the longer I stood here, the harder it was to see my way to a solution.

I took a deep breath. It didn't matter—I'd figure it out. I was going to survive this, I just had to be smart. And I had to accept the worst-case scenario. The worst that could happen was being captured by the Imperator and the Bastardmaker. I was in their home, but...I didn't think they were here. Neither would expect me to come to their country—so the chances of them tracking me here were slim. And if, on the off-chance they were actually following the trail of akadim to my sisters—they'd be following a path north, not west.

Rhyan and I had set out only two nights before. At best, my worst enemies had reached Cretanya. They were moving with their soturi, and considering neither man would be anywhere near the frontline, that also meant they had to be moving slowly.

It was a small thing. But it would buy me time.

I looked around the room again. The bed was perfectly made, cold-looking, untouched. Brockton and his friends had been in Bamaria, at the Soturion Academy. If I'd had to guess, they'd been sent out with everyone else to find my sisters, or they'd been sent by the Imperator to track and capture me. Neither of those would have led him here though.

Fuck. Had we really been that unlucky? We'd escaped the Shadow Stronghold, avoided a legion of soturi, and escaped nine nahashim. And all so I could be captured by Brockton fucking Kormac, son of the Bastardmaker, disobeying orders to come home and party with his friends. Failing to do his duty as a soturion.

Squeezing my eyes shut, I tried to temper the nerves exploding in my belly. If I was in Brockton's bedroom rather than the prison, then there was a small chance only he knew I was here. If he'd reported me, I'd be in a dungeon being watched by a guard. I'd have been stripped of all my weapons. But I could feel my dagger against my thigh. My sword scabbard was empty—I was pretty sure my sword was back on the cliffside with the nahashim.

I would have been insulted he'd thought me so little a threat that I didn't need a guard or to be separated from my dagger. They'd failed to disarm me in the Shadow Stronghold, too. Yet they weren't wrong this time. Because here I was, tied up and unable to reach my weapons. Unable to escape. Again.

I desperately tried to parse out what it meant—why I was alone, why I was in his room. Was he keeping me secret so no one else knew he was here? Or did he have some other reasons?

My arms shook, and the door creaked open.

Brockton passed through the threshold. His beady black eyes slid over my body, landing on my face last. He looked startled to see I was awake.

"Thought I'd have to throw water on you." He carried a log under his arm and tossed it into the fire, rubbing his hands together as the flames receded and then flared back to life, popping and crackling. "At least you don't snore."

"No," I said quietly. "I'm awake."

His back remained to me as he locked the door, the bolt making a thick metallic thud as it fell into place. The sound echoed, making my heart pound. When he turned, a wolfish grin was on his face, and his eyes wandered over me again.

My skin crawled at every place his gaze landed.

"What do you think of my pole?" he asked, eyebrows lifted.

"It's cutting off my circulation," I said, affecting my best heir's voice. "And it doesn't match your décor."

He licked his lips. "You remember when you were whipped? I do."

I swallowed a growl. Of course, I remembered. I'd pay a small fortune to not have to remember, to unhear Aemon saying, "I'll do it," to erase the moment the Imperator cruelly decided to add another lash—one that had nearly destroyed me.

My stomach twisted at the thought of others being tied here—of his past victims suffering in my place.

"What do you want?" I asked.

"Right to the point, huh? No small talk? No pleading?"

My nostrils flared. "No one knows I'm here, do they?"

He looked surprised. I tucked that away as a win. I'd guessed correctly.

"What makes you say that, Lady *Asherah*?"

I ignored his attempt at insulting me, and lifted my chin, as I gathered all my thoughts.

"One, that your uncle is leading the Emperor's task force to hunt akadim. You're not at the Academy in classes. And you're clearly not on the hunt. So, I'm guessing, you're not even supposed to be here. Second, I was locked in prison by your uncle. And I escaped." I stared him down, pretending I wasn't terrified. "You found me. Something tells me that protocol demands I be kept in your dungeons, but I'm not. I woke up without even a guard in place and my weapons still on my body. And I'm in your bedroom."

He shrugged. "Dungeons? Guard? Come on now. You're engaged to Lord Viktor. You're not a prisoner here."

"The cuts on my wrists and these ropes say otherwise," I gritted through my teeth.

He shrugged again, stepping closer. "Well, like you said—you escaped. Thought you might be a flight risk. Couldn't take any chances."

"So why not remove my weapons?"

He frowned, his lips pouting. "Are you able to reach them?" he asked, his voice mockingly sweet, like I was a child, Like it was the dumbest question ever asked.

I glared. "Then tell me, why your room if not a dungeon? As you said, I'm to be engaged to Lord Viktor."

He frowned. "He's not here."

I stored that information away, too. "Is this how you treat your future cousin-in-law?"

He laughed. "Come now, Lady Asherah. Or shall I call you Lady Lyriana? Soturion?" He shrugged. "We both know you have zero desire to marry him."

"I wasn't aware Ka Kormac cared what others wanted or desired."

Brockton smirked.

"Even so," I said, "won't he be mad that you have me tied up like this?"

His eyes narrowed, and he turned away from me and began pacing up and down the room. He stopped suddenly in the center of the room and walked toward me. His roughened hands gripped my chin, forcing my face up to his.

"You think your mind games are going to work on me? Huh?" He spit in my face, and I resisted the urge to gag as his spit slid down my cheek. "I found you on my land. In my country. Surrounded by nine dead nahashim. I didn't come to your fucking country and pass out, now did I? Nor did I bring any monsters with me."

No. But your uncle brought fucking akadim. I tried to twist out of his hold, but he only held me tighter, his nails pinching the corners of my mouth.

"You did that," he snarled. "You came here. You escaped the Shadow Stronghold—I assumed to get away from my cousin or uncle. I assumed to go after your sisters like the idiot you are.

But, no, I find you here, and with nine fucking snakes. I want to know why."

"I'm trying to find my sisters," I shouted.

"And what makes you think they're here?" he asked, his neck flaring with color.

I watched him carefully. He seemed to be genuinely asking his question. Like he wondered what I knew that he didn't. Like he'd been left out of some crucial detail others had been privy to. Or like he was about to be in trouble—I was positive he wasn't supposed to be here now.

"What makes you think they're not here?" I asked, wondering just how much he knew, if he knew anything at all. I had no idea who'd taken my sisters and written me that letter. It could have been Imperator Kormac. But then why make the exchange in Glemaria? I'd think Rhyan's father sent the note—except for the fact that he had the key.

"I'd know," Brockton spat. "Why come here for them?"

"Because I don't know where they are," I said desperately. "I'm just searching. I just want to find them."

"Alone?" he asked.

I tugged on my binds. "Obviously."

His fingers dug into my chin. "Where's your forsworn bastard?"

I bit the inside of my cheek. "I have no idea where Soturion Hart is."

Without warning, he slapped me across the cheek so hard my head snapped to the side. The sting of pain was so sharp, I cried out before I could stop myself. Tears burned behind my eyes.

"That's for lying," he gritted.

I sucked in a breath, my cheek vibrating.

Focus on the pain. The pain in my cheek, the pain in my wrists. Stay present. Stay calm.

"Where. Is. The. Forsworn?" he asked again, punctuating each word with such force more spit flew from his mouth.

"Why do you want to know?" I asked. "What is he to you?"

An angry flare in Brockton's aura swiped out. "You seem to be forgetting, my *lady*. I have you tied up. You're at my mercy." His hand lowered to my neck, his fingers digging into my flesh hard enough to bruise.

My hands began to shake as his hand kept moving lower—over my armor, down my sternum, to my waist. He hooked his fingers into my belt, and I instinctively sucked in my belly, leaning back, trying to put any level of distance between us that I could. I was desperate to avoid his touch even if it was only through clothing.

"Now try to remember," he said, his voice lowering to a dangerous pitch, "I ask the questions. Not you."

I exhaled through my nose, my mouth clamped shut. He tugged on my belt, his knuckles against my belly.

"How did you get out of prison?" he asked.

I stared ahead, refusing to answer. Another wolf howled outside the keep.

"I said," Brockton yelled, "how the fuck did you get out of prison?" His hand lifted inches from my face. His palm was still red from hitting me.

"I paid off a guard," I lied quickly.

"Last I heard, Ka Shavo couldn't be paid off."

"You heard wrong."

"I don't think so." His eyes narrowed. "What about the Ready?"

"What about my arkturion?" I asked defensively. I knew his reputation was in ruins—but did people believe he'd freed me?

"He let you out?" Brockton asked.

"No."

Brockton stepped back, pulling his hand from me. He scratched his chin, his black eyes moving slowly across my body. "See, that I almost believe. Because I don't think you could just get out of there. You were locked up for a week before and didn't escape. No one let you out. Not your limp-legged father. Not your aunt. And we all know what little Lord Grey did for you." He pouted, his face a mockery of sympathy. "How he gave over his ring for you. And how that didn't even free you, because Ka Shavo doesn't just let their prisoners go, do they?"

I tried to control my breathing.

"We all know the forsworn bastard got you out. The question is how. A question I was asking myself for two days. Until I saw something very interesting this morning."

My heart pounded. "I paid off a guard," I said again. "He opened the gate. I ran."

"What guard?"

"I don't know!" I cried.

"Because he doesn't exist! Because the forsworn did it." Brockton turned his head, the movement preternaturally slow as his black eyes held mine. "And if Ka Shavo doesn't release their prisoners...then the only way out of the Stronghold with all its shadow magic and wards...is traveling." His eyes darkened, as his mouth widened into a vicious grin. "I finally figured it out. How he runs so fast. How he's always everywhere you are. He's vorakh."

My heart was in my throat. "You're delusional."

"Then tell me why I stumbled onto the borders of Korteria today and saw you with him. And then watched him vanish into thin air?"

My eyes widened, sweat beading at the nape of my neck. Tell the truth...truth to hide the lies. "The snakes were after him," my voice shook. "Sent by his father, by Imperator Hart. I sent Rhyan away, to keep him safe. So, I could kill the snakes myself."

"Wrong answer."

"How is that the wrong answer? It's the truth!" I yelled. "I did kill them! And you, like a fucking coward, stood back and did nothing. You just watched me fight."

His fist was in my hair, pulling my head so far back I thought my neck would snap.

"I'm not lying!" I shouted.

He tugged harder. "And I'm not a coward. I stood back because it didn't concern me."

"Fine. But that's the truth. Now let me go. I answered your questions. I don't know where anyone is. I'm only trying to find my sisters. Bring them home. Like everyone else in Bamaria. And if I'm not a prisoner, release me from these ropes. Let me go."

"I can't do that. My uncle had you locked up for a reason. We need to keep you safe."

My chest was squeezing in on itself, my stomach twisting. I was going to throw up. I had nothing in me, and still I was going to be sick.

"Then at least...at least, untie me. Give me a proper place to stay—befitting of a lady of Ka Batavia. With a female attendant."

Brockton cracked his knuckles. "A female attendant," he howled, nearly bursting with laughter. "No, I can't let you go. And I can't change your room. Not yet. Because you're right. No one knows you're here. Or that we're here. So, I think we'll take a few days, before we make that announcement. And maybe your bastard will show. And I'll hand you both over. But in the meantime, you're going to be family. We should get to know each other better."

"We?"

There was a knock on the door. And my heart pounded in response.

"We." Brockton looked me up and down before heading to the entranceway, unlatching the bolt, and admitting three more soturi, the ones who'd been with him when he'd found me.

I'd never spoken to them before, but I recognized their faces. They all had pale skin, blonde hair, and beady black eyes. They were apprentices studying at the Katurium, always following Brockton and Viktor around. Always watching me. And all three had the cruel look of the Bastardmaker.

The arkturion had only ever publicly claimed Brockton as his son. But I would have bet my life the others were his brothers. The mannerisms, the cruelty, those eyes—they were all too similar.

One, I thought was named Brett. He was taller than the others. The second...the second was called Geoffrey. He was the most muscular of them. And the third...his hair was longer in style like the Imperator's...his name started with a T.

The wolves crowded around me, not speaking but somehow all knowing where to stand, like they had an order for this sort of thing, like they'd done it before, had a practiced ritual.

There was an unmistakable scent in the air. Predatory. Cruel. Hungry.

Aroused.

"Get it out of her yet?" asked Brett.

Fuck. Fuck. All four of them had seen. Had witnessed Rhyan using his vorakh.

"She was just telling me the brave story of how she killed those mean snakes this morning."

"You saw me kill them," I said, my voice shaking. "And Rhyan left."

"Rhyan now?" Brockton purred. "Not *Soturion Hart*?"

My throat dried. "The point is..." I shook my head. "The point is you know how fast he is. He ran. Not my problem if you weren't paying enough attention to see him go. Maybe check your eyesight. Because he ran away, and that's the end of the story."

Brockton shrugged. "Okay, we'll play your game. Let's pretend for one second that you're not a Godsdamned liar, and your forsworn bastard doesn't have a vorakh. Why didn't he come back for you?"

Geoffrey smirked, sharing a look with the third wolf. Trey. That was his name.

"How could he come back for me? You took me! He doesn't know where I am!"

"We waited," he said. "We waited some time out there on the mountain, wanting to see what he would do. Whether or not he'd come back. We even went looking for him. Sent wolves to scout. Shouted at him that we had you. That we were taking you prisoner."

"I thought I wasn't your prisoner."

This time Trey stepped forward. "Still want to play that game? You're a fucking prisoner. Deal with it."

Brockton bared his teeth. "The forsworn bastard who can't keep his eyes off you—who loses his shit if someone so much as looks your way. That one? The one who risked everything to break you out of prison...he just left? Left you all alone and helpless? You really expect me to believe that?"

"It's what happened!"

"And after we combed the entire mountainside, we found no sign of him."

"Because he left."

"That story is almost as believable as saying he isn't fucking the shit out of you every night."

"What? No."

"What?" Geoffrey mocked. "No."

The wolves all laughed.

"Face it, Batavia," said Trey. "He's fucked. He comes for you, we turn him in for vorakh. He comes for you, we turn him in for breaking his oath, and taking advantage of his poor innocent novice."

Brockton laughed. "Let's find out, shall we? Get the truth out of you at last. We'll wait for him to come. And...have some fun along the way."

He stepped behind me, his breath disgustingly hot on my neck, his hands reaching for the ties of my tunic. I jerked, my body going taut, my breath coming short, but he only pulled harder. His fingers began to unlace the top, loosening the fabric. I felt the clasps of my armor unbuckle, the metal loosening, no longer a protective shield around my body, no longer a barrier between me and my enemies. With a loud clang, it fell to the floor.

"Brockton, stop," I pleaded, shaking, trying to twist my head back, to see him, to somehow stop him. "Please! Please."

"Just making you a bit more comfortable."

I couldn't breathe. Couldn't breathe. Couldn't escape.

The laces loosened further, just like they had when I'd been whipped. Brett, Geoffrey, and Trey leaned forward, their nostrils flaring, as their eyes lit with excitement.

I squeezed my eyes shut, trying to hold back my tears and panic. They knew about Rhyan, and there wasn't anything I could do.

The rope dug into my wrists—cutting, brutal.

Rope. Rope. Tear the rope. Tear the rope apart....

I opened my eyes to look around the room for anything I could reach to use as leverage or a weapon. But I could barely move with my bonds. And my protections were leaving me, piece by piece. My belt was off. My remaining Valalumir stars lying helplessly out of reach.

I realized then why I hadn't been stripped of my dagger and armor before. Brockton was crueler than I'd thought. He'd left them to give me false hope—to see how I'd react when they were taken. He'd wanted to witness me losing my protection, losing my weapons. See me awake, see me suffering.

But there was one weapon left.

I still wore Asherah's armor. He thought it was a necklace, and he'd left it behind.

Could I call on her twice? Was it possible?

Heart hammering, I began to chant the incantation under my breath: *Ani petrova kashonim me ka el lyrotz, dhame ra shukroya, aniam anam. Chayate....*

But I felt nothing. None of the diamonds were glowing, and I felt no sense of power or connection. Asherah's blood was dormant. I'd only called on our kashonim hours before. The magic was only ever meant to be used on rare occasions, once-in-a-lifetime moments, not twice in one day. And the magic between me and her, it was unlike any other kashonim.

Rarer, unknown. Something told me that calling on it again, so soon, would be worthless even if she knew what was happening, even if she wanted to help me.

There was my kashonim with Rhyan. His blood ran through my veins. And I already knew what he would say.

Call it. Use it. Take everything he had.

But I couldn't.

I didn't know where he was—if he was in danger or if he was on his way to find me. Either way, he needed all his strength, if he even had any left after this morning. I couldn't risk his life nor the slim possibility that he'd gotten my message. That he knew I'd been taken. That he was going to find me.

Brockton's hands were on my back again, the tunic completely undone, hanging loose before me. My back was vulnerable and exposed.

How many times would I be scarred by Ka Kormac?

I twisted in the ropes, knowing it was pointless but unable to remain still. Unable to stop fighting even if it was useless.

"I'll scream," I said. "And then they'll know I'm here. They'll know you are, too! They'll know you're here without leave."

"Please do. I want to hear you. For the longest time, I've wanted to hear you make the same sounds you made before," he snarled. "The sounds you made when the whip cut through your skin, forced your back to bow, your mouth to open. Make sure you scream as loud as you can. It won't make a difference. The walls in Vrukshire are thick. Especially in my bedroom. Wolves are light sleepers." His hand ran down my back, and I nearly gagged. "And in the meantime," he said, "maybe your vorakh lover will show. I hope he does."

"And what will Lord Viktor say," I asked, my panic rising, "when he finds out you hurt his future bride?"

The wolves laughed again.

Brockton walked over to the chest and removed a whip.

I couldn't breathe. I was powerless. Helpless.

"He won't mind. If he were here, he'd be doing this himself." He stroked the leather of the whip, which buzzed with the faintest hint of magic—magic designed to cause pain and injury. Made to cause wounds that did not easily heal on magic bodies. "Ready to feel this on your back again?"

"Please," I cried. "Please don't."

"I wouldn't," he said, his voice teasing, "if you'd told the truth."

"What truth? I told you the truth."

"But I want to hear it from your mouth. I want to hear you say that you're also forsworn—that you broke your oath, and I could have you stripped and exiled for that alone. Or how about the truth that your forsworn bastard isn't just fucking you—but that he's a vorakh, too. Why else were there na-hashim trailing you? Why else were you left alone? And why else did you come here? We'll find out. He'll come for you sooner or later. And when he does, I'll be handing him over."

Brockton moved behind me. I was having flashbacks to that night. The torches, the cruel laughter. The blinding pain, and feel of blood rushing down my back as I was torn apart. He cracked the whip against the floor, the sound making my knees buckle, my head fall forward.

"Brock, come on," said Brett suddenly. "Don't do that to her back. It's been through enough." He winked at me.

Geoffrey grinned. "Do her tits."

I balked. "No!"

Brockton laughed cruelly, coming to stand in front of me. His hand slid down my leg before I could react. I kicked, but he caught my ankle in his hand and tugged until neither foot was on the ground and the rope was so tight around my wrists, I thought it would snap off my hands.

Then he stood before me, one hand gripping my ankle, the other slicing what remained of my tunic down the front as I writhed and twisted away from him. He cut me, sloppy with the blade. Then I was only covered by the shift over my breasts, my riding pants, and boots. My entire body was shaking, as I tried to twist away from him, and my skin burned as blood dripped down my stomach. My body was still suspended in the air.

"And get that necklace off her. It's in my fucking way," said Brett.

Brockton released my foot, and I awkwardly fell back, my knees wanting to bend to brace my fall. My arms nearly snapped before I found my footing. The wolves howled, and then I felt the cold air on my collarbone as Asherah's armor hit the floor.

"NO!" I yelled.

My shift was all that covered me, all that concealed my breasts. My dignity.

"Brockton," I cried. "Please. Please. Don't do this. Don't."

"Sorry, Asherah." He slid his blade down my chest, and the thin material shredded in half.

I squeezed my eyes shut, feeling the moment I was exposed, feeling the disgust of their eyes on me.

"Godsdamn, Batavia," said Trey. "You've been holding out on us."

"What the fuck," Brockton said, his voice deadly serious.

For a second, I wondered if my Valalumir was acting up. Could they see the gold star between my breasts? Did they know I was in contract with the Afeya?

Then something pulled against my neck, and I opened my eyes to see Brockton holding the vadati stone in his hand.

It was blue, bright with light shining through its golden case. It was connected. Rhyan. Rhyan had been listening the whole time.

"Who's on the other end?" Brockton asked. "Who?"

I kept my mouth shut.

"Is this the forsworn bastard?" he roared into the stone. "Is it? This you, Hart? Well, guess what? You better get your ass to Vrukshire. And do it quickly. Alone, without your weapons. Cause we're going to fuck your girl. We're going to do it until you get here."

He dropped the stone, still attached to the chain around my neck. I watched it plunge back between my naked breasts, the light fading until it was clear. My heart sank.

Then Brockton's hand was on my breast.

I cried out, my skin crawling with disgust as he squeezed. And just as quickly, he stopped, his body freezing up as the wolves all turned their heads. Something passed by the window, the torches on the balcony flaming out.

A dark shadow crashed through the window. The glass shattered, the sound piercing as hundreds of broken shards shot forth into the room.

Brett, who was closest to the window, fell to the ground first, screaming as he covered his head. Glass covered his back, but before he could get up, a soturion stomped their black leather boot on his neck.

Rhyan pulled back his hood, his eyes locking with mine, as he took in the scene. His expression feral, his body terrifyingly still as his anger pulsed through the room. His aura was a rage

I'd never felt before. There was a sword gleaming in each of his hands. A third blade strapped to his back.

Burning cold from his aura swept across my skin. There was no mistaking his fury. And all at once, the fires stopped burning, the logs in the fireplace hissed as they iced over, and the wolves began to shake as the room darkened.

"Take your fucking hand off her," Rhyan snarled, "or I'll cut it off myself."

CHAPTER
TWENTY-NINE

"Bind him," Brockton ordered, reaching for my blade. But Rhyan was faster. He hauled Brett up from the ground by the hair, still managing to hold both blades—one behind Brett's head, the other at his neck. Pieces of glass were stuck to Brett's cheek and hands.

Geoffrey and Trey were moving forward, rushing to attack to Rhyan, to come to Brett's defense.

Rhyan only watched Brockton, who still had his hand on me. "You'll die for this." There was something savage in Rhyan's voice, something almost inhuman. His lilt was heavy and his face red. He stared with utter hatred at Brett, pushing the sword against his neck. His head turned slowly, his green eyes stopping on every wolf in the room, assessing, threatening, before they landed back on the wolf he'd trapped.

There was no warning. Rhyan's sword struck like lightning as it slashed across Brett's throat. Blood gushed down his tunic as he fell to the floor.

"Fuck!" Brockton shouted. He was so stunned, he finally let go of me, and I leaned back, trying to put distance between us, to conceal my nudity from the others.

Rhyan responded by kicking Brett's lifeless body, and watching as his corpse rolled grotesquely over the broken glass. He stilled, dead.

Geoffrey and Trey stared at each other, silently trying to communicate and plan. Rhyan lifted both arms, both swords, the points aimed perfectly at their necks. There was a dangerous gleam in his eyes. One I'd never seen before.

"My oath, my soul," Rhyan said, his voice so full of vengeance, and power.

"Shut up." Brockton jerked his chin at the two remaining wolves.

"It's the motto of Ka Hart," Rhyan said, in the same violent tone. "Thought you should know. So when I tell you now, that I swear to all the Gods that every pathetic excuse for a man in this room who dared lay a hand on Lyriana, who touched her, who threatened her, who fucking *looked* at her, will die, I want you to know that my oath will be fulfilled. And that you have, at best, five minutes left in this world."

"Slice his throat," Brockton ordered. "Now!"

I balked as Geoffrey surged forward, sword and dagger raised, but he only made it two steps before Rhyan cut through his weapons with ease, his blade pushing right through Geoffrey's throat.

The wolf gurgled, creating this horrid, wet choking sound. Blood spilled from the sides of his mouth like drool before Rhyan kicked him in the stomach, pushing him off his sword. And then he fell with lifeless eyes, his body crumpling on top of Brett's.

Trey didn't hesitate. Rhyan spun, his swords swinging in a circle around him. He lunged, but Rhyan struck, his blade finding the exact spot it needed to under his armor. His sword pierced through Trey's back, before he retracted, and left Trey for dead, bleeding out on the floor.

Brockton bared his teeth, holding my dagger to my neck.

"Stand back," Brockton said. "One step," he warned, "one step, and she's next."

Rhyan's eyes met mine. Slowly he set down his swords, standing with both of his hands up in surrender. "You don't need to hurt her," he said.

I could hear the barely contained rage in his voice. He'd done this so many times—pretended to be indifferent, shut down his emotions. But they were always boiling just below the surface.

I could barely breathe. Brockton pushed the dagger against my skin, the blade cutting into me. Tiny beads of blood dripped down my bare collarbone.

Rhyan's eyes tracked the blood, and his aura, icy and deadly, raged out even as he kept his face schooled into a neutral expression. And then he vanished.

He reappeared in the space between me and Brockton, his head slamming into Brockton's. Rhyan grabbed Brockton's arms, recovered my dagger, and swung it in an arc above his head, cutting my ropes.

My arms collapsed to my sides, helpless and numb as I stumbled back. My wrists were burning and bleeding. My strength was gone.

"Tell him to stand the fuck down," Brockton said, "if you want to know about Jules." His dark eyes bore into mine.

I stilled, my heart slamming into my throat.

"Shut the fuck up," Rhyan said.

"No," Brockton sneered. "Because if you kill me—you'll never get her back."

"Get her back!" I roared. "She's dead!"

"Is she?" Brockton asked.

Rhyan shook his head, looking at me carefully. "He's trying to mess with you. If he lives, we die."

But I needed to know. I shook my head at Rhyan. He didn't change his hold. I turned my attention back to Brockton. "Tell me."

"Lyr," Rhyan said, a warning note in his voice, but he did as I asked, and held Brockton tighter.

"If you kill me," Brockton said, "I won't get to tell you about how I fucked her."

"You mean raped?"

"Ask me when I did it," he said. "Because it's not when you think."

My chest was heaving. I'd heard enough. "Give me a sword," I demanded. "Give me a sword. Give me a fucking sword." I didn't recognize my voice. I didn't recognize the rage that was boiling inside me. The humiliation. The fear. The absolute need for revenge for years of Ka Kormac's torment, for what they'd done to me, to Rhyan, to my country.

To Jules.

Rhyan stared at me with fear in his eyes I'd never seen from him before.

"Give me a sword!" I yelled again.

"Partner," Rhyan said.

"NOW!" I screamed.

Rhyan's eyes moved back and forth across my face before he nodded. Keeping Brockton restrained with one hand, he pulled the third sword from behind his back and handed it to me.

I stepped forward, half-naked, blood running down my neck and breasts, dried nahashim blood and venom covering my arm. I felt farther than Lethea. I looked farther than Lethea.

"You rapist!" I screamed.

Brockton's face paled, but he spit. "Bamaria will burn for this. We've already infiltrated your land. And just as sure as I drove into Jules's body, our soldiers will drive into yours before it's over. My uncle has all the pieces in place. Go ahead and kill me. I'll still have my revenge with your puppet aunt on the Seat."

I gripped the hilt, my knuckles white. "Rhyan swore that none of you would walk out of this room alive," I said, my voice filled with a deadly promise. "And he never breaks an oath. But he never specified who would kill you."

"If you do, this will mean war," Brockton said.

"Maybe it would have," I said, my hand shaking, "if you'd actually told anyone I was here. Or if you were supposed to be where you were."

"GUARDS!" Brockton screamed. His nostrils flared, and I could smell the fear pulsing in his aura.

"Lyr," Rhyan said. "I'll do it."

I shook my head. This man, this monster, had violated me, stripped me, humiliated and touched me. I'd believed he'd raped Jules, and he'd tortured Rhyan in the habibellum.

This one was mine.

Behind Brockton, Rhyan's shoulders tensed as he gave me a sharp, single nod. It was time to end it.

"You bitch!" Brockton spat, blood flying from his mouth. He leaned forward, somehow escaping Rhyan's hold, produced a dagger I hadn't seen, and thrusted it forward. Pain sliced through my leg. I felt the blood running down my knee and calf, pooling in my boot as I stumbled.

Rhyan's hands moved to Brockton's head. He was going to snap his neck.

I felt dizzy, and as I stepped forward, I nearly stumbled. He'd cut my leg, and I was already bleeding heavily. I wasn't going to be able to stand much longer. But I was going to end him.

I had both hands on the hilt of Rhyan's sword and my eyes on Brockton's heart.

"She's alive," he spat. "But if I die, she dies, too."

I thrust the blade beneath his armor, in and up, grunting as I pushed it through, surprised at the effort needed. I used all the strength I had left, my fingers numbing as I twisted the sword, tears blurring my vision.

Brockton's eyes closed, and he fell with a thud, nearly taking me with him. I was barely standing as it was.

Rhyan jumped out to help me, his arms wrapping around me from behind, his hand guiding the sword free from my loose grip.

"The hell's going on?" came a shout from outside the door. "Lord Brockton?"

"We need to go, Lyr," Rhyan said quietly. "Now!"

I nodded, seeing what we'd done. What I'd done. The gruesome deaths. I looked back at the pole, at the sliced ropes, the ends of which were still around my wrist. I looked back at what had almost happened.

Footsteps marched down the hall.

Rhyan was racing around the room, sheathing my dagger, bunching up my ruined shift and tunic, hastily wrapping my cloak around me, buckling my armor, reclasping Asherah's chest plate around my neck.

He wasn't just collecting my things, I realized. He was removing evidence—removing all signs that anyone aside from the wolves of Ka Kormac had been inside this room.

I used the moment to grab a blade, and sliced what remained of the ropes from my wrists. I let them fall on Brockton's body.

After Rhyan made a final sweep, he scooped his arm beneath my knees, heading for the window. "Don't look, Lyr," he said. "Close your eyes."

I wrapped my hands behind his neck, buried my face against him, and squeezed my eyes shut, feeling my heart try to pound its way through my chest. Rhyan raced for the broken windows. I opened my eyes just long enough to see him stepping around the dead soturi. Trey, Geoffrey, and Brett.

Holding me with one arm, he leapt onto the windowsill, his boots crunching on the shattered glass pieces. He grabbed for the upper ledge, holding on for balance, before dropping down onto the balcony.

The cold dry air was harsh against my face, and I could hear the breaking of metal—the slamming open of the door, and the shouts of alarm the wolves of Vrukshire Keep discovered the carnage we'd left behind.

Rhyan raced across the stone, staying close to the keep's outer walls. The balcony twisted and turned and around a turret. Alarm bells from within began to ring. Down below, soturi were hollering orders at each other, organizing into units, heading to the gates to keep anyone from leaving. Others were being sent inside. It only took a minute before a massive search party for the killers—for us—was underway.

CHAPTER THIRTY

RHYAN RAN FASTER AS more alarm bells sounded. The keep of Ka Kormac was on full alert.

"Almost there, partner." Rhyan pulled me tighter against him. "I've got you. We're getting out of here."

We reached a corner, the balcony rounding the bend. From there, Rhyan traveled. I clutched him as tightly as I could, my stomach feeling like it was being pulled out of me. His knees bent, his boots hitting the frozen grounds. We were just outside the gates. Vrukshire Keep behind us.

I never wanted to see it again.

My entire body was covered in goosebumps. The night was freezing, but I also knew I was going into shock. My skin was somehow clammy, itchy, and freezing all at once. And every injury, every cut, the nahashim's bite, made me feel like I was being torn apart.

"We're leaving this place," Rhyan said. "I'm going to take care of you. You're alright. You're alright. Just hang on. A little longer."

"Why aren't you traveling again?" I cried. "Why are we still here?"

"Sorry. I'm sorry. Don't have much power. And it's hard to use this far west. Just close your eyes. I've got you. It's over now. No one is going to hurt you. *Me sha, me ka*, Lyriana."

I buried my face against his cloak, desperate to inhale his scent, to feel his aura wrap me up and hide me from the world.

He kept running, his speed increasing with each step. The wind blew against my face and through my hair. A pack of wolves howled, and my heart leapt into my throat until the sound suddenly stopped. There was another tug on my stomach. Another jump. We appeared at the bottom of the mountain, and in the distance, there was a horse the color of moonstone—an ashvan—tied to an aged silver moon tree. Glittering leaves left tiny lights across its back.

Rhyan slashed the rope tethering the horse, and hauled me up onto its back before climbing up behind me, one hand steady on my waist.

He made a shushing sound at the horse as it shifted its body in agitation. Still gripping me, Rhyan rummaged through his bag and pulled out a cloth.

"Can you bend your leg for me, Lyr?" he asked. "The injured one?"

Grunting, I settled against him, pulling the leg up onto the horse's back.

"There you go, just lean back against me." Quickly, Rhyan wrapped the cloth around the wound and tied the ends together.

His body tensed behind me as noise sounded in the distance, getting louder with the wind. Soturi marching. They were close.

I shook my head. No. No more. No more Kormac. Not tonight. Not ever.

Rhyan slid his hand up my leg and helped me ease it back over the ashvan's side so I could ride. He wrapped one arm around me, his palm flat against my belly, while the other took the reins. His thighs flexed, securing me into place.

Leaning forward, keeping my back pressed to his front, Rhyan stroked the ashvan's mane.

"*Vra*," he said, urging the ashvan to go. "*Vra!*" he called, tugging on the reins, his hand pressing into me. The horse whinnied, and took off.

I leaned back against Rhyan, tears falling freely, as he urged on the horse, ordering it to run faster. The surrounding trees passed by in a blur until the woods grew thicker, darker, the trunks and branches more closely knit together. But Rhyan wasn't slowing down.

My stomach turned as he shouted again at the ashvan.

"*Vraya! Ya!*" The ashvan was racing now. "*Volara!* Fly! *Volara!*" He leaned forward, commanding the ashvan to go faster. "*Mahar! Mahara!*"

The ashvan picked up speed, its pace only possible through magic. Rhyan tightened his arm, as the horse rose up on its hind legs, and then we took flight, racing up beyond the tree branches, and then into the sky.

With a resounding neigh, blue sparks of light flashed beneath us with each step the ashvan took, galloping faster and faster at Rhyan's urging.

"*Mahara!*" he commanded, his thighs tense around mine. His arm remained locked into place, holding me against him.

I gripped his arm, my nails digging into his sleeve. I'd been flying my entire life, but only inside the carriage of a seraphim. I'd never been on the back of an ashvan before. Being so exposed to the elements, knowing there was nothing beneath my feet, reminded me of the night I'd broken my blood oath, fallen from the carriage, and nearly plummeted to my death before Rhyan had saved me.

Rhyan leaned forward, his breath against my ear. "Alright?"

I sniffled in response. I was too tired, too wrecked, to speak.

"Just breathe, we're almost there," he said, his thumb rubbing up and down my stomach. His other hand turned the reins, guiding the ashvan. "We're over the Cretanyan border," he said. "We need to go back down. And I'm going to travel us back to our room at the inn."

"Cretanya again?" I wanted to cry. This whole day had been a waste. Three days down, and we were still south of the capital. Nowhere near Glemaria. Nowhere near saving my sisters. And I'd almost been...almost....

"It's okay," Rhyan said. "We'll make up for it. One thing at a time. We're going down now. Hang on, Lyr." His tone changed as he shouted out to the horse. "*Dorscha*," Rhyan said, ordering the descent.

I closed my eyes, feeling the horse angle downward, the gallop slowing as we descended. My stomach flew into my chest. The moment I felt the hooves touch the ground, I exhaled, feeling Rhyan release me from his arms. One hand remained on my back, keeping me steady as he jumped down from the ashvan. I only realized then that our bags had been strapped to the horse and Rhyan had three swords because he'd recovered mine. He must have found it with the slain nahashim.

He moved to the front of the ashvan, stroking its face and murmuring to it in High Lumerian before he reached for my waist and gently pulled me down toward him.

"Last jump for the night," he said.

I could see for the first time the devastating exhaustion and worry and fear painted across his face. He'd been fighting for me all day, doing everything he could to restore his power, to use it sparingly in a country where magic was weak, to pick the right moment to save me because if he'd acted too soon, we could have both been caught. His vorakh exposed. Our broken oaths used against us.

I hugged him to me and watched as the ashvan and trees vanished, and then we were back at the inn, in the same room as before.

Rhyan dropped our bags, stumbling backwards, looking ready to faint.

That was when the sobs came, wracking my chest with their force.

"Lyr," Rhyan cried. He was letting his guard down now, too, holding me tightly to him, burying his face in my neck, inhaling deeply as his shoulders shook. Then he stilled, swallowing roughly and pulling back, pushing my hair from my face. "I almost lost you today." He blinked quickly before taking a deep breath. "I'll get you cleaned up. Let's get in the shower."

I nodded wordlessly, feeling numb as he led me to the bathroom. He turned on the water and began methodically undressing me. He removed my armor and cloak then bent down and held my waist as he stepped my feet out of each boot. He did the same to slide down my socks and untie the bandage. Reaching up, he grasped the waist of my pants and gently pulled them down.

"How's your leg feel?" he asked.

"It hurts."

"Try to keep your weight on the other foot for me." He stood, keeping his eyes on my face as he pulled the remains of my tunic over my shoulders, letting it slide to the ground at my feet.

His nostrils flared in anger as he saw my ripped shift, the cuts down my sternum. There was a bruise above my breast—fingermarks. His eyes reddened as he reached inside the stall, checking the water's temperature. He turned back to me, his gaze at first lifted to my face, but after a moment, his eyes wandered down my body.

His fists clenched at his sides. He was visibly restraining himself, the anger in his aura palpable, and for a second, the shower water seemed to pause as if he'd frozen the pipes, but then the water continued flowing, and steam began to fog the small mirror that had been nailed above the sink basin. Rhyan's neck reddened, his nostrils flaring, before he closed his eyes, taking a deep breath.

"You're covered in blood." His voice was gruff.

"It's not all mine."

"I know." He ripped off his cloak and armor. His weapons clattered to the ground at his feet, as he rushed to remove his boots. "I'm coming in with you," he said, a worried look in his eyes. "Is that alright? I want you to hold onto me, keep weight off your left leg."

I nodded again, still numb. A pit formed in my stomach as he removed his pants and tunic. He was in only his short-pants. "These are staying on," he said, watching my face.

I tried to give him a smile, knowing he was trying to make me feel safe, to reassure me this shower was about cleaning. But I couldn't smile. I wasn't sure those muscles were working. His eyes searched mine before he stepped into the stall with me, positioning me beneath the stream.

Hot water splashed down on my skin, hitting the back of my head, and rolling down my neck and shoulders. I felt Rhyan reach for my underwear.

"Lyr, is it okay if I take these off? Just so you can get clean."

"Okay," I said, my voice small.

He moved slowly, carefully, keeping his eyes lifted as much as possible, the muscles in his jaw flexing as he untied the ribbons on either side of the material. I felt the callouses of his fingers against my hips as he pulled the cloth from between my legs, and tossed it onto the bathroom floor.

The moment it was gone and I stood completely naked, something shifted inside me. My chest started to heave. I was completely naked, vulnerable—in the state Kormac would have eventually gotten me into. In the state I imagined Jules had been in. The water was too hot, and Rhyan was too close, and I just wanted to scream, and—

"Partner." He reached for my face, cupped my cheeks, stared into my eyes. "You're okay. It's just me. We're just going to get cleaned up. Okay? You're safe now."

Grabbing a washcloth, he went to work, lathering it in soap and taking my arm in his hand. It was stained almost completely from elbow to wrist in black and red blood. Mine, and the nahashim's.

I watched as the blood dripped down my body, mixing with the water and turning pink before running down the drain.

I felt Brockton again, cutting through my tunic, cutting open my shift. I felt all of the wolves watching, laughing, leering. Brockton's hand on my bare skin.

"NO!" I yelled.

Rhyan stopped at once. "Did I hurt you?"

"No," I cried.

He kept his eyes on my face. "Lyr, you're okay," he said. "You're safe."

I burst into tears, shaking my head. "No!" I pulled back my arm, trying to cover my body, cover my face.

Rhyan immediately released me.

"I don't want to be seen. I don't want anyone to see me like this."

"No one can see you, Lyr," Rhyan said gently, stepping into the spray. "There's no one here. It's just me."

"I don't want you to see me," I cried. "I just...I can't...."

His face fell, a look of anguish in his eyes. "You don't want me to see you?" He bit his lip. "Okay. That's okay." He glanced at the edge of the stall. "Do you want me to go?"

I grabbed his hand. "No."

"I won't," he said, but he sounded so sad and hopeless.

"I'm sorry," I cried. "I know I'm not making any sense. I just...."

"Can I hold you?" he asked.

I nodded, and he stepped forward and wrapped his arms around me, his hands carefully placed on my back.

"Shhhh," he said. "I've got you. You're safe. I swear to the Gods, you're safe now. They can't hurt you. Never again. You're safe with me, Lyr. I swear."

"I know," I said. "I know. I just, I don't want to be seen right now. They all saw me, they were all...." My shoulders shook. I could still feel their eyes, feel the arousal in their auras. The violence. The hatred.

"We've got to get you cleaned up and bandaged," he said desperately. "What if I keep my eyes up the whole time, just on your face? I won't look at you, at all. I won't look anywhere else."

"No." I covered my eyes, sucking in a pained breath. I knew I was being unreasonable. I couldn't think straight. The horror of the night was too much, too confusing. Rhyan was my safe place, he always made me feel the safest I'd ever felt. But it wasn't enough right now. Because I felt anything but safe at the moment.

I wanted to get this blood off of me. I wanted to wash away Brockton's touch. I wanted to burn it off my body, and I wanted Rhyan to do it—and at the same time, I didn't. I just knew I didn't want any more eyes on me tonight, not after I'd been assaulted and humiliated, not after I'd heard what they'd done to Jules.

Not after I'd taken a life. I'd killed. I'd killed with my own hands. Not an akadim. Not because I was forced to in the arena. But a life. A living, breathing soul.

But even with all of that, I didn't want Rhyan to leave. What I wanted was for none of this to have happened, for me not to have to deal with the consequences they'd forced on me. I wanted to curl up into a ball. Feel his arms. Not be seen. Not remember. I wanted to forget any of this had happened. Live in the world where it hadn't.

But it had happened, and I was here now, and nothing felt right.

"Lyr." Rhyan's voice was low and calm. "Listen to me. You're having a panic attack. It's okay. You've had them before. And I've helped you. Remember? I'm going to help you again. You're going to be okay. We're going to get through this."

"I feel like I'm dying." The water was too hot and too cold. The shower was too small. Our room was too many stories up. The wind outside was howling too loud.

"I have an idea," Rhyan said. He stuck his hand out past the curtain and brought in a towel. "I'll cover you with this and clean you up. I'll work around it. You'll be covered the whole time. Does that feel better to you?"   More tears fell. The towel was getting soaked. It was so stupid. But it was the best thing he'd suggested. "Okay."

"Okay." Rhyan stepped back. "Keep your hand on my shoulder." He wrapped the towel around me, tucking the ends beneath my arm. "Good girl," he said, pressing his forehead to mine. "You're doing so good. This shouldn't have happened to you—you didn't deserve it, but you were so brave. I just need you to be brave for a little while longer. Can you do that for me?" He brushed my hair out of my face, soaking wet from the stream.

"I killed him," I sobbed. "I'm a killer."

"No, you're not. You had to do it. He was...." Rhyan's mouth tightened. "He was going to do Gods-awful things. He's already done worse. They all have. But you don't have to carry this. Give it to me. I'll carry the guilt. I would have killed him myself. I swore I would. It's mine. Let me bear it for you. I'll bear anything you want."

I shook my head.

"Lyr." Rhyan gripped my face, his thumbs moving slowly, soothingly across my cheeks.

"You can't. Because I did it. And I did it for you, too. And I feel sick to my stomach. Because I would have killed him again if I could have."

His throat bobbed. "Look at me. Breathe with me. Listen to my voice. Listen."

I shook my head, feeling hysterical.

"Lyr. Lyr. *Ani janam ra.*"

I stared into Rhyan's eyes, my breath slowing. "I know you."

Rhyan nodded encouragingly. "I know you. And I love you. You are good. You did what you had to do to survive today. You didn't do anything wrong. You saved yourself. You saved me. You had no choice. Okay? I see you. I see exactly who you are. Nothing today has changed how I feel—and nothing has changed who you are, or who I see in front of me."

"And who am I?" I asked.

He stroked my cheek. "My partner," he said gently. "My heart. My Lyr. My love. My—" His throat worked. "Everything."

I sniffled and nodded, and for the first time since we'd left Vrukshire, Rhyan looked relieved.

"Good. Take a deep breath for me, okay?"

I did, slowly inhaling and exhaling, using his breaths as a guide.

"Good, Lyr. You're doing so good, I promise. You're in control. I'm going to tell you everything I'm doing. If you say stop, I stop. You want me to leave, I'll leave. Whatever you want to do here. You have the power."

I nodded again, feeling just the slightest bit of tension leave me.

"We're going to get you all cleaned up in the shower, then bandaged, and dressed in anything you want to wear. And then I'm going to get you food—whatever you want to eat, I don't care, I will find it. And then you're going to climb into bed and rest. Let your leg heal. And I'm going to watch over you."

"The stone was blue all day. Did you hear everything?" I asked.

Rhyan nodded slowly. "Everything."

"You were with me the whole time."

"The whole time. I was fighting every second of this entire day to get back to you. To find you. I was always going to come for you. You know that." He leaned forward, kissing my forehead. "I would have killed every wolf in Lumeria to get you back. Burned the Empire to the ground to reach you. Nothing was going to stop me. I just wish I'd been faster."

I exhaled again, staring into his eyes, finding comfort in them. "I'm ready."

Rhyan smiled and got to work, adding more soap to the washcloth and scrubbing off all the blood, using the towel around me to get my middle and backside. He got onto his knees to get the bottoms of my feet, careful around the cut Brockton had made on my leg, and even shampooed my hair, massaging my scalp and carefully brushing out the tangles with his fingers, and adding oil.

We climbed out of the tub, and Rhyan switched out my soaking towel for a dry one, all while keeping his eyes on my face. He patted me down and led me to the bed where he went to work applying sunleaves to all my cuts and bruises and then covering everything in bandages, wrapping the last one tight around my calf.

"Do you want your own pajamas tonight? Or mine?" he asked.

"Yours."

He smiled. "As you wish."

"I'm sorry...about the shower."

He shook his head. "No apologies. I told you, whatever you want tonight, you get."

A few minutes later, I was tucked into bed wearing his gray knit-pants and swimming in one of his soft sleep shirts.

"Food?" he asked, throwing on a long-sleeved tunic and boots before promising to return with hot soup and bread. It was all I wanted—something simple, something warm.

I scrunched up beneath the blankets, hugging the pillow to my chest, trying to take deep breaths as I waited for Rhyan to return. I'd never had a problem being alone before. But now...my heart was hammering, and it didn't stop until he stepped back inside the room. He was carrying two large silver trays and a pastry box. As he set down everything on the bench before the bed, I slowly climbed out from under the blankets, inhaling the spices and watching the steam rise when he released the covers.

We ate in silence, me sitting on the edge of the bed, my feet propped up on the bench, while Rhyan sat cross-legged on the floor. When I'd cleaned my bowl and inhaled my last piece of bread, he handed me the pastry box with a shy smile.

"What's this?" I asked. It wasn't from the kitchens at the inn.

"I made a short trip into the city while our soups were cooking. Had to try three different bakeries, but I found it."

There was a white ribbon around the box, which I untied, and lifting the lid, I found a fresh lemon cake.

"Here you go." He produced two forks and joined me on the bed.

I inhaled the sweet, sugary lemon scent. My favorite. And saw Brockton's body falling. The wolves dead on the floor. A flash of Jules screaming. Blood and broken glass.

Rhyan cut into a piece of the cake and moved the fork to my mouth. "Whatever happened today, you still deserve to have this."

A tear rolled down my cheek as I opened my mouth to take the bite, savoring the icing as it melted on my tongue. It was half heaven. Half hell. Something was niggling at the back of my mind—something I wasn't ready to deal with yet.

With Rhyan's help, I finished the cake. Afterward, I was too exhausted and emotionally wrought to do anything else but fall asleep as he watched over me. Exactly as he'd promised.

Hours passed before I woke from a nightmare. The images I saw were moving too quickly for me to interpret. There had been flashes of Haleika, Leander, my father, my sisters, Jules.

I opened my eyes and let them adjust to the dark. I'd woken alone. I stretched out my arm, finding nothing. Rhyan's side of the pillow was cold like he'd been gone for hours.

CHAPTER THIRTY-ONE

I SAT UP, PANIC washing over me, my stomach twisting.

"Rhyan?" my voice croaked.

At once I heard his breathing, and I turned, catching sight of his silhouette in the moonlight. He was wearing the usual soft knit pants he slept in, and sitting on the edge of the bed, as far from me as he could be. His back was bare; the black gryphon tattoo spread across his skin seemed to come to life as he moved. Its wings spanned across his arms. Beneath the beast were the snowy mountains of Glemaria, our destination. A torn rope wrapped around the gryphon's leg.

His shoulders shook. He was crying.

I pushed back the blankets, crawling across the bed to him, my leg aching fiercely. "Hey." My hand rubbed up his back, up the tattoo to his shoulders. His skin was cold.

He coughed and rubbed his eyes, turning to look back at me. "I didn't mean to wake you. How are you doing?"

I wiped at the tears still welling in his eyes, tracing the soft path of wetness down his cheek. It mingled with the pink of his scar illuminated in the moonlight. Sometimes I forgot it cut through not just his eyebrow but also his cheek, as it was so faint there. "You didn't wake me. How are you doing?" I sat beside him.

His shoulders stiffened. "I asked you first." His voice cracked, his words rough like he'd been crying a long time.

"Rhyan, talk to me. What's wrong?"

His face fell, fresh tears welling. "I just keep thinking about what was going to happen. What they were going to do to you if I hadn't gotten there in time. I cut it too close. Too fucking close. And it was my fault you were taken—I was an idiot, wasting my power. You were almost—" He swallowed hard. "I almost didn't make it."

I crawled into his lap, and his arms instantly tightened around me as he buried his face in my neck. I felt him inhale deeply as I hugged him. "But you did make it. And they didn't...."

"I know. I know." He swallowed roughly, his hands moving up and down my back. "I'm sorry. I don't want to put this on you. You've been through enough—too much." His chest heaved against mine. "I just can't stop picturing it. You with them. What he said about Jules. The absolute terror of exhausting my power, of being too late. Of failing again."

My heart hurt as he spoke. I knew he was speaking from experience, speaking of atrocities he'd witnessed at home with his mother. I knew if the roles had been reversed, if I'd found Rhyan tied up like that, nothing in this world would have tempered my rage. I'd barely controlled myself when I'd learned he'd been tied up years before. And much as I was struggling with the knowledge that today I'd taken a life—I didn't...didn't regret it. And to protect Rhyan—I'd do it again.

I wound my fingers through his hair, stroking the curls at the nape of his neck. "You got to me in time. I'm okay. We're okay."

He cupped my cheek, his thumb brushing my skin, his bottom lip shaking. "You left me," he said.

"I had to." I searched his eyes. "You were almost empty. They were going to take you."

"I know you saved me, Lyr. I know that. You're amazing. But the fear I felt, knowing you were in danger in another country, the absolute helplessness of being unable to reach you—"

"It's over now. We're safe. We're together."

"Never again," he seethed. "No more parting."

I nodded. "Never again."

"Where you go, I go. *Me sha, me ka.*" He pressed his fist against his heart, tapping it twice before he flattened his palm over his chest.

"Me sha, me ka," I repeated the words, repeated the gesture.

Rhyan leaned his forehead against mine.

"Do you want to come to bed now?" I asked.

He shook his head, our foreheads still connected. "I'm scared to sleep. Scared with what happened, even with you beside me, that the nightmares will come, that they'll be worse. Tonight reminded me of things I've seen. Things I've done. I've killed before. Too many men. I don't want to disturb you."

"I want your nightmares. I want you to disturb me. I want whatever you need." I pressed my lips to his, kissing him softly, slowly.

I inched forward on his lap, pulling his body against mine. The kiss deepened, as he held me closer against him and flipped us over onto the bed, a sudden rage in his aura. He shifted me back onto the pillows, his weight settling over me as he kissed me possessively, like he was claiming me, reminding me I was his, reminding himself. He touched me as if he was proving I was there, I was safe, I was with him.

Rhyan moaned into my mouth, one hand tangling in my hair, the other sliding down my waist leaving goosebumps in its wake. His fingers slid beneath my shirt, his callouses making me utterly aware of where his hand was, and where it was going. He grazed my bare skin, sliding up and up my rib cage. His hand closed around my breast.

"No!" I shouted. I was back in Vrukshire, tied up, helpless. Brockton's hand was on me, bruising. Humiliating.

Rhyan rolled off me at once, throwing his head into his hands. "Fuck. I'm sorry. I'm sorry. It was too soon."

I pressed my palms to my temples in frustration, pulling my knees up to my chest.

"Shit, I'm sorry, Lyr. Shit. I can sleep on the floor," Rhyan said quietly, turning away from me.

I grabbed his hand. "No. Stay by my side. I meant what I said before. I want you here. I want you. I just," I sighed, tears burning behind my eyes. Not only had Brockton and his wolves tortured me, they'd ruined this for me, too. Fucking rapist bastards.

"You need to take it slow," he said, squeezing my hand. "It's okay. You're not ready."

I swallowed. "Come closer."

Rhyan rested his head on the pillow next to me, and I took our joined hands, took a deep breath and pulled them beneath my shirt. Gently, I pressed his palm to my belly, to the spot he so often claimed as we slept.

"I'll get past this," I said.

Rhyan's lips quirked up, but his eyes were still sad. "I know you will. You're the strongest woman I know. A warrior. But...only when you're ready. There's no rush from me. No schedule you need to be on, no expectations on my end. When it feels right for you, I'll be here."

My fingers traveled up his arm. He kept his hand still on me, letting me be in control.

"You're sure I can do this?"

"Completely sure," he said. "I had to do it, too."

"What do you mean?"

"It wasn't the same," he said quietly. "But I had something...." His jaw tensed. "Something happened to me."

I froze.

"You wanted to know why I'd been called a whore." His fingers flexed against my stomach.

I continued dancing my fingers across his arm in a soothing pattern.

"I was nine. The senator from Hartavia was in Glemaria, some official state visit, and, well, my father had never paid attention to me. Never in a good way. The senator did. He sat with me at dinners, joined me for visits to the gryphon dens. Made me feel special. Gave me the affection that I now know I was lacking."

I inched closer to him on the bed, having too clear an image of this Rhyan in my mind. I'd met him for the first-time during this period of his life. When he was ten. I'd seen this Rhyan who was afraid of his father. This Rhyan who was lonely and loved gryphons and wanted one as a pet because he desperately needed a friend. This Rhyan who spent his time alone in a cold fortress following around the Master of the Horse, taking care of gryphons, and training them despite the fact this task was far below his station as Heir to the Arkasva and Imperator. This Rhyan who was so angry and reclusive that it had been a big deal for him to read beside me on a random afternoon, sharing lemon cake.

"A few weeks into the visit, the senator announced that he'd invited a singer to the fortress. She sang ancient Lumerian poetry—stories of the War of the Light. I'd mentioned to him I was reading the stories on my own. My father wasn't enthusiastic but said I could attend the concert. My mother, though, she was against it. She didn't want me to go." His voice caught, and he shook his head. "I threw a fit. I demanded. And she relented under my father's eye. I went. We were the only ones there. It was a private concert, the senator said, because I'd impressed him. I don't remember much. Just that the senator kept inching closer and closer to my seat. Whispering about her songs, talking over her performance, asking what I thought about this verse or that. The ones he was asking about, they were all—all verses about Auriel and Asherah, their affair. About sex. I didn't know anything at the time beyond the basics. But I wanted him to continue being impressed with me. I pretended I knew what he was saying. But I didn't, and then the concert ended, the singer left. And we were alone."

My stomach twisted, and Rhyan's hand twitched, agitated against me. A small burst of cold filled the room, a snowflake on my nose. And then the cold faded.

Rhyan continued, "He asked me again about the verses. Then asked...if I touched myself. If...I'd ever touched a man." Rhyan shook his head. "I knew something was wrong. I'd made a mistake coming there alone with him. I told him, I hadn't. And it was late, I should go, my mother expected me in bed. But then he asked me if I wanted to...to touch...one."

I rested my hand on his arm, barely daring to breathe.

Rhyan shook his head again, his eyes watering. "I said no. But I was nine, and he was a senator. He took my hand and placed it...over his tunic, just held it there, for a few seconds. That was all."

"That was too much," I said violently.

He coughed. "The door opened, and sentries came in with my father. I didn't know what I was doing, but I knew it was wrong, and thought I'd be in trouble. I was always in trouble. I pulled my hand away. But my father saw. I know he did. I know he knew what happened. He looked at me and frowned and chided me for keeping the senator from more important duties. And," Rhyan laughed, the sound hollow and mirthless, "he *thanked* the senator. Thanked him for entertaining me, admitting I'd needed the attention, said he'd been charitable to even look at me. He sent me to bed. I washed my hands. Washed them a long time. But even after, my palm itched. Sometimes it still does."

I'd seen him itch his hand before when he was upset about his father, when he fell back into the mindset of the old Rhyan, the Rhyan who had been powerless and alone, the Rhyan who hadn't torn the rope yet.

I traced the veins of his forearm back under my shirt, to where his hand still rested against my stomach. He stilled as I took his hand in mine, and rubbed circles against his knuckles with my thumb.

"I only ever saw the senator a few times after that, mainly at state dinners, Valyati, a handful of Revelation Ceremonies. He never approached me again. And I didn't face him until I was forsworn. I...I don't know what I was thinking, I had no plan—just get out of Glemaria, past the border, past my father's soturi. I thought I might find sanctuary in Hartavia—I had familial connections, an aunt and uncle. I didn't want to stay, I just wanted an arkasva to vouch for me, to add one more step between me and my father." Rhyan took a deep breath, watching me carefully.

I continued stroking his hand.

"But the High Lord of Hartavia publicly called me a whore, and the senator watched me from the Seating Room with horrified eyes, acting like I'd victimized him. Accusing me of propositioning him, convincing him to protect me in exchange for favors. That's how the rumor started. That's the whole story. I guess it took a while before it made its way down south. It was small, and I know it's nothing like what you—but...."

"No. Don't." I pressed my lips to his palm—to the places he tended to scratch, the places where the senator had defiled him—wanting to kiss away every itch, every memory, every touch he hadn't wanted. "Don't minimize it."

"I never told anyone about that—what happened." Rhyan shuddered against me, and I kissed him again, down his palm to his wrist and forearm, before he grabbed my chin and pulled my lips against his.

"I'm so sorry," I told him. "It wasn't your fault. And it matters. It's not too small a thing, what happened to you."

A fresh tear fell down his cheek.

"We're in this together," I said. "We're going to get through this together."

"We are," Rhyan said.

I swallowed. "Do you think...do you think anyone suspects...anyone knows anything? About earlier?" We were already on the run from Bamaria. But Rhyan breaking me out of the Shadow Stronghold to find my sisters was quite a different crime than him killing the son of Korteria's warlord, and three of his men.

"I went out," Rhyan said quietly. "After you fell asleep. Stalking around the city, listening. Word just reached here of their deaths."

I sucked in a breath. "Fuck."

"Our names weren't mentioned. The official story is that they attacked each other. Brockton allegedly tracked the soturi that were hiding from the akadim fight. I was listening—all day to them through the stone. You were right—he wasn't supposed to be home. I don't think he told anyone about you."

"What if the others did? Or someone in the keep saw? Servants see so much more than they get credit for. They talk." That was why we had to send all of ours away after Meera's vorakh was revealed.

"Then we'll deal with it," he said.

"Rhyan?" My voice shook. I'd been thinking over Brockton's words again and again.

She's alive. But if I die, she dies, too.

We'd never seen a body or proof of her death. I'd just accepted it. Everyone had. She'd gone through exactly what we'd been told would happen to vorakh our entire lives.

But Brockton's words....

Rhyan was watching me carefully.

"Jules," I said weakly. "Do you think..." My chest heaved, I could barely get the words out. "Do you think we were lied to? That she's alive?"

Rhyan's eyes grew distant, and he took a long time to respond. "I want to say no. But...I don't know anymore. If she is, then...." His chest heaved, and he had a haunted look on his face. Then we'd let her suffer alone for two years.

He squeezed my hand. "Anything is possible."

CHAPTER
THIRTY-TWO

FIVE DAYS PASSED SINCE Vrukshire. Despite my anxiety about losing a day of travel to Glemaria, neither me nor Rhyan could get out of bed the following day. My leg was cut up from Brockton, and Rhyan had truly depleted himself by traveling. Even if we'd wanted to, neither of us were physically capable of moving. I'd learned a few more details about Rhyan's day in his waking moments. How he hadn't eaten, hadn't slept. Hadn't allowed his power to restore because he'd been tracking the hours since I'd been gone. Speaking my name softly into the vadati every quarter hour to keep the connection alive. He'd been waiting for clues. He knew I was in Korteria. But he needed an exact location, and he'd needed time to get back to the country.

The extra sleep had been welcome. And we'd both been so deeply tired, neither of us had dreamed. Rhyan woke from time to time to go out for food, making sure I ate, and changing the bandage on my leg. But that was it. We didn't talk beyond that. Didn't do anything, but hide beneath the blankets.

And then we set out the following morning after dawn. We were both quiet. Not discussing what had happened, not mentioning all that we'd shared with each other. Rhyan hadn't suggested running while my leg healed, but I was able to walk on it. And while his energy was returning, he still didn't seem like himself. We were both moving slowly, tiring more quickly, sleeping later, sitting down more often.

Our days were spent walking in silence, huddling together against the wind and the cold and the occasional flurries of snow, making only small jumps into secluded areas.

My feet were aching and numb with cold by the time we reached Numeria, Lumeria's capitol, home of the Emperor. Brockton's great uncle. When we did get close to civilization, we heard the same story Rhyan had. Brockton was a hero, chasing down his friends who'd left the akadim to hide. Only to be betrayed.

Rhyan kept our compass pointed east, allowing us to reach the trijunction of Numeria with Damara and Aravia. The tight eastern borders meant we wouldn't have to spend the night in the capitol. I'd always been curious to see it in person. But now, it was the last place I wanted to go to and I was happy to stick to the trees.

Once we reached Aravia, we were officially in the northern half of the Empire, in the countries ruled under Rhyan's father. Rhyan no longer had allies or inns he was willing to trust, even if he checked in alone and disguised. The odds of someone recognizing him were too risky.

We spent our first night officially camping at the mouth of a cave he was familiar with. He'd spent weeks living in it when he'd first left Glemaria. Through the night, we took turns staying awake, resting our heads in each other's laps for warmth, sharing one cloak as bedding and the other as a blanket.

In the morning, Rhyan traveled to the nearest town to buy us breakfast and coffee. He even stopped to pick up spices—which he still insisted on keeping hidden from me—to turn our cups into Secrets of the North. It was a small thing, but it gave me my first genuine smile since Vrukshire. I had been missing it.

While he'd sorted out our meals, I'd poured over the notes I'd been sent along with my mother's journal. I'd read it again and again the night before by the torchlight, trying to memorize her words, understand what I needed to do, find new meaning in what had been engraved into the stone.

We unlock for blood, soul, and key. Power is restored, with these three.

I'd probably read the passage of my mother's visit to the seraphim statue at least a dozen times.

Rhyan sat across from me in the cave and bit into a hardboiled egg. I still had the journal out along with the key from Rhyan's father and Asherah's chest plate. The diamonds in the star centers of the armor were all fiery red—even the ones that had been smashed and restored.

"The only thing I'm worried about," I said, picking up the key, "is the soul part. The key is obvious—it fits in the carving my mother described. And your father basically confirmed as much. But do I need to somehow give part of my soul? Or is it enough that I contain it—hold part of Asherah inside me?"

"I'm still not used to you being a goddess. I mean," Rhyan lifted his good eyebrow, "I always thought you were a goddess. Metaphorically. But a literal one? That's different." He bit his lip, something playful in his expression. "I should really add that to my resume. Bodyguard with experience protecting heirs to the arkasva and an ancient goddess."

"One would think only a god could protect a goddess," I teased.

"Partner." His lips quirked. "Are you calling me a god?"

"Maybe. If you were, which one would you be?"

"Rhyan, God of Bodyguarding." He puffed out his chest, exaggerating his accent.

I giggled. "Not Auriel?"

His face fell, and his eyes returned to studying the text before me. Coughing a little, he said, "I think you being the reincarnation of Asherah is enough to fulfill the soul part—you use the key, and you can open the seraphim."

I returned to studying the items, wishing I hadn't said anything about Auriel, Asherah's soulmate, her *mekarim*—two bodies that were one. Ramia had hinted other gods were present, reincarnated now. Even Moriel could have returned.

Had Auriel? The thought simultaneously made my heart pound, and my stomach twist. Would I feel anything if I met him? Would I even want to? I guessed Rhyan was worrying over the same thing.

"What about the blood?" I asked, trying to lessen the tension. "Is it enough that it's running through my veins? Or do you think I need to spill it?"

Rhyan's shoulders tensed. "I don't want you spilling blood unnecessarily. We'll try the key first. Then we'll go from there." He gestured at the chest plate. "The stars also contain her blood. Maybe we just need to smash one." He bit his lip. "The writer of the note didn't offer any further instruction. But he expects you to provide the goods. So, I'm guessing we'll be able to figure it out—unless it's all a trap."

That was still a possibility, but too many coincidences made me feel certain that the clues would add up to what the note described. They had to.

Still, I hadn't missed the moments Rhyan had gone quiet since we'd left Bamaria, his face drawn like he was deep in thought. I knew what he was doing—planning. If this was just a trap, he wouldn't hesitate this time to grab me and take me as far from the danger as he could. Out of the Empire.

But we couldn't do that without my sisters, so all of our stores of power had to be contained. No unnecessary traveling over long distances, and no calling on kashonim. Not unless it was life and death.

Rhyan packed up our things and put out the fire. We began our daily hike, moving through the wilds of Aravia, mainly dense patches of moon trees whose leaves glittered with silver and dripped with melting snow. Thanks to Rhyan's navigation, Aravia was the final country we had to pass through to reach the Glemarian border. We were bypassing Eretzia and Sindhuvine, both west of Aravia and full of forests, which made them top hunting grounds for akadim. And more and more often, we were seeing evidence of their existence. Torn clothing left in the middle of the woods. Small trails of blood. Abandoned camp sites full of raggedy cloths, and trophies the akadim had taken from their victims. Soturion armor, mainly northern leathers. Some silver jewelry.

I was trying my best not to think about it. Not think about who those things belonged to. What had happened to them. Or if they were akadim now.

And I tried most of all not to think about Morgana and Meera.

Rhyan took my hand as we entered a clearing. The sun was unusually bright, but in that moment, a dark shadow soared from the horizon, casting shadows over us.

I squeezed his hand, but he laughed.

"Lyr," he said, genuinely smiling again. "Look up. It's a gryphon."

Wind blew against my face as I stared up in disbelief. Its massive form flew directly over us, its feathers and fur a beautiful rippling mix of bronze and brown.

"Gods," I laughed. "They're enormous. You weren't exaggerating." Three seraphim could have fit on its back.

He lifted his good eyebrow. "I never exaggerate about size."

I felt a wave of desire in his aura. I swallowed, my throat suddenly dry.

Rhyan smiled ruefully and turned his gaze back up, watching the gryphon soar, its tail trailing behind it.

"Are they all that big?" I asked.

"They are once fully grown."

"They're beautiful."

"They are," he said again, his voice hoarse.

"We'll see more, won't we? Maybe even see one up close?"

He nodded. "Once we hit the Glemarian border, you'll see so many, you'll be sick of them."

"Were you ever sick of them?"

He made a noise low in his throat. "Never."

We continued on until the temperatures fell so low with the setting sun that we were forced to make camp inside another cave Rhyan had discovered.

The next day panned out much as the first and ended in another night in a cave. The farther north we went, the colder it grew. We'd just had our coldest winter in Bamaria, yet it was mild compared to Aravia. Nothing had prepared me for the true cold of the north or how thick the snow fell. I had to actually lift my legs up and down as we walked through a clearing that contained two feet of snow—and this was the more walkable trail that Rhyan had scouted. To combat the frigid temperatures, I doubled up my riding leggings, added a second pair of socks beneath my boots, and wore a second shirt beneath my tunic.

Still, I couldn't stop shivering through the night and barely got any sleep. It felt like the cold was in my blood. Rhyan seemed fine, of course. Even when Bamaria was cold, it was still too warm for his liking. This was comfortable weather for him.

By the end of our fourth day of hiking through the freeze, I was fantasizing about the feeling of the sun on my skin. I was also fantasizing about showers. Long, hot showers. Now that we were no longer staying at inns or brothels, bathing was starting to become an issue. But Rhyan swore he knew a cave close to the Glemarian border with a hot spring.

However, it was not the cave he brought us to that night. We hadn't gotten as far north as he'd planned, partly because I was slowing us down—my leg just now healed, and partly because he didn't want to risk us being exposed.

"Wait right here," he ordered at the mouth.

Unfamiliar with this particular cave, Rhyan wanted to do a quick sweep to check for danger or other inhabitants. He'd done the same every other night, as we could never be sure if we were truly alone, but he'd always been quick, retaining intricate knowledge about their layouts.

This time, I found myself growing uneasy as the minutes passed. I burrowed into my hood, leaned back against the stone wall, and hugged my arms to my chest. I even shook my hips in an attempt to create warmth.

"Lyr?" Rhyan's muffled voice came through the vadati under layers of my clothing.

"Rhyan?" I yelled back, trying to squeeze my hand through my layers of armor and clothing to find the stone.

"Lyr!" Rhyan said, his voice more urgent. "Are you there?"

"I'm trying to be!" I'd just managed to pull the golden chain out from my multiple shirts and tunic when Rhyan appeared right in front of me.

"Gods!" He gripped my shoulders.

"I'm okay," I said. "The stone was buried in my clothing."

His jaw tightened. We'd been making an active effort to keep things light, to not delve into the horrors of Vrukshire Keep, but these small moments when Rhyan worried about me were happening more and more frequently. He always tried to cover them up, not wanting to worry me with his own anxieties. But we knew each other too well. One look was all I needed to know if he was in distress.

I reached for his arm. "You don't have to hide this from me," I said.

He shook his head. "No. I'm going figure this one out, too. It's just...still too soon."

"I know." Everything felt too soon.

"You know it doesn't change how I feel about you."

I narrowed my eyes, suddenly insecure. We'd barely touched in any kind of intimate way since that night. We held hands, we kissed a little, and Rhyan almost always slept with his hand on my belly. But that was it. Everything we'd been progressing toward, almost racing into after so many months of deprivation had come to a screeching halt. "What do you mean?"

"I still see you as a warrior. As an accomplished soturion."

I nodded, my stomach untwisting.

"I just...worry about you," he admitted.

He feared losing me. And I feared being naked and vulnerable. Rhyan had been warming water by the fires, creating makeshift baths so we could be clean each day. I'd tried to pretend it was the cold keeping me from fully undressing even when he turned his back to give me privacy. But every time I removed my clothing now, I saw Brockton cutting off my tunic, cutting through my shift. The wounds he'd inflicted had long scabbed over and healed. The bruises faded. But I knew exactly where they were. They were invisible now, but he'd still left scars.

We both just needed time.

"Was everything okay inside the cave?" I asked.

One eyebrow furrowed. "It appeared empty. But I found something strange—something I think you need to see." He extended his hand.

"Far?" I asked, knowing the gesture meant a jump.

"It's okay. I can handle it."

I stepped into him, wrapping my arms around his waist. By now, I was used to the tug on my stomach I got when traveling. It no longer bothered me, but I still felt startled every time my feet touched down somewhere new.

A lit torch was stuck in a crevice of the stone wall where Rhyan had left it. He pulled another stick from his bag and lit it then waved the flame before the cavern wall.

I gasped. A series of paintings were before me. They'd been stylized in a very familiar way. The broad brushstrokes, the use of color, the technique in which the eyes had been drawn, the way the paint was texturized—I wasn't exactly an expert in art, but I knew one artist's work when I saw it.

"These look just like Meera's paintings." I clutched at my chest, staring at the lines.

"That's what I thought, too." Rhyan had only seen them once, the night of Meera's last vision—right before Morgana scrubbed the walls clean.

"These can't be hers!" It hadn't been a month yet. It was too soon for her to have had another one. But we were on the verge.

Gods. The thought of her having a vision alone, scared, surrounded by akadim, made me sick. And that was still the best-case scenario—that she was alive.

But she was supposed to be in the Allurian Pass. In Glemaria, not Aravia. West, not east.

"Do you think they came through here?" Perhaps they'd had to stop along the way, camp in different caves to reach their destination.

Rhyan squeezed my hand. "They could have. But it's also possible someone else with vorakh made this painting."

My stomach twisted. Would Jules have painted like this, too, after visions?

She's alive. But if I die, she dies, too.

I pushed the thought down. He was trying to mess with me. To manipulate me, to stay alive. That was all.

Rhyan's eyes scanned it again, focused and intent. I was reminded of a night months ago, before we were kashonim. I'd wandered into the Temple of Dawn and found him there alone, staring at the pictures adorning the walls and ceiling. The art told the story of Auriel and Asherah, of them becoming Guardians of the Valalumir, forbidden to be together, but falling in love anyway—until Moriel betrayed them, and Asherah was banished for the affair. Rhyan had explained each painting to me, pointing out details I'd never noticed before.

There was a pang in my chest watching him now. Rhyan was the one with the true appreciation for art. An appreciation he hardly got to sit with.

"It was actually the subject matter that made me call you at first," he said. "But then I noticed the style."

I stared at the series of images. There was something a little off, something that was missing Meera's essence, making me feel certain it wasn't her. But was it possible all vorakh painted the same way? She'd never painted before her visions. I wanted to believe it was her work just as much as I prayed it wasn't, that I hadn't missed an opportunity to be there for her and help her. And that fear in the back of my mind, that it was someone else's work—no. I couldn't go down that road. I just couldn't.

Rhyan stepped back, and I moved with him, taking in the entire scene.

A white seraphim watched as five bodies fell from the sky. One was a female with raven hair and an orange dress rustling in the force of her flight. Another was a male with equally dark hair and indigo robes tight against his falling body. There was another female with white hair, her dress a vibrant blue. And another female with gold hair and a gown painted violet. Beside her was another male, his limbs flailing, his robes yellow.

Rhyan waved his torch up, and I could see that they'd fallen from the stars. From Heaven.

"Auriel's Bane," I said. "These are the fallen Guardians banished from Heaven. Ereshya in the orange, Moriel wearing indigo, Cassarya in the blue, Hava in the violet, and Shiviel wearing yellow."

"You're right." Rhyan stepped to the right, moving the torch with him, and we both saw in the same moment that the mural expanded. Sitting opposite the white seraphim was a black gryphon, also watching the fall. And farther down still was another image: a golden-haired god carrying a red-haired goddess in his arms. The goddess's eyes were closed, and the god wore a look of utter devastation on his face.

I met Rhyan's gaze. The god was adorned in green. His eyes painted a vibrant emerald that reminded me of Rhyan's.

In the next image, he had laid the goddess on top of a white stone. He was sinking to his knees.

"By the Gods," Rhyan said, his chest heaving.

"What is it?" I asked.

His mouth fell open as he looked at me with a distraught expression nearly identical to the one in the painting. "Gods, I forgot, you can't see the pictures moving."

I'd forgotten Lumerian paintings came to life. I was so used to seeing pictures remain still, unable to see the true magic of them without my own magic power.

"What do you see?" I asked. "What is it?"

"That's Auriel. And that's Asherah. He places her not on the white stone, but inside it. There's a lid, and when he closes it, the stone takes form. It becomes a seraphim, just like the one on Gryphon's Mount." His face had paled, his eyes haunted and distant, before he looked back at me. "I don't think the statue of the seraphim is simply holding the shard. Lyr, I think we're heading for Asherah's tomb."

CHAPTER THIRTY-THREE

"HER TOMB?" MY EYES began to water, some emotion I couldn't explain overwhelming me. Like a memory, or a knowing. A sense of...of another life. But one I couldn't grasp. One I was now afraid of. "You mean...her body is there?"

"I'd read that Auriel buried her in some stories. There's so many, but I never knew where, or if that was the full truth. Her tomb had never been found, just as none of the gods' or goddess' burial places had. Just as the shards have been lost for centuries. No one's seen them, only speculated."

"Is there more?" I asked, dread rising inside of me. I had only vague memories of Asherah. I hadn't yet felt the pull toward her, the emotions of being her, the love she felt for Auriel. But I could feel it now. I'd known the name Auriel my entire life. I couldn't think of a time I was not aware of him, of his existence. But he was a god. A legend. A story. And now...I felt...tenderness. Hearing his name differently in my mind. My heart warming. My chest swelling.

Auriel.

I looked to Rhyan and realized nothing had changed there. I still loved him, still felt the same. But now I felt...more. Like my love had expanded. My heart was nearly bursting. And then the dread sank in. I wasn't sure I was going to be able to open the seraphim. How could I be expected to open my own tomb. Even if it wasn't really me...something had shifted. It felt like me.

And I felt the truth of this in my soul. Her soul. Every vision Meera had had, even the visions of my mother, they all showed the same thing: Asherah was asleep on Gryphon's Mount.

It was her body that was there. She was only awake now because I was. Because I'd taken her blood—my blood—into me.

Rhyan's finger reached for Auriel. "His eyes," he said.

"Just like yours," I whispered. Rhyan's eyes had always been extraordinary, greener in color than any other eyes I'd ever seen.

"Hmmm." Rhyan frowned uncomfortably then glanced ahead, waving the torch. His chest heaved, his eyes glazing over before he turned his away. "There are more paintings up ahead."

"How old are these, do you think?" I asked. The colors were vibrant, not faded, but the magic of Lumeria could have easily preserved the paintings for hundreds of years. These had certainly been painted after the Drowning. No Lumerians would have been on these shores yet. That gave me a window of a millennium. They could have been ancient. They could have been painted weeks ago.

"Not old," Rhyan said, waving the torch forward. He revealed a small alcove and jars of paint on the ground. "Not even close."

"Meera!" I shouted.

Rhyan placed his hand over my mouth.

"Lyr," he hissed under his breath. "It's a nest."

My eyes trailed forward, and I saw piles on the floor—blankets and stacks of hay.

Up ahead on the dirty stone wall was another painting in the same style. It depicted a god wearing indigo robes with dark shadows around him. His aura. There was a cruelty in his eyes, a darkness. And an uncomfortable familiarity. He reminded me of death.

A golden crown sat on top of his head, and the seven-pointed Valalumir glittered above him.

"Lyr?" Rhyan asked, his voice shaking. "Can you see the words?"

"No, I don't see any." I squinted.

"It says, *Moriel vaspa el bar dia. Teka el bar. Halavra el omae negrare. Teka. Teka. Maraak Moriel.*"

I repeated the High Lumerian in my head, quickly working through the translation. "Moriel has returned to his body."

Rhyan nodded. "Kneel before him. Death to all who deny. Kneel. Kneel. King Moriel."

"He led the army before," I said, my stomach hollow. "For months now, the akadim have been acting strange. Growing in numbers, organizing, moving south. Evolving. What if this whole time it was because their leader returned?"

I thought now of the letter. Had it been him? Moriel reincarnated? Moriel who took out my mother's journal, left it on Ramia's desk for me to find? Moriel who'd taken my sisters?

But who was he? Whose body had he been born into?

"We need to get out of here," Rhyan said urgently. "Now."

"We can't. What if Meera's here? Morgana?"

"Lyr," Rhyan said again, his jaw tensed.

"No! We have to search the rest of the cave."

Rhyan's nostrils flared, his shoulders tensed. "Lyr."

I shook my head. "No!"

He closed his eyes slowly. "Okay. I'll look. Just stay here, and I'll search for them."

"No, I have to come, too. I need to know." My heart was pounding.

"Lyr, please," he begged, his voice desperate. "Please let me protect you. Let me do this."

"But they're my sisters," I pleaded, squeezing his hand.

His eyes shut slowly. "Stay behind me," he ordered, squeezing my hand in return. He drew his sword and held it before him as I reached for my dagger.

We moved forward, our steps slow and careful.

"Swear," he said under his breath. "Swear you won't let go of my hand this time."

"I swear."

The cave began to wind, the walls narrowing and the ceiling lowering.

And then a growl rumbled low in the distance. The sound echoed off the walls. A sharp breeze, like breath, came through the opening we stood beneath.

There were footsteps. Loud and uneven.

I stopped breathing, my eyes meeting Rhyan's as his grip on my hand turned vice-like.

"Stay back," Rhyan said, his voice low. "Lyr. Dagger. And sword." He released me as I removed my weapons, securing them in my hands.

The akadim came into view. Male. So tall, its head hit the ceiling, making the akadim at least ten feet tall. Its eyes were red, its body covered in dirt.

Rhyan ran, racing straight for the beast. He leapt forward, his sword aiming for the akadim's arm. Blood spurted as Rhyan landed behind it, his boots crashing into a puddle. But the akadim seemed undeterred by its injury and uninterested in fighting.

Its red eyes were on me, and it pointed a long, filthy claw.

"Asherah!" it roared. *"Teka! Teka! Maraak Moriel!"* The giant raced toward me as I held my ground, my sword and dagger thrust out.

"LYR!" Rhyan screamed, racing back and throwing himself onto the akadim's back.

The scent of death and decay coming from its breath filled my nostrils. I moved to attack, my eye on the target—the same spot Rhyan had cut.

But like the other akadim I'd faced, it went right for Asherah's chest plate sparkling around my neck.

Good. It would react as the others had: hurt, scared, screeching in pain. I'd use the opportunity to attack.

But the akadim's spiked finger pressed right through the stars, undeterred.

Its claw was met by my Bamarian armor. The Valalumir inside me began to heat.

"Rhyan!" I screamed.

He had climbed up on the monster's back and gripped its neck before his sword sliced through it.

Blood gushed. The monster was deeply wounded, but not dead. Akadim could only be killed in three ways: by fire, by beheading, or by being stabbed through the heart.

The akadim stumbled forward, roaring in pain. I backed up, feeling the heat of my contract with Mercurial spread through my torso like I was on fire. It was then I noticed the akadim seemed to be wearing some kind of necklace. Almost like a choker. Silver, with a red dot in the center. Blood red.

"Lyr, get back!" Rhyan yelled as the akadim fell forward. Its forehead smashed to the ground, its blood mixing with a puddle. Rhyan jumped to his feet. Standing over the beast, he threw down his sword and severed what remained of its neck. The head rolled forward as Rhyan rushed to my side. "You okay?"

"It's burning," I said, hand to my chest. "It's happening again."

"Asherah!" came a low hiss.

Rhyan clutched me to him. "Lyr, I don't think your sisters are here. We've got to go—now!"

I wrapped my arms around him. "Go."

My feet thudded outside the cave, right where we'd arrived. Rhyan grabbed our bags, hoisted them over his shoulder, then grabbed me again. My stomach tugged, and my boots slipped as we landed on icy snow on the cliff of a mountain. A frozen lake was below us. Rhyan pressed me back against a wall. Ice and snow nearly burning with cold against my head. A freezing gust of wind blew so hard that if we weren't careful, it could blow us off the mountain.

"Shit! Shit!" Rhyan cursed. "Is it still burning?" He turned toward me, shielding my body from the wind.

"It's fading," I said, feeling the heat die down. "I don't understand what caused it or why the akadim didn't react to my armor—like the others did." The first one that had attacked me couldn't stand the touch. And it had bothered Haleika so much so, she'd shattered three of the stars in the arena.

Rhyan frowned. "Could it be because you have her blood in you? With the kashonim?" He shook his head. "It doesn't matter right now. We have to find cover for the night."

"Did we go far?" I asked.

"No. We're nearly at the Glemarian border—if we find somewhere nearby to camp, we'll cross into Glemaria first thing in the morning." He brushed hair from my face, staring into my eyes. "I'm sorry. I shouldn't have brought you there."

"You couldn't have known." My teeth chattered more fiercely than before. "It's worn off, and now I'm definitely...really...fucking...cold."

"Come on then."

But a set of growls erupted from ahead on the path. My heart stopped. More akadim.

"Fuck! Fuck!" Rhyan roared. His sword was already back out as I tried to reach for my dagger, but my fingers felt like ice.

We were on the edge of a cliff, the path not wide enough for both of us to move forward. It was just enough for Rhyan, so I stayed back. He charged ahead as two more akadim came into view, their bodies shadowy in the dark, their large arms rising, their eyes glowing red. There was a catch of silver on one. A choker—identical to the last akadim's.

"Asherah." The monstrous hiss came from behind me.

Steeling my nerves, I turned to face another one. This time, I reached for my sword, praying my fingers would find purchase in the cold. I heard the metal sing as I slid it from its sheath. The akadim swiped its claws out at me, and I jumped back, my torso just out of its reach. I lunged forward and slashed, slicing through its arm. Blood trickled onto the side of the mountain, bleeding into the frozen patches of snow.

"*Teka!*" it roared. "Kneel for Moriel!"

There was a thud behind me. I turned, unable to stop myself. One of the akadim had fallen, defeated by Rhyan. It had been decapitated, and its choker rolled off the side of the cliff. Rhyan was already fighting the next beast, his boots scraping against the icy snow, his cloak swirling out behind him, his arms raised, swords gleaming.

In my distraction, the akadim I fought grabbed me around the waist and hauled me to my toes. I plunged my sword into its hand, kicking and twisting. But he lifted me up and up, my feet dangling above the cliff, as he squeezed me.

I held onto my sword, grunting as I used every muscle I had to turn my body around, to face the monster. When I did, inhaling its putrid breath and staring into its eyes that promised death, I pulled my sword from it, and with both hands, I slammed the blade down, screaming as I used all my strength to break through its chest, pushing and pushing the sword into its heart.

It roared in pain, its eyes widening in disbelief. I needed to retract the blade, move away from it, get to Rhyan, but my sword seemed fused inside the akadim's body. I pulled harder, my muscles burning, my hands nearly slipping from the hilt, and then it was free. Blood oozed from its chest, as its face went slack. A low groan from deep in its throat escaped its mouth as its arms lowered and its grip on me faltered.

I stared down at the cliff's edge, leaning my body to be closer to the wall, to make sure the akadim set me on the ground. If he set me down too close to the ledge, I was in danger of slipping and falling. But I couldn't seem to get out of its grasp, or direct its hand.

Then a light flickered in its eyes. It held my gaze, the red blazing like fire, as if it'd had another life stored inside and had suddenly called it forth. Its hands slid up from my waist until its claws wrapped around my neck. Blood poured from its wound as it held me up again, lifting me higher and turning, walking to the edge, its arm extended, my legs dangling helplessly over the side of the mountain. Nothing between me and the frozen river below.

"Rhyan!" I tried to cry out, but my voice was hoarse, barely loud enough for me to hear.

The sounds of his battle were drowned out by a wintry gust of wind.

The akadim stumbled, weakened by its blood loss. Its back slammed into the wall, bringing me with it. I kicked violently, trying to bring myself back over the edge, to grab hold of the akadim's arms without losing my sword. I was starting to panic. Desperate to reach the wall, to get out of its grip.

Its eyes started to close, death finally coming for it. But its hand squeezed and the beast looked up at me one last time, as my feet dangled helplessly.

"Please," I begged. It too wore a silver choker. A red center that seemed to flash with light, before the monster bared its teeth, and the light went out.

"Teka, Asherah."

Then it threw me over the edge.

A hollowed scream left my throat. My stomach bursting into my heart. My feet kicked and arms flailed, but there was nothing to hold onto, nothing to save me as I plunged down and down and down until my feet hit the ice, my legs shaking with the impact. I collapsed to my knees, my hands smashing into the frozen river, my skin burning with the cold.

"LYR!" Rhyan yelled with a force I'd never heard before.

I thought I saw a shadow flying over the edge.

I shifted, and the ice cracked beneath my feet, and then I was falling again. My chest tightened. My heart stopped. My breath ceased. There was just burning, ice-cold fire filling my lungs as I plunged into the river. The current pulled me down beneath the ice, and I kicked my feet, straining to see the surface, to find my way out, to keep the river from taking me. I swam like I'd never swum before, reaching my arms up and up and up. But I found only darkness, hit only hard, cold ice, again and again, Until I couldn't see. Couldn't feel. Couldn't breathe.

I reached up, one last time. My palms smacking against thick solid ice.

And then the cold took me, as I drowned.

CHAPTER THIRTY-FOUR

THERE WAS ONLY DARKNESS. Only cold. Then something slammed into me, hands dug into my arms, pulling my body backwards. I was pressed to something hard and sturdy. Then there was more darkness.

My eyes sprang open. Everything felt tight, stiff, frozen. I was no longer in the water. I was in a cave. One lit torch jutted from a stone wall, illuminating the cavern, its fires crackling and popping amidst my ragged breathes.

I gasped in pain, trying to sit up, but there was a heavy pressure on my chest keeping me down.

Rhyan.

Rhyan's hands were over my heart, pushing down, pumping. His eyes caught mine. He stopped and hugged me to him.

"Thank the Gods," he cried.

I opened my mouth to speak, but I couldn't. I was too cold. I was shivering everywhere, and it was hard to move. My muscles felt like they'd frozen under the water.

"Lyr, I've got you," Rhyan said, still sounding worried. "I need to get you warm," he said quickly, his accent heavy and blurring his words together. "I took you to the cave, the good one. The one with the hot springs. You're going to be okay. You're going to be okay."

I nodded slowly, only then noticing that there was water behind me. Steam rose from the surface of the spring, and the scent of salt permeated the air.

My armor had already been discarded, both Asherah's chest plate and my Bamarian metal. Now Rhyan was frantically pulling off my boots, socks, belt, and pants. Layer after layer, all soaking wet, freezing, and stuck painfully to my body. My legs were bright red, itching and burning, as if they were on fire and freezing at the same time. My tunic came off, then my shirts, until I was in nothing but my underwear, my teeth chattering.

"I'm sorry," Rhyan said. "Lyr, I'm sorry. I know you don't like this, but we have to. Okay? You're doing so good, so good." His breathing was heavy, uneven, his voice strained.

I closed my eyes, feeling him sit my body up then ease my legs into the water.

I hissed at the contact.

"I know it hurts. It's going to feel better soon," he said urgently.

I started leaning back, too weak to hold myself up, but Rhyan's hand was on my spine immediately, propping me upright, keeping me supported.

From the corner of my eye, I saw his soaking wet clothes hit the ground, piled beside all of his layers of armor, his weapons, and boots.

He'd been under the water, too. He'd frozen, too, to get me out. He slid next to me on the edge, the gryphon tattoo on his back a deeper black than I'd ever seen it against the slightly blue tinge of his skin, skin that was always shades paler than mine.

I caught sight of the curve of his ass, only realizing then he was naked before he plunged into the water, hissing and cursing under his breath.

He waded toward me, wrapping his arms around my waist. "I've got you. I'm going to take the rest off. Okay?" One arm remained around me, holding me up, as he untied my shift.

I stiffened, stopping him with my hand, my nails digging into his forearm.

"Lyr...I'm sorry. We need to get you warm. You need to take this off."

I squeezed my eyes shut, the pain so bad. I knew he was right.

"Okay," I said, my breath heavy, and labored.

Rhyan nodded, and threw the material into the pile of soaking clothes. Then his hand lowered, his fingers finding the ties of my underwear. "This, too. Just to get warm."

I sucked in a breath as I felt the material loosen from me and a slight jolt of panic in my chest. But Rhyan's eyes were on mine the whole time as he tugged the material away from me, lifting me slightly to get it free. The cloth vanished. He pulled me into the water.

"Fuck," I yelled, pins and needles stabbing every inch of my body.

He laughed in relief, tightening his hold on me. "Worst hot spring ever." There were tears in his eyes, and I knew they were from my outburst. If I was well enough to curse that loudly, then I was strong enough to survive.

But I was still so tired and having trouble keeping my eyes open.

"Need to get more of our bodies under," he said, pulling me down with him.

The heated water pricked at my stomach and ribcage until I was submerged to my neck. Rhyan was squatting below the surface and brought me closer, pulling my body against his. He reached around me, careful to keep only my chest against his. But it wasn't enough. I needed more warmth. My teeth were still chattering.

Suddenly his hand wrapped around my ass, pulling against his stomach. My legs wrapped instinctively around his torso, and I could tell, he was purposely keeping me lifted, well above his waist. Making sure I felt safe now that he was also naked.

My chest heaved. Breathing was getting easier, and I could feel that my body was thawing. Wrapping my entire body around him was exactly what I'd needed, but I still wanted to close my eyes.

His arms ran up and down my back, his eyes watching me carefully as he held me.

"Talk to me, Lyr," he said.

I buried my face against his neck.

He stroked my nape, and gently pulled my head up to meet his gaze. "Stay with me. No sleeping. Not yet. Okay?"

"Okay," I said weakly.

"You killed another akadim," he said. "You know that? You killed it. You're a powerful soturion, even without magic. Do you know how many soturi don't have even one kill under their belts?"

"How many?" I asked.

His lips quirked. "I actually don't have the numbers. But I can promise you, it's a lot."

"When we get back to civilization, will you figure out that number for me?"

"I'll make it my mission. And don't forget, you're a nahashim slayer, too," he said, moving us through the water, keeping the warmth from stagnating. "You're so fucking strong, Lyr," he said. "You're the strongest warrior I know."

I shook my head. Or I tried to. I wasn't sure I was moving much yet. "That's you," I said.

"Right now, it's you. And you know what that means?"

"That Mercurial was right?" I croaked. The Afeyan messenger had once promised I could be the strongest soturion in Lumeria.

Rhyan pressed his nose against mine, and the feeling of warmth he brought with him made me sigh in relief. With his magic intact, he was definitely recovering faster, his body warming against mine. "No. It means you're going to be fine. You're going to get through this. You're so brave."

My eyelids felt heavy, and my head dropped forward again.

Rhyan lifted my chin. "I know, partner," he continued. "I know you're tired. But you've got to stay with me."

"I'm trying," I said. "Keep talking."

There was an uncertainness in his face, before he said, "Did Jules ever tell you we were friends?"

At this, my eyes widened. "No."

"That summer." He smiled. "She knew how I felt about you. But she also knew I was protecting you by staying away. Or trying to, at least."

"I can't believe I never knew that." Of course, I had known they'd talked, that they were friendly, but I'd had no idea they'd considered themselves friends rather than noble acquaintances. My heart warmed at the thought. I could almost see it—Jules being her fun-lovingly dramatic, over-the-top self, while Rhyan, quietly amused by her antics, tried desperately to maintain a serious face. She'd known all about my crush on him, and I'd bet anything she'd been secretly working to bring us together that whole summer.

"I didn't want you to know," he said seriously. "I thought it was for the best. I thought it would keep you safe—safe from my father. The last time I saw her, I told her that leaving you and pretending that kiss had meant nothing to me, had broken my heart."

"I didn't know."

"You weren't supposed to. I wanted to make it easier for you. But leaving crushed me." He rubbed his nose against mine. "Because I already knew. Knew I loved you from that first kiss."

"What did Jules say when you told her?" I asked.

He chuckled. "Well, she finally stopped yelling and cursing at me for breaking your heart. I believe she called me a gryphon-shit asshole."

Tears filled my eyes, and I laughed. "That sounds like Jules."

"And she also said...she was rooting for us."

The tears were falling now, even as I smiled. "She never told me that."

My heart started to warm, and I'd never been more grateful to Rhyan in my life. He knew exactly how to keep me distracted, knew the one topic that would keep me from succumbing to the cold and falling asleep.

"Jules kept her promises," he said. "She was a really good friend."

"Do you think...?" I started to ask, but a sob cut me short.

"Don't do that," Rhyan said quietly. "Don't start overthinking or worrying—not until we have more information. Not until we know something real."

"Okay."

"Right now, we're just going to get warm. We're going to get through this night. And then we're going straight to Gryphon's Mount and getting your sisters back."

I tightened my arms around him, leaning my cheek against his as he continued moving us through the water. The sounds of our breathing growing into a steadier rhythm mixed with the tinkling of the spring and the popping of the torch flames echoing against the walls.

After some time, I was no longer in pain. In fact, I was warm, reminded of the hot soaks I'd been able to take at the Katurium after training, reminded of the relief my muscles always felt in the heat.

"Warmer?" Rhyan asked.

"Yes. You?"

"Very."

"How long did I freeze?" I asked.

"Less than a minute. The second I saw you go over the edge, I didn't think. I just jumped. I only traveled at the last second so I wouldn't hit the ice and fall in with you. You were moving so fast, so far from where you fell in. I knew I needed to be quick. I couldn't miss, or I'd freeze and never get you out. Once I was sure of your location, I traveled under the water, grabbed you, brought you here."

"You must be so tired," I said. "I'm sorry."

"Shhh. You did nothing wrong. All that matters is that we're okay." He glanced around the cave. "But, uh, we're not going to have clothes for a while."

I eyed the completely soaked through pile of our gear.

"What do we do? Just stay in here all night?" I asked. The cave was the warmest one we'd been in yet thanks to the spring, but after nearly freezing to death, I knew we couldn't simply be out in the nude, especially not after being wet.

"No. I stayed here before. I think—I hope—I have some blankets that I stored here once. Assuming some other poor soul hasn't found them. I'll get a fire going, put our clothes out with them, but," he pressed his forehead to mine, "body heat is what's going to get us through the night." Rhyan pulled back, his hands running up and down my spine.

He'd adjusted me against him, still careful to be sure my pelvis was against his stomach, and I only realized then how much effort and care he'd taken to keep this from turning into anything else.

But now, with his own body temperature regulated, Rhyan was feeling a different kind of heat, the evidence of which had risen up to poke me in the ass.

I stilled.

"Ignore that. You stay in the water," he said, voice hoarse. "I'm going to find the blankets, start the fire."

He set me down, careful to keep certain parts of himself from grazing my body. Then he vanished.

The difference in temperature with him gone was almost shocking. I clutched my arms to my chest and sank low into the water, moving my legs as much as I could to build up my own heat. But my stores were weak.

Rhyan reappeared a minute later holding a pile of blankets in his arms. From the looks of it, there were around three—all hanging just so, leaving his modesty intact. His eyes followed my gaze down to the pile of blankets, then his gaze held mine again, and suddenly, I was feeling just a touch warmer on my own.

"Found them. Can't believe they're still here," he said happily, dropping all but one on the ground. The last one, he wrapped around himself. There was already a mix of fire logs nearby, a pile started from someone else who had crossed through here—hopefully someone with no intention of returning tonight. Rhyan gathered more logs and debris by the walls, building the pyre to double the size of our firewood piles from our previous nights of camping. He brought the torch down and let the fire catch. Then he laid out all of our clothes and emptied our bags, spreading the contents by the fire, which was now flaming and powerful enough for me to feel its heat rushing toward me.

"Ready to dry off, partner?" he asked, coming to the side of the spring.

I nodded, moving toward the edge. Rhyan held the blanket out for me to cover myself and use as a makeshift towel. As I stepped out of the spring, he swept me off my feet and carried me before the fire until we were both completely dry. Then he brought me to our "bed" for the night. He folded the blankets a few times to pad the ground then laid me down and curled himself around me.

Our bodies were pressed tightly together in a way they never had been before, with nothing between them. The warmth radiating from him was addictive, so different from the usual cold he projected. I sighed contentedly, feeling warmer and safer than I had in days.

"You know, partner," he said, rubbing my back, "I didn't realize just how desperate you were for a bath that you'd jump into the first river you saw."

I pouted. "It's not funny yet."

His laugh was low in his throat. "No. It's not funny at all," he said. "But if I don't joke, I'm worried I'll succumb to the absolute terror of what it was like to see you go under. Feel that fear of losing you."

I stroked his cheek, rough with stubble. "I feel like we keep almost losing each other."

"But we keep finding our way back," he said.

"You're doing a little more on that end than I am."

Rhyan pushed his knee between mine, tangling our feet together, stirring more heat between us. "You're worth it."

"Am I? I feel like I keep screwing everything up. And you've sacrificed so much to be with me. To help me. And I'm here, not even...."

"Not even what?" he asked softly as he brushed a strand of hair behind my ear, only slightly damp now.

"I don't know. I'm freaking out about being exposed, and then making decisions that get us into trouble, or hurt...and I'm still keeping our relationship from...being more."

"Lyr, things happen on the road. Do you know how many times I've fucked up? Or was hurt? You're doing really well. And...I don't need anything like *that* from you, especially with the stress you're under. Remember what I said on Valyati? Before everything happened? Holding your hand was the best gift I'd ever been given. And make no mistake. I want you. I want you so fucking bad that sometimes I feel like I'll die from desire. But if all I was going to have in this life was touching your hand, that would have been enough. That would have been a moment I treasured my entire life. There's nothing you need to be doing. No timeline. No rules to follow. No expectations. Just whatever you want, and when you want it."

My breath came fast. "I think sometimes I still feel like I'm failing everyone. Letting everybody down. In all ways. All the ways it counts. I'm failing my sisters. Failing Bamaria. I could be failing," my throat dried, "her." I couldn't say Jules. Not now. "And tonight, I feel like I should have been faster. I should have realized the danger, not forced you to risk your life like that."

"Oh, partner. You couldn't be further from the truth. I know the life you lived made you feel like you had to be perfect. Like you had something to prove. But that's not it, not how I see you. If you want me to spell it out for you, I will. Whatever is getting into your head right now, it doesn't need to be there. So here it is." He sucked in a breath. His eyes were so green as they stared into mine. "I loved you the first time I kissed you and you didn't know how to kiss me back. I loved you when your confidence grew and you took control and left me wild and full of need. I loved you when you didn't know how to move against my body to take your pleasure. And I loved you when your hips rolled against mine and made my cock so hard, I thought I'd burst against that tree.

"I've loved you when you've dressed up in your jewels with your hair curled and shiny, your eyes dark with make-up, and your lips red as berries. And I've loved you when you wake up in the middle of the night, your hair messy, your face bare, and your jewels off.

"I've loved you when you've water danced, your hips moving so sinuously, I could stare at them all day. And I've loved you when you could barely run without a cramp. I loved you when every sword fell from your hand. When you grew the strength to hold one. When you were a little girl who thought I was a rude nuisance and you still let me sit with you and share cake and stories. And when you were a woman, smart and kind and beautiful. I've loved you when your skin smells like vanilla and musk. And when you smell like vomit because you made yourself sick from fighting. I loved you when you saved me from the nahashim. And I loved you when I stormed into the keep to get you back.

"I loved you when your sword pierced through that fucking asshole who touched you. And I loved you when I slayed his wolves for daring to look upon you."

Tears filled his eyes. His voice had gone hoarse, and I felt my own heart pounding, swelling. My entire body vibrating with love, with his love, and mine for him, his essence, his heart.

"Do you get it yet? Lyr, I love you. In all your forms and all your stages. And I always will. No matter what you do. No matter what you give me."

I traced the line of his scar, my finger skimming down the contour of his cheek and jaw then up to his lips. "What if I want to give you all of me?"

"Then I'd give you myself in return."

My heart was beating a rhythm loud enough to burst through my chest, my stomach fluttering, and yet a feeling of peace had suddenly washed over me. A certainty. A knowing. A confidence I hadn't expected. I trusted Rhyan implicitly, loved him so much, and wanted him just as badly as he wanted me.

"Rhyan." My voice was barely above a whisper. "I love you. I don't want to spend one more night not knowing what it's like to experience this with you."

His eyes searched mine, vulnerable, questioning.

"I can't go one more night not knowing you, not joining my body to yours."

"Lyr, you...you almost drowned earlier. And you...you've been through so much." His chest was rising and falling against my own—against my bare breasts, which now felt full, my nipples peaked not from the cold but from wanting. The buds were sensitive rubbing against him, and heat was coiling through me, surging between my legs. Maybe in a perfect world we would have been doing this for a long time already. And maybe in the world we were in, it would have taken me weeks, months or more, to get past what had happened at the keep. But we were here now, and everything felt suddenly perfect. I knew exactly what I wanted, beyond any reason, any doubt.

His eyes were hooded, dark with desire as he watched me, still so vulnerable, so unsure.

"Rhyan, I want you—more than anything. I've never been more positive. And because of everything I've been through…. That's why I can't wait. I feel fine. Thanks to you. Always thanks to you."

He closed his eyes, his breaths heavy, a flush spreading through his chest and neck. His grip on me tightened, his fingers pressing into my flesh with want, with possession. But also, with love. The way he managed to convey all of those things at once, that was exactly why I wanted him. Needed him.

Rhyan groaned, his jaw working. "I want you. I've wanted you for so long. But don't…don't make this choice out of fear. Or because you fear tomorrow."

I kissed him, moving my lips softly against his. He was still, letting me be in control, letting me set the pace. But I was hungry, full of need and desire, and I deepened the kiss. My tongue stroked his, and I kissed him until he gasped for breath.

"This isn't out of fear," I said in between kisses. "This is out of love. This is because I want you. I always have. You took possession of me that night all those years ago. That kiss…that sealed it for me, too. It just took me longer to remember. But for me, Rhyan, it's always been you." I kissed him again, and this time he kissed me back with a ferocity that left me panting. His hands tangled in my hair and cupped my cheek, his body straining to be closer to mine. His cock stiffened, thick and hard, pressing against my belly.

Rhyan groaned into my mouth and angled my head up, kissing down my jaw to my neck, grinding into me, gently rolling me onto my back. His body slid over mine, his arousal causing friction between my legs that left me moaning and desperate for more. The heat he offered me left me nearly delirious with pleasure after having been so cold.

"Are you sure," he panted, kissing me again, "this is what you want?"

I was slick with need, could feel it coating my sex. I undulated up, rubbing myself along his length, rolling into him so he could feel just how sure I was.

"You feel that?" I asked, my voice husky as I pulled him down to me. "How wet you make me? I want you inside me. Rhyan, please. Fuck me."

He twitched against me. "Gods, Lyr. Where did you learn to speak so fucking dirty?"

I bit his bottom lip. "I had a good teacher."

And with those words, it was like a leash had snapped. His hands and mouth were everywhere, kissing, licking, biting, groaning into my skin. He tilted my hips up, shifting the blankets beneath me, not only creating a cushion against the floor but elevating my hips to meet his, deepening the sensations.

He lowered his head, drawing my nipple into his mouth, flicking the sensitive peak with his tongue.

I bucked beneath him, my skin humming with pleasure as his hand cupped my other breast, his thumb brushing my overly sensitive nipple. His other hand moved down my body, the callouses of his fingers teasing me as he slid them between us, adding pressure I hadn't known I needed.

I threw my head back, crying out, my fingers digging into his back.

He growled. "Keep making those sounds, partner, and this is going to be over very quickly." He shifted his mouth to my other breast, as he, at last, pushed a finger inside me.

I gasped, immediately clamping down around him. "I want to touch you."

"Partner," he breathed against my skin. "I want that, too. But I'm not sure I have the control right now. Let me touch you first." He added a second finger, slowly fucking them in and out of me.

In that moment, I seemed to realize that this was really happening. We were finally at this moment after all the years, all the oaths sworn, all the promises made, all the attempts to fulfill duty and honor. Finally, we'd arrived at the place that felt as if it had always been inevitable, always fated. Like we were somehow always this—always together, always this natural.

He was moving his mouth lower and lower, kissing his way down my breasts and my stomach, his tongue brushing against my belly button. His eyes rose up to meet mine, dancing with a fiery emerald light as he continued his descent.

I arched up, and suddenly, a wave of shyness fell over me as I realized where his mouth was going next. I hadn't expected...hadn't been prepared. I reached for his head, my fingers tangling in his curls.

"Rhyan, wait," I said breathlessly. "Are you....?" I couldn't get the words out, too full of desire, even amidst the vulnerability.

"Am I what?" His eyes filled with mischief, a hungry smile on his face. "You know what I'm going to do, partner. You know I want to drink my fill of you. And I'm about to savor every last drop."

My stomach tightened, as his hands gripped my ass.

"It's just...." I stared up at the ceiling, watching the reflection of water and fire shine in the stones above us. "I've never done...that...before."

Rhyan stilled before climbing back up, resting his chin on my belly, stroking my skin with his thumb.

I looked down and caught the surprised look on his face.

"Your choice?" he asked carefully.

I could hear the implication. If I hadn't done this before, it was because a certain someone—that I was positive neither of us wanted to name in this moment—hadn't done this for me. In truth, he'd been willing. I'd been the one who'd refused, always hiding my body, always trying to keep him satisfied while keeping him from seeing my scars, my wounds, and the truth of who I was, the secrets I was forced to keep. And maybe...maybe some part of me had also been insecure—worried he wouldn't think I was perfect. I'd never been perfect enough. Not for him. Not for myself. Not for anyone.

I could feel that old habit rearing its head. That old fear. The sudden panic, the need to hide, to protect. For too many years, my body hadn't been my own. Too many had tried to possess it, use it for their various needs.

But Rhyan had helped me feel like I could reclaim it. Like I could be in control. Even if the attack earlier this week had set me back.

I nodded. "It was my choice. At the time it...felt too vulnerable. And I was too nervous to be seen...like that."

Kissing my stomach, he said, "That makes sense." He pushed up onto his elbows, sliding farther up my body until his head was over mine. He kissed my lips again. "We don't have to, if you don't want. But you have nothing to be worried about with me. I swear."

I squeezed my eyes shut, taking a deep breath. "I want to. It's just...I think I just needed a second."

He smiled softly. "Take all the seconds you want."

"Maybe I should also tell you that this," I gestured between us, "is my first time."

Rhyan was too slow to hide the second look of surprise on his face.

"Is that okay?" I asked, unsure of his reaction.

His face softened. "Of course, it's okay." His voice was so gentle, so reassuring. "I just didn't know. But I'm glad I do now." He brushed my hair behind my ear, tracing the curve of it with such tenderness I shivered. "I'll be gentle," he said. "You don't need to feel nervous. You know you're safe with me, right? And that you're always, always in control?"

Fresh tears were in the corners of my eyes. "I know."

"Thank you for telling me." He kissed me again, his hand slowly stroking between my legs. "Is this okay?" he asked.

"It's good."

He was quickly rebuilding the fire that had stalled in my sudden panic.

"Mmmmm," he hummed. The corner of his lips lifting. "Now here's what I want you to do. You're going to lay back, and relax, and let me get you ready." His thumb pressed against my center, as he lowered his head.

"You're sure you want to...do that?" I asked.

Rhyan almost snorted with laughter. "Want to? Lyr, I dream about the taste of your lips. And not all those dreams are about the ones on your face."

I blushed, squeezing my eyes shut. "Gods."

"Trust me," he purred. "I want to taste you. Can I?"

"Yes," I gasped, already writhing beneath his ministrations.

"Good." He lifted his good eyebrow. "Now open your legs for me, partner."

I did, watching as his body slid down until his mouth was right up against my sex, his eyes wide and hungry. His hands wrapped around my legs, pulling me even closer as he pressed his nose to my inner thigh, breathing deeply. He offered a kiss there, and then he was against my center, inhaling my scent, his breath alone making me want to melt.

I bucked, nerves getting to me again. This was so intimate. I'd never felt this exposed, this vulnerable.

"Partner," he warned. "Don't get lost in your head now. Stay with me for this." He pressed a soft kiss over me and nuzzled my sex before he finally licked me from the bottom to the apex of my thighs.

My back bowed, the sensation almost too much.

"Like that?" he asked.

An unintelligible sound was my only reply.

And then Rhyan unleashed himself, and my core pulsed and spasmed. I was no longer in control, no longer able to stop myself from writhing, bucking, thrusting my hips against his mouth one second and squirming to get away the next because it was just too good.

I felt like I could barely breathe. My fingers dug into the blankets, and then they were digging into his hair. The heat inside me was building, growing, coiling into a mindlessly crazed crescendo of pleasure.

I was screaming nonsensical words, yelling Rhyan's name as my orgasm began to crest with an intensity I wasn't expecting, a force I didn't think I could survive.

I bucked, throwing my head back, as his mouth closed on my center, sucking and licking, two fingers sliding into me, hitting the spot inside me that—

"I can't," I yelled. "Fuck." My toes curled, my legs shaking. I had to get away. It was too much. Too good.

"No, you don't," he growled. "I'm not done with you yet."

His arm clamped down over me, his palm pressing over my belly, locking me in place, and somehow it felt even better.

And then I...Gods.

Rhyan was relentless, kissing me, stroking me through every last spasm, and even as the shocks of my orgasm slowed, he continued to lick, almost reverently, worshipful.

My eyes shut, and I was reminded of my first day of training when my muscles had liquified, when I'd been sure I was never going to be able to get up or move any part of my body again. That was nothing. This had melted me.

Rhyan covered my body with his, stroking my cheeks and kissing me, his lips soft and full and slick with my arousal.

He moaned, and I could taste myself on him. I finally found the strength to move my arms and hug him to me. One final aftershock rumbled through my center.

"Partner, you still with me?" he asked, deepening the kiss. One hand moved behind my head, cradling me as we kissed.

"Mmmhmmmm," I said, not sure I trusted coherent words to leave my mouth.

"Fuck, that was good," he said, kissing me again and again, his tongue sensually gliding against mine, the motion exactly what he'd done between my legs. "It's official," he murmured. "You win."

I opened my eyes. "Win?"

He smiled wickedly. "I concede. The months-long debate is at an end. Bamarian cuisine is far superior to Glemarian."

"Seriously? You decided this now?"

He dragged his lips over mine. "I just tasted the best meal of my entire life, and it was from Bamaria."

"By the Gods," I laughed.

"Mmmm." He took my hand in his, threading his fingers through mine. "You taste," he said, staring into my eyes, "like my favorite thing in the whole world."

My cheeks heated. "And what's that?"

He smiled, holding my gaze. "You." Then we were kissing again. He settled between my legs, his cock heavy against my belly. I reached between us, gripping him, reveling at how silky he was between my fingers, and how hard.

He jerked.

"Was that okay?" I asked. "I haven't gotten to touch you yet."

"It's more than okay," he said hoarsely.

He propped himself up on his elbows as I brought my other hand down to simultaneously cup him while I stroked from base to tip. Rhyan shuddered, throwing his head back. "Lyr. I need you."

I leaned up to kiss him, feeling his hands move beneath me, readjusting the blankets, adding more padding beneath me as he settled between my legs.

I slid him up and down my entrance, feeling his shoulders shaking, as clenches of desire pulsed through me. With a growl, he grabbed my hands and pinned them over my head. His hips flexed as he controlled the movements between us.

"Lyr," he said. "Before we...I just wanted you to know. I'm protected. I had the spell performed years ago. You won't be able to get pregnant from me, not until I reverse it."

I squeezed my eyes shut in embarrassment. I was so wrapped up in him, I was barely thinking about that.

"Good," I breathed.

"You ready?" he asked, reaching between us. He slid one finger in, then a second, his thumb circling, creating a new ache between my legs. A new need. A new desire.

But I swallowed, my nerves ratcheting up again. He released my hands, and I gripped his back.

He exhaled slowly, reading me so well. "Don't be scared. It's just me. I'll be right here with you the whole time."

I nodded.

"You decide when. Or if you've changed your mind—"

"I haven't."

His hips twisted, and I started to cry out, but he swallowed it with his lips. "You can tell me to stop at any time. You can tell me anything. If it feels good, if it doesn't. If you want more, less, it's yours. I swear."

My inner walls clamped around his fingers. "Now," I said.

He positioned himself, his forehead pressed to mine. Our breaths mingling as he stroked me one last time. His green eyes bore into me, and then he pushed in, almost immediately coming to a halt as I tightened.

I sucked in a breath.

"Breathe," he whispered. "Breathe, and let me in."

I gasped, my heart racing, and then I breathed out, feeling my inner walls stretch as he pushed in, and in, and in, feeding himself to me slowly until he was fully sheathed.

I froze, my body tightening and clenching around him. Rhyan remained still above me, small tremors in his arms. He groaned, the sound a mix of pain and pleasure as he stared down at me, and I watched, my heart swelling, something in my soul reaching out to his. I wasn't prepared for the sheer intimacy of it—of how close I felt to him, not just physically but on every level imaginable. I felt a thread between us, ancient, unyielding. Like this had always been the way, like we'd always been meant to find ourselves in this moment.

"Lyr, you okay?" he asked urgently. "Am I hurting you?"

I shook my head. I was so full—full of him, full of emotion, full of love—I was finding it hard to speak. At last, I managed, "No. It's just...a lot. Pressure."

"I think it'll help if I move. I'll go slow." He arched back, his movements even and precise before he thrust even deeper into me.

Sweat began to bead around my forehead and neck—a miracle after I'd nearly frozen before. Then he thrust again, and this time, I gasped, a sound of pleasure escaping me.

He grinned mischievously. "Like that?"

"Yes."

The pressure was fading as he ground down, rubbing against me until I was on fire everywhere, inside and out. We found a rhythm, my hips lifting and rolling, seeking out that friction between us again and again. With each thrust, I clenched around him, that coil of desire tightening inside of me.

My hands slid down his back, my feet locked behind him, as I pulled him closer, urging him to move faster.

He rested his hand under my head, brought my lips to his, and kissed me before he began to thrust, sliding in and out, moving harder, faster, almost frenzied. I met his movements, the sensations of pleasure building inside of me, the tension rising, everything coiling tighter and tighter.

Gold light sparked between us, the light emanating from my chest.

The Valalumir. It was glowing, sparkling, filling the entire cave with golden light.

Rhyan's hair no longer looked dark but golden. His eyes widened, so green, so bright, it was almost hard to look at him. "Is it burning?" he asked

"No," I gasped. "Just lighting up." I moaned. "Don't stop. Don't. I'm almost there."

For a second, some emotion flashed across his expression, and his gaze grew distant before he seemed to shake it off and stared back down at me.

"Lyr," he moaned. "Lyr."

I shuddered, ready to explode, burying my face against his neck, biting down on his shoulder.

He was now pounding into me, relentless as my legs wrapped around his hips.

The feelings of pleasure rippling inside me were growing, tightening, and expanding until the coil snapped, and I screamed, my entire body shivering and shaking.

The star was still glowing, and Rhyan was watching me as he moved wildly against me, stoking the inner flame again until I was nearly undone. I was riding the wave of another orgasm as his muscles flexed, his entire body going taut, before he gritted his teeth, throwing his head back and growling.

He reared back and pushed into me one last time before he yelled, "Fuck. Fuck. Lyr," as he spilled inside me.

I clutched him to me, holding him through his tremors until he finally went still, his forehead resting against mine, his breaths heavy.

Slowly Rhyan pulled himself out, and gathered me in his arms, kissing my forehead and nose before planting a gentle kiss on my lips. "Are you okay?" he asked.

I nodded. "I'm good. You."

He hummed in response, and reached between my breasts where the light was slowly fading. Then his eyes returned to mine and he brushed his thumb against my cheek. *"Mekara,"* he murmured. *"Mekara."*

My soul is yours.

I reached for his face and stroked his jaw, my heart bursting as I answered, *"Rakame."*

Your soul is my soul.

He shuddered, a tear in his eye. "My soulmate." Then his lips were on mine, soft, gentle. "That was...everything," he said breathlessly, hugging me tighter. His hand ran up and down my arm. "Are you sure you're okay? Do you need anything?"

I snuggled against him, reveling in this feel of him holding me, of holding him. "I'm good. Not sure I can get up anytime soon."

"Don't. I'm not letting go of you, not for the rest of the night." He leaned in to kiss my forehead.

His hand trailed down my chest, once more over the golden star, whose light was now dormant. Shakily, he traced the seven rays.

Rhyan flattened his hand against my chest. "When this started to glow, there was a moment when I saw you...but not as you are now. Not as Lyr." His jaw tightened. "I saw you as Asherah."

"What?"

"It's like, for a second, I was gone, and then I was back. It happened so fast. I was terrified I'd traveled by accident, but...I'm almost positive, it was a vision. Or a memory. One I never knew I had." He shook his head. "It was familiar. I saw a beach, golden sand. You were walking on it, wearing the chest plate, the diamonds gleaming in the sun. Your hair was red, so red, and blowing in the wind, your face was yours but not...you were glowing, so full of light, and you turned to me, took my hand. And then you said...." His chest heaved, and he wore the same haunted look as before.

"What did I say?"

"You called me Auriel."

CHAPTER THIRTY-FIVE

I GASPED. "WHAT?"

Rhyan swallowed roughly, his eyes watering, as he shook his head. "You walked right up to me, took my hand, looked me in the eyes, and said Auriel. Lyr, have you...have you ever had any visions of her, or memories of...the other life?"

I nodded slowly, still stunned by his words. "Only a handful of times. They're vague. More like flashes. The first time...it was just my hand. I was on a beach with golden sand, holding up my hand as if to block out the sun. That was it. But it wasn't my hand...at least, not how it looks now. My skin was darker. My hand was larger. I've never...never seen anyone else in the visions. Do you think...that...do you think you were remembering?"

"I don't know. I don't.... It felt that way. I've wondered," he said. "There have been moments in my life, where I felt...not myself. There was no explanation. The first time...it was that summer I visited. Uncle Sean took me to see the Guardian of Bamaria. And there was one moment when I touched the statue and...I was suddenly so full of power and strength...I accidentally threw Sean across the sand. I was bound at the time, so I shouldn't have been that strong. And I wasn't after. Then it wasn't until later, after I started soturion training, that the feeling returned. Sometimes on the rare days when Glemaria was hot, I had this...strange sense of another time. I thought maybe I was remembering Bamaria. But it never felt the same." He stroked my hair. "Since I found out about you...a part of me has wondered..."

"Wondered if you were Auriel?"

He shrugged. "I think that part was wishful thinking. But...I've started to think—what if that was why my father wanted me back. Why all this time, he let me live. He knows who you are. He's always known. And, with how he treated me...he always wanted control, yet never once did he force a blood oath on me. At least, not until the night that...." He exhaled sharply, and looked up toward his scar. "I thought for so long he wanted me dead. That one day he'd slip, and my life would be over. But that never happened. He wanted me alive. And for years, I've tried to piece out why. What value was I to him? What could he want from me if he hated me?"

"Rhyan." I touched his cheek.

"It's okay. It is what it is. But there was something my old bodyguard Bowen once told me. He said that my dying was the last thing my father wanted."

I cupped his face, my finger tracing the scar through his eyebrow to his cheek.

Rhyan sighed. "I'd say it doesn't matter—and until a few weeks ago, I'm not sure I would have truly believed it possible—even if I suspected it was true. But considering you're Asherah, and we've heard more than once now that Moriel may have returned, I wouldn't put it past the realm of possibility."

"Did you mean what you said?" I asked. "When called you me, *Mekara?*"

"Yes," he said fervently. "Gods, Lyr. Yes. I didn't say that because of the vision. Or any speculation. That was me. That was all me. Even if I'm not him, I don't care. I couldn't care less. My soul is yours." He took my hand and pressed it to his heart. *"Me sha, me ka, Mekara."* He kissed my fingers. "I swear it."

"I don't care if you are either. Because I meant what I said, *Rakame.*"

"Good. Now come on," he said, propping us up into a seat. "Let's get you cleaned up." His slid my arms around his neck, lifting my ass into his lap, before he stood gracefully. "Back into the spring."

Sinking into the water now felt glorious, warm and soothing. And this time, Rhyan wasn't trying to hide his growing erection or maintain a respectful distance between our bodies. The boundaries between us, the ones forced on us by the Empire and the ones we'd created to protect ourselves when we'd needed them, were finally gone.

We swam around, reveling in the heat and being able to enjoy it, not simply need it to survive. Then our lips met in a kiss so deep, it seemed like we were still on the blankets, still joining our bodies together. My arms were around his neck, his thickening length against my belly.

Suddenly, Rhyan was rushing toward a smooth rock formation at the edge of the spring. Fresh warm water trickled onto my shoulders and down my breasts as he leaned my back up against the rock, he was already fitted to my entrance.

"Can you take me again, partner?" he breathed, his voice hoarse, sliding against me.

Reaching down between us, my fingers wrapped around him, hard and ready. Slowly, I slid him in and in. I groaned at the sudden pressure, clenching around him as he trembled against me, giving me time to adjust to this new angle.

"Fuck." He pressed his forehead to mine.

I gripped his shoulders, undulating against him, our eyes meeting as he thrust up, his fingers digging into my waist. I circled my hips, rubbing against him, building that fire again until it felt like it was blazing through my limbs, sparking every nerve in my body.

"Do you know how many times I fantasized about this?" Rhyan asked. "How many times I thought about throwing you over my shoulder, stripping you naked, and taking you in the baths of the Katurium?" He pumped up into me, growling with each thrust. "In our training room? In my apartment? In yours? How much I fucking wanted you everywhere?"

I dug my nails into his shoulder, my inner walls beginning to pulse, the sensations overwhelming.

It felt like I was going to go over the edge. I'd never come so many times before. Never this powerfully. I'd never been this sensitive. I started to tense, worried a scream was about to rip through me, and I pushed forward, burying my moan in his shoulder.

"No, partner," he said wickedly, pushing me back against the rock, one hand restraining my arms above me. "No hiding. I want to hear it. Hear everything. Hear you scream."

He was completely in control like this, fucking me, while I could do little more than lay back on the rock and take it.

My breath came short, and my moans echoed across the spring as he pumped into me again and again and again. Years of pent-up desire, of longing, powered each thrust. And my own need for him, my own years of sacrifice and denial, were hungrily taking every stroke. With nothing to hold onto, I writhed and thrashed against the wall, moaning and cursing, my heels digging into his ass.

I didn't even recognize my voice anymore or the sounds I was making.

Rhyan's eyes bore into mine. "Yes, Lyr. Yes." He released my wrists, sliding his hand to my breast.

I couldn't take it anymore. The orgasm ripped through me, shattering me all over again as I screamed, keening right into Rhyan's own release until his yells of pleasure were all I could hear.

He tensed, his abdomen flexing as he pumped into me one last time. Then he gathered me into his arms, kissing me and dragging me back into the water.

"Can I apologize in advance if you're sore tomorrow?" He kissed my shoulder.

"I'll probably make you apologize then, too," I said. "But...worth it."

"What if I swear I'll make it up to you?" he asked.

"And just how are you going to do that?"

He grinned. "I can think of lots of ways." His finger traced a line to my breast, and he lowered his head, tugging my nipple between his lips until I gasped, arching back. He tightened his hold on me. "Might start with worshipping these."

"Well, it's a start," I said breathlessly as he kissed his way up to my lips.

My chest was still heaving as he held me, and so was his—something that didn't usually happen even after our most intense workout and training sessions thanks to his god-like strength.

I swallowed, looking down at my chest, at the faint gold of the star. It hadn't lit up that time.

Rhyan's gaze followed mine, one eyebrow furrowed. "I wish I knew what triggered it. What it meant."

I brushed a loose curl from his forehead. The water and perspiration gave him tighter curls than usual. "Did you see anything that time?"

"No. Only you. Only my Lyr."

I smiled. *"Rakame."*

"Always."

Sometime later, he carried me out of the spring, taking care to dry me and rearrange the blankets so we could actually sleep and stay warm. He laid me back down in our nest of blankets while he added more debris to the fire.

When he was finished, he started toward me, but stopped suddenly in his tracks, staring down, a goofy smile on his face.

"What?" I asked.

"Just...you. All of you. I was so frenzied, needed so badly to touch you, to take you, I didn't have the chance to just look and admire you. How fucking beautiful you are."

My breath caught. I'd certainly been naked before in front of others. But in pieces. In the dark. Or in the bathing room where it was understood we didn't openly stare and gawk.

And at this point, Rhyan had undressed me more times than I could remember, but always respectfully, always with an attempt to keep his eyes on my face until he had permission to look. Now he had it. And he was taking full advantage, his eyes raking me from head to toe.

The impulse to cover myself or to shift positions surged through me, but I tempered it down and stared back, realizing I'd also been denied the same opportunity. I'd seen everything at this point, but not like this—not in full where I could take it all in, appreciate his physique, his strength, all of him.

"You are, too, you know," I said. "So fucking beautiful." And he was. Every last inch of him was utter perfection in my eyes, his muscles so defined yet elegant. I'd once dreamt of him naked in the temple, but my imagination had nothing on the reality of Rhyan.

He winked at me. "Get your eyeful now, partner. I'm starting to get cold and need you to warm me."

I laughed. "Before you get in here, turn around."

"What?"

"Turn around," I ordered. "I need a good look at that ass."

He bit down on his lip, his eyes narrowing, but he turned for me, flexing his perfectly sculpted cheeks until I was giggling helplessly.

Glancing over his shoulder, he gave me one of the stern looks he often reserved for training. "First you objectify me, and then you laugh at me, all while I'm standing here shivering," he warned, using his overly affected northern accent. His good eyebrow sloped down in admonishment, and then he turned, jumping on top of me, and kissing me until I wasn't giggling anymore.

He pulled the blankets up around us, our bodies tangled together, his pine-and-musk scent cocooning me as his hand found its usual place to rest on my stomach. His calloused fingers stroked my skin as our breaths slowed and synchronized. I felt myself falling into unconsciousness, warmer, safer, and more contented than I'd ever been.

Just before I dozed off, he whispered, *"Mekara,"* one more time.

I sighed happily, tucked away in the most delicious blanket of warmth, Rhyan's arms around me, his knee between my legs. The last of our fire crackling against the slow rush of water in the spring. Every part of me was tired. Some parts of me were sore, as I'd expected. But it was a surprisingly welcome soreness, reminding me of every intimate touch, every moment that had happened between us. I could almost feel him still throbbing inside me.

I was lying on my side, Rhyan wrapping around my body from behind, and I could feel very clearly that even if he wasn't awake yet, some part of him was. And it was very ready to continue what we had started last night.

Unable to help myself, I arched my back, rubbing against him, forcing his hands to tighten and pull me flush against his chest, his arousal even more obvious now, pressing against my backside.

"Mmmm," Rhyan moaned sleepily, his fingers on my belly stirring. His lips found my neck, pressing tiny kisses up the curve to my ear. A soft growl erupted low in his throat as he playfully bit at my earlobe. "Morning, lover."

I turned in his arms, unable to hide the grin taking over. "Morning."

His gaze moved across my face. "Most beautiful sight to wake up to." He cupped my cheek, pulling my lips toward his, as he gently rolled me onto my back.

My hips lifted automatically as he moved over me. I reached for his ass, pulling him down.

He stilled, leaning forward to kiss me softly. "Are you sore?" he asked, running a hand down my leg.

"Maybe a little."

"Sorry," he said, but even as he apologized, he rocked his hips forward, gently sliding against me, with such slow precision, I bucked.

Warmth burrowed between my legs as I slowly rolled up to meet his thrusts.

"You know," I said, digging my fingers into his forearm, "It doesn't look like you feel too sorry."

"Doesn't it?" he gritted through his teeth. "What about my apology offends you?" he growled, sliding back and forth so deliciously slow, his abdomen taut, sweat beading on his forehead.

"Customarily, an apology...doesn't consist...of repeating...the thing...one must—" I gasped, "apologize for."

He gripped my ass, gently lifting me, the new angle even more intense. "Come on, partner. Give me the definition then, teach me the custom."

"Fuck," I panted, my brain too scrambled with pleasure to return the banter. He wasn't even inside me and still, he was....

"That doesn't sound like a definition," he teased.

"It is now. What you're doing." I was panting.

"This?" He rolled his hips.

"Yes," I cried. "Now don't you dare stop apologizing."

He bent his head to my nipple, sucking it between his lips, before kissing me again, wrapping my legs around his waist as he continued slowly, torturing me. "Sorry," he murmured against my lips. "Sorry. So fucking sorry."

After Rhyan finished his apology, and then apologized again with his...favorite meal, he laid on his back and pulled me over him, lazily rubbing circles up and down the length of my spine. "I don't want to leave this cave."

"Me neither."

Leaving meant leaving behind the place where we'd come together. The place where it had felt like our souls had met. Outside was dangerous and cold. Full of akadim and duty and Glemaria.

"Are you nervous to be back in your country?"

His throat bobbed, an unusual amount of vulnerability in his eyes. "I'm terrified."

I hugged him tighter to me. "I'll be there with you."

"That helps." He continued stroking my back.

"We're almost at the border, right?" I asked.

"We'll be at Gryphon's Mount by nightfall. We're going to need to walk all day though, because the only way to make sure we're not seen is to travel to the cliff where it resides. The mountaintop connects to the keep. So, I'm going to store everything I have."

"That makes sense."

We stared at each other, both knowing we had to move, to get up, to get dressed, but neither wanting to. The fire Rhyan had started last night was still lightly crackling and smoking, but was surely dying down. Mainly burning embers at this point. It made sense to go, not try to start a new one. And we were now less than a week from the deadline to reach the Allurian Pass.

A sudden wave of guilt washed over me. What the fuck was I doing? My sisters....

"Lyr, don't. You did nothing wrong. You're allowed pleasure. You're allowed pleasure no matter what else is happening. You can't suffer enough to save them. You're doing the best you can. And we're almost at the last part of the journey." His thumb rubbed a crease between my brows, frowning as he gazed around the cave.

"Almost at..." I didn't want to say Asherah's tomb.

Rhyan's eyes fell on the star between my breasts. And the weight of last night seemed to settle between us. Not just how we'd connected, but...what that connection might really mean.

"All right, partner. How about on the count of three?"

A short while later, we were out of the cave. All the food we had been carrying with us had been ruined when it had gone underwater, but, luckily, our clothes had dried. My mother's journal had been miraculously protected by its case, and the notes I carried from my "supporter" were safe inside my cuff with Meera's vision log.

Though it was out of the way, Rhyan insisted we head to the nearest village for food. We were likely going to be moving the rest of the day without stopping, and he had to be sure his magic was at full strength. We quickly found a restaurant, one of the few that seemed to exist there, but the moment we decided to get food, the Aravian clock tower rang, the bells a low hum that sent my pulse racing. From the corner of every building, tree, and bush, a soturion that had been in hiding stepped out. It was a changing of the guard.

Even the villagers seemed startled at this, many stopping in their tracks and staring as a dark aura of fear and tension rose into the air, all tinged with the cold of winter. The soturi wore the brown leathered armor of Aravia, close in design to Rhyan's Glemarian armor, meant to protect against the snow and winter. The sigil of the country's ruling Ka, Ka Lumerin, displayed a silver ashvan soaring over the moon, similar to the sigil of Ka Elys.

Rhyan kept his hood down, and I adjusted mine. I'd been careful to keep my hair concealed whenever we were out-side, especially since the Elyrian woman had caught my hair at the brothel. Since then, I'd been sure to keep it covered every hour of the day until night fell. The morning sun was pale from the gray winter sky, but it would be enough to bring out the true Batavia red I was known for and give us away.

Rhyan and I didn't have to say anything to each other; we both knew there was only one reason for this number of soturi to be present and on guard in a tiny village. They were looking for us. What wasn't clear was who'd sent them. Imperator Hart had to have known exactly where we were going the minute Rhyan had stolen the key.

We'd been betting on reaching Glemaria first—on Rhyan's father being slowed down by politics and Arianna's conse-cration—but there was nothing stopping him from putting out an alert to find Rhyan. To find the forsworn murderer, and thief, and bring him back to his father for justice.

If they found me, I'd be brought before Arianna and locked up without any chance of escape, or any chance of finding my sis-ters, finding my power. Or I could be sent to the Imperator and forced to marry Viktor—assuming they still believed Brockton and his wolves had killed each other.

For a second, there was a flash in my mind of my sword going into Brockton. The light leaving his eyes.

Rhyan squeezed my hand, immediately sensing my distress, but said nothing. We'd moved into a crowd, and he took a few steps back, placing us behind an Aravian family of mages huddled together and staring at the soturi, their starfire blades gleaming with flames even in the shallow rays of the sun.

His other hand reached for me, sandwiching mine between his. His thumbs rubbed soothing circles on any bit of my skin he could touch. "They don't see us," he said under his breath.

I nodded shakily.

It didn't really matter whose orders the Soturi of Ka Lumerin were following or who they'd allied with. Anyone catching us immediately stopped us from everything we needed to do.

But it seemed we'd escaped detection. The green cloaks were fading, as the soturi stepped into their new placements.

I heard several of the villagers moving on, muttering to themselves about the ridiculousness of so many soturi on guard, especially during the day. Northern soturi spent more hours guarding in the night, protecting against the akadim hiding within their borders.

As the crowd dispersed, my eye caught on one soturion standing in the center of the village who wasn't moving or hiding. His brown leather was a sharp contrast to Rhyan's black armor, and his cold eyes were an icy blue I could see even from a distance. He wore his hair cropped severely short, reminding me of Aemon, except this man was blonde, and he kept turning his head, glaring at everyone like he was searching for someone.

For us.

"Pretend to look at apples," Rhyan said quietly, directing me to a fruit stand.

We both had styled our soturion cloaks to cover our armor, to keep any sort of identifying features hidden. No one could see that Rhyan was Glemarian or that I was Bamarian. But they'd know we were soturi, and if anyone decided to talk to us, we'd need to leave immediately.

I was tempted to say fuck breakfast. We needed to go. But our entire mission was dependent on Rhyan's magic, and that was dependent on his energy. If he didn't eat, we weren't going to get very far.

"Let me get the food," I said. "You need to get out of here. Your face is more recognizable than mine."

"No."

"Rhyan, please. If I'm caught, I'll most likely be safe and sent back south. If you're caught—" I shook my head. "You can't get caught."

"I can skip breakfast."

"No, you can't."

He'd only just recently gotten his full strength back, and then immediately, we'd fought akadim, gone under a frozen river, and traveled. Plus, there was everything else that had happened last night....and this morning.

"I'll get the food. I'll call if I run into trouble," I said, affecting my voice with the command of an Heir to the Arkasva, something I hadn't done in some time.

I supposed I no longer had a right to do it. Not until I fixed things. But I was right about this, and he knew it. He was just stubborn and protective.

But so was I.

He nodded, a look in his eyes warning me to be careful.

I walked inside the restaurant, full of wooden chairs and tables, and made my way to the bar to place an order for food we could take with us. The hall was packed, I supposed because it was so close to the border and all of the soturi who were stationed here. Luckily, that made me less noticeable, and I was able to pay for breakfast and exit without speaking to anyone aside from the restaurant staff. I'd tried to speak in a low voice, not wanting to emphasize my lack of a northern accent or draw any more attention my way. Somehow, I'd been lucky.

An hour later, the border was in sight. Soturi were on guard, standing every few feet, the way I'd expected them to be in Bamaria after the akadim attacks. Some were obvious in their stance while others blended into their surroundings thanks to their cloaks. But the fact that so many were out in force, a mixture of black and brown leather, had my nerves on edge.

This felt like a direct threat from Imperator Hart. Like he was taunting us, trying to convince us he would win.

Rhyan paled at the sight of the wall of soturi. They couldn't see us—we were too deep in the dark of the closely knit trees of the Aravian woods, our cloaks blending us to near invisibility. But we had a clear view of them.

"I'm going to guess this is not a typical amount of soturi for border patrol," I said.

"Certainly not during the day. This is even overkill for the night watch against akadim."

"Travel?" I asked. This was starting to feel like one of those times where it was going to be necessary. If there were this many soturi in Aravia, on the Glemarian border, the likelihood of there being soturi waiting for us on Gryphon's Mount was high. Though, considering the secrecy of what hid there, we were both hoping the number of soturi sent by Rhyan's father would be limited.

Rhyan had spent the morning leading us to where the Aravian border had been the least protected from what he remembered, where he'd been able to get through with his friends before he'd left the north, but there were no openings for us to slip through now.

"I think we have no choice," Rhyan said. "We shouldn't linger." He was still pale, his scar pronounced. "Come here to me."

I stood in front of him so the toes of our boots touched and wrapped my arms around his back. His hands slid down my sides and back to grip my ass, squeezing as he pulled me against him.

"I'm not going to let go," I said, locking my fingers together behind him.

He rocked against me, his eyes darkening. "Just wanted an excuse to touch you."

My body instantly responded to his, and I gasped. "You're going to have to apologize to me again."

"Happy to do so. I didn't get to spend enough time worshipping this part of you." He caught my earlobe between his teeth and gently tugged.

"You have so much to be sorry for," I hissed.

"I'll start groveling...on my knees."

With that, my stomach tugged, and my boots left the ground. We landed on the other side of the border. I felt the crunch of snow beneath me and sticks and brambles from the dense forest trees around us. Rhyan let out a small moan and leaned back against the nearest sun tree, which was ancient looking with pale white-gold bark. His shoulders were rising and falling rapidly, his gaze distant.

There were no soturi in sight, nor akadim or anything else I could see from a quick scan of the Glemarian trees stretching over us. Nothing specifically that could have caused his distress.

I took his hand. "You okay?"

His shoulders shook fiercely, his body trembling. I pressed my body back to his, my arms around his shoulders. "Breathe, Rhyan. Breathe for me. You're okay. You're okay now. I've got you."

I could see his flirtation beyond the border now for what it was. A distraction. A distraction he'd desperately needed before crossing the threshold to return to his home after over a year away, after being forced into exile.

I'd seen Rhyan's moods go to extreme lows, and I'd seen him rage. But I'd never seen him have a full-fledged panic attack before. I could only imagine what he was feeling, being here for the first time since his mother had died and he'd been named forsworn. This was his home. The placed he loved and missed. His birthright. Yet it was the place where he'd suffered the most, the place where he'd lived under his father's worst mental and physical abuse.

"Rhyan, I need you to look at me." I ran my hands down his arms and took his hands into mine.

He nodded, staring into my eyes. But it was clear he could only half see me.

"Rhyan, I need you to take a breath. Can you do that for me? Ready? You're going to inhale. Good. Now let it out. Nice and easy. I'm right here."

His nostrils flared, his breath coming up short. I tried again, pressing harder against him, nodding in encouragement. At last, he followed my breathing pattern.

"Good, you're doing so good. Keep looking at me. Good. Squeeze my hand."

He did, gently, most likely afraid he'd break it if he squeezed too hard. He'd once told me to squeeze his as hard as I could, that I wouldn't break him. But with his strength, the reverse wouldn't be true—not until I had my power.

I looked around for something else he could focus on, but I had a feeling the entire country of Glemaria, the very knowledge he was on his ancestral soil, was bringing this about. Though he'd never said it, I was pretty sure he found traveling overall to be triggering for his anxiety. Especially when here, especially where he'd been punished for it.

He needed a distraction, but there was nothing—only trees, only Glemaria.

I unhooked my armor, letting it fall to the snow, and unbuckled my belt. I grabbed his hands and shoved them up my tunic, inside my shirts to my bare skin. I shook off a small shiver, allowing the cold under my clothing. His aura was wild now, storming around us, nearly as bad as it had been the first time I'd learned he had such debilitating nightmares.

He stilled, his eyes widening, truly looking at me now. His fingers pressed into my belly and I breathed slowly, in and out.

"You're okay," I said, as his storm intensified around us. "I'm here this time. We're staying together. I doubt your father's even in the country. And even if he is, he can't hurt you. He can never hurt you again. Remember? Rhyan, you got away. You escaped. You're stronger than him. And you're stronger than you were back then. You tore the rope. Anything else that happens, you will survive. You can fight, and you can win. You can tear that rope again and again. And this time, I'm tearing it right along with you."

He squeezed me, rougher than his usual touch, but I welcomed it. I welcomed anything that would help him feel better.

"Remember who you are," I said, rising on my toes to kiss him. *"Rakame."*

The blizzard ceased. His aura was calming. Finally, he let out a solid, heavy breath, sliding his arms around me.

"Gods," he groaned. "Sorry."

"You're okay," I said. "Nothing to apologize for. How are you feeling?"

"Ready to do this." He looked down at my discarded armor and belt, lifting his good eyebrow, before kissing me. "Thank you." Bending down, he picked up my belt, then fixed the pleats of my cloak.

By the time I was armored up and ready to go, there was a growling screech in the air, and then another, the sounds like a seraphim turning into a lion.

"Look." Rhyan pointed, and in the sky, three gryphons flew by. Their fur and feathers were a mix of bronze, silver, and gold. "Told you. They make that sound all the time when they're together," he said ruefully. A boyish smile spread across his face.

I smiled in return, so grateful to see him returning to his usual self, even though we couldn't stay here. Any lingering was especially dangerous for us. I hated that he couldn't simply enjoy Glemaria—at least, the parts of Glemaria he could enjoy—but that day would come. When his father was gone.

"To Gryphon's Mount?" I asked.

"To Gryphon's Mount." His lips tightened, and he had a look of determination in his eyes, which were blazing, focused. And we were off.

Rhyan kept us to the trees, to the wilds—off the beaten paths—which meant my first trip to Glemaria involved me not getting to see any of his country, so my impressions of it basically came down to the fact that it was cold. The coldest country of the Empire by far. The snow here was the heaviest and thickest. And every path Rhyan took us on was uphill, so my calves were burning.

But the air smelled fresh. Like pine. Like Rhyan. And that softened my feelings toward Glemaria by a considerable degree.

We hiked through lunch as the late afternoon sun faded. The Soturi of Ka Hart were extremely present, but none seemed to venture too deeply into the woods. Rhyan's father may have warned them to look for his son, but he was never going to reveal Rhyan's vorakh and the likelihood of him getting into the country the way he had, so him entering these woods unseen was probably beyond the realm of their thought.

The woods filled with shadows as a fresh bout of snow began to fall. I huddled as close to Rhyan as I could, my soturion cloak hooded over my face, catching the snowdrifts.

Just as the sun set—the sky darkening with the night, the gryphons on patrol, and the snow falling even harder—we reached the bottom of Gryphon's Mount. The giant creatures glided through the sky, and the nearby chatter of soturi trying to distract themselves from the plummeting temperatures could be heard easily at the mountain's base.

Rhyan sucked in a breath, scanning the horizon. We couldn't just travel to the seraphim. We were going to need to travel in small bursts, checking for soturi at every landing to see just how many guarded the statue.

"I'm not sure if we're going to get through this without more blood on our hands," he said quietly. "So fucking stupid. My father using them for this."

I followed his gaze up. "We'll do our best."

Wrapping me in his arms, Rhyan closed his eyes, and we took our first jump.

CHAPTER THIRTY-SIX

MORGANA

MY EYES FLEW OPEN, and immediately I knew I was lying in a bed—a proper bed with pillows and sheets and blankets, not scraps of hay tossed over a pile of dirt. My chest tightened as I stared up at the ceiling.

Rock.

My eyes burned, a pit sinking low in my belly. I was still in the cave, still prisoner, still trapped. I squeezed my eyes shut, shivering. Fear and cold were consuming me. I was freezing. The air felt so much colder than it had before. Damper, too. My arms were covered in goosebumps, and my teeth chattered as I tried to get my bearings.

Gods, I wished I were still sleeping. That had been my only reprieve since I'd been taken. I'd had no dreams or nightmares. In my sleep, I had ceased to exist. I had been in nothingness, which was far more preferable to my reality.

Strange. I used to fear the idea of nothing, of being an un-formed soul, of the world not yet created. Now I'd take that over this, over being captured by akadim, in a heartbeat.

How long had it been? Days? Had actual days passed? A week? I'd spent so much time sleeping and waking in the alcove where I'd been tied up, I had no concept of time.

My stomach roiled. Nerves. Terror. And I was starving. When was the last time I'd had food? Two days? Three? Longer? I knew I hadn't eaten a thing since I'd been taken. I vaguely remembered dirty water being shoved down my throat when I'd been half-conscious on the rope. I'd nearly gagged, it had been so disgusting. But I'd been thirsty, my throat so dry I'd thought it'd kill me.

How long could a Lumerian survive without food?

And where was Meera?

I pulled my hands through my hair. My fingers got stuck; my hair was a knotted, tangled mess.

Groaning, I pulled my hands out, my broken fingernails tearing some strands from my scalp. I wiped them off on my dress, which was caked in dirt and sand and bodily functions I was becoming far too fucking aware of by the smell wafting toward my nostrils. I pressed my fists against my temples, trying to breathe through my mouth. For the first time in as long as I could remember, I didn't have a headache—it was literally the only thing I hadn't suffered from since my capture.

Where had this bed come from? Did I dare leave it to find Meera?

The girl I'd seen earlier flashed in my mind. Naked. Assaulted. Tortured. Probably an akadim by now. She'd be taller, her body full of red stretchmarks, her skin paler, her nails elongated into claws.

I stared down at my own hands, dirty and disgusting but human. Lumerian. Not the hands of a monster.

My shoulders shook. If what had happened to the girl I'd seen in that alcove happened to Meera, I'd never forgive myself.

I pushed back the covers and stood. My legs wobbled, weak, not used to bearing weight.

Then a thought entered my mind, clear and sharp, painful. *Morgana?*

It was Meera. She was awake. She was alive.

My whole body was sore, and walking felt foreign, but I moved from the alcove, too afraid to call back and draw attention to myself. I had to get to her. I had to find my sister.

I passed through the threshold into the cavernous hall around me. The rock formations— their color, their scent—felt different. This wasn't the same cave as before.

A chill ran down my spine. We'd been transported again while unconscious.

Morgs! Where are you?

I walked more quickly, peeking into the different alcoves. More beds like the one I'd been in—proper beds—appeared, but they were all empty.

Come on, Meera, give me a clue. Give me something to work with.

They're taking me.

I ran, energy that I shouldn't have had firing through my legs. I peeked inside every alcove, around every corner, until I found myself going down a long narrow hall leading downward, deeper and deeper into the cave.

Stupid one-way vorakh.

Terror was ringing through Meera's aura. I had to be getting closer—I could always feel her at a distance, but this was too powerful. I ran farther, going deeper, the lights of the torches dimming. There was a salty, mineral-like scent in the air, and it was growing warmer, humid.

Gods. They're taking my clothes. I can't fight them.

I slowed, opening my mind. I needed to see what she was seeing. I needed a location, a view, something to help me find her.

Then I was in—seeing through her eyes. Blue waves glowed against the cavern wall and low ceiling. Warm water pushed like a tide against her feet. An akadim gripped her. It was the girl I'd seen. Murdered. Changed. Now, it was tall, its eyes red, its skin torn, its teeth fanged.

But there wasn't any hunger or violence in its eyes.

Meera struggled against it, fighting to keep her dress on, filthy and disgusting as it was.

"Stop!" she screamed.

I could hear her—with my ears, not my mind.

I kept going. I had to reach her.

"Clean you!" roared the akadim.

The floor sloping beneath me evened and became damp, the stones growing warmer and warmer. I saw Meera ahead with the akadim, which was no longer fighting to undress her but simply sliding its clawed nails through the fabric until it fell from Meera's body in shreds.

She was naked, her body pale and thin, wide swaths of her skin bruised and cut.

"MEERA!" I screamed, racing forward. "Get your hands off her!"

The akadim ignored me, gesturing to the water beyond.

"You, too," said another akadim. Another female.

"Bathe," it ordered.

"What?" I asked.

"BATHE," it roared.

I stumbled back, my heart pounding. Then I realized where we were. It was a hot spring. A bath. A warm bath.

We were being cleaned. There were no male akadim in sight.

"Why?" I asked. "What for?"

"He's coming," said the akadim, its voice gravelly.

"Who's coming?"

"Maraak," it said, its voice lowered in reverence. "He wants you both bathed for the meeting."

"Maraak?" I asked, my mind flitting through High Lumerian for the translation. Fuck, Lyr would know. Then I remembered. It meant king. I narrowed my eyes at the akadim. "Who is your Maraak?"

"Moriel," it said.

Moriel was a god. Moriel was gone. Moriel hadn't walked this earth in centuries.

But neither had Asherah.

"No," I yelled. "I will not bathe for him. I do not take orders from dead gods."

"BATHE," the akadim roared, now coming for me, its claws out. I was going to be stripped, too, my dress torn to pieces.

I glanced over my shoulder to see Meera being herded into the water, her body vanishing beneath the clear blue. Her akadim kneeled at the edge, grabbing her hair and pulling her back, forcing her head under water.

"STOP!" I screamed.

But then it pulled Meera back up and removed a bottle of shampoo from a basket I hadn't noticed. It was actually bathing her.

I'm okay, Meera thought, trying to add a note of bravery to her thoughts. *It's strange. But I'm okay. I think it's safe to get in.*

A part of me wanted to. I desperately wanted a bath. A hot one. And soap. I wanted rooms full of soap to rub against my body. In every scent that ever existed. I wanted to bathe for a week. I'd never felt this disgusting in my life.

But I'd be damned before I let one of these monsters force me into the water, bathe me against my will like a child, touch me with their undead hands.

"I will not," I roared. "If your Godsdamned King Moriel wants me bathed, then he can clean me himself. Until then," I gestured at my soiled dress and hair, "he caused this mess. He did this to me. If he really is here, if he really has deigned to walk the earth again, and he really wants to meet me, then the least he can do is smell the stench of what he caused."

The room suddenly darkened, not from lack of torchlight, but an aura. One that was familiar. One I'd felt thunder through Bamaria more times than I could count. It was shadowy, deep, dark, and full of death and rage.

I could feel something ancient, too. Something unleashed that hadn't been there before. Something that had been hidden, tempered for years, and was now free.

The akadim fell to their knees, prostrate and whimpering.

Boots echoed down the hall.

You were saying? The thought entered my mind, sharp as a knife, clear as it had been the first time he'd spoken to me this way.

My hands were shaking. My knees were buckling.

This couldn't be. He couldn't be—

He stepped into the cavern. *If you want me to give you a bath, kitten, you know I'd be more than willing. But you should also know that after I scrub the dirt and grime from your body, I'll be feasting on it. Exactly the way you like it.*

"No," I cried. "No. No." He couldn't be. He couldn't have done this. "I trusted you!"

Men lie, he thought. *You knew that well. But here's what you didn't know, Morgana. Gods also lie.*

You fucking bastard!

My head was swimming. His thoughts like dark shadows beating against every corner of my mind. And somewhere in the back of it, I could hear Meera. Hear her shock. Her disgust. Her betrayal as she recognized his face.

His eyes darkened as he walked toward me, the akadim still bowed, cowering in fear.

"You!" Meera yelled.

But he only shook his head. "Later."

I felt his aura sweep around me in black shadows that hid us from the world. The cave was gone, and so was Meera and the spring. It was just me and him.

"Come," he said, taking my wrist in his hand. I was so filthy, the gesture pushed the dirt caked on my wrist toward my hand. "You wanted me to bath you. Then I will."

"What about Meera?"

"She will not be harmed. And neither will you. Come. I will explain."

I let him lead me away, the shadows plunging me into darkness that didn't lift as we walked. Somehow, he knew his way around, and when he let the light return, I found myself in another cavern. A large bed, fitted with sheets and pillows lay in the center. And beyond it another spring, far smaller than the one Meera had been forced into. This one was closer to the size of the bathtubs we had in Cresthaven.

"Get in," he said.

"I'm not fucking listening to you," I said, snatching my hand from his grasp.

He brought his hand to his nose and sniffed, making a face of disgust. "There. I've given you exactly what you wanted. I've smelled what I've caused. And I am sorry. Now let me fix it, and explain."

"No!"

"Kitten," he said, a warning in his voice. "Did you not demand I bathe you myself? Come, I know how much you want this."

He brought his hand down before me, and my dress fell, shredded to pieces at my feet.

I stood in silence as he removed his armor and stripped off his shirt, standing before me, his muscular chest beautiful, strong.

A god incarnate.

He took my hand and led me into the waters.

Instantly the feeling of heat soothed my skin, but even better was the sensation of the layers of filth lifting from my body.

He sat at the edge of the spring, producing a wash cloth and soap. Fuck. The scent of clean. I almost cried.

Fucking bastard.

He pushed my hair off my shoulders, running the washcloth down my back.

"I told you before to be prepared to do anything."

I snapped back from his touch. "I didn't know that anything included being kidnapped with my sister by akadim! That it included being ripped from my home, tortured and assaulted by monsters, starved and left in filth for days."

He lifted my chin in his hand, bringing the washcloth down my cheek. "I will make it right." Then he returned to my back, running soap across my shoulders. "The akadim are brutish but a necessity that you will understand soon. No soturi will rise up against the Emperor. And despite the twelve countries all belonging to the Empire, we are far from united. You know this."

I stared ahead, refusing to answer, as he lifted my arm to wash beneath it.

You don't have to speak, he thought. *As long as you listen.*

"Thanks for the fucking choice."

The washcloth slid across my collarbone. *Here is your choice. If we are going to do what we said, if we're going to liberate the vorakh, rescue Jules, allow our kind to have any semblance of a future in this world, then we need an army that can vanquish the Emperor's forces. He doesn't just have the largest number of soturi behind him. He has vorakh, seeing the future, reading everyone's mind. Traveling his spies from place to place.*

The Empire has turned on our people, keeping them as slaves, serving in the palace where it sucks out their life and power for its own purposes, siphoning their magic, torturing, imprisoning and murdering them—all while the Empire makes a profit in the end.

I scented a fresh wave of soap. A mix of herbs and flowers. The dirt was moving into the water, off my body as he moved his ministrations lower, scrubbing gently across my breasts.

But you and I? We can change this.

I shook my head. "Why me? Why choose me when there are others? Why put me in this role? I never asked for any of this."

"You are special, Morgana." He lifted my other arm. "You always were. The time has come for ancient promises to be fulfilled. For ancient wrongs to be righted. For primal enemies to meet their due."

"Stop! Stop speaking in fucking riddles. This isn't you! Just speak plainly, because I'm holding on by a fucking thread."

Isn't it? Isn't this me? Haven't I spoken to you this way since the start?

He had. But only in my mind. Out loud, at Court...he'd been straightforward. And I'd never mistaken that *him* for the *him* who visited me alone. Who plotted. Who concealed his vorakh. Who helped me tame mine from time to time.

He turned me to face him. "Then I'll speak plainly. Did you think it a coincidence that you were born the sister of Asherah's reincarnation? Did you not think you might have the divine in you as well?"

"No. No. I didn't." I'd barely believed it of Lyr. Barely understood any of this. Gods were gods. Not mortals.

"Seven Guardians of the Valalumir," he said. "Seven cast from Heaven. Seven burdened with mortality, with materialization, with reincarnation again and again until our Empire devolved into the cosmic joke it is today. I've known a long time who I am. I remembered. And now, Asherah has awakened with light from the Valalumir inside her body once more. Now all of the ancient players will remember who they are, will know they've traveled through the cosmos to play their parts once again. To finish what was started."

"And I'm one of them?" I yelled. "A part in this play?"

"You are more than a part. You are the center."

His thumb moved across my cheek. and I flinched from his touch.

His eyes narrowed. "My akadim could not touch you. Blood-cursed, they call it. It's not your vorakh. It's your connection to the light—to the Valalumir. To the part of you who once walked on water, who reigned in Heaven as a goddess. It was awakened inside you the moment Asherah was. You know. You've felt your vorakh more intensely than ever. You saw it in Meera's vision. You saw the goddess wake up, looking through the eyes of your younger sister. And you, you will soon come to know who looks through yours."

My heart pounded. *Looks through my eyes?* I shook my head. "Who then? Who am I?"

He grinned. "You were once called Ereshya. Goddess of the Orange Ray. Your hair was raven black, much as it is now. You were beautiful but forbidden. Regal and intelligent. Crafty, sometimes cruel. Unlike Auriel and Asherah—*we* showed control. We performed our duty. But not on earth—on earth, you were mine."

My heart was hammering. I shook my head, the truth of his words piercing some inner piece of my soul I didn't yet understand. Tears burned behind my eyes. This couldn't be happening. Couldn't be true. And yet.... "And Meera? What part is she playing in this little play of yours? Why did you drag her into this? You should have left her alone."

"I have my reasons. In time, you will know every one of them."

I scoffed, looking away.

Do you doubt who I am? he asked.

The twisting in my stomach, the gut-wrenching knowing intensified. I didn't doubt. I believed he was who said as much as I believed Lyr was Asherah.

But me? Ereshya?

"What exactly do you want me to do? And what the hell do you mean by 'finish what we started'? I started nothing! I was the second daughter of the arkasva. I've been a noblewoman my entire life—meant to be in the fortress, to look pretty and serve on the Council. I've done nothing to deserve this. And I don't remember any of what you're talking about. If it's true—it's not me. It was someone else. No one has ever called me Ereshya, because I'm not her. She's dead. Like Asherah was dead. Like you're supposed to be dead." A tear rolled down my cheek. Fuck. Fuck.

He nodded, brushing it away with his thumb. "I know. Yet here I am, reincarnated. As are you."

"So fucking what! I'm not a goddess now. Why bring me into this?"

"Give it time. Your head's been so full, but your memories are going to return. Everyone's are. Together, we can restore the Valalumir. We can reforge the light, reclaim our divinity, and take the Empire down into the bowels of hell where it belongs. The first of the lost shards is about to be discovered. For centuries it's been buried, but soon, it will shine again. Restore me. Restore you. Asherah is bringing it herself. If my scouts are correct, she will be approaching the shard by nightfall."

"You mean Lyr?"

He nodded.

"You fucking asshole! You know Godsdamned well her name is Lyr. Not Asherah."

"Lyriana is her name now. But you will find in time, that the names merge, and there is little difference between them. It is the soul that matters—the soul that lives on."

"Is she safe? What have you done to her?" I seethed.

"Nothing," he said, sounding amused. "She is safe. I swear. She has just entered Glemaria with her lover. You know how he keeps an eye on her. I have seen the reports. She is coming, believing she will rescue you and Meera. Do not worry."

"Believing? What does that mean?"

"I offered her a trade. Your lives for the shard."

"Fuck you," I said.

"Hmmm," he said. "I've missed you."

"If you think I'm coming to your bed after this—"

"You will. But I'll wait until you're ready."

In the distance, metal bars rattled as if someone was being held in a cage. Magic hummed over the sound as if trying to conceal it. I recognized the sound as a magic ward. If I was hearing correctly, there were several of them. The room darkened and lightened.

He tilted my head back, washing my hair.

The bars rattled again, the metallic thuds echoing through the spring. The wards buzzed as if in distress, as if some power was fighting them. Weakening their defenses.

"What is that?" I asked.

Prisoner, he thought simply.

"Another reincarnation."

"No. Something far more dangerous."

I closed my eyes, trying to keep myself from panic, from the verge of tears. And I desperately tried to keep my mind blank as he washed the weeks' worth of grime from my hair. I was lathered, shampooed, and conditioned, until for the first time in as long as I could remember, I felt clean. Almost like myself.

A mage stepped into the cavern, carrying a tray. "I have her food, Maraak."

"You bitch!" I yelled, recognizing her at once. This was the chayatim, the mage with the sigil of the Emperor tattooed across her cheek. The vorakh who'd herded me and Meera to the beach—to the very spot where the akadim took us. She wasn't working for the Emperor. She was working for *him.* For Moriel. She'd tricked us.

I felt his hands wrap around me, a gentle restraint.

The mage sneered, but set down the tray on a small table by the bed with her stave. Pointing it back toward the entrance, she muttered an incantation and a silky black dress floated into the room as well.

"For you to wear when you're clean." She bowed. "Is it time?"

He nodded. "Go now." Then stroking my hair, he said, "All clean." He reached for some oils scented with jasmine. My favorite, and began rubbing the oils through my hair.

The same noise from earlier sounded again. Like prison bars rattling.

"I'm going to check on that," he said, standing and pushing his tunic back over his head. He brought fresh towels from a table to the spring and patted them. "Dry off when you're ready, kitten. Get dressed and eat. Then we'll talk some more."

"And what if I decide to leave?" I asked, staring at the open cavern. No guards were present. And other than Meera, and that bitch who'd betrayed us—Parthenay. I'd pulled her name quickly from his mind, there were no other Lumerians here.

"My akadim will not let you."

"They can't touch me."

"They couldn't," he said. "But now they can. I've shared my blood with them."

"What!"

"Call it a kind of kashonim. It gives them the ability to fight the blood-cursed, those with divine blood, those who were Guardians. And it allows me to draw on their strength. You'll never get out."

I squeezed my eyes shut. The bars rattled in the distance, more violently forceful than before. The sound echoing.

"Where's Meera?" I demanded, worried he'd lied again—that she was now behind bars.

"She is safe. Fed. Clean. You have my word. I'll be back soon."

I waited for him to leave, before I stood and toweled off, still rubbing at my skin until I was raw and red.

My stomach growled, and I couldn't resist any longer. I slipped into the dress and sat down to eat the food Parthenay, the chayatim girl, had left.

I opened my mind, imagining the obsidian walls parting, allowing in any thoughts I could find. I needed to know who else was here. Who was prisoner. And where Meera was, if she was really okay. But I could only hear her faint ramblings. She was far, her mind quiet. But she seemed content. Cleaned up, and eating—just as he said. Her heart was racing with what she had seen. Who she had seen. But it was a far cry from the way her heart had been racing in terror since we'd been taken.

The rattling became more persistent and I closed my eyes, straining my ears. Who was it? Who else was here?

Not Lumerian. I couldn't hear their mind. Akadim? Or was I simply weakened from being here? Was it possible they'd taken the elixir?

No. That wasn't it. It was that the prisoner wasn't human—I was locked out of their mind. There was only one other race of Lumeria who could evade my thoughts—the Afeya.

All at once, the ceiling filled with glittering Valalumir stars. They fell slowly into the water. I turned, seeing hundreds upon hundreds of stars spinning and glowing with light. It was the presence of an aura. It wasn't Lumerian. Only Afeya could cast their auras out like this.

Be careful. A thought forced itself into my mind. *He'll fuck you and soothe your body with oils and perfume. But if your sister is successful in coming here, you'll be just as much a prisoner as I am. Even if your bars are invisible.*

Mercurial? I asked.

First Messenger of Her Royal Highness, Queen Ishtara of the Star Court, High Lady of the Night Lands.

You fucking bastard. You— My thoughts cut out—something in his powers able to freeze my mind.

Killed your father? He taunted. *Forced your sister into a deal? Do not speak on matters you do not yet understand. He may call you Goddess, but you are not yet. Not to me.*

And what about him? He imprisoned you—didn't he! I thought Afeya were more powerful than Lumerians.

He purred in my mind. *You thought correctly, my raven-haired lady.*

I narrowed my eyes. *Then how were you imprisoned?*

I was not captured by a Lumerian. But a man testing his God-power. It's very dangerous to mix your blood with akadim. He will pay a price for this. Moriel should know better.

Great. *What the fuck do I do?*

Ah, ah, ah. Even while I am imprisoned—I am not one you should ask questions to. You are not beyond a deal with me yet.

And I will not be here much longer. His magic grows weak. If you ask me anything again, I will require a bargain.

I would never deal with you.

Mercurial laughed in my mind. *No. You never did want to. Do what you wish, my remembered Ereshya. My prison bars are thinning by the hour. The very magic he wants to restore his power will release mine. His window to keep me is fast coming to a close. And by the Gods, and the stars upon my queen's head, he will pay.*

I have no doubt, I thought.

Never forget, I am immortal. And I am by far, the most destructive force in this cave. You would fare much better with me.

No.

I leave you to your choices. As always. But, consider this a favor from an old acquaintance. A piece of advice, if you will. If you do not get out soon, I promise you, he will trap you for eternity.

THE THIRD SCROLL:

THE RED SHARD

CHAPTER THIRTY-SEVEN

LYRIANA

THE WAXING MOON SHINED above as my feet hit the crunch of snow on Gryphon's Mount. Rhyan had taken us up the side of the mountain, and we rested on the edge of a cliff. We were still, searching for soturi in silence. Rhyan had bypassed the usual way of reaching the seraphim—coming from his father's keep. The snow and flatness of the mountain's base made it impossible to walk or hike up. It could only be climbed, and there were soturi in place to spot anyone who attempted to do so.

But landing where we had—almost halfway to the top, where there was no truly viable entrance—we found ourselves alone.

The cliffs were sharp with jagged edges, uneven and rough. A valley surrounded the craggy, snow-capped mountains, and against the wind and falling snow, gryphons called to each other. Their screeching and growling so much louder now that we were off the ground. Intense gusts of wind threatened to blow me back, all generated by the powerful force of their wings.

With a quick nod indicating we could continue forward, Rhyan moved ahead, leading the way. This was a mage-made path that had been created over time, and used for patrol. But it ended abruptly and would force whoever was here to stop walking and start climbing—exposing them to the soturi at the top.

When we reached the edge of the path, we traveled again, landing higher on another ledge, and higher until we were as high as we could go without being in the center of the mountaintop, the center where the seraphim dwelled.

Down the long and winding pass of Gryphon's Mount was Glemaria's fortress, where Rhyan had grown up. Within it was a smaller keep called Sea Tower; we had a Sea Tower in Bamaria, too. The main keep was made of thick stone walls and turrets. Simplistic in design, it was known as Seathorne.

Somewhere in there was Rhyan's old bedroom, the place where he'd wished for his own gryphon. The place where he'd grown up.

My heart panged.

But in that moment, three gryphons soared over Seathorne, their screeching calls roaring over the wind as they formed a row and flew right over our heads.

Rhyan hugged me to him, one eyebrow furrowed with worry, as we tried to remain unseen beneath our hoods. "I feel strange."

"How so?"

"Like I'm about to travel, or like I already am traveling, but my body's still here."

I ran my palm over his forehead. "Maybe you should sit down?"

He nodded shakily; his expression haunted. "No. Let's just get this done. I don't want to be here any longer than we need to, and we still need to find our way west to the Allurian Pass."

"Just take a breath," I said, holding his gaze.

He peered ahead, silent, his nostrils flaring as his eyes roved around the mountaintop.

Six soturi were standing guard.

Rhyan cursed.

"What is it?" I asked.

"Dario's here," Rhyan said, his voice heavy.

"Your friend?"

His jaw tightened. "Used to be. Before I left." He stared at his boots, shaking his head. "I can't...I can't kill him. I already killed one friend. Killed.... Shit. I can't kill him, even if he wants me dead now." He looked ready to panic again.

"Then don't," I said. "You're not killing anyone else tonight."

"Lyr, we can't decide that for sure, no matter how much I want it to be true. Battle is battle. Death happens. He may very well have orders to kill me."

I took his face in my hands. "No, he doesn't. Remember, your father wants you alive. And I don't believe he could kill you if he was your friend."

"You don't know what I did to him. Things change."

And seeing myself kill Haleika, I knew he was right.

I swept my fingers over his eyebrow. "You'll work it out. For now, we just need to knock them unconscious before they see us. You know how to do that. Pretend it's a habibellum."

Rhyan continued watching me, his breath uneven.

"Look at me," I demanded. "You've got this. Time for *you* to get out of *your* head. It's dark, you have the element of surprise in your favor. You've taken down five soturi at once, all while bound. Rhyan, you're the strongest soturion I know—the most skilled. You can do this, and I'll be right there with you."

He nodded again but didn't look fully convinced. He knew these men. It was different, I understood that. "We have to be quick so they remain silent. If one screams, they'll alert the others."

I looked up, eyeing the shadowy outlines of their cloaks, blending in and out of the trees on top of the cliff. "Which one is Dario?" I asked.

Rhyan pointed to a soturion at the edge. Keen eyes, lined in black with thick lashes, watched the cliff. His skin was slightly darker than Rhyan's though still pale by Bamarian standards. Thick dark curls fell to his shoulders, the front pieces braided back with silver beads threaded into the knots. Even through his armor and cloak, his build was impressive. I had a feeling back in the day, he and Rhyan were evenly matched at their academy.

He was going to be the problem—he was the most out in the open. If we attacked him first, we'd alert the remaining soturi. But if we waited too long, he'd notice something amiss.

I pulled Rhyan's face to mine and kissed him. "We've got this," I said.

"I'll start on the right. You take the soturi on the left. Leave Dario for me. He's dangerous."

I nodded, noting he was giving me only two of the five soturi, the ones who weren't standing before the seraphim. Each one was by a tree or small growth.

"They're taller than you, so you're going to need to jump high. The minute you hit their back, take your cloak, wrap it around their head, and choke them. Use both your arms, tight as you can around their neck. You'll feel their head go down first. When that happens, don't let go. You're going to jump back and ease them to the ground so they don't wake."

I'd learned this before in training. But had yet to test my ability to choke someone out. Rhyan had offered, but I could never do it to him. My chest tightened, and I steadied myself, my eyes on my targets. "Ready," I said.

"I'm going to take you to the first one. Be quick and run to the second. I'll run interference if you get into trouble."

Rhyan came up behind me, his arms around my hips, positioned to lift me as soon as he reached our destination.

"Go," I said.

We jumped. My feet were airless, weightless, and then Rhyan's boots hit the ground, and he hoisted me up. I latched onto the soturion's back. Before he could finish his shout of surprise, I had the edge of my cloak over his head, shutting his mouth, my arms around his neck, squeezing as tightly as I could.

He went slack almost instantly. But I kept holding on, feeling him stumble backwards, about to fall. Keeping my arms tight, I kicked back, my feet hitting the ground with a soft thud as I carefully laid him down and removed my cloak from his face.

He was out. My heart pounded, guilt gnawing at me. But he would be okay.

One soturion down. Five to go.

I had to get to the next one. Through the trees where I'd been concealed, I could see the shadow of Rhyan already choking out his second soturion.

Three remained.

A sudden snap of movement caught my eye—Dario had shifted, his keen gaze now alert. He sensed something amiss. I felt his aura reaching out, probing. Suspicious.

I ran to my next target, staying on my toes as much as I could, and then I leapt. He yelled out before I could cover his mouth by throwing my cloak over his head. He was faster than the other, his arms reaching for his neck to block my attack. But I just managed to squeeze in, my arms choking him before he could stop me. My left arm kept the right secure as my grip tightened, and just like the first, he went down.

I gently laid him in the snow, and in the distance, heard Rhyan shift, laying down another soturion.

We were almost there.

A blade slid across my throat as I was grabbed from behind. I held my arms up in surrender, my breath still as Dario lifted me to my feet.

Rhyan was in front of us a second later.

"Take your hands off her, Dario," he snarled.

"Hello, to you, too, Rhyan."

"Release her, now!"

"Why? She mean something to you? Also, welcome back." His accent was deeper than Rhyan's, as was his voice. "You have some real fucking nerve."

"Dario, I'm sorry." Rhyan sounded desperate. "I want to explain."

"No doubt. I expect you have a great story to tell, a legendary tale to back up your crimes. Tell me, *friend*, why I should let her go? Huh? Why shouldn't she receive the same fate you afforded Garrett?" He squeezed my arm, the blade digging in—not deeply enough to cut but enough to leave me trembling. "You afforded my father." Dario spit.

"Please. I don't want to hurt you."

"Just like you didn't want to hurt anyone else here, right? It was all one big fucking accident?"

"Another time, I can explain to you. To Aiden, How fucking sorry I am. What really happened. And...I'll let you take your swing at me. As many you want. Aiden, too. But this is bigger. Please! Who ordered you here? What did they say to you?" Rhyan asked.

"You think I'd tell you? A forsworn of Glemaria? How about you drop your weapons?"

Rhyan's face fell. "I'm so fucking sorry." Then he was gone. Dario yelled as Rhyan wrenched him off of me, kicking away the blade as he subdued him to the ground. With a grunt, Rhyan tightened his hold. Dario kicked, struggling to free himself, but Rhyan was too strong, and at last, his eyes closed.

"Fuck!" Rhyan gritted through his teeth, pushing his fingers through his hair, staring in horror at his old best friend. "Fuck!"

I took his hand. "Rhyan—"

His chest rose and fell with rapid breathes. "I should have expected this. Come on. They won't sleep for long." He was already running away from me. "The seraphim's over here."

I ran to catch up to him, as Rhyan pointed ahead.

I squinted, seeing nothing but piles of snow.

"Right there," he said, taking another step forward. He took my hand, pointing my own finger at what seemed to be a build-up of ice until a blue flash caught my eye. Moonstone.

I ran ahead, finding the seraphim's head. She was positioned much like the Guardian of Bamaria—lying on her belly with the front of her body propped up by wings as she stared out toward the Lumerian Ocean.

I started pushing off the snow that covered her body, in some places shoving off heaping slabs of snow that had frozen solid.

I touched a smooth white wing, now free, and glided my hand over her back. There was a sudden jolt of energy, like a spark had burst from the statue, that exploded into my arm. I sucked in a breath as the energy raced through my body.

Heat rose in my chest. A faint golden light peaked out from my armor and tunic.

"It's lighting up." I clutched at the armor on my chest in alarm, groaning in pain. "And it's burning this time." Sweat broke out behind my neck, as my knees buckled. This felt different from the other times though. The sensation was denser somehow, and I felt nauseous on top of everything else.

Rhyan rushed to my side, catching me. Gasping, I pulled my hand from the stone, and the flames inside my heart cooled.

Rhyan reached out his palm, touching the seraphim's back right at the spot I'd touched. His face paled.

"I feel it," he said, his eyes far greener than I'd ever seen. "This surge of power." He pulled back, flexing his fingers before his face. Then his nostrils flared, as determination blazed in his aura. "Let's find the opening."

I placed my hand back on the seraphim, feeling the magic again, my arm shaking with it. Sliding my fingers over the smooth stone, I searched for the words my mother had found or any sign of an engraving.

Rhyan found it first.

"Ha zan aviskan me shyatim, cain ani chaya tha o ha yara," he read the High Lumerian inscription. I rushed to his side to peer at the words. At first, I couldn't see them, then as I moved my head, changing the angle of my line of vision, there was a flash of blue, the moonlight illuminating the words.

The sun revealed my secrets, so I hid them with the moon.

There, right below the engraving so faint, I could barely believe my mother had seen it on her own, was the seven-pointed star, its rays curved like the sun. Exactly like her rendering. Exactly like the key Rhyan had stolen from his father's sword.

"Let's see if this works," Rhyan said.

I sucked in a breath as he fished through his pouch, producing the ruby red star. He held it out to me.

I was suddenly terrified. What if it didn't work? What if this had all been for nothing?

And then...my other fear. What if it did?

Either way, we didn't have long. One of the fallen soturi was already stirring.

I held the key in my hand, finding the inscription on the stone's star.

Aniam aviska sol lyrotz, ka, e clavix. Shukroya mishverach, o tha trium.

We unlock for blood, soul, and key. Power is restored, with these three.

Asherah's soul had reincarnated into my body. Her blood was my blood. And I held the key in my hand.

More snow fell. A gryphon screeched in the distance, followed by an answering roar. Rhyan's gaze turned up.

"A scout." His voice darkened. "Hopefully, it's not looking too closely."

My hand shook as I fitted the red Valalumir-shaped key against the lock. It hovered above the carving then seemed to be sucked into the statue like it had been part of it all along. I could no longer see an edge, find the places where the key ended, and the statue began. A red light flared behind it. Batavia red.

Rhyan cursed under his breath in surprise, his eyes widening.

My heart was beating so hard, so fast.

But nothing else happened.

"Look for the opening," he said. "The key's in. So the tomb should be unlocked. We just need to lift the lid."

Frantically, I moved my hands across the statue, and just as my mother had described in her journals, there was an indentation, it was slight, but I could feel where the tomb was meant to be opened. I grasped what I believed to be the lid and I pulled, but there was no give.

"I'll try with you," Rhyan said.

He placed his hands beside mine. The moment he made contact, the star fired up, flames burning like the key was made of starfire.

Rhyan cried out in pain. A sob full of agony on his lips, as he fell to his knees, his hands slamming into the frozen snow beneath us.

I knelt beside him. "What's wrong? What happened?"

His breathing was heavy, his eyes glazed over and distant, his mouth open in horror.

"Rhyan? Rhyan?" I reached for his face, trying to lift him up, to get him to see me.

Tears rolled down his cheek. His lips shook, as he sat back on his heels, kneeling before the seraphim, before Asherah's tomb. His hands were in his lap, opening and closing helplessly.

A strange feeling washed over me. An uncomfortable familiarity. I'd seen this before. I'd seen Rhyan fall onto his knees and sit back on his heels. I'd seen it in my dream just after our kashonim had formed. I'd walked into the Temple of Dawn, a dress made of water. And Rhyan had fallen from the sky, naked. In anguish. His skin red and smoke swirled around his bared body.

The paintings of Auriel and Asherah had come to life and it was the first time, their clothes fading away after Auriel placed the red light into her heart. Into my heart.

Rhyan opened and closed his hands, making fists, just as he had in my dream. Everything looked and felt so eerily the same, I felt myself being pulled into my own dream-like state. A feeling of warmth on my cheeks. Golden sand, and a burning in my heart as light entered.

Auriel walking toward me.

"The fuck are you doing here?" One of the soturi had woken up, and I was immediately pulled back to reality.

But Rhyan hadn't been. He was still on his knees, still somewhere else, not seeing what was before him.

I unsheathed my sword, facing the Glemarian soturion. "I don't want to hurt you," I said.

"Don't worry," he said. "Because I'll be hurting you."

Our steel clashed just as another gryphon soared overhead, screeching into the snowstorm. I swung out, stepping away from the statue, not to retreat but to draw the soturion away from Rhyan. I needed him to stay clear of him until this vision or whatever was happening had passed.

The soturion charged at me, snarling.

But I blocked him easily, pushing his sword back. Using the moment of his surprise, I spun out and attacked again, my boots sliding in the snow.

With a swift lift of his arm, our blades crashed, ringing until I pulled back. His gaze fell on Rhyan.

I raised my sword over my head, breathing deeply, my breath on the air, my fingers tightening and loosening over the hilt. I couldn't miss. I didn't have much time.

I lunged to crash my sword on his shoulder, but his blade blocked me, the impact so forceful I nearly crashed into the seraphim. I grunted in frustration and spun on my heels. He'd widened his stance and had a derogatory look in his eyes, like he didn't believe I could take him.

But what he thought didn't matter. I knew how hard I'd trained, knew I'd slain two akadim, and I ran at full speed.

The soturion just barely dodged my attack that time. Had I been on grass, I would have met him, but the snow kept slowing me down. He was used to the terrain and using it to his advantage.

I swung again, using both hands, turning the sword so quickly he was forced to retreat.

And I threw out my foot, tripping him. He rolled to the ground, spinning away from me. His sword fell into the snow. He scrambled for it, but I was on him in a second, my blade poised beside his neck. I pressed it into his skin, not enough to cut him, but enough for him to take me seriously. "Stand, and I let you live."

He snorted. "You didn't kill me the first time."

"I can always correct that mistake."

"Can you, little girl?" He held up his hands in surrender, rolling his eyes as he stood. He glanced around the mountaintop.

"I've killed before," I said.

"Is that so?"

Brockton's eyes flashed in my mind. The light leaving them. I didn't want this. But if he threatened Rhyan's life, threatened mine—I could do it again.

Instead, I tossed my blade into my left hand, catching the hilt.

"Don't tell me," he said, his voice full of derision, "you're really left-handed, and now you're going finish me?"

I fisted my fingers, resting my thumb on top, just as Rhyan taught me all those months ago.

"No. I'm right-handed," I said, and punched him in the face.

He stumbled back. "You bitch." Blood spurted from his nose. He held his hands over his face.

I turned the sword in my hands, palms carefully placed around either side of the blade, the hilt pointed to me. Just as he removed his hands to see what I was doing, I struck him—exactly where I'd punched him.

He collapsed, his eyes closing.

I rushed back to Rhyan's side, sheathing the blade at my hip. "Gods, Rhyan! Rhyan!"

But he still wasn't responding. I reached for his face, cupping his cheeks, and pressed my forehead to his.

He sniffled, his chest heaving, and suddenly he was looking at me, really looking at me. His eyes filled with the same recognition I'd seen in Meera's when she was finally free from a vision.

"You're okay?" I asked. "What happened?"

"I remembered," he cried, his eyes searching mine. "It was like last time. But I couldn't control it. It took me, and I had...I had another memory. I know for sure, Lyr...I was him. I was Auriel. And it's all coming back."

Tears ran down my face, the truth of what he was saying plunging through my heart. Every pull I'd felt towards him, this sense of destiny, this hold he'd had on me, even before we ever spoke, before we were even able to form such a connection...his soul had been calling out to mine. And I'd been calling back, tugging on the thread that bound us together. That had linked us for centuries. For millennia. For lifetimes.

"Lyr," he said, his voice raw with emotion. His voice deep, layered, like he was somewhere in between himself and Auriel. Like his love for me had just grown, surpassing this life, encompassing the other, the first. I was sure of it, because that was how I felt in that moment, too.

I pulled him closer to me. "What did you remember?"

He shook his head, squeezing his eyes shut before looking at me again. "I was here. I brought your body—Asherah's body to this place—and I...I'm the one. I'm the one who put her to rest at the end. I—" His voice shook. "I used my magic to create the tomb. I used my magic to seal it. I'm the one who made the inscriptions. The one who created the key. Red. Batavia red." He covered his mouth with his hand. "Asherah's red."

Tears were falling down my face. "So it really is my tomb?"

Rhyan wiped at his eyes with the palms of his hands before pushing his fingers through his hair. "Whoever sent you that note, I don't know if they truly understood—or if they'd planned it this way. For me to also be here. It was never supposed to be you who opened it. It was me. Auriel's blood. Auriel's soul. Auriel's key."

"But Auriel's blood," I said urgently. "We don't have that."

Pinching the bridge of his nose, he said, "We do."

I shook my head. "How?" Awakening our memories may have connected us to our souls. But blood was blood. Blood was physical, material. "Rhyan, you don't..."

"No, I don't." Rhyan took my hand, his thumb stroking my skin. "But you do. You have it. Auriel's blood was in Asherah's. They were kashonim after he fell. Kashonim when they battled Moriel. Her blood is in your blood. Which means his blood is, too." He unsheathed his dagger, handing it to me.

I understood. I had do it. He couldn't. Wouldn't harm me. And was still trying to give me a choice, as little as I'd had one since my sisters were taken.

"It's okay," I said softly. "How much?" I grasped the handle.

"Only a drop," he said, looking distant, as if he were reviewing notes he'd studied for a test. He moved closer beside me, his shoulder pressed to mine, before his arm wrapped around me. "We'll open it together."

I pressed the blade to the tip of my finger and, hissing through my teeth, pushed it into my flesh.

A single drop fell into the snow, the color spreading like a blooming flower, before I held my finger over the star. Rhyan retrieved the blade, and sheathed it, as I squeezed the tip of my finger, drawing out another bead.

This one fell onto the center of the key, and all at once, the indentation of the lid flared to life, glowing bright red.

Rhyan was breathing shallowly as he pressed his finger to the key, pushing it into the stone. Into the tomb.

Magic hummed, and fires erupted around us, melting the snow. I clutched at Rhyan as the flames rose and spread, wild in the cold wind. Within seconds, we were surrounded by a ring of fire. The buzzing of a ward around the tomb flared before fading. The tomb was unlocked. And I watched in shock as the lid floated up and up and up.

I squeezed Rhyan's hand, not wanting to look, not ready to face myself, to see my old body, my death.

"It's okay," Rhyan said. "She's in a coffin. You won't...you won't see any of her, just a carving of her likeness."

My throat was dry as I stepped forward. Asherah's coffin inside the tomb was made of gold, her entire body sculpted. She was beautiful, and the details of the carvings of her face reminded me of my own. My own likeness. Her eyes were closed, and her arms folded across her chest. Space had been created in the carving beneath her arms, and tucked into them was what we'd been sent here for.

One of the original seven shards of the Valalumir, lost for centuries, was now within my reach. The crystal was the length of my forearm. It was shining and dark, pointed at the end like a sword. Gleaming beneath the fires that surrounded us. I felt an instant pull toward it. An ancient fear, like a warning in my heart. The power within this crystal, the trouble it had caused. The way it had directly led me to be standing here at this very moment...I could feel its power. Feel its strength. Feel its danger. Otherworldly. Divine. Beautiful.

And terrifying.

But then my eye caught on something beside it. A stave, unlike any I'd seen before. It was long and thin, made of the wood of a dark sun tree embedded with starfire diamonds. Someone had broken it into two pieces.

And out of nowhere a sensation overwhelmed me. A feeling of ownership, possession.

Mine.

I remembered my own stave, snapped in half by Aunt Arianna when she'd cut me off from the life I'd dreamed of—the life of a mage.

I reached for the pieces, and my hands closed around the smooth wood. *Asherah* was etched into the side in the old letters of High Lumerian.

And that was all it took. One touch. And I was her. Rhyan's face vanished, as did the fires of Gryphon's Mount. The seraphim, the tomb, all gone.

I was in battle, holding up the stave—the tip of which sparked red light—in one hand, and in the other hand holding a sword as I charged forward. Shouts rang in my ears, and in the sky agnavim, with wings of pure fire and light, soared forward against the enemy.

Then the vision was gone. And I was back on the cliff, with Rhyan, with Asherah's tomb, and six soturi who were going to regain consciousness any second. Unless the fires found them first.

I gripped the stave in both hands. I knew it was common practice for a stave to be broken upon a mage's death to prevent another Lumerian from using it. I had been one of the rare exceptions—my stave broken while I still lived, before I could ever find my magic.

"Lyr," Rhyan warned.

Smoke was billowing around us, the flames growing higher and higher.

We had to get out of here. And I saw in that moment, the fires weren't spreading out, they were moving in. Getting closer to me, to Rhyan, almost as if they were a fail-safe. Were the tomb to be opened, the fires would trap the thief.

Rhyan reached for the crystal, for the shard of the Valalumir in Asherah's arms. But nothing happened. He gripped harder, grunting, his knuckles white as he pulled. He couldn't take it.

"Is it stuck?" I asked.

"No," he said slowly. "It's not. It has a spell on it. My—Auriel's—doing as well. It's you. Only you can remove it."

I stepped forward, my palms sweating, and at last, I reached for the crystal. Light burst from it, so bright I stumbled backwards, almost falling into the flames before Rhyan grabbed me.

The lid of the tomb sank down, and the tomb resealed itself, making the seraphim statue whole again. As if we'd never been here, never touched it. The lines of the lid vanished, becoming smooth, untouched moonstone, and the key fell into the snow. Rhyan grabbed it, quickly stuffing it back into his pouch, as I felt the weight of the shard in my hands.

Fire exploded inside of me. The flames inside my heart crackling and dancing, burning me from within. Sweat poured down my face. Pain worse than I'd ever felt—worse than when Mercurial had put the Valalumir in me—brought me to my knees.

And right as I thought of him, his aura filled the mountain. Stars fell from the sky.

And his anger rumbled across the ground.

Had I broken our deal somehow? He'd threatened the Valalumir to burn me from within if I ever did. A sense of dread washed over me. And then I was gone. The flames vanishing once more, Rhyan's voice muffled. I was plunged into another memory. Back to the golden sand.

Auriel stood before me, a light in his hands too bright for me to look at with my newly mortal eyes.

"You shouldn't have come, Rakame."

"Oh, how I've longed to hear you call me that again."

"I didn't want this for you."

"And I didn't want this for you, Mekara. Please. Take this. Before it's gone. Before it's corrupted like the rest. We don't have time."

"I can't. I can't. Auriel, please. It's my fault."

"No, Asherah. The fault is mine. Please, you must. It's all that remains. It's yours. You're the only one strong enough to keep guarding it, to protect it."

I shook my head.

"It's part of the red ray of light. Yours to protect yours to guard. It has to be you. You're the fire."

The red light came toward me. Consumed me. Filled me.

Rhyan lifted me to my feet. I was dizzy, the fire still inside me.

Then Asherah appeared on Gryphon's Mount. She walked through the flames. Her hair was red, her white dress flowing and untouched, as she passed through the ring of fire.

"Use the crystal," she said, speaking in High Lumerian. But I could understand her as if she spoke plainly. "Restore the stave. Claim your magic. You were not meant to come this way. This was a mistake. Your magic was withheld because I was punished, therefore you were punished—only protecting the Valalumir would restore power for you. Doing your duty. Now it's in your arms. Protect it. Take your power now. It is your only chance to survive."

She vanished, billowing into wisps of smoke.

And as if some force beyond my control had taken over my body, I touched the crystal's edge to the stave in my other hand. Flames licked at the wood, dancing up and down it as the crystal brightened. A force beyond me opened my hand, and the sun-wood stave flew up into the air, the two halves coming together.

Red light—Batavia red—sparkled around the breaking point until the two sides were fused together, and as one piece, the stave fell back into my palm.

Magic surged through my body. Power itched inside of me, crawling, ready to explode, to be expressed.

And I pointed the stave at the flames entrapping us, ready to perform my first act as a mage.

"Ani petrova augnishi." The flames before me snaked into smoke, and I turned, pointing the stave around the entire ring of fire, extinguishing the circle into nothing more than a hiss.

"Lyr," Rhyan said in awe. "You...by the Gods! You have your magic?" He stepped closer to me, his green eyes wide. "Your aura! Lyr! I can...I can feel your aura."

I stared down at the stave, warm in my palm. It no longer said *Asherah* in the ancient text. It read *Lyriana*.

I was a soturion. But I was also a mage. And I held the first of the seven lost shards of the Valalumir in my hand.

It was time to get my sisters back.

CHAPTER THIRTY-EIGHT

RHYAN WRAPPED HIS ARMS around me, kissing my forehead, my nose, and my lips. "You have magic! Lyr! Do you feel different?" he asked.

"I do. I can feel it thrumming inside me, itching to get out."

Someone moaned behind me. And a second voice joined it. The soturi were waking up.

"Now," Rhyan said, sobering. "We need to go."

But something squeezed my waist from behind, too violently and sharply to be Rhyan or the sensation of travelling.

I looked down, and saw rope. Black bindings were snaking around our bodies, pushing us closer together.

"The fuck!" Rhyan's eyes widened as he struggled to hold onto me, and there was that familiar tug on my stomach—the one that signified traveling—the one I felt every single time Rhyan had taken me away from danger, or taken me somewhere new. But this time it was only the feeling. We didn't actually move from where we stood. We couldn't. We had both been cut off from our magic.

I met his frantic gaze. "I thought only soturi patrolled up here." And this had clearly been performed by a mage.

"They do," Rhyan seethed, then he looked beyond me. "My father wants *me*. Let her go, and I'll come willingly."

"Unfortunately, I wasn't sent by your father." A mage was on the mountain with us—she seemed to have appeared out of nowhere. She was thin, her body swallowed by her blue mage robes, her gold and silver stave shaking in her bony hand.

"Who the hell are you?" Rhyan asked.

"I'm not who you need to be worried about," she said.

"What do you want?" I asked.

She smiled, turning her head, her eyes flicking to the seraphim. "What I want, you cannot give me, unfortunately." Light caught her cheek, and a golden Valalumir tattoo—the sigil of the Emperor—shined on her face.

One of the Emperor's servants. My pulse spiked. Was she going to bring us to him?

But she shook her head. "I no longer work for him."

"What?" Rhyan asked.

And then I realized—she'd answered my question. The question that was in my mind. No one but Morgana had ever done that before. She was vorakh.

The mage grinned at me. "Exactly."

My heart pounded. *We won't tell anyone you're vorakh,* I thought desperately. *If you let us go. I won't tell anyone, not even him. I swear. Please.*

Rhyan was struggling against me, trying to break free of the ropes, his hand straining to reach for a blade, his other using all the muscle he had to simply break free. He'd done it before. Torn the rope apart—broken free of his bindings when we were in the arena, when Haleika had turned and was after me.

The shard in my hand began to glow, brighter and brighter and brighter. I had to close to my eyes and gritted my teeth as it warmed in my palm. Spots danced beyond my eyelids.

"Ah, exactly what he said would happen," said the mage.

The heat around my body from the ropes vanished, and I stared down, the spots still obstructing my vision. The shard had torn through the rope. The piece of the Valalumir in my hand was too powerful to be contained by mere mage magic.

Rhyan noticed in the same moment, his grip on me tightening.   "Go," I hissed. "Just go."

But claws dug into my hips as I was wrenched away from Rhyan's arms.

"LYR!" he roared.

I watched in horror as an akadim appeared behind him, its claws around his waist as he was lifted into the air.

"Rhyan!" I yelled, as I was lifted up by my own akadim. "You beast!" I hissed, holding the shard against it, but nothing happened, either because akadim were immune to magic or because they were stronger than the Valalumir's thrall. I kicked helplessly in the air, its claws digging painfully into my stomach.

I tried to remain logical. I could escape. I'd fought akadim before without magic, and now I had it. But my muscles weren't cooperating. I felt sluggish, sleepy, like I could barely hold my head up. My body was going still.

The mage watched us, completely undisturbed by the presence of akadim. Her eyes seemed merely curious, roaming back and forth between me and Rhyan. "I told you I wasn't the one you should be worried about."

Rhyan landed a punch against his captor, and the akadim roared, its red eyes full of violence. I saw then, it wore a silver collar—just like the akadim in the caves had.

"Now, now," the mage said. "No harm, remember." She wasn't speaking to Rhyan, but the akadim. And it seemed to listen, bowing its head.

"Why can't I move?" I asked, terror overwhelming me. I felt paralyzed, and for the first time ever, Rhyan was losing a fight.

"The binding," she said. She spoke with a sweet voice that left chills running up and down my spine. "He knew it wouldn't contain the shard. But it was a good distraction for the akadim. And a nice way to subdue you. My ropes held a simple muscle-relaxing spell, layered over the binds."

I heard the sound of flesh hitting flesh and managed to turn my head enough to see Rhyan getting punched in the face.

"NO!" I yelled. "Don't touch him. I'll kill you if hurt him!"

"He was struggling too much," the mage said, looking at him curiously. "Very strong, this one. But he'll be subdued."

"Let us go!" I could feel the akadim squeezing me, its claws digging into my flesh, bruising me, starting to draw blood.

"Don't worry. You'll be asleep any second. Time to leave."

A gryphon flew nearby, soaring straight for Gryphon's Mount. I could no longer move my arms or legs. The gryphon lifted back onto its hind legs, turning its body vertical as it came in for the landing, blowing gusts of ice and snow against me.

"Lyr," Rhyan said, his voice faint. He was losing the fight.

I watched helplessly as the girl crawled onto the gryphon's back. Rhyan's akadim mounted the gryphon next.

I kicked, trying to pry my captor's arm from around my waist, but I had no strength left.

I was carried onto the gryphon's back. Its wings spread. There was no carriage, nothing to hold onto, as its wings fluttered in powerful thrusts. Fear gripped me like a vice, as we were plunged into icy cold air, soaring higher and higher into the night's sky. Gryphon's Mount was below us, moving farther and farther away. The seraphim's moonstone vanishing into the snow, the six soturi stirring and standing.

My entire body began to shake with cold, with fear. I felt almost as cold as I had when I fell into the ice.

My stomach sank, the gryphon turning, flying faster and faster. The wind whipped violently through my air, and I could already feel the skin on my face turning red and raw with cold. I caught Rhyan's eye.

"Lyr," he said, his voice weak, the sound almost heart-breaking. "It was the scout," he said. "This gryphon. I should have known." His head fell forward, the spell finally taking down his body, his strength, but he kept his eyes on me, fighting to keep them open. Like he always did. Always fighting. Always protecting. "I'm sorry," he mouthed.

I tried to say it wasn't his fault, I tried to say it was okay, but my mouth wouldn't move, and then my eyes closed.

CHAPTER THIRTY-NINE

I FELL IN AND out of consciousness. My eyes opened to wind blowing against my face, an endless dark sky, and the shuddering pain of the cold. Even asleep, my limbs had been shaking, absorbing little heat from the gryphon's back, and even less from the akadim that held me captive. I found Rhyan's eyes. He was awake, held by an akadim on the other end of the gryphon's back.

I could tell he was trying to conserve his energy, to remain calm, keep his aura close. But he had a feral, almost crazed look to him. His eyes were on every place the akadim touched me. Noting every place its claw landed against my belly.

He didn't have to be here now. He was strong enough to break free, or simply strong enough to travel, but I knew he'd never leave without me. Getting me free from the clutches of my captor wasn't going to be an easy feat, and it was too risky to attempt while flying as quickly as we were through the night.

Plus, the mage was still watching, her stave out, her back unnaturally straight. She was so strange, unblinking, unmoving. Emotionless.

But she was also a problem. I could almost see the wheels turning in Rhyan's mind—working out every possible escape scenario.

"No," the mage said suddenly. She shook her head at Rhyan. "You'd fail."

He glared.

"Not enough time," she said, reading his mind, trashing his escape plans. "I wouldn't worry. She holds a piece of the Valalumir. She will be protected."

Why all this trouble? Why not just take the Valalumir from me? Why take us, too?

She shifted her gaze to me. "He has his reasons."

You couldn't take it from me, could you? I thought. The Imperator and Brockton had both captured me, and both left me with my weapons. Both times because they assumed I couldn't use them, couldn't reach them effectively. They underestimated me. Not realizing I wore a vadati, that I was one word away from the greatest weapon in the Empire. Rhyan.

But this mage...she should have taken this one from me. It was far too valuable, too powerful. And if she hadn't there was only one reason. She couldn't.

Her nostrils flared, telling me I was right, and she looked pointedly back to Rhyan, shooting down another one of his plans to save us.

"For fuck's sake!" he snarled. "I get it."

"If it entertains you, keep plotting. As long as you know that each one will fail."

Rhyan hissed under his breath, his shoulders shaking with cold. His eyes found mine, and his nostrils flared.

"It's okay," I mouthed to him, "I'm okay."

He nodded once, and closed his eyes for a long minute. And then he opened them, the same feral look spreading across his features. His eyes conveying all his concern.

I couldn't tell how much time had passed, maybe hours, of Rhyan and I simply staring at each other, reassuring ourselves the other was there still-alive, not hurt. But after sometime, the sky began to brighten with hints of color. Dawn approached with a faint reddish golden glow, and I felt my akadim tighten its grip on me out of distress.

"Day," it growled at the mage.

"Yes," she said in her oddly sweet voice. "It's almost time."

"Hurry," it said, its putrid breath blowing past me. I gritted my teeth, resisting the urge to gag.

Rhyan was still, watching me almost as unblinkingly as the mage. I was pretty sure that once the initial spell had worn off, he'd barely gotten any sleep, not trusting himself to be unconscious around the akadim and not trusting them to be alone with me. His hands were fisted against the restraint of the beast's arm, and his knuckles were white, his entire body brimming with a predatory stillness he only had when he was truly furious. He'd been keeping it at bay, but now that dawn approached, he was starting to slip.

Given the opportunity, he'd murder everyone on this gryphon to reach me. But I knew he wouldn't strike until we were on land.

The gryphon's head dipped down, one wing lifted, and suddenly we were racing downward, my stomach in my throat.

"It's okay," Rhyan said. "They descend fast."

Tears burned behind my eyes. Of course, gryphons descended faster than seraphim, their larger bodies and weight bringing them down. I couldn't believe this was my first time riding one—against my will, captured by akadim, and terrified.

I gave him a small nod, trying to thank him for the reassurance—for being the sort of person who, even when his life was threatened, still protected me with every tool he could possibly use.

His good eyebrow lifted, and the wind blew through his hair, turning the curls he'd had earlier into long, loose waves, bronzed gold as the sun rose.

Golden like Auriel's.

Auriel....

He looked pointedly ahead with a small jerk of his chin. An ominous-looking mountain loomed ahead. The sides of the mountain were smooth as a wall—no areas of flatland, no paths. The only way past it was to fly over it or cross through the tunnels and caves that had been created before Lumerians had reached these shores.

This was the Allurian Pass. Morgana and Meera were in there.

I looked down at the crystal I still held, trying to get a better sense of what it could do. It seemed like it should have been glowing a bright red, but other than during those first moments when I'd taken it in my hands and when I'd had the vision of Asherah telling me to use it, it had been dormant.

Rhyan's eyes were on the crystal and then on my face, as if he were thinking the same thing.

The mage waved her stave around the beast, and a dome of white light formed, creating a protective barrier to keep us from crashing. We were nearly at the ground, and our gryphon hadn't slowed.

I resisted the urge to grab hold of the akadim. To hold onto anything. Instead, I narrowed my eyes, glaring at the mage. "I thought magic didn't work on akadim."

She shrugged. "It doesn't. If they fall, they fall. But the shield will catch you."

I swallowed, only realizing then my ears had popped. The gryphon finally slowed, and we touched down.

The mage stood, staring curiously at Rhyan, who was being hauled to his feet. Immediately, he sprung into action, twisting out of the akadim's grip and reaching for his sword.

"Now's not the time to play the hero," she said, as black glittering ropes burst from her stave and wrapped around him.

Rhyan growled under his breath, his face red.

I hated to see him like this, knowing what the ropes meant to him. I turned on the mage. "You said the Valalumir would just break through it anyway."

She shrugged. "It would. That's why you get the akadim holding you prisoner."

Rhyan's captor moved to my side, growling under its breath. Its fangs poked out from its mouth as it grabbed my arm, hauling me to my feet. The one who'd held me took my other arm, and together they lifted me. Pain shot into my underarms.

"PUT HER DOWN!" Rhyan roared. "You'll break her arms."

The mage shrugged again. "She has her magic power now. She'll heal."

I kicked to no avail as the akadim stepped away from the gryphon. The mage walked ahead with one look over her shoulder, signifying Rhyan was to follow. Glaring, he walked ahead, his muscles bulging as he tried to break free from the ropes. She emitted a small light from her stave, and the akadim holding me dragged me forward until we were all inside the mouth of the cave.

I couldn't see much beyond her light—none of the torches were lit, and she made no effort to light them, clearly reveling in keeping us in the dark. I kept my eyes on Rhyan ahead of me. He kept glancing over his shoulder, making sure I was still there, making sure I was unharmed.

It felt like we'd walked an entire mile before the tunnel opened up. Then with a grunt from the akadim, I was dragged into a cavern large enough to rival the Temple of Dawn. It was full of torches and three black poles. They were about the same size as the one in the Katurium, larger than the pole Brockton had in his bedroom.

A shiver ran through me.

So much had happened since then. And for one night, I'd been allowed to forget. To feel pleasure. Love. Safety. But this...this was my life.

The mage, now in the center of the room, removed her blue hood, and the fires made the golden tattoo on her cheek sparkle.

In the light, I could see she had sunken-in, bright blue eyes and a gaunt face that made it hard to tell her age. A third akadim emerged from the shadows, growling, its eyes red. It stood around eight feet tall—small for an akadim but still enormous. Its arms extended, its claws out, as it headed straight for Rhyan.

Rhyan looked to me, his nostrils flaring—as if debating whether to fight or give in. Bound as he was, I believed he could fight off one akadim. Even two.

But here, even if he freed himself from the binds, he'd then have to fight through three akadim to get to me before the mage cast another spell.

I shook my head sadly at him, knowing from the defeated look in his eyes he'd made the same calculations.

The akadim grabbed the rope binding Rhyan and tugged him toward the first pole, where it tied Rhyan's arms above his head.

I felt sick. It was the same position he'd been forced into in the arena. The same one Brockton had forced on me.

Two more akadim emerged from the shadows, their arms out before them. And I realized then, they all had the silver collars. Every single one.

I peered more closely, finding the red centers glowing against the silver, as they moved into the firelight and I realized with horror that they were carrying my sisters. Unconscious.

"NO! Meera! Morgana!" I yelled, rushing forward only to be yanked right back into place. I hissed, knowing I would be covered in bruises—if we survived.

"Shut up," snapped the captor to my left. Its hair was long and black, and looked like it hadn't been washed in months. It smelled like it, too.

Its claws dug into my arms, and Rhyan's gaze seared into the spot where it touched me.

The akadim dumped my sisters onto the ground. Neither moved. Gods. Were they alive?

"What happened to them?" I yelled. "What is going on?"

The mage turned to me. "Akadim are sloppy. But your sisters are alive. Just asleep. Same spell I used on you and your lover."

My cheeks flamed at the fact that she'd pulled those thoughts out of me. That for hours she'd been invading my mind, and Rhyan's. I knew he'd figured out what she was—but even after a year with Morgana's vorakh—I still slipped. Still let her into my head.

The mage had no right.

She rolled her eyes. "It was quite titillating. Especially seeing the spring... through his eyes."

"Fuck you," I snarled, as Rhyan growled a string of curses.

The two akadim with Meera and Morgana hoisted them up to a seat, lifting their arms and tying ropes around their wrists. Their wrists secured, the akadim pulled on the ropes, forcing Meera and Morgana—still unconscious—to their toes, their heads lolling to the side.

"*Teka!*" yelled the mage. "He comes."

Shivers ran through my body. Moriel. Moriel was coming.

The akadim fell to their knees. The two who still gripped my arms forced me onto the ground. My knees hit the stone at the same time, and I cried out. And yet, somehow I still held the shard of the Valalumir. Still held possession of my stave—tucked into my belt.

Even the mage fell to her knees. She lifted one eyebrow at Rhyan as if to say, *Well?*

He only glared, tilting his head apologetically with a sneer. "Sorry. Tied up."

"Maraak Moriel," said the akadim. "Maraak Moriel." It was a chant. To my horror, more fires blazed to life in the cavern, popping and crackling with smoke. The light revealed row upon row of akadim. My entire body stilled. My heart threatening to hammer through my chest. One akadim terrified me. Dozens...there were dozens in this room. Even if I called on kashonim, even with my magic power...we stood no chance. Not with Rhyan bound.

Dozens of the monsters all fell to their knees, their growls echoing, their red eyes all focusing on one thing.

A throne made of black obsidian.

We were in a Seating Room. A Seating Room full of monsters. Monsters who would not hesitate to murder us, tear us apart, or worse, turn us forsaken. Turn us into akadim.

My heart was pounding, and my stomach turned, the sound of the beasts unbearable.

"Maraak Moriel," said the akadim, chanting louder, faster, their fists banging on the ground like death drums. I felt like I was going to faint.

Footsteps echoed, the sound coming closer and closer. The chants stopped abruptly. Silence fell upon the room, and then dark shadows slid along the walls, and an aura filled with darkness, anger, and thunder roared into the Seating Room.

My stomach tightened like a vice—to the point where I felt sick. I swore I knew that aura. I swore I'd felt it a thousand times before. Powerful. Strong. Deadly. The aura of a God of Death.

Moriel entered the Seating Room. His red arkturion cloak flowing behind him. His golden Bamarian armor shined to perfection.

And I looked up into the furious eyes of the Ready.

Moriel was Aemon.

CHAPTER FORTY

No. No. No.

I was going to be sick. Aemon! Aemon who had been like an uncle to me. Aemon who had vouched for me to the Imperator, secured me a place in the Soturion Academy when I was powerless. Aemon who had helped me to avoid exile. Who'd quelled the rebellion and placed my father on the Seat. Who'd overseen my protection and safety for years.

Tears welled in my eyes. My heart shattering all over again. And something cold and hard settled over my heart.

He was also Aemon who had whipped me. Who had rushed forth when the Imperator demanded a lashing. Rushed forth when he had never done so before, when it wasn't his job as arkturion to dole out punishments to novices. When he'd said, "I'll do it."

I'd thought he was saving me at the time.

Gods! I'd thought he was saving me, by hurting me. Because someone else would have hurt me worse.

Rhyan had never forgiven him for that. Too late I realized, Rhyan had been right.

Fuck!

I tried to breathe as Aemon moved into the cavernous Seating Room, his aura—heavy and full of shadows—always angry, always full of power and rage. It swept over me, tiny shivers erupting across my body, my heart hammering, my stomach turning over and over. His dark eyes fixed on me, even as he passed by where I'd been forced to kneel, even as he made his way to his Seat. He didn't look anywhere else. Not at the mage who'd brought us here. Not at my sisters, or Rhyan. Or the dozens and dozens of akadim that filled the room.

There was something openly hungry, and greedy in his gaze. Something possessive.

The Valalumir in my arms began to glow, a faint, dark light. Almost like it was answering his call.

He wasn't looking at me. He was looking at the shard. At his prize.

I squirmed, feeling the fire of my anger bursting inside. All I'd been through—all I'd suffered to get to this.

I wanted to yell, to scream, to run at him. And all this time—all this fucking time—he'd been the one who took my sisters. He'd been my enemy.

But the only thing that came out of my mouth, was a quiet, pitiful, "No."

"Bring her forward," he commanded.

"NO!" Rhyan roared, "fucking bastard!"

The two akadim holding me prisoner, hoisted me up by my arms, my feet dragging on the ground before they dropped me again at Aemon's feet.

"I knew I didn't fucking trust you," Rhyan shouted, his face red.

Aemon ignored him, watching me carefully. He wore the stern, deadly face of the Ready, the face that had been so familiar to me. The face I had always trusted.

"You're Moriel?" I demanded. "You're the reincarnation!"

"As you are the reincarnation of Asherah, and just as before, I see you have broken your vows, forsworn yourself of your oath with your lover. It's always the same. Every time. Every life. You never change. It's always him. It's always Auriel."

My chest tightened. All the fears and anxieties I'd carried for months as my feelings for Rhyan grew deeper and deeper rose to the surface. All the time I'd spent hiding it from Aemon, fearing the punishments we'd receive if he ever knew. Worrying about betraying him, betraying his trust. Trying to bury my feelings. It had been for nothing.

He'd known before we did. It was all so clear in my head now. He'd made the choice to let Rhyan stay. To make us kashonim. He knew what we meant to each other—and he'd made it a punishment for us to be who we were, to feel how we were always destined to feel.

"You put us together," I shouted. "You made us swear those oaths!"

Aemon shrugged. "Were you not well matched? Has he not taught you to fight like a warrior? Have you not killed my akadim as a result," he snarled, his voice darkening. He leaned forward in his Seat, his hand reaching for the Valalumir, glowing warmer and brighter against my arms.

"I swear to the Gods, if you touch her," Rhyan growled.

But Aemon fisted his hand and pulled back, not touching the crystal. Not touching me.

The ground shook beneath my feet, as the cave darkened. My heart jumped. And for a moment, the entire room seemed to shake, the torchlights flickering in and out. It was like the cave was going to collapse, like the walls were going to fall in. It was the same feeling I so often had during my panic attacks.

But this time...it wasn't me. The room really was shaking. Like there was an earthquake.

"I wouldn't worry about that," Aemon said smoothly. "I've had a guest for some time. But now with the Valalumir present, I expect he's preparing to leave as we speak."

"And at what point might I prepare to leave?" I asked.

"When you hand over what I asked for."

"And you'll give me back my sisters?"

Aemon only stared at me. "I will release them from their imprisonment."

"And me?" I asked, not trusting his wording. "Will I be free to go? Rhyan?"

"My lady, I agreed to your sisters for the shard. Anything further will require another negotiation."

I sniffled, trying desperately to assess all the information I had. Rhyan and I were not going to walk free. Of that, I was sure. And if he honored our bargain, and released Meera and Morgana—what were the odds of them being released safely? Or the odds of me and Rhyan eventually escaping...unless...if Rhyan broke free from his ropes...we could travel. We had a chance.

I stared at Aemon's face. The face I thought I could read—that had guided me, and protected me. Helped me make impossible choices when the Imperator threatened me.

Had taken over security for me and my sisters. Of course, he had. I remembered him specifically asking for it—to be in charge of their security. Not because he cared. But because he'd wanted to make it easy to reach them. He'd even given me time in the Shadow Stronghold. Time to call Rhyan. Time to escape. We'd done everything he'd wanted. We'd walked right into his trap.

"When did you know?" I asked. "When did you know who you were? Who I was?"

"I've always known about myself. I can't recall a time I haven't. A time I wasn't aware of him, and his life. And I knew you the moment you were born."

"But you protected me," I said dumbly.

"Not when you fucking lashed her," Rhyan roared.

"Hart," Aemon snapped. "I'm sick of both your internal and external outbursts. You never let that little incident go—reminding me ad nauseum in every single meeting. And yes, I know you were suspicious of me from your first akadim kill. Congratulations—your suspicions were correct. Now enough. I'm well aware of how you feel. Believe me. I've been aware for a millennium. So, for once, in one of your Godsdamned lives, shut up."

I eyed Aemon carefully. "Internal?" And I understood. "By the Gods." I shook my head. "Aemon, you're...you're vorakh?" *You knew? You knew about Meera? And Morgana? Rhyan? All this time you knew? And never said anything?*

Aemon nodded. "How often your mind conceived of me having two faces. One of Aemon. One of the Ready. A God of Death. I suppose that's fitting for Moriel. But you never truly understood or saw. I always wore the same face. Only sometimes I was in too much pain, too overloaded by the voices to contain myself any longer. And a warlord cannot simply drink and smoke himself to oblivion every day. But never once, did you put two and two together."

"But you—" I shook my head, torn between my anger, and sympathy for him. I understood. I'd seen the pain it caused Morgana. I didn't understand how he could be doing this. "Aemon, you were on our side. All these years, defending us, you knew, and you were keeping our secrets." Some part of me was desperate, grasping onto anything I could conjure up, holding onto hope that he wasn't my enemy. That I hadn't been betrayed again. That we could all walk out of this alive.

"No, Lady Lyriana," he said slowly, his aura striking with such a force I leaned back. "I was never on your side. You assumed I was. You assumed because I hate the Imperator that I was on your side." He rose from his throne, towering over me. "You assumed because I supported your father over Arianna in Tarek's rebellion, I was on your side." He shook his head, the gesture stern, like that of a disappointed teacher. Or a warlord. "You need to learn. Your enemy's enemy is not your friend, nor your ally. Just another enemy. Everyone who is not behind your cause is against you." He unsheathed his sword. "I've never cared for one second who ruled in Bamaria. I could just as easily have sat Arianna on the Seat all those years ago, placed the golden laurel on her head, let Tarek live." He stepped forward. "It was never about your father or your mother's final wishes. Nor was it ever a matter of seating the true heir. I did what I thought was going to keep me closest to you, Asherah. I was ready to fight and kill and do whatever I had to do until the day you revealed yourself powerless. Until the day you confirmed to all who suspected exactly what you were. I've waited years for this. Lifetimes, all for this moment. Everything I've done, every choice I've made, was never in support of you. But simply to be near you."

"Including lashing me?"

His eyes darkened, and then he carefully sat back on the throne, the black obsidian glowing with red firelight. "You had that coming ages ago. So when the opportunity came, I couldn't resist. But remember well, I never struck you on my own."

"I guess that makes it okay then," I shouted. But then I shook my head. My vision blurring. "Why?"

"For this." He gestured at the Valalumir shard.

It was glowing even brighter than before. But there was something strange about it. The color was beginning to reveal itself. And to my horror, it was not red. Not even close.

The shard was glowing indigo.

The room shook again. And this time, golden Valalumir stars fell from the ceiling, sparkling and glowing.

"Enough!" Aemon said, his voice full of the violence and darkness that consumed him when he was the Ready. A God of Death.

Moriel.

"That shard is mine. Moriel was the Guardian of the indigo. Not Asherah."

The akadim who imprisoned me inched closer, as if sensing I was preparing to escape. I had no idea what I was doing—only that I'd be damned before I gave the crystal to him willingly.

The beasts on my sides squinted, clearly pained by the shard's light. Slowly, I got to my feet, and stepped forward, my heart racing. "If your whole plan was about getting this, then why haven't you taken it yet?"

His eyes flicked beyond me. "That would be Auriel's fault. He made it so I could never again take it with my own hands. No one could. Not from its final resting place. Not from anyone without Asherah's blood. And her blood was supposed to die with her. The Valalumir was meant to be lost in shards for eternity. But Auriel was deceived. He hadn't counted on the immortal Mercurial. Hadn't foreseen the Afeya finding the chest plate, and preserving it. But the magic has held up so well, even Auriel reborn could not remove the shard. Only you, Asherah."

"And you can't take it. I have to give it to you willingly," I said.

"If you want your sisters to live, you will do so."

I closed my eyes. I didn't know what to do.

"Do as I ask," he said, reading my thoughts.

"And if I don't?" I seethed.

"Meera goes first." He snapped a finger, and the akadim at her pole, tugged on the ropes, lifting her body, her head rolling.

"Lyr!" Rhyan yelled. "Don't."

Thunder crackled in the Seating Room, every light blinking out as the smoke and shadows of a powerful aura nearly suffocated me. The akadim at my sides released me. Everyone in the room seemed to lose consciousness at once. I was alone, the only one untouched. Even Aemon was silent. His head had fallen forward, but his fingers were twitching as if fighting back against this.

Then, through the darkness, Morgana approached. Valalumir stars fell from the ceiling, and an angry, feline roar echoed across the walls.

I stopped thinking. I ran for Morgana, throwing my arms around her and bursting into tears.

"Morgs! Gods, Morgs! Are you hurt? What's happening?" I tightened my hold, so relieved to see her, to hold her. To know she was okay. But she pushed me off.

"It's Mercurial. He's escaping. Causing a distraction." She narrowed her gaze, as if communicating with the Afeya. "It's because of the presence of the shard," she continued, her expression focused. "It gave him the strength to escape. Aemon isn't at full power yet. Not at his god-strength, but he will be soon, if he possesses this."

"But he was already powerful enough to control Mercurial? To control akadim?"

Morgana shook her head. "He's controlled akadim for years. Something he remembers from his past life allows it. And he's started to create kashonim with them. Trading blood—giving them silver collars like armor—siphoning their power. The akadim couldn't touch Asherah's blood before. But they can now. They can touch the blood of any Guardian reincarnated."

"I know. I encountered a few. Morgs, let's go. We can escape. We just need to get Meera and Rhyan. He can get us out." I took her hand, squeezing tight.

Morgana looked back at Aemon, his wrists turning against the black armrests at his sides, his body twitching, fighting to awaken.

"Come on," Morgana said, running toward the poles. "We don't have much time." She pulled her stave from the folds of her black gown.

"You were able to keep your stave?" I asked in surprise.

"I was kidnapped and held prisoner by akadim before today. It was useless against them." Quickly, she began muttering under her breath, pointing the stave at Meera, and then at Rhyan. At once, their ropes dissolved and they both slumped against the poles they'd been tied to.

She chanted again, and Meera's eyes opened, hazel, wide and in shock. She sat at the base of the pole, stunned, her eyes looking at Morgana with betrayal.

"What?" she asked. "What happened?"

As Rhyan's eyes opened, he moved quickly, traveling to our side, his eyes assessing, seeing the akadim were down, seeing Aemon's head falling forward on his throne.

"We need to go," he said. "Now!"

"Can you carry all three of us?" I asked, hating I had to put that on him.

Rhyan sucked in a breath, seemingly adding our weights up in his mind.

"How much time we do have?" he asked.

"Less than a minute," Morgana said.

"I think I can do it."

I nodded, and Rhyan reached immediately for me.

But Morgana shook her head. "No. You risk using too much power. Take us one by one."

Rhyan's eyes fell on me, unsure of the request, but without time to argue, reached for me again.

I shook my head. "No. Meera first. Please." She looked so frail. I had to be sure she was free.

"Lady Meera," he said, sweeping her into his arms. A second later they were gone."

I stood with Morgana, my stomach twisting. *Were you hurt?* Then I suddenly remembered, she couldn't hear my thoughts anymore. I opened my mouth.

"I wasn't," she said. "And I can hear you. It wasn't the Vala-lumir that stopped me hearing your thoughts. Aemon...he gave you an elixir that night at Cresthaven. It protected your mind from mind-reading—like a shield over your thoughts. I should have known." Her aura darkened, flaring out around me, and my stomach twisted.

"An elixir?" I asked. "To protect against vorakh? Morgs, there's no such thing."

She nodded solemnly. "There is. I should have told you a long time ago. There was a reason I didn't know about Arianna's treachery. And I'm so sorry. We found out...after they're tested in Lethea, the vorakh who can read minds are sent to the Emperor. Their magic is siphoned, creating an elixir that keeps their thoughts hidden. Arianna was taking it. That's how she tricked me."

"What?" I asked. "Morgs...no. No. That's not.... They take vorakh to the Emperor?"

Rhyan reappeared. The lights were flickering, and I could feel it. Mercurial's magic, his chaos, was beginning to wear off. Aemon would open his eyes in seconds.

"Rhyan I don't think we have time for two trips," I said. "Can you manage both of us?"

His jaw tensed. "I'll manage. Neither of you can let go of me."

I took his hand, our fingers threading together, but I needed to adjust my grip on the Valalumir. The indigo shard was becoming so heavy in my arm.

"Wait, we have to do this right," Morgana said, her voice shaking. "Lyr, hand it to me. I'll help."

I passed the shard to Morgana.

She waved her stave, a protective dome of white light around her.

"Morgs!" I shouted. I reached for her, only to hit the magic of her protection spell. "What are you—"

"Morgana, no!" Rhyan hissed.

I shook my head. "Morgana, don't. Just come here!"

"I'm sorry! Tell Meera, I'm sorry. But I have to do this." Tears streamed down her cheeks. "I've been lying to you, Lyr. For months. I've been on a mission. I found out, it wasn't just the mind-readers they were taking to the Emperor. It's all vorakh."

"All vorakh...Morgs! Stop just—"

She offered a grim smile. "They have them enslaved, and they're using their powers, stealing all of it. Mind-readers, travelers, and those who see visions."

"Visions?" Like Meera. Like....

Brockton's words pounded through my mind.

She's alive. But if I die, she dies, too.

My heart stopped beating, my body going still. *Jules. No. No.*

Morgana nodded. Once. "She's alive."

"And you knew!"

"Lyr," Rhyan growled.

The torchlights returned, hundreds of fires flaming to life, crackling as they ripped across the cave. Aemon sat up, his eyes open, his aura exploding like a hurricane. And all at once, the dozens upon dozens of akadim, rose to their feet, their red eyes all focused on me.

"Asherah!" They all seemed to be shouting at once.

"Goodbye," Morgana said.

"MORGS!"

Rhyan wrapped his arms around me, dragging me back, pulling me away from her.

"MORGS!"

My stomach tugged. And we were gone.

CHAPTER FORTY-ONE

"LYR," RHYAN SAID GENTLY. "Lyr?"

I stared at the grayed winter sky, my face numb with cold.

Rhyan leaned forward, patting the fur of the gryphon beneath us. "Tovayah," he praised it. "Tovayah." He replaced his arm around me again, and took my hand in his. My other hand sat between Meera's palms.

Hours had passed since we'd escaped. Rhyan had moved quickly; he'd loaded me and Meera onto the back of the same gryphon who'd taken us in the first place. The beast was moody at first. But a few strokes from Rhyan, and soothing remarks in High Lumerian, and the gryphon completely changed allegiance, doing whatever Rhyan wanted.

"Partner, please. Say something."

I sniffled. What was there to say? We'd been betrayed by Aemon. And in the end, I hadn't been able to save Morgana. Nor had I been able to save the shard of the Valalumir.

And Jules...Brockton had been telling the truth. All this time... She was alone, suffering...scared. Being tortured.

Meera shivered against me. "Are we landing soon?" she asked.

"I know a system of caves nearby. We'll be safe there for the night," Rhyan said. Then massaging my hand, he looked to me. "Partner. Please."

"My, my, my," drawled a feline voice.

I stiffened and looked up to see Mercurial balancing on one foot, standing on the head of the gryphon.

"Get off him!" Rhyan snapped.

"I weigh nothing, my not-lord," Mercurial purred. "He doesn't feel a thing. And...I do apologize for all the times I could not come when called. I was, as you know, a bit *tied* up. Thank you by the way, for asking after my well-being. I, too, was a prisoner of Moriel. But no, don't ask how I'm doing."

"Have you come to call in your favor?" I asked, my voice dull. It was the first thing I'd said since we'd escaped.

Rhyan's eyes snapped toward me.

"My favor?" Mercurial asked, his voice teasing. "Why, that would imply my remembered goddess, that you had fulfilled your end of the bargain."

"Haven't I?" I asked. "You said I was to claim my magic power. And I did! No thanks to you. I suppose not the way you wanted either, but I did it. So go ahead, call in your fucking favor. So I can be done with it."

He switched feet, giving his hips a shimmy, the diamonds on his skin glittering, as he returned to balancing. "You got your wish, you could try to look happy about it."

"What do you want, Mercurial?" Rhyan asked, his hand now rubbing up and down my back. He remained seated, but his entire body had tensed, leaning toward me protectively.

"Be careful, my not-lord. That almost sounded like a question." His violet eyes fell back on me. "And no. I am not calling in a favor with you. Because you're still not ready. You think an immortal would waste his time on the simple magic of Lumerians? I never meant for you to be finding your Lumerian magic to be the point of our deal. So basic." He wrinkled his nose in disgust. "When I said you were going to claim your magic—I didn't mean Lyriana's. I meant Asherah's."

"I found her tomb," I shouted. "My tomb! I touched a shard. And I have her stave."

"Which makes you not only a fine soturion, but also a mage. Congratulations. But no!" he snapped. "Neither is what I spoke of. What I intended. I meant for you to claim your power as a goddess. And now, because of your foolish, idiotic, stupid, mortal, rash decisions, you will have no choice in the matter."

"Stupid? Rash! Moriel kidnapped my sisters! What choice did I have? Especially when you were gone!"

"You could have thought— you could have used your Gods-damned brain!"

"Enough," Rhyan shouted. "Say your piece, and go! You're not welcome here."

"So rude, Auriel. As always."

"Yes, well, some of my memories are coming back. And I'm not too fucking happy with you either."

Mercurial bowed. "Then I'll say my piece. I warned you not to do this! Ramia told you—this was a bad idea. Even yourself knew. Did not Asherah come to you? Speak to you when you called on kashonim? Tell you at her own gravesite, this was not the way?"

I balked, remembering when I heard her voice in Korteria.

"Do not head for the stars. What you seek is with the moon," I said. "How was that a warning?"

"She was referring to the Afeyan Courts. The star court lies beyond Glemaria. You were heading for the stars. Heading north. You should have been going south. The secrets to your power—your true power—not this weak mage shit—is in the Moon Court. Ramia had made arrangements on my behalf. And you've ruined them all."

The sun revealed my secrets, so I hid them with the moon. I groaned. The answers had all been there, but I hadn't been able to see them.

"Fuck off," Rhyan snarled. "You put the Valalumir in her, you made it painful, made it burn her. We had no choice. We had to act. And we did the best we could with the information available. Including the information you failed to provide."

Mercurial vanished, reappearing before Rhyan, pulling him to his feet.

"You put the Valalumir in her, Auriel. A thousand years ago—you—not me! I simply returned it! And I did nothing to it. Do you want to know why it burned! It was lighting up for the other Guardians. Whenever one of them got their hands on our Lyriana, got them a little too close to her heart...the light recognized them. And it got, shall we say, excited."

I blinked. Remembering now the first time it had truly burned, I was kissing Rhyan in my room at Cresthaven. His hands were on my breasts. Gods. And after I'd lost my diadem, I'd run into Aemon, he'd grabbed my shoulders.

The light was recognizing Guardians.

Mercurial dropped Rhyan beside me.

"It was burning in Meera's room," he said, his eyes widening. "When Morgana took your chest plate."

I stared at Mercurial. "Morgana? She's...she's a Guardian, too?" I asked.

"Ereshya, goddess of the orange ray," he said. "Looks like history has repeated itself in more ways than one. She's betrayed you, and run to her lover Moriel's side, again."

My chest heaved.

Mercurial snaked his head, his neck rolling. "I have to go now. You two have caused far too many problems I must fix, or it will spell doom for everyone. But when I find you again, you better be ready this time. Ready to listen. Ready to become Asherah. Because you just handed Moriel all he needs to become a god. It's only a matter of time before his full power returns. And believe me, you won't want to see what that looks like."

The ghost of a smile spread across his blue face. And with that, he was gone.

I thought of what Rhyan had told me that night in my room weeks ago. That his father said I had the potential to unleash more power and destruction than anyone in the Empire ever has.

He'd been right. I'd just unleashed Moriel back into Lumeria.

A laugh like bells chiming sounded in my head. *Oh Asherah, your full power as a goddess will be even more destructive.*

I squeezed my eyes shut, willing him out of my head.

"Lyr..." Rhyan said. "We're going to figure this out."

"How?" I asked. "I've just given the most dangerous god to walk Lumeria his greatest weapon."

Rhyan nodded. "You're more powerful. Look what you've done. We defeated him before. We're going to do it again. There's the two of us, together. But first..." His eyes blazed emerald green, so full of light and determination. "We're going to rescue Jules. We're going to get her back. And then, we're sending Aemon, Moriel—whatever he wants to call himself—back to hell."

I squeezed his hand.

"And Lyr," Meera said softly. "You're not alone in this. We outmatch them right now. Three to two."

Us against Morgana. How was that even possible?

"Three to two?" I asked, finally hearing her words. "But Meera, only Rhyan and I...."

She shook her head. "I touched you first," she said. "That night, when I was having my vision. I reached for you, and you started to burn—that's when you called Rhyan. I think...I think based on what Mercurial just said, I'm also a Guardian."

CHAPTER FORTY-TWO

MORGANA

I SAT ALONE ON my bed, my gown spread across my legs. Aemon sat in his throne room...I supposed I could think of him like that now. As Aemon. As the Ready. Now that our relationship, now that this thing between us, was no longer in the dark.

The room glowed with indigo light, the darkest of the rays. I had kept the shard. Betrayed my sisters. All because I knew what I wanted. More than anything.

I wanted to bring the Empire down.

And as much as I fucking loved Lyr, as much as my heart was torn in two leaving Meera, as much as I wanted to die every time I saw Lyr's face in my mind—saw that look of betrayal, saw the devastation I'd caused by telling her the truth about Jules, I wanted something more. So much more. Something I knew I'd never get if I went home, if I'd gone with them. If I'd continued following the rules, playing the same games.

I wanted change.

And I didn't care at this point how I got it.

I was going to get Jules back. And I was going to take the Empire down as I did so. The vorakh which powered the Emperor's forces were going to turn on him. Soon, they were going to stand behind me.

My two-faced goddess, he'll demand the shard from you, sooner or later, you know. Mercurial's thoughts pushed into my mind. He'd told me he'd create the diversion. That it was my one chance to get out. To leave Moriel, Aemon. But I'd never trusted the Afeyan. I saved my sisters. Even Rhyan. I'd done enough. Now, it was time for me.

You're a fool. You don't even know what to do with the shard. How to use it, wield it. Or how to keep it. Stop underestimating him. Because before you know it, he's going to make a trade you can't refuse. He's going to demand you hand it over freely. And when he does, you won't have a choice.

I rarely have. At least when he does—he won't be bargaining with my sisters' lives.

You underestimate him again. He can, and he will. And he will do worse. The immortal's cruel laugh rang through my mind. *You'll wish you'd come with me when I gave you the chance. Understand now, that the line has been drawn. I gave you a moment. You refused. Mercurial does not give second chances. You are my enemy.*

Wasn't I always? I shrugged, staring into the crystal, as I turned it in my hands. The lights shined across my skin, and vanished as I turned it over, and over, and over. I had to hold it as long as I could. I had to refuse Aemon's demands to hand it over as long as possible. Nothing else mattered.

But Mercurial whispered in my mind. *Consider this my final act of service to you. My final piece of advice for the sake of our long history together. You chose wrong, Ereshya. Again.*

WARRIOR OF THE DROWNED EMPIRE

The Story Continues in the
DROWNED EMPIRE SERIES, #4

SON OF THE DROWNED EMPIRE

RHYAN'S STORY FROM SOLSTICE
CONTINUES IN THE DROWNED
EMPIRE SERIES, #1.5

THE GUARDIANS
OF THE
VALALUMIR

ASHERAH, GODDESS, GUARDIAN OF the Red Ray
  Ereshya, Goddess, Guardian of the Orange Ray
  Shiviel, God, Guardian of the Yellow Ray
  Auriel, God, Guardian of the Green Ray
  Cassarya, Goddess, Guardian of the Blue Ray
  Moriel, God, Guardian of the Indigo Ray
  Hava, Goddess, Guardian of the Violet Ray

GLOSSARY

Names:

Lyriana Batavia (Leer-ree-ana Ba-tah-via): Third in line to the Seat of Power in Bamaria

Morgana Batavia (Mor-ga-na Ba-tah-via): Second in line to the Seat of Power in Bamaria

Meera Batavia (Mee-ra Ba-tah-via): First in line to the Seat of Power in Bamaria (Heir Apparent)

Naria Batavia (Nar-ria Ba-tah-via): Niece to the Arkasva, not in line to the Seat

Arianna Batavia (Ar-ree-ana Ba-tah-via): Sister-in-law to the Arkasva, previously third in line to Seat, Master of Education on the Council of Bamaria

Aemon Melvik (Ae-mon Mel-vik): Warlord of Bamaria, Arkturion on the Council of Bamaria

Rhyan Hart (Ry-an Hart): Forsworn and exiled from Glemaria. Previously was in first in line to the Seat of Power (Heir Apparent)

Haleika Grey (Hal-eye-ka Gray): Tristan's cousin, and one of the few friends and allies Lyr has in the Soturion Academy

Hava (Ha-vah): Guardian of the Violet Ray

Auriel (Or-ree-el): Original Guardian of the Valalumir in Heaven, stole the light to bring to Earth where it turned into a crystal before shattering at the time of the Drowning

Asherah (A-sher-ah): Original Guardian of the Valalumir in Heaven. She was banished to Earth as a mortal after her affair with Auriel was discovered.

Mercurial (Mer-cure-ree-el): An immortal Afeya, First Messenger of her Highness Queen Ishtara, High Lady of the Night Lands

Moriel (Mor-ree-el): Original Guardian of the Valalumir in Heaven. He reported Auriel and Asherah's affair to the Council of 44 leading to Asherah's banishment, Auriel's theft of the light, and its subsequent destruction. He was banished to Earth where he allied with the akadim in the war that led to the Drowning.

Ereshya (Air-resh-she-ah): Goddess, Guardian of the Orange Ray

Shiviel (Shiv-ay-el): God, Guardian of the Yellow Ray

Cassarya (Cah-sar-ree-ah): Goddess, Guardian of the Blue Ray

Theotis (Thee-otis): Current Emperor of Lumeria Nutavia. Theotis was previously from Korteria, and a noble of Ka Kormac. His nephew, Avery Kormac, is the current Imperator to the Southern hemisphere of the Empire, and Arkasva to Korteria.

Avery Kormac (Ae-very Core-mac): Nephew to the Emperor, as Imperator, he rules over the six southern countries of the Empire, as well as ruling Korteria as the Arkasva.

Afeya (Ah-fay-ah): Immortal Lumerians who survived the Drowning. Prior to, Afeya were non-distinguishable from other Lumerians in Lumeria Matavia. They were descended from the Gods and Goddesses, trapped in the mortal coil. But they refused the request to join the war efforts. Some sources believe they allied with Moriel's forces and the akadim. When the Valalumir shattered, they were cursed to live forever, unable to return to their home, be relieved of life, or touch or perform magic—unless asked to by another.

Ramia (Rah-me-yah): Half-Afeyan librarian

Zenoya (Zen-oy-ya): Half-Afeyan librarian

Places:

Lumeria (Lu-mair-ria): The name of continent where Gods and Goddesses first incarnated until it sank into the Lumerian Ocean in the Drowning.

Matavia (Ma-tah-via): Motherland. When used with Lumeria, it refers to the continent that sank.

Nutavia (New-tah-via): New land. When used with Lumeria, it refers to the Empire forged after the Drowning by those who survived and made it to Bamaria—previously Dobra.

Bamaria (Ba-mar-ria): Southernmost country of the Lumerian Empire, home of the South's most prestigious University and the Great Library. Ruled by Ka Batavia.

Korteria (Kor-ter-ria): Westernmost country in the Empire. Magic is least effective in their mountains, but Korteria does have access to Starfire for Lumerian weapons. Ruled by Ka Kormac.

Elyria (El-leer-ria): Historically ruled by Ka Azria, rulership has now passed to Ka Elys, originally nobility from Bamaria.

Lethea (Lee-thee-a): The only part of the Empire located in the Lumerian Ocean. Ruled by Ka Maras, this is the country where criminals stripped of powers, or accused of vorakh are sent for imprisonment. The expression "Farther than Lethea" comes from the fact that there is nothing but ocean beyond the island. Due to the Drowning, the idea of going past the island is akin to losing one's mind.

Damara (Da-mar-ra): A Southern country known for strong warriors, ruled by Ka Daquataine.

Glemaria (Gleh-mar-ria): Northernmost country of the Empire, ruled by Ka Hart. Imperator Devon Hart is the Arkasva and Imperator to the North. Rhyan Hart was previously first in line to the Seat.

Prominent Creatures of the Old World Known to Have Survived the Drowning:

Seraphim (Ser-a-feem): Birds with wings of gold, they resemble a cross between an eagle and a dove. Seraphim are peaceful creatures, sacred in Bamaria, and most often used for transport across the Lumerian Empire. Though delicate in appearance, they are extremely strong and can carry loads of up ten people over short distances. Seraphim all prefer warmer climates and are rarely found in the northernmost part of the Empire.

Ashvan: Flying horses. These are the only sky creatures that do not possess wings. Their flight comes from magic contained in their hooves. Once an ashvan picks up speed, their magic will create small temporary pathways to run upon. Technically, ashvan cannot fly, but are running on magic pathways that appear and vanish once stepped upon. Residue of the magic is left behind, creating streaks behind them, but these fade within seconds.

Nahashim: Snakes with the ability to grow and shrink at will, able to fit into any size space for the purposes of seeking. Anything lost or desired can almost always be found by a nahashim. Their scales remain almost burning hot and they prefer to live near the water. Most nahashim are bred on Lethea, the country furthest out into the ocean, closest to the original location of Lumeria Matavia.

Gryphon (Grif-in): Sky creatures that are half eagle, half lion. Extremely large, these animals can be taken into battle, preferring mountains and colder climates. They replace seraphim and ashvan in the northernmost parts of the Lumerian Empire. They may carry far heavier loads than seraphim.

Akadim (A-ka-deem): The most feared of all creatures, literally bodies without souls. Akadim kill by eating the soul of their victims. The demonic creatures were previously Lumerians transformed. Akadim grow to be twice the size of a Lumerian and gain five times the strength of a soturion. Immortal as long as they continue to feed on souls, these creatures are impervious to Lumerian magic. Akadim are weakened by the sun and tend to live in the Northern Hemisphere.

Water Dragon: Dragons with blue scales that live deep in the Lumerian Ocean. Previously spending their time equally between land and water, all water dragons have taken to the Lumerian Ocean and are usually spotted closer to Lethea.

Agnavim (Ahg-naw-veem): Rarely sighted in Lumerian lands. These red birds with wings made of pure flame favor the lands occupied by the Afeyan Star Court. Lumerians have been unable to tame them since the Drowning.

Terms/Items:
Birth Bind/Binding: Unlike a traditional bind which includes a spell that ties a rope around a Lumerian to keep them from touching their power, or restricting their physical ability to move a Birth Bind leaves no mark. A Binding is temporary, and can have more or less strength and heat depending on the mage

casting the spell. A Birth Bind is given to all Lumerians in their first year of life, a spell that will keep them from accessing their magic power whenever it develops. All Lumerians develop their magic along with puberty. The Birth Bind may only be removed after the Lumerian has turned nineteen, the age of adulthood.

Dagger: Ceremonial weapon given to soturi. The dagger has no special power on its own as the magic of a soturion is transmuted through their body.

Ka (Kah): Soul. A Ka is a soul tribe or family.

Kashonim (Ka-show-neem): Ancestral lineage and link of power. Calling on Kashonim allows you to absorb the power of your lineage, but depending on the situation, usage can be dangerous. For one, it can be an overwhelming amount of power that leaves you unconscious if you come from a long lineage, or a particularly powerful one. Two, it has the potential to weaken the mages or soturi the caller is drawing from. It is also illegal to use against fellow students.

Kavim (Ka-veem): Plural of Ka. A Ka can be likened to a soul tribe or family. When marriages occur, either member of the union may take on the name of their significant other's Ka. Typically, the Ka with more prestige or nobility will be used thus ensuring the most powerful Kavim continue to grow.

Laurel of the Arkasva (Lor-el of the Ar-kas-va): A golden circlet like a crown worn by the Arkasva. The Arkasva replaced the title of King and Queen in Lumeria Matavia, and the Laurel replaced the crown though they are held in the same high esteem.

Mekarim (Mee-kah-reem): Soulmates

Mekara (Mee-kah-rah): Term of endearment, translates to "My soul is yours."

Rakame (Rah-kah-may): Term of endearment, translates to "Your soul is mine."

Seat of Power: Akin to a throne. Thrones were replaced by Seats in Lumeria Nutavia, as many members of royalty were blamed by the citizens of Lumeria for the Drowning. Much as a monarch may have a throne room, the Arkasvim have a Seating Room. The Arkasva typically has a Seat of Power in their Seating Room in their Ka's fortress, and another in their temple.

Stave: Made of twisted moon and sun wood, the stave transmutes magic created by mages. A stave is not needed to perform magic, but greatly focuses and strengthens it. More magic being transmuted may require a larger stave.

Vadati (Va-dah-tee): Stones that allow Lumerians to hear and speak to each other over vast distances. Most of these stones were lost in the Drowning. The Empire now keeps a strict registry of each known stone.

Valalumir (Val-la-loo-meer): The sacred light of Heaven that began the Celestial War which began in Heaven and ended with the Drowning. The light was guarded by seven Gods and Goddesses until Asherah and Auriel's affair. Asherah was banished to become mortal, and Auriel fell to bring her the light. Part of the light went into Asherah before it crystalized. When the war ended, the Valalumir shattered in seven pieces—all lost in the Drowning.

Valya (Val-yah): The sacred text of recounting the history of the Lumerian people up until the Drowning. There are multiple valyas recorded, each with slight variations, but the Mar Valya is the standard. Another popular translation is the Tavia Valya which is believed to have been better preserved than the Mar Valya after the Drowning, but was never made into the standard for copying. Slight changes or possible effects of water damage offer different insights into Auriel's initial meeting with Asherah.

Vorakh (Vor-rock): Taboo, forbidden powers. Three magical abilities that faded after the Drowning are considered illegal: visions, mind-reading, and traveling by mind. Vorakh can be translated as "gift from the Gods" in High Lumerian, but is now translated as "curse from the Gods."

THE EMPIRE OF LUMERIA

THERE ARE TWELVE COUNTRIES united under the Lumerian Empire. The 12 Ruling Kavim of Lumeria Nutavia.   Each country is ruled by an Arkasva, the High Lord or Lady of the ruling Ka.

All twelve countries submit to the rule and law of the Emperor. Each Arkasva also answers to an Imperator, one Arkasva with jurisdiction over each country in either the Northern or Southern hemispheres of the Empire.

In addition to the Emperor's rule, twelve senators, one from each country (may not be a member of the ruling Ka) fill the twelve seats of the Senate. The roles of Imperator and Emperor are lifelong appointments. They may not be passed onto family members. Imperators and Emperors must be elected by the ruling Kavim. Kavim may not submit a candidate for either role if the previous Imperator or Emperor belonged to their Ka.

Imperators may keep their ties to their Ka and rule in their country. An Emperor will lose their Ka upon anointing and must be like a father or mother to all Lumerians.

Empiric
Chain of Command
Emperor Theotis, High Lord of Lumeria Nutavia

The Emperor rules over the entire Empire, from its capitol, Numeria. The Emperor oversees the running of the Senate, and the twelve countries united under the Empire.

Devon Hart, Imperator to the North

The Imperator of the North if an Arkasva who rules not only their country, but oversees rule of the remaining five countries belonging to the North. His rule includes the following countries currently by the following Kavim:

Glemaria, Ka Hart
Payunmar, Ka Valyan
Hartavia, Ka Taria
Ereztia, Ka Sephiron
Aravia, Ka Lumerin
Sindhuvine, Ka Kether

Avery Kormac, Imperator to the South

The Imperator of the South is an Arkasva who rules not only their country, but oversees rule of the remaining five countries belonging to the North. The sitting Imperator is also nephew to the Emperor. His rule includes the following countries currently being ruled by the following Kavim:

Bamaria, Ka Batavia
Korteria, Ka Kormac
Elyria, Ka Elys (previously Ka Azria)
Damara, Ka Daquataine
Lethea, Ka Maras
Cretanya, Ka Zarine

The Immortal Afeyan Courts*

The Sun Court: El Zandria, ruled by King RaKanam
The Moon Court: Khemet, ruled by Queen Ma'Nia
The Star Court: Night Lands, ruled by Queen Ishtara

Afeyan Courts are not considered part of the Lumerian Empire, nor do they submit to the Emperor, however, history, prior treaties, and trade agreements have kept the courts at peace, and working together. They are the only two groups to have shared life on the continent of Lumeria Matavia.

THE BAMARIAN COUNCIL

Each of the twelve countries in the Lumerian Empire includes a 12-member council comprised of members of the nobility to assist the Arkasva in ruling and decision-making.

The Bamarian Council includes the following:

Role,	Name
Arkasva,	Arianna Batavia
Master of the Horse,	Eathan Ezara*
Arkturion,	Aemon Melvik
Turion,	Dairen Melvik
Arkmage,	Kolaya Scholar
Master of Education,	Pending
Master of Spies,	Sila Shavo
Master of Finance,	Romula Grey
Master of Law,	Kiera Ezara
Naturion,	Dagana Scholar
Senator,	Janvi Elys
Master of Peace,	Brenna Corra

*Eathan Ezara was named the temporary arkasva and ruled with the silver laurel for a full day before transferring power to Arianna Batavia. Arianna's move to become Arkasva Batavia, High Lady of Bamaria has left an opening for the position of Master of Education on the Council. The selection of a new Master of the Horse is imminent and with recent developments, several other new appointments are expected to be made.

TITLES AND FORMS OF ADDRESS

APPRENTICE: THE TERM USED to describe a soturion or mage who has passed their first three years of training. As an apprentice their time is divided between their own studies and teaching the novice they are bound to. This is done to strengthen the power of Kashonim, and because of the Bamarian philosophy that teaching a subject is the best way to learn and master a subject.

Arkasva (Ark-kas-va): Ruler of the country, literally translates as the "will of the highest soul."

Arkasvim (Ark-kas-veem): Plural of Arkasva

Arkturion (Ark-tor-ree-an): Warlord for the country, general of their soturi/army.

Emperor: Ruler of all twelve countries in the Lumerian Empire. The Emperor is elected by the ruling arkasvim. They are appointed for life. Once an Emperor or Empress dies, the Kavim must elect a new ruler. The Emperor must renounce their Ka when anointed, but no Ka may produce an Emperor/Empress twice in a row.

Heir Apparent: Title given to the eldest child or heir of the Arkasva. The next in line to the Seat of Power or First from the Seat.

Imperator: A miniature Emperor. The Empire always has two Imperators, one for the Northern Hemisphere, one for the South. The Imperator will also be the arkasva of their country, they have jurisdiction over their hemisphere but also act as a voice and direct messenger between each Arkasva and the Emperor.

Lady: Formal address for a female, or female-identifying member of the nobility.

Lord: Formal address for a male, or male-identifying member of the nobility.

Mage: A Lumerian who transmutes magic through spells. A stave is used to focus their magic. The more focus one has, the less a stave is needed, but the more magic one can use, the larger the stave may need to be. Arkmages (the high mages) tend to have staves as tall as them.

Maraak: High Lumerian for King

Novice: The term used to describe a soturion or mage who is in the beginning of their learning to become an anointed mage or soturion.

Soturion: Soldier, magically enhanced warrior. A Lumerian who can transmute magic through their body. May be used as a form of address for a non-noble.

Turion: Commander, may lead legions of soturi, must answer to their Arkturion.

Your Grace: Formal address for any member of the ruling Ka. Anyone who is in line to the Seat of Power must be addressed so, including the Arkasva. A noble may only be addressed as "your grace" if they are in line to the Seat.

Your Highness: Reserved as formal address only for the member of Lumerian nobility serving as imperator. The term of address has also been adopted by the Afeyan Star Court.

Your Majesty: Used only for the Emperor or Empress. Previously used for the kings and queens of Lumeria Matavia. This can also be applied to the King and Queen of the Afeyan Sun and Moon Courts.

ACKNOWLEDGMENTS

It's official. Lady of the Drowned Empire was my hardest book to write, but I feel like it's the book where I learned the most about myself, including what I'm fully capable of—and it's also where I learned how to fully trust my intuition. I will probably need this lesson again though....

I picked the release date of February 14 for a significant reason (Valentine's Day was just icing). I remembered looking ahead in the calendar for a date that felt far away enough from Guardian's publication that I'd have plenty of time to write and edit (but not too much time), and I liked that this was a Tuesday, and close to the original date of my first book Daughter of the Drowned Empire which I published on 2/22/22. Also—OMG—one year ago today, I didn't have a single published book. Today, I have four (Solstice counts even though we'll still call it a novella).

However, as usual, my plans went awry, and I became convinced about a hundred times that I wouldn't be able to finish this book on time, or at all for dozens of reasons. Every time I felt resigned to pushing the date back, something would happen that miraculously put it back on schedule. And I'm pretty sure that it's the spirit of my grandfather, Frank who kept this whole production on time. Frank was my grandfather, and namesake. He was a psychologist, and a writer of mystery and detective stories. Frank passed before I could meet him on February 14, 1981. I've always loved my name, and loved that we're both writers—and now I feel closer to him than ever.

February 14 was also the day my brother was born. Happy birthday, Michael. So it just feels really special to continue adding meaning to this date in my family.

I also have some other people who were absolutely crucial to Lady currently being in your hands.

Donna Kuzma, seriously—thank you, thank you, thank you. You are the synopsis queen, and somehow have the magic ability to make an offhand comment about one aspect of a chapter not working for you that inspires me to rewrite everything and get it right—all because you can pinpoint the one tiny thing that's off. Your editorial notes are unmatched. I love your insight. And can't wait to dig deeper into the next novel with you (especially since we're officially in brand new territory). Also I tried, but couldn't work it in—so here you go: "I have two modes. I go to the library. And I punch monsters in the face."

Asha Venkataraman, you are a life saver. I felt like I was writing blind at points—especially toward the end, and you just swooped in like a super hero to beta read and offer insight and encouragement. I don't think I could have finished without you.

Marcella Haddad, as always, you keep me focused, you keep my mindset where it needs to be to do the work, and your unwavering belief is contagious and always reminds me on the hard days that I can totally do this. However, I will still require at least one hundred more reminders.

Danielle Dyal, you are a miracle worker and every time you figured out the editing schedule again and made it happen (even when I wrote way more than I'd planned to, and took way longer to do it), I was in even more awe of your skill and work ethic. Thank you as usual for amazing copy edits!

Stefanie Saw, this is the best cover yet—other than the futures ones. You just keep upping your game and I'm honored to work with you.

Mom, prophecy fulfilled. Write, write, write.

Elissa, I think I finally understand statistics! What?

Jules, so proud of you! And thank you as always for your support, especially with uploading .

Eva, thank you for the constant support.

Miguel, thank you for always checking in, and listening!

Michael, thank you for sharing your birthday with my book.

Dylan, Blake, Hannah, Dani, my heart belongs to you four.

Steve Kuzma, as always, thank you for protecting the digital realm.

Huge thank you to the Drowned Empire ARC Team. Thank you to everyone who has been on this journey with me now for four books, and thank you to everyone who has joined the team. I am so grateful to you all.

And of course, last but not least, the chaotic, the meddlesome, but the always amazing street team—Forsworn Mayhem! Thank you, thank you, thank you! Especially: Kirsty Claassen, Olivia E. Fraga, Bethany Hayes , Jaycee Webb, Cassidy Karge, DeAnna Hill, Jenessa Moore, Krystal Spooner, Emma Reece, Stacey Rae, Lauren Richards, Sydney Skye (Squid), Kalynn Trammel, Alisa Huntington, Tasha Jenkins, Kristianna Weppler, Iliana katana, Emma Russell, Molly Fabricatore, Megs Ley, Andrea Brondige, Victoria Webb, Christine Stewart, Bekah Abraham, Rachel Cunningham, Yanet Aguirre, Lucy Heckla, Calli O'Sullivan, Zoë J. Osik, Megan Cristofaro, Sandra Jean Glazebrook, Heather Creeden, Meghan Hughes, Katie Hunsberger, Chelsea Taylor, Danielle Plant - Read wRite Run, Marisa Alsua, Kyla Clarkston, Shana Heinrich, Srishti Nair, Nadia Larumbe , Tandia Dudman, Sarah Heifetz, Jade Lawson, Brittanie G, Céline Yzewyn, Courtney Washburn, Kiah McDaniel, Courtney Stosser, Jennifer Walsh, Mercurial's queen , Brynly Kapelanski, Kayleigh Foland, Heather Corrales, Christine Stewart, Iliana Katana, Zoë J. Osik (After Reading), Alisa Huntington, Brianne Glickman, Izzy, Lara K, Lila, Madi Healey, Audra Jones

And thank You for reading!

Love,

Frankie

ALSO BY THE AUTHOR

ABOUT FRANKIE DIANE MALLIS

Frankie Diane Mallis is the bestselling author of the fantasy romance Drowned Empire series. The books became #1 bestsellers on Amazon in Greek and Roman Myth their debut year. She lives outside of Philadelphia where she practices yoga and belly dance, and can usually be found baking gluten free desserts. To learn more, visit www.frankiedianemallis.com, and join the newsletter. Follow Frankie on Instagram @frankiediane, and on TikTok @frankiedianebooks.

Made in the USA
Monee, IL
17 February 2023

28114661R00298